Road to Fargo

Road to Fargo

Maggie Kelley and JP Ronan

ISBN: 1-4196-6315-1
ISBN-13: 978-1419663154

Visit www.booksurge.com to order additional copies.

Road to Fargo

Figures:

Introduction

The old west was a collection of large territories that spread from the Missouri River west to the Pacific Ocean, north to Canada, and south to Mexico. The only civil law enforcement personnel permitted to cross these boundaries was the U. S. Federal Marshall.

The more successful marshal's ranged over the wider regions of jurisdiction. Following the worst of the outlaws to greater lengths became the hallmark of the best marshals of the U.S. territories. These premiere law officers had to be more capable on horse back, better at navigating the open range, intimate with the tribal etiquette of the many indigenous nations, and capable of dispensing justice with a hand gun.

The mature federal marshal had to survive many gunfights, apprehend numerous badmen, and adjudicate crimes where courts could not be reached. Here we find such a marshal upon an especially long hard trail pursuing one of the deadliest villains ever to pass out of Texas. We share the hunt and the many experiences of the officer along the track to justice.

Heroines, scalawags, small town officials arise and bring alive tales of the old west that may well have been true.

Loci:

Two Bears...mountain valley
Sweet Creek...small town south west of Fargo
Eighty Eight's....road house south of Fargo
West Liberty...farming town south of Fargo
Wagon Spill...country village south east of Fargo
Silver Spoon...mining town west by north of Fargo

Personae:

Curly and Seth Adams...ranchers
Averill Alderdyce...gambler from Ohio
Agnes Barnby...ranch cook
James Bayfield...medical doctor
Homer Bodley...owner country store
Roy Bowler...farmer
Wayne and Rita Bugel...owners of the trading post
Dave Chorba...freight hauler
Jeremiah Cloug...chicken rancher
Frank and Jessie Coulter...deputies

Verna Cox...mountain recluse
Bog Don...war counsel to the Nez Perce
E J Doyle.... Preacher
Clive Ferguson...English gambler
Wade Fite...trapper
Marcus and Shanti Fletcher...ranchers
Bill and Mary Freedman...owners of the roadhouse
Hasna Gova...native warrior
Many Horns...chief of the Nez Perce
Sewa Kac...medicine man to the Nez Perce
Sheb Ledbetter...senior cowboy on King Ranch
John Bryant Ledford...gambler
Anna Kingler...sheriff of Red Creek
Joe Kingler...younger son
Luke Kingler...first son
Marty Kingler...husband to Anna
Linda Lee...widow
Van Lemmon...outlaw
Inot Mai...native princess
Mara Nar...grandson to Many Horns
William McElroy...retired army officer and gambler
Billy Lewis...town bully
Little Owl.... native child
Lucy Patterson...San Francisco gambler
Peaches Pauli...mountain guide and tracker
Pelts Pauli...tracker
Will Richardson...widower
Jessie Rodgers...elderly widow
J D Sumner...sheriff of West Liberty
Joel and Kate Schmuer...neighbors to King Ranch
Frank Simms...gun fighter
Carl and Susan Meirs...neighbors
R D Weir...gambler from Milwaukee

Dedicated to the always inspiring Antoinette Tolomeo.

Chapter 1

A Farm House

In the dimming western sky a violet band of light hangs just above the horizon. So marks the ending moments of the sunset.

The dark night sky is not yet fully arrived. The stars may not yet appear.

Upon a distant knoll in an isolated high valley of a western territory, a warm glow emerges through the shutters of a lone house. This single earthly beacon answers the presence of Venus and Saturn.

The silhouette of this low cabin of log with sod roof sits as the sole haunt of worldly life.

This cool late spring night, the approaching night reveals this structure to be full and busy.

Motions of merry making within are glimpsed from without. Sounds of surging cheer accompany.

Gathered at this outpost are the families from the neighboring ranches and farms. Two dozen souls are common in celebration for the end of the time of heavy snows and cold rains.

The Kingler Ranch is presently host to this annual tradition. Food, dance, drink, and tobacco are shared while fiddle and banjo give music.

The gathering's enthusiasm will last through the night. Only with the rise of the new sun will the assembly quit. Visiting souls will begin to recede to their individual homes at day break.

In the main room of the Klinger's home the assembly is partitioned.

Women and food are combined around the serving tables near the cooking fire.

The men sit off to the far side. Here they huddle comfortably before a large open fireplace with smoke and samples of whiskey.

All children are retired to the bedrooms to play.

"Where's young Joe?" Wayne Bugel asks.

"Up near abouts the valley of Two Bears...been gone over a week now...his ma's getting on the anxious side for his coming back." Marty Kingler responds.

"Still after lost foals?" Joel Schumer from the first homestead nearby inquires.

Marty sips his first taste of a clear liquid poured out from a jug held by Joel.

"Damn fine stuff!"

Marty speaks through his puckered lips. "Woooee...that's awful good."

"It's the best squeezings you've made so far!" Wayne lips smack in agreement.

The Schumers have been brewing a pure soft distilled liquid for generations.

"What of your boy Joe?" Wayne resumes.

"Last year he roped nearly a dozen stray foals off those rising meadows. Says he won't settle for less this year." Marty replies proudly.

"Don't those natives up there mind him wandering near to their summer camps?"

"That boy takes his string of gathered horses right over to Many Horns' lodge. The chief holds a heap of magic over them new ponies. His braves won't hunt those fields until summer."

"Many Horns is a fine honest man...does good business." Wayne adds. "He and his people are always welcome at my store. Can't say that about all natives."

"Wayne, that trading post of yours must be the largest this side of the mountains," Joel prophesizes.

"I'd like Joe to bring some of his foals on over for trading one spring."

"His business is his own, Wayne. Them Nez Perce hold big magic with them ponies of Joe's. They're eager to trade for'em." Marty replies.

"Hell Wayne, all you have to do it ride up there when them strong spring thunder storms pass over them slopes and find yourself some mare what's got herself struck dead with lightning. Easy enough to rope a newborn what's don't know how to leave their fallen mother's side." Smirks Joel.

"Damn few men can walk a horse through them open mountains slopes let alone cut out a running foal at a full gallop." Wayne responds agitatedly.

"That boy of yours gets his horsemanship from his native blood." Joel guesses.

Marty Kingler is proud that his maternal grandmother was a member of the Nez Perce Nation.

"It don't hurt a bit when you goes stomping about them

hills on your own." Marty points to the deer skin shirt crafted by his native grandmother that hangs above the fireplace.

"Them signs Na Na stitched into that dress shirt 'er big magic to them Nez Perce. Shows this ranch be part of the Nez Perce Nation." Marty adds.

"Some one better get Carl Meirs to slow down on that whiskey...he's guzzling like it's his last chance at a drink." Marcus Fletcher interrupts.

The Fletchers have traveled the furthest distance to tonight's festivities.

"No ones seen that man without a drink in his hand in last twenty years." Wayne adds.

"Or sober!" Joel chimes.

"His daddy and his grand daddy died of the drink." Marty reminds.

"At least two of his kin been locked up in the local jail house over on the other side of them mountains." Joel reports.

Wayne whispers. "Hear tell at least one of his kin's been hung some wheres in the Dakotas."

"Not right drinking like that in front of the women and young-uns". Marcus is unhappy. "Ought to be asked to leave!"

"Can't rightly...his woman is one fine hard working lady... she's earned her right to join in...mo matter what." Marty replies.

"If'n he gets rowdy we'll help him out to a bed in the barn real gently but permanently like."

❧

"Put that ham down on this here board." Anna Kingler instructs.

"That's one grand roasted hunk of meat Kate." Anna adds

"The Schumers raise the finest hog in this part of the territory." Adds Agnes as she begins to slice.

Agnes Barnby is the cook for the Kingler Ranch.

She is a large bulbous woman of great strength and unyielding health.

"My people were pig farmers back in Germany. They brought their own stock to the new world with them. That there oink maker is a result of generations of breeding," Katy Schumer says.

The Schumer woman is mighty good natured and always wears a generous smile.

"It'll eat like a champion I'm a betting." Laughs ninety year old Jessie Rodgers. "Hope there's bacon from that there pig in the morning."

"Mother you've been eating like a soldier ever since I can remember." Anna jabs as she hugs Jessie.

Anna is long and slender in form as is her mother.

"Set that boiled sausage between the ham and the fried chicken along with them venison steaks...hope there's enough chicken?" Anna questions. "Oh, the roast needs put on that large platter."

"Got seventy some pieces of chicken. Should do!" Shanti Flecther responds.

"Girl where did your parents get a name for you such as Shanti?" Rita Bugel asks.

"My mother read that name is a newspaper what come all the way from San Francisco when she was a child. Some entertainer actress from over the sea had an advertisement in that paper for her evening show. My mother was struck with that name and give it on to me...don't know rightly if'n it means anything important or interesting. Always liked it though."

"Girls all the meat is ready...let's get the rest into the serving bowls." Anna commands.

The woman will serve in large crock containers; green beans warmed with stuffing, fried potatoes and onions, sliced red beats with hard-boiled eggs in a vinegar sauce, peas and butter mixed in mashed sweet potatoes, long noodles in meat gravy, baked beans in a honey and ham sauce, creamed sweet corn, steamed brown rice with black beans, dumplings in a thick chicken gravy, hot pepper soup, and baked yams in a mustered-honey sauce.

A mound of hot biscuits is set on a large warm griddle and covered with a clean cotton cloth.

A punch is made from cool spring water, honey, ginger root, and a bit of seltzer.

Hot coffee and tea, cold milk and varieties of liquor are arrayed as well.

"Deserts to the long table at the rear!" Anna signals.

A tray of steamed apples in sweet cream is placed next to patties of fried dough covered with honey and cinnamon.

A large plumb pudding glazed with a vanilla sugar icing sits behind a heavily frosted three layer chocolate cake.

Fudge, hard-boiled taffy, and stick candy lie out on assorted plates.

Pies from rhubarb, pecans, and chocolate pudding find a home.

"Bittles be ready." Agnes confirms as her hands rest upon her wide hips while a large much soiled kitchen towel hangs over her round shoulder.

"Ladies we will take a plate filled to our own man folk...then we'll call the children over to the table and fix'em each a bite to take back to the bedroom." Anna announces. "Then ladies we will be free till the music starts. The men can take some desert on their own mostly!

The ladies busily gather and commence loading fixings to be consumed. Each man will be served hardy portions."

"Seems the young Schumer girl and your Luke be looking after one another" Notes Jessie.

"My Mary has always had eyes for you Luke!" Kate affirms.

"Mary's turned into a beautiful young woman." Anna replies.

"Look like them two be near to courting." Shanti observes.

"My Mary has set her hopes for Luke since early choosing." Kate smiles.

"Well if'n she can stand a bedroom full of mud and muskets then she'll be right for Luke, Lord knows I can't get him to live civil in that room of his." Anna moans. "No one knows how he finds anything in there. How he can live in there?"

"Agnes, fetch Sheb a plate with a bit of every thing...don't know that he's particular any?" Jessie asks.

"That be your new hired hand?" Rita inquires. "What his full name? He's new to these parts! Ever been married?"

"Sheb Ledbetter...from Texas...don't know" Anna smirks coyly. "Marty sits a whole lot with his work, his word, and his privacy!"

"Bet he's good with a hand gun, and a rifle!" Kate nods her head. "Them Texan cowboys learn shooting and fighting from the time they begin to walk I hear tell."

"Hear tell they need to." Quips Shanti. "Lots of wild crazy characters down there...so say the newspapers."

"Hear tell them Texans be mighty capable with the women as well." Rita Bugel adds. "Not a bad looking man either."

"Shucks, never meet a Texan what couldn't ride, rope, or eat any four legged critter that be known." Jessie chimes.

"Mother are you ready for your glass of whiskey...I'll bring it to your rocking chair." Anna is concerned with her mother's comfort.

"Just one...I suppose! More gives me indigestion." Jessie receives from her daughter a full sized mug of moonshine. "Hate getting old!"

Jessie takes a first long sip of the clear liquor.

"Jessie, why don't you tell us how Sweet Creek got its name?" Rita asks.

"Shoot! You don't want to hear that all legend told again."

Jessie is more interested in her hard drink.

"It's the way you tell it that keeps it fresh and interesting." Katy begs.

"Mother, the girls always look forward to your tales...bet that's why they come all this way." Anna enjoys this account as well. "You know that all your best stories will be asked for tonight."

"Oh well if you insist but this here tale gives but a piece of the whole truth. However what's to be told be most of what's knowd."

Jessie rocks slowly. Her mug is set to her side.

Her eyes drift off into the distance. The old woman's memory moves back in time.

Her expression is relieved. She enjoys the innocence of the earlier times.

"My daddy and his two brothers came out to these parts when they where still just boys."

All the women measure her uncomfortable look.

They briefly pause in their dinner's preparation.

"They brung a mess of mules out to sell to the trappers and hunters. Dumbest creatures the Good Lord every invented... the mule."

Jessie's look of frustration passes quickly.

"During their travels they came upon an old shelter in the bend of a stream. A place much used by travelers in times when they had cause to hold up for a spell. Daddy said it were just a mess of rocks plied up with some logs throwd on top. Couldn't stand up inside or move around...more of a shed than a proper home. Kept a body warm and dry if need be."

Jessie laughs at the thought of three tall boys stuck tight inside with 6 or 8 belligerent mules tethered on the outside.

"Them mules ate up all the profits. Easier to break a wild horse then be a getting anything useful from a stubborn mule."

Jessie frowns.

"My daddy had a mule so dumb that it didn't have the brains to turn around to go backwards! One day that critter walk hind end first into the entrance of our cold cellar...fell in and got it's hind quarters stuck in the ground...and my dad and his brothers wasted a whole day digging the fool animal out of the ground."

The women laugh hysterically.

They desire more of the same.

Jessie rocks with agitation with her recollection.

"My daddy rode that mule to a big poker game, gambled that damnable fool of a mule in the table stakes, and lost that poker hand intentional. My mother wanted to shoot the critter and sell its hide. My daddy was too soft".

"What was your choice Jessie?" Rita asks.

"Hell I offered to pull the trigger...my daddy was too good hearted"

Jessie's eyes water. "Was my mother that had a hard edge?"

"That ole shed stood where Bugle's trading post stands now."

Jessie is quick to pick up more of the tale.

"The creek makes a big bend there...Sweet Creek...the natives give the stream that name in their typical fashion of hiding things. Seems there were two tribes lived on either side near to that bend. Been so long ago that the names of them nations be lost. The Nez Perce says they have lived here forever but before forever these two small tribes occupied the lands around that bend."

Jessie stops for a sip of whiskey. Her eyes brighten with distilled delight.

"My dad traded with some braves that claim to be descendants of them early peoples but he couldn't be sure though. Least ways these two neighbors came to feuding over a special young maiden. I guess this native gal was a real beauty what broke the hearts of many native warriors...one too many it seems."

The rocking stops as Jessie continues.

"The feud came to full out war. There passed a major battle in that there bend where the town now stands. So many died and so much blood was shed that the water in that creek turned red. All the dying and injured natives what crawled there to ease their thirst just gathered in piles along the shore. The number of the slain reduced both tribes to such a weakened condition that they could not defend themselves from any other tribes what where about. Them two nations soon perished from the face of this earth."

"Mother what happened to the maiden what caused all the trouble?" Anna asks.

"No one knows but I'm betting she joined the Black Bear

Tribe. Lord knows that bunch has been making trouble as long any can recall."

"What makes you say that?" Asks Kate.

"Same reason Cain's descendants caused all that trouble in the bible...bad seed is all."

Jessie's strong sentiments give assurance to the ladies.

"That native maiden must have been like that widow maker, Linda Lee...hear she's marring again this fall to old man Richardson." Rita says.

"What makes a woman to keep on marrying like each man was for the first?" Shanti asks.

"A woman never quite feels so feminine as when a she's being touched by the hands of a strong man." Susan Meirs confidently states.

The women collectively sigh.

"She has two boys; one 16 years and another 13 years." Anna figures. "One from each of her two dead husbands...how does a woman kill men off like that?"

"The Good Lord made a version of woman that don't never see another's need, nor feel another's hurt, nor gives to relieve another's want...all that kind sees in other folks is a reflection of their own desires...that kind be powerful good at taking away from others. Can get so bad a body can't rightly live with that kind...they is bound to die sooner than they should" Jessie comments.

"Why would any mature man want that kind of a woman?" Shanti asks.

Jessie replies." Marriage is a union of two souls...many have the need just for the companionship."

"Lonely...the man is just alone too much is all." Rita senses.

"Nothing be lonelier than being dead!" Jessie snorts.

The girls laugh.

"Jessie how's about the rest of the story of Sweet Creek's founding?" Kate reminds.

"The native peoples keep off that there bend in the stream...least wise from living there as they fear the spirits of the dead what dwell there. Never been any theft or trouble from the natives there's about The town of Sweet Creek grew up easy cause the natives left the place to the homesteaders."

Jessie smiles broadly. "My dad traded many a mule to them Black Bear. Them people had the good sense to eat'm...there's nothing else them mules 'er worth."

Jessie's audience gives much laughter.

"Looks as if them ladies are getting ready to feed us boys." Marty announces as the girl's amusement draws the attention of the men.

"Sheb you in for a real treat...bet they don't celebrate spring time down there in Texas the same way?"

"Mr. Kingler them Mexicanos have a real good time come early May...lots music, dancing and festivals." Sheb answers. "Never seen such fixings as them woman folk have ready over there."

"Winters can be hard and long here." Wayne states. "Them what survives here abouts be real happy at it's end."

"How does a Texas boy get all the way up here?" Asks Marcus.

"Well I been hankering for a good while to ride the up into Canada and see the sights." Sheb words are soft and slow. "Just was riding back t'other side this fall when I came upon the Kingler's spread and signed on."

Sheb's thin arms and long fingers motion one direction and then back to the other.

"He's a fine hand...a hard worker...respectful like!" Marty gives his seal of approval.

"Haven't seen you in town...or nears." Wayne directs to Sheb. "You'll have to stop in the trading post."

"Let's sit!" Marty is motioning towards the dining table. "Them young-uns hunger won't keep much longer."

After the men start eating, the children gather in a single procession.

The line passes through the kitchen area where the women fill each child's plate to the individual's taste.

The ladies then assist the youngsters in their return to the bedrooms where the children will consume their supper.

❧

The women watch the men folk and wait.

"Marty's always been a good eater. Don't never put any weight on that tall frame of his." Anna remarks to the other women.

"None of his male kin carried any weight...thin as grass all of'em." Jessie recalls. "Hard workers them Kingler folk. Came from England the original one did. Kinglers was here with the first of us."

"His grandmother, Little Deer was a small woman." Anna states.

"Small and as round as that rain barrel outside catching water...when she was young she was as tiny and as pretty a gal as had ever seen in these parts." Jessie nods.

"How did Marty's grandpap come to wed a Nez Perce?" Shanti asks.

Ann looks at her mother. "Best you tell the story."

"Back in them days the hills was full of bears...big'uns. Now 9 out 10 grizzly bears what takes a man's scent will stalk 'em. No such thing as a grizzly bear what not's hungry." Jessie's rocker kicks into motion with her excitement.

"Now them natives use a bear grease to cover them selves when they be out of their village. Them bears won't stalk their own kind cause they don't be sure how big might be the other bear. Natives mostly fool the nose of a grizzly."

Jessie holds up one hand and shakes one finger at the ladies.

"Where they be getting all that bear grease?" Rita asks.

"From a donor bear?" Jessie laughs. "Course that donor is usually dead at the time."

All the ladies add to the laughter.

"Keeps the bears away...and just about any other living thing as well." Jesse's nose flinches with revulsion at the remembrance of the odor of bear grease.

"Some use a small bell strapped on them so's a tinkling sound is made with each step. Keeps bears away but a bell's no good for use against two footed predators what hears that sound."

"Marty's grand pap was one fine hunter and trapped all over the valleys in those mountains." Anna interrupts. "He use to say a grizzly always walks behind it's prey until it gets a chance to get close and strike one powerful blow with it's giant paw."

"Bear will walk down wind natural like. If a horse gets a scent of a bear, it'll break into a run right quick." Kate adds.

"The bear will get scent of a hurt animal and come a running from miles off. Man what's skinning a deer or elk or any critter had to be mighty quick in them days. Not so many bears about here now...a few but nowheres near like the old days." Jessie assures. "Gots to go well up into the mountains for big bear hunting."

"Any ways, seems Marty's granddad was being stalked after the man shot an elk. He was just skinning the thing when that bear swiped him from behind. Never saw or heard the thing. The bear drug that elk off and let him be...that elk saved his life." Jessie reports. "Bear will attack a person's head and neck first...a heavy fur hat saved that man."

"What happened then?" Shanti asks.

"Native found him hurt real bad...heap of magic for a man what lives through a bear attack. Natives held Marty's granddad in high esteem ever since. Let the man recover in the lodge of Little Deer's father what be the chief at that time. Mr. Kingler figured out native courtship quick enough to get himself hitched."

"They must have loved each other right off!" Kate insists.

"Oh! Them men be near done eating." Agnes informs.

The girls get busy readying their meals after ridding the men's leftovers.

The men return to the large fireplace and refresh their drinks.

"What's the news from Sweet Creek?" Marty asks.

"Miners 'er moving this a ways...some fool's done writ about a gold find nears about." Wayne responds. "Many's tried but there just no gold in these parts...Going to sell a bunch of hardware to those willing to try."

"How's the hunting this spring?" Marcus asks.

"Been a bumper crop of furs taken from the looks." Wayne notes.

"Trappers in early are they?" Marty asks.

"Several camps already set up outside Sweet Creek... seen'em on our ways over here." Joel reports.

"They'll be trading for whiskey and raising hell in town early this year...tell the sheriff!" Wayne proffers. "Oh yeah! Let the sheriff know that Roy Bowler come to town on his lonesome early this week."

"Best to let the sheriff know first thing in the morning...it'll keep till then." Marty replies.

"Seen any bear hide, Joel?" Wayne inquires.

"Hear they be only young bears what been taken and mighty few of 'em." Joel tells.

"No one brings in hide of big grizzly?" Marty is surprised.

"Last few years mostly teenage bear...mostly black bear." Wayne responds. "Just one trapper gets large grizzly anymore... a man named Pauli...strange little man...don't know much about him. Got a family though over to next county."

"Where he's getting his bear?" Marcus asks. "Them bear hides are fetching top money if'en they be full grown grizz."

"Up on the highest rocky slopes...Pauli is the best tracker in them parts...No one else can." Wayne announces.

"The only time bear gets that high is when they go to hibernate!" Marty puzzles. "Hard to find a bear then."

"Well Pauli do and regular like...expect him to bring in some good hides by the end of spring." Wayne assures.

"That reminds me of a fella what use to dump the waste from his cabin instead of burning it. He'd throw it down in a holler back behind his place...stuff would pile up and rot. Bears got use to feeding on his trash. Come late in the spring he'd wait up top and shoot himself a couple fine specimens." Marcus says.

"What happened to that fella?" Joel wonders.

"Well one night he was a sleeping in his cabin...kept his rifle loaded at his side at all times...when a mighty big grizzly come up to his door. Suspect it followed his scent from near that holler. That bear pushed in the cabin door and came right for the man."

All listen with grand anticipation.

"That old boy grabed his weapon and fired without aiming...no time to lift the riffle up to his eye for sighting." Marcus continues.

"What happened then?" Wayne is impatient.

"Hit that bear with the one shot and the critter ran off into the night." Marcus concludes.

"Well what else?" Prompts Joel.

"Tar nation, that old boy was a feared to go to sleep for expecting another grizzly bear to come up anytime day or night after him...after two or three days the man had to give up his farm for fear of sleeping through a bear attack and dying." Marcus smiles." Don't pay to be lazy around bear."

"Bear prefers to take a woman. Couple years back, a man and a woman where stocked by a grizzly. Killed the woman but left the man alive." Marty recalls.

"Yes sir I recall that happening. Some tenderfeet farmers south a ways from here." Wayne recollects. "Neighbors got together and hunted that there bear down and shot it. I sold its hide!"

"Seems to me there was a woman what killed a bear that broke into her farmhouse with a wood ax she kept in the kitchen by the hot stove." Marty recalls. "Just her and a baby home at the time. Believe I read the account in the paper back when I was younger."

"Them wild stories get picked up by the papers back east

and they keeps folks from coming out to the west." Wayne says agitatedly.

"Don't stop them with gold fever from a coming." Sheb states dryly.

"No telling what kind of fool gets to risking his life on gold finding." Marcus adds. "They be coming wild eyed and reckless...causing all kinds of trouble."

"Well them natives up in them hills won't take kindly to them miners tramping over their burial sites and disturbing their hunting grounds. Likely to be some native trouble to come." Marty adds.

"Many Horns is reasonable man...the army will have to keep them miners outa the natives' sacred places." Wayne insists.

"Them young warriors might not listen to Many Horns counsel. Best let them miners know when they get to buying at your trading post Wayne...could save someone's life." Marty advises.

"Last time there was trouble with miners up in the mountains, it happened over drinking water. Them fools fouled the water at several of the natives drinking holes...mess of folks died until the army rooted them miners outa them parts." Marcus recollects.

"Not to change the subject...but Will Richardson is a going to marry the widow Lee." Wayne announces.

"Fine looking woman." Marty states. "Hard working too!"

"What can she see in that old goat Richardson...he's as cheap as any what ever come across the Missouri River...when his wife died what bits she left he sold or burnt...never gave one thing to the needy about here." Joel does not like the man.

"He's got his hands full with Linda Lee...that's for sure. She tells everybody she's a going to live to be one hundred years old...not a day less." Wayne reports.

"Most women don't figure they can make a life for themselves...that be why they choose a man for...seems this lady likes the sort of life she'll be taking on when she marries." Sheb remarks.

Marcus scratches his head. "How many times she been a widow up to now?"

"Twice since she come here...no one knows if'n she was widowed before." Wayne shrugs his shoulders in doubt.

"Well seems to me that two dangerous forces are coming together and only one's a going to survive!" Marty jokes.

"How's about a bet on the one to survive that marriage?" Joel suggests.

"Well let's have a show of hands what thinks Old Will can last five years as a newly wed?"

Wayne counts only the hand of Marty as it is raised.

"Now how many think that widow Lee will be holding another funeral for her husband fore too long?"

Wayne, Marcus and Joel raise their hands.

"The bet is Mrs. Lee outlives Will Richardson with odds 3 to 1 in her favor."

All the boys hoot with mischief.

"Well every man needs a good horse and a good woman!" Carl blows forth in a sober moment.

"Good horses needs to be out on the open range...good woman needs housed up real sound like. Be hard for a man to keep his horse and his woman satisfied all the time." Marty gives his final words.

"Easier to keep a horse happy...that be why some men stay in the saddle." Wayne concludes.

Sheb notes aside to Marty." That boy of yours has not touched one bit of food or drink yet. He's a sitting spell bound in that corner with a cute blond filly."

"That's the Schumer girl...Luke always been sweet on her. Since she's come to be a full grode woman he's pickled dumb just at the sight of her. He's not a hearing one thing she's a saying over there. He'll sit there stupefied as long as she looks at him."

Both men smile with amusement.

"Ever been married, Sheb?" Marty asks.

"Once! Back when I were near to your boy Luke's age." Sheb nods affirmatively.

"Lost' em all...three kids one at a time with fever. My wife and I buried all her reasons for living. My woman just wasted away then...I buried her and got up in my saddle and rode off. Been riding my horse ever since."

"Must have been hard for you Sheb! Must be hard yet." Marty sympathizes.

"Lost all expectings from life. Just a living one day...one hour at a time. Got no cause to be a worried over much." Sheb's head hangs a bit low.

"Tell us how you like our territory." Marcus interrupts.

"Like it fine." Sheb responds.

"Man what's been traveling all that time must have seen a mess of places." Marcus continues.

"Seen my share...hope to see a bit more." Sheb answers.

"Seen much gun play?" Marcus persists.

"Some...most folks live peaceful like." Sheb assures.

"Must have held many a job during that time." All the men are interested in Marcus thoughts.

"Always work for someone who's willing to get dirty." Sheb confirms.

"Ever come across a gun what's been hired on?" Marcus is anxious to hear.

"Seen a few...mostly near about a place where there was a range dispute. They get hired to go after cattle rustlers, settle troubles over water rights...even hire on to fight natives in rough times." Sheb recalls.

"You ever hired on for gun work?" Marty asks.

"Riding as a hired gun is short work...damn few men can make a living that a way...outlaws mostly...and law men. Bet no one in Sweet Creek ever hired a gun fighter...or ever seen one most like." Sheb dismisses the notion.

"Well some years back we had a gun fighter drift through... a man named Frank Simms...always wore a side arm...distant type." Wayne recalls.

"Folks left him be...he never caused no trouble here... moved on after couple days." Joel reminds.

"That fellar was moving on to the Dakotas...He was a

waiting up here till some others joined him. Was some trouble over there with homesteaders." Wayne states.

"Nothing here to fight over." Marty reasons.

"Could be if'n they ever find gold!" Marcus fears.

"Never going to find gold...damn near every creek and holler been searched." Wayne insists.

"It's been peaceful here since the U. S. Calvary keeps the Nez Perce lands clear of trespassers. Has been some gun play but thieving be only cause of trouble nowadays." Joel notes.

"Gun fighters always be taking the advantage...prefer killing someone easy like". Sheb closes. "Best to be ready...don't take too much to start trouble...just a fool with a gun."

"You must have crossed through many of the native lands." Wayne affirms.

"Plenty! I were raised near Apache lands in the south west." Sheb replies. "Seen a whole assortment of natives...most be friendly."

"Here tell them Apaches be fierce fighters." Marcus offers.

"An Apache can tract anything over any type of ground. Settlers will tract any critter what leaves good sign but there be some signs only the Apache can read."

Sheb points to the ground before him. "We stayed out of their sacred hills...they might make off with an occasional horse of our'n or kill a steer when they be hungry but otherwise they let us be."

"Ever been tracked by a native what was looking for your scalp?" Wayne asks.

"Did some scouting in Oklahoma lands for the army...been chased right good!" Sheb nods yes.

The women take their turn at dining.

Each lady samples the others' prepared food.

"Try this chicken Agnes made mother." Anna suggests.

"Don't give me no little piece...like my chicken pieces big." Jessie warns.

"Bet you have a chicken story Mrs. Rodgers!" Shanti prompts.

Jessie smiles at the thoughts being recalled.

"When I were first married my husband...a sweet man mind you...came home with a box of peeps from old man Ward's dry goods. Harold Ward be the man what owned the trading post back in them times. He had the ugliest wife ever seen in these parts but he loved her like a queen. The more that woman pecked on Mr. Ward the more he loved her. All us children called her Pig-nose Ward. She did the school teaching in them days...give her own the best marks."

The women sit spell bound.

"Any way, them peeps what my man brung to the farm turned out to be mostly roosters...come day break dozen of them critters came to calling out so loud seemed like the whole U.S. Calvary were a charging up to go to war. The loudest damn pile of noise ever any body ever heard. Couldn't get that man to take a hatchet to a one of 'em. So I done rid the place of'em all at one time."

"How did you do that mother." Anna asks holding back her laughter.

"Got up before sun rise. Went out under the tree where them bandy rosters were a sleeping up on a branch. Shot all of'em down with your father's shot gun."

Tears fill the women's' eye from laughter as they continue to dine.

"Got any taters left warm yet?" Mrs. Rodgers holds out her plate for another helping. "Them be mighty good eating Agnes!"

Jessie likes potatoes mashed, fried, boiled, baked or scalloped.

"Thank you, Mrs. Rodgers." Agnes responds. "It be a pleasure to serve fixens to a good eater like yourself."

"Always been a big eater...all my folks eat hearty." Jessie nods affirmatively.

"Reminds me of a time my Uncle Pat came to live with us. Uncle Pat wasn't married and wasn't working regular. Came to our farm looking for employment."

Jessie glows warmly at her remembrance.

"Fine looking, fine built man was my Uncle Pat. Didn't take to farm work or hard work for that matter." Jessie's eyes beam with delight as she looks on to the ladies.

"Damn nation, it be hard to find a job when you don't take to work natural like." Jessie laughs.

"That man could talk on with one captivating story after another with no end in sight. If'n he could have gotten paid for talking he'd been rich in a week."

The ladies laughter does not end their need for more gossip.

"Spent his time entertaining the lady folk." Jessie eyes water. "My mother loved Uncle Pat. The man could do no wrong in her eyes. Mother could care less if'n he ever did a lick of work."

"Well! If Uncle Pat wasn't talking then he was a eating. Saw personal, my Uncle Pat eat six helpings of sausage and biscuits, then sit down to a full meal one hour later with no loss of an appetite. "Jessie pauses for emphasis." Ate near a whole pie afterwards"

Jessie looks in disbelief to her audience. "Never used a bit of his energy in labor. Must have talked his weight off."

Many laughs are given in agreement.

"What happened to old Uncle Pat?" Anna asks.

"Married a rich widow woman who was heading back to St Louis after burying her husband."

Much sadness comes to Jessie. "Never saw my Uncle Pat again. Died young in the big city. Marrying be a risky business."

Suddenly Jessie bends over convulsed in laughter.

Smiles return with Jessie's endless wit.

"My dad would get awful mad at Pat for staying in bed while the rest of the men folk went off to work. One hot summer day, Pat stayed in bed a terrible long time. My dad came in the house and lit a large fire in every fireplace. Pat got so hot in bed he came out of his room a sweating and a puffing and a running around mighty confused. Never saw my dad laugh so hard. He just couldn't breathe and he couldn't stop a laughing. "

Jessie stands to relive the cramps returning from her experience.

She continues.

"Here was my dad and my uncle both full out hysterical. Mother went panic-stricken as well a trying to cool off Pat, shush pap while a worrying if dad would ever breathe again. I was a looking from one out of control adult to the other. All them grown ups were a twisting about beside themselves with uncontained unnatural aspirations and little me just a helpless and a wanting to cry and laugh at the same time."

Tears fill all the ladies' eyes at the extreme of their amusement.

The long open trail rises gently over a meadow's crest to fall quickly into turn.

Steady on rider and mount step slowly with rarely a quickened pace.

Balance and ease in motion of the joined pair gives way to a steady onward progress.

There is no haste.

The rider sits tall under his broad Texan hat.

His long over coat gives way at the stirrups to snake skin boots with spurs.

The rifle, rope, saddlebag and other gear tell of a long trail ahead.

The earth covering horse and rider give say to a long trail passed.

Heavy dusk gives no cause to their travel's halt.

Failing light keeps the horse on the road as the robin yet stalks on the meadow's floor.

Day yields way to night.

The screech of a distant owl is carried on gentle breeze.

Rider and horse breathe deeply of the sweet warm spring air.

The man's mind drifts to thoughts of pleasant times past.

He recalls a boyhood ride from a long hunt to his mother's house and his favorite meal.

His mother's image is of a young strong woman.

His mount was a fast Pinto stallion named Rags.

His mother was the first to use this name when the foal took to pulling on her laundry as it hung in the sunshine.

He remembers his grandfather and the difficult trails they rode together.

His first lessons in tracking game were given from these adventures.

Grandfather would point his finger to his old head and then to the center of his aged chest.

"When all else is the same, it is one's head and one's heart that will make the final difference." The old man would say.

His mount then was called Ruff Box and his grandfather's horse was called Graveyard. They animals were born identical twins.

Graveyard was the stronger steed and his was grandfather's forever-favorite ride.

Dreams of his young wife enter his thoughts.

He had married a good gentle woman.

She loved to ride a white mare named, Snow bank.

His wife gave this name. The choice was made because of the large round hindquarters that dominated the animal's shape.

All thoughts of the before now pass through his soul with joy.

The loss of his mother, grandfather and wife no longer give pain. His love for his people transcends the present emptiness of the sky and the open range.

His heart is warmed.

As the eastern sky blackens, the rider approaches a split in the trail.

The horse gives an abrupt snort and takes a quick turn. The beast comes to a complete stop indicating a preference.

The rider studies the direction following each branch in the divergence of the road.

"Yep! You got more damn sense than most."

The rider acknowledges as the horse moves down the fork into the leftward divide.

"Seems to be a piece or two of light shining out on the flat of the horizon there...Ranchers most likely!"

The rider pats the neck of the horse.

"You smell a barn that aways do ya?"

The rider glances about the sky.

"Will sashay down and ask for to stay the night. Perhaps you'll enjoy some equine companionship?"

The mount begins the passage to the day's end with youthful strides.

The rider's memory continues.

"Old Hat Box!"

That was the name of the horse his mother used with her carriage to get to the shopping in town.

Fine small mare that was as gentle as could be. Ma never lost a package for having that critter bolt and run away.

He recalls a tale from his grandmother of a time when she was pregnant and standing out next to the corral on his granddad's farm.

Someone waved a towel to shoo a fly out the door of the homestead.

The only horse in the corral was extra skittish.

Took to a panic from that towel a moving.

That pony scrammed out of that enclosure right through the fence knocking his grandmother to the ground.

There was another horse for which his dad had paid good money. When that mare got tired of being under a saddle she would lay right down and refused to move.

She was a beautiful healthy strong filly.

Had gold hair with white locks and dark nose.

"Can't recollect her name."

Dad was mighty happy to trade her off.

The laughter of the women strays the men from their conversation and drink.

"Old Jessie! Her stories never lose their freshness." Marty beams. "Heard them all many a time and look forward to a hearing them all again. Her humor keeps Jessie...keeps us all mighty young."

"How old is Jessie" Sheb asks.

Marty scratches his head.

"No one's rightly sure. Her folks didn't put names in the bible. Some say she got to be ninety, some say that she be much older. Jessie don't know herself and Jessie doesn't care a bit."

"How long has she been a widow?" Sheb's interest persists.

"Jessie had been widowed forty years by my count." Marty offers. "Her men died from a natural disease and on the much too young side. Not unusual in the harsh seasons we have out here."

"Must be one strong gal, old Jessie!" Sheb concludes.

"Them what survives many years in these parts be powerful strong. That goes for man or beast." Joel adds.

"There's a tale told by the natives of one trapper that lived heres about for well over one hundred years." Marcus recalls.

"That be the one they call Stump?" Asks Marty.

"The same!"

Wayne answers. "Never married. Never ate meat. Kept cats! Couldn't ever get along with people."

"Why did they call him Stump?" Asks Sheb. "Did he lose a leg?"

"No! He liked to fire his rifle off a stump what he used for support. Put stumps all over abouts his cabin. He was a dead shot from far off when he fired from one of them stumps. Natives where mighty respectful of his skill that aways and never would venture near his home." Marcus replies.

"How'd he come to live so long? Did he have a secret?" Sheb wonders.

"I heared he attributed his long life to just enjoying himself. Living as much like as when he was a juvenile as he could." Wayne informs.

"Liked his whiskey!" Joel adds.

"There was a time that not one native could remember when old Stump first showed up here abouts. Stump out lived the entire native population that first greeted him.

"How old was he when he died?" Sheb quizzes.

"No one knows! He just stopped turning up. Even the natives lost sight of him." Marty replies

"Anyone ride over to his cabin to check?" Sheb suggests.

"No one had poor enough judgment to try with all them stumps available for his use." Joel jokes.

"My grandfather had a mule what lived for 38 years. That jackass out lasted grandpa's time as a married man." Sheb reports. "Knew that mule better than any of his kin...preferred it over his kin most likely."

"I sell a whiskey what's been 50 years in the barrel before the bottling and it been sitting in my store for 20 years more." Wayne advertises.

"Say lets all go together and buy that old whiskey for the next wedding of any family what's here. We'll all consume that liquor the night of the wedding." Joel teases.

"Shoot! When my boy Luke gets hitched I'll buy the whole bottle. Just us that be here tonight will sit down and enjoy it together." Marty promises.

"Most of cats live but a year or two as most die a violent death" Marcus injects. "My ma had a cat that was 25 years old when it got run down by a stage coach. Ma could never forgive herself for that old cat a dying before its time."

The men laugh at the irony in the joke.

❧

"Mother do you want to taste any of the deserts?" Anna asks.

"Don't care for deserts. Never did!" Jessie states. "Believe I'll have a half glass more of whiskey before the dancing commences."

"When I was a growing up all the folks had a bit of whiskey including the young adults." Jessie nods." Might get some deserts on a Sunday or other social. Whiskey kills the taste for sweets."

Jessie nods again. "That be the way the Good Lord intended it."

Many smiles arrive to the attending women folk.

"In some families when they sat down for the evening together they be no words spoke until the whiskey got poured out to all." Jessie continues. " No one there knew how to make conversation being full sober."

Laughter is quick from the ladies.

"Old lady Marsh hated the stuff being that her husband was a drunk and beat her often." Jessie recollects. "Can't hardly remember seeing that woman without a bruise somewheres on her face or body."

The mood of the women turns somber.

"Old man Marsh came along home from the still one cold winter night so drunk that he fell down outside in front of his own doorstep. Froze to death right there. His wife found him all stiff at first light."

Jessie pauses. "Every year since then on the anniversary of that night, Widow Marsh drinks one teaspoon full of whiskey in her hot tea as way of celebrating."

Convulsive hilarity ensues.

"What about the Baker's hog?" Anna asks for another tale of drink.

"Them Bakers were never farmers." Jessie returns. "Made mighty fine sour mash whiskey."

"Fed the pulp waste to the one hog" Jessie's mind revives the details of her intending account.

"Baker's pig got so big no body could go near it for fear's

sake. Grew to be near 14 feet long and close to 2000 pounds in weight. The swine turned plum wild. Ran the county tearing into stills. It were drunk most of the time. Men folk got too scared to go into the woods after it. That hog died of liver failure."

Kate Schumer falls back off her chair in hysteria.

The women abandon all sense but the uproarious.

"That swine put a dent in the local whiskey business for years. Baker went broke and lost his ranch." Jessie keeps on.

The women wave to Jessie begging her to stop.

They fear losing complete control of themselves.

Anna runs away laughing while holding her bladder.

"Whole tribe back in them hills got mighty drunk on the bacon and sausage they got from Baker in trade."

All the women but Jessie follow Anna out into the fresh air.

❧

The late evening rider nears the farm house.

The women have taken flight to escape Jessie's merciless humor.

The eruption of loud noise from the ladies as they emerge from the cabin startles the nearing horse and rider.

The man pulls back on the reins to bring the motion of the horse to a stop.

"Be some kind of riot over to that ranch."

The rider stretches high in the saddle to gain advantage to his look.

"Appears to be all women in some mighty big fuss."

The sounds of collective merriment from the ranch's front arrive at the distance much like the chaos heard in warfare.

"Women!" The rider announces.

"A whole bunch of them be powerful disturbed."

The rider dismounts.

He begins a slow walk in the direction of the ranch.

The horse follows at his side.

"No sense hurrying over there just to get caught up in some serious feminine unrest."

"Years back when I were still a boy my ma sent me into one of the local villages."

The rider is to explain the need for caution in the present circumstance to his mount.

"Well all the men folk had made off for the day fishing together or out after some other sport."

The man's free hand moves with agitation in the direction of the farm house.

"Some neighbor ladies took the opportunity to express their mutual disappointment with each other. Their comments got right serious and deeply hurtful."

His mount attempts to take meaning from the gestures of the man.

"Words started more wars the gunpowder!"

The horse is keen to hear the sounds from the man and snorts in response.

"As they be no manly restraint anywhere's about the town at that time, some other of the women folk joined in taking one side or the other. The tossing of bitter words gave way to objects being thrown from back and forth."

"Just in a flash water jugs, empty bottles, sticks, any bit that served as a missile was launched in the assault. Women where a running, and a throwing and a screaming as loud as they could be."

"Never been as scared as that moment."

The man points his finger empathically toward his attentive horse.

"Never saw a bunch of folks go berserk instantaneously before. They scared off every dog, cat, bird, and critter about."

The horse nods and pounds the ground repetitively with one hoof in response to the man's demeanor.

"Took to hiding right off. Couldn't leave a watching for I was spell bound over the goings on."

"When the voices and arms of them women folk went

numb. Then order was restored just as sudden as the fracas erupted."

"That's why we'll stay away. Things get normal like then we'll get to your barn."

Marty instructs the men in preparing the main room for dancing and music.

He plays a fine fiddle and Wayne is an accomplished banjo player.

The music will ebb and flow with the energy of the dancers young and old.

Jessie will dance with the little ones.

Girls will dance with girls and occasionally pull a man into a hoedown.

Square dancing, jigs and reels, circle promenades will be held. The wholesome crowd will try line dances, and two steps of every known form.

Interrupts for food, drink and relief are frequent but will not stint the festivity.

When the musicians rest, songs from a chorus or solo will flow.

Everyone will choose to dance.

Everyone except Anna because in her rush to the outside, she took a fall and injured her ankle.

She won't dance, walk, or ride for some days.

Anna will however play the small piano and sing through out the night.

Luke Kingler and Mary Schumer have yet to separate company.

"Let's go outside for a spell so's we can be alone?" Asks Luke.

"We need some privacy!" Mary responds as she similes in delightful anticipation.

"I want to hold you Mary...quiet and sweet like." Luke implores in a whisper.

Mary holds Luke's hands in hers.

Her eyes shine brightly.

Her smile is lasting. "I can't. We have to wait!"

"What for...you wanna...I wanna?" Luke's frustration shows.

"My mother has been watching me all night. Her eyes never have a rest. You'd think she'd have more to fret over than me." Mary's frustration shows.

"Your mother knows that I'm honorable. She likes me I'm sure."

"It's me she's worried about." Mary frets. "Wait until they play the Louisiana Reel. Then we will slip outside. Mother goes crazy when they play that tune and then she will forget about me."

The Louisiana Reel is the most popular tune played locally for dancing.

All able bodies will participate.

The dance is also one of the longest and may continue uninterrupted for half an hour.

"There she is again looking at me until she catches my eye." Mary knees bounce to relieve the boredom of their wait.

Luke stares at the face and lips of the pretty attending girl. "I can't wait till we are alone."

"I can't wait until we are married?" The girl replies and waits for a response.

Luke's silence dismisses Mary's smile.

Her face is questioning.

"You do want to marry me...don't you?" Her words are pointed.

Luke is 19 years of age.

His dreams are of ranch and farm.

Thoughts of a wife and family are distant.

"Sure...yes...will get married...sometime."

Luke's answer does not satisfy.

"I'm 14. My mother and my grand mother were wives and mothers by the time they were 15." Mary needs understanding.

Again Luke misinterprets the meaning of Mary's complaint. "Them was earlier times...frontier times. Not like now."

Luke is sure his words will comfort. "I'll speak to my folks and then I'll speak to your folks."

"You haven't told you parents about our feelings for each other?" Mary is unhappy. "What are you waiting for? You haven't committed to our future. Your not sure!"

Mary's eyes tear.

"We've been busy with the end of winter and all. Lot's a mending before the summer comes."

"Your thoughts should be of us first. The ranch, the fences and the livestock should come second." Mary is angry and withdraws her hands.

Mary is not sure she wants to be with Luke at this moment.

The first chords of the Louisiana Reel play out.

A great commotion of high stepping country folk fills the dance floor.

Mary notes her mother's complete distraction.

She seizes Luke's hand.

"Now!" She delivers as she pulls the boy toward and out the front door into the night.

Around to the side of the cabin the pair steps briskly.

Luke moves close to the front of Mary.

There is little space to separate their bodies.

Luke's two large hands find Mary's tiny waist.

Her hands gently slide up Luke's arms towards his shoulders.

Her grip is soft and barely felt by Luke.

His grip is full and tight.

Mary is enraptured by his close presence and the musk of his firm body.

Luke is excited by the softness of her form.

Mary's yielding look arouses Luke to aggression.

Luke's insistent response lifts Mary lips toward his.

Luke's mouth closes upon hers in a full long tender kiss.

Mary steps fully into his embrace.

Upon this moment of full desire Luke utters "I want you for my woman."

After an examining look Mary reaffirms. "I want you for my husband."

The horse and rider have recombined to the one.

The harmony of the music has made peaceful the night.

Their approach to the Klinger Ranch is concluding.

Luke is undisturbed by the sound of the rider's arrival to the front of the cabin.

Mary's passion is silent. "Some one's out there. I hear a horse."

Hesitantly Luke listens to her request.

He recognizes her concern. "Horse and rider are about to come in."

"Who's that what be coming this late?" Mary asks. "Is your mother expecting any one not on time?"

Luke peeks around the corner.

"No one that I know of. It's a lone rider." He states as he grips Mary's arm and leads her back inside. "Best I tell dad...in case it be trouble."

As the rider enters the ranch, several men stand on the porch of the cabin.

Rider and horse are aware of the greeting to come.

The men study the tall thin rider.

"Anybody recognize the horse or the rider?" Asks Marty.

Unanimously they agree that a stranger is coming.

The lone traveler and mount stop to give and to take best view.

"Howdy!" The rider declares.

Marty steps out.

"Welcome stranger. You're traveling late!"

"My respects to all." The rider does not dismount. "Got a ways to go."

"Can I help you?" Marty's eyes do not depart the man, his horse or the rider's hands.

"Need a place to throw down for the night."

The rider's hands remain up on the saddle in full view." My mount took wind of your barn there a while back. Be happy to pay you for your bother."

"He's in need of some companionship I'm supposing." Marty responds. "What's you business in these parts? If'n you don't mind the asking."

"Passing through. Going to stop in Sweet Creek to see the sheriff then I'll be on my way."

"Not much room? The barn will have to do." Marty accounts.

"I'll be just all right out to the side. Fine night! I'll keep well." The rider says.

"Sheriff won't be in town tomorrow." Marty adds.

All the other men have been taking carefull note of the conversation.

The rider waits for more information.

Marty ponders.

"You're welcome to stay the night." He points to the barn. "Stable your mount. Plenty of feed...we don't charge for common curtsey here abouts."

Marty waits for a response.

The rider nods his head in agreement." Know where I can meet the local sheriff?"

"Stop at the kitchen here tomorrow. You can have breakfast and the sheriff will be here." Marty assures. "First light! They be a lot of a hullabaloo then as the festivities break up."

"I sleep light. I'll be awake before dawn either way." The rider shows appreciation.

"Be welcome to join in. Music, dance, something to eat...a bit of whiskey...all free in keeping of springtime come."

Marty is taking a liking to the man.

"Won't interfere. I'll get to bedding down." The rider nods again in appreciation and to take his leave.

"Can I ask your name?"

"Legs!"

The rider responds as his horse trots off to the barn.

"Seems like a descent sort." Wayne comments to Marty.

"Powerful determined to be out here on the range late like." Joel adds.

"Not much of a bother...him sleeping out...wish I could have offered better." Marty instructs.

"You were most hospitable to the man." Marcus concedes.

"Never heard the name Legs in these parts." Adds Carl.

"Any one ever heard of a man named Legs?" Wayne asks.

Sheb has been quiet and retried during the encounter. "That there be U S Marshall Legs."

All have the hired hand's attention.

"His full name is Wooden Legs." Sheb tells.

"I didn't see no sign of a lost leg on the man." Carl sneers.

"Strange name for a fellar!" Joel comments.

"His grand pappy give him that name." Sheb retorts. "His grand pappy was a big war chief of the Sioux. Story is that as a baby his legs never tired. Never needed resting."

"Seem to know a lot about the Marshal, Sheb." Marcus notes

"He's famous down Texas way. He be up this direction for only one reason. Chasing a mighty bad hombre for a long way." Sheb assures.

"Well! We will not talk of this tonight. The morning will be here soon enough." Marty requests.

The Marshall is glad to have his horse take some needed comfort.

He takes his gear to the far side of the barn away from the ranch house.

Here he'll sleep in the company of the stars and the open sky.

A small black cigar is produced.

This tobacco gives the Marshall a sense of relaxation when smoked.

As the fumes are exhaled the Marshall reviews the look and style of every man upon the porch that was there to greet him.

The marshal is up long before dawn.

He has inspected all the animals gathered by the night's attendants.

All is found to be correct about the place.

He will stand afar and watch the folks as they depart to ensure all is correct with the lodgers.

The men folk emerge at first light to rein carriage to horse.

The children wash and gather belongings as the ladies reheat meat, cook eggs and prepare a hearty breakfast before departure.

Marty Klinger steps to the barn to seek the marshal.

"Good morning. How did you rest?"

"Right fine!" The stranger nods.

"I come to bring you to breakfast with the sheriff."

"Don't like to disturb folks. I'll be fine here. Be over after all the folks have gone off." The stranger nods again.

"Suit your self but we will save some eggs for you. The crowd will be leaving any minute"

Marty returns.

The marshal wants to study the folks without their notice.

He particularly wishes to observe Sheb.

About the time that a black cigar has been completely smoked by the marshal, the Klinger estate is returned to normal.

The marshal walks to the door of the Klinger Ranch.

Young Luke opens the door.

"Greetings! My folks are waiting at the table. Coffee's hot."

The marshal is seated with Mr. and Mrs. Klinger.

Food and coffee are produced.

"What can we do for you Mr. Legs?" Anna asks.

"Mam, I'm a federal officer in pursuit of a criminal wanted down Oklahoma way for killing a deputy marshal. I need to make some inquires. I'd be obliged if you would let me speak with your sheriff."

"Well that's easy marshal. You're talking to her!"

Chapter 2

A Bath House

Sheriff Anna Klinger has directed the marshal with whom to make general inquires in the town of Sweet Creek.

She has also requested of him to investigate the whereabouts of Mrs. Roy Bowler.

The marshal has been in the saddle for many a day with only the comforts of field and steam.

He is anticipating a stay with ease in Short Creek.

A soft bed indoor, and warm food in a cafe will make the coming experience a welcomed holiday.

Albert Heberle's shop is in the midst of the community

of Sweet Creek. It's a large stone building with a handsomely decorated front. Bright colors and European style buttress and arch tell the visitor of the shop's quality and the owner's success.

Marshal Legs dismounts and ties his horse to the hitching post in the store's front.

He begins to brush the dust form his cloths.

Hs eyes study Heberle's store.

"Someplace right out of the old world." Marshal Legs remarks to himself.

A thin grayed hair man; neatly dressed and in a manner that is exact to every detail emerges.

"You are new to here! Yah?"

The owner quickly inspects the form of marshal and his horse. "Is much traveling with you? You need a place to stay until roads north are open!"

The thin man stands with his back erect and awaits a response.

"The sheriff tells me you rent out of rooms." Marshal Legs inquires.

"Yah, Yah! It's good here for the traveler. The beds are just like you find in Germany, large and soft!" The proprietor smiles knowing that the quality he offers will be enjoyed by all his customers.

Marshall Legs nods once in acknowledgement.

"There is no woman to stay here. Only men take lodge... The women are too demanding and too much trouble. Besides my wife is always with jealous ideas."

"Just me and my horse." Responds the marshal.

"Good! My wife Brigette will show you to a room. The entrance is around back."

The owner points to a path that wanders around to the rear of the building.

"There is a stable just behind. My son Günter will see to the care of you animal while you are guest of Heberle." Again the required direction is pointed out.

"Sounds real fine!" Marshall Legs again nods in agreement.

"There is below a basement room for privacy. There is the shower with running hot and cold water. There is the sink and washroom again with hot and cold water. There is the toilet with running water for flushing. It s no large room but it's built just as you would find in Germany like the Romans constructed there."

"Didn't get your name?" The marshal responds.

"Albert Heberle! I am the owner. I studied engineering in the old country. My wife and I came to America to escape the plague in Germany. Here I make the living as the butcher. It's good honest work. My family and I are very proud of that which we have built up here."

Albert sends a very pleasant smile in welcome to his newly arrived guest.

The marshal likes the man. "As soon as I've settled my horse I'll try you indoors plumbing."

"There is the good food at the café!" Albert points down the lane that runs through the village to a small yellow house.

"The food is good and not expensive. Yah?"

Another nod comes forth from the marshal.

"You shall want three nights stay before you can travel north!" Albert informs.

The expression on Marshall Legs' face shows his disbelief.

Albert does not miss this.

"There is heavy flooding ahead. It's always this way at this time of year. The roadway is closed at the bridges.

I have inspected these myself and they are not safe when the water is high."

The mood of Albert is most serious and confident. "Every spring when there is heavy storms on the upper hills there is flooding, and there is dying by those who should heed warnings but do not."

The marshal offers a final nod then he points in the direction of the rear access.

"Bridgette! Rouse!" Albert calls to his wife.

"Yah! A buxom and handsome woman appears at the door

"This man requires a room." Albert informs her.

"Yah Yah! Just go around then I meet you to open the door." The woman smiles at the marshal.

❧

Marshall Legs is unaccustomed to the finery of the privy at hand.

He relishes however the challenge to soak and clean thoroughly.

His clothes are piled upon a small bench.

His hat rests atop at the side and his boots just at the floor below.

His guns and holsters are mounted above on a peg near to the door of the shower.

The water flow of the shower is generous and comfortably heated by early Roman tile and flue design.

In the manner most efficient the shower's spray and sound are contained within the stall.

Exterior noise and distraction do not penetrate.

The soap provided by the Heberle's is made in the traditional German style with the strong fresh scent of pine.

In a short time Marshall Legs is lathering and relaxing in body and soul as the gentle water relieves the harshness of the open road.

The present occurrence recalls to the sheriff his time as husband and provider.

His wife had never experienced as rich and luxurious a shower.

He's not sure if anyone he's ever known has had a similar cleansing.

"Worth the long ride!" Marshall Legs tells himself as the water continues to fall over his sore body.

Few minutes turn into many as his need for relief of dust and sweat persists.

"I'm a gone to wash my duds up and make the day sweet and fresh. Might have young Günter give my horse a wash down at the river. We will both start up refreshed together."

The bather achieves a large portion of satisfaction.

While the shower is being occupied, a number of women are visiting the privy and are quick to begin washing some needed items.

They are unknowing and indifferent as to the shower's occupancy.

As they become busy about the needs that compel their attendance, one young lady takes note.

"There is some man's close piled over here." She calls to her companions. "I think there's a man in that there shower."

Uncontrollable curiosity moves the girls into the small corner to inspect the cloths and chance to peek at the shower's user.

"Wait calls out their leader!"

Too late!

Her peers close upon the male artifacts and knock about the lady carrying a bucket of a cleaning solution made of a strong acid.

The bucket falls free with its contents spilling over the hat, boots and vestments of the marshal.

"Oh no!" Shrieks one girl

The moment is frozen as the ladies examine the unintended disaster.

"We've ruined this man's garments." Announces another woman.

"It's my fault! I wasn't strong enough to hold the dang bucket." The guilty party is staring with anger at the mess that she has just created.

"Listen to me!" The leader gathers everyone's attention.

"We are all responsible! No one of us is to blame." The collective look upon the ladies is disconsolate.

"What shall we do?" They all ask.

"Ill wait for the man, apologize, explain everything, and ask his forgiveness." The principal female states to the others.

"He's going to be really made at you...us that is!" Another girl gives comment while looking at the empty bucket. "Let's clean up and get out of here at once.

"That's a fine idea." The responsible voice agrees.

Just as the majority of women are departing the chamber the marshal is exiting the shower.

The sheriff is stunned at the sight of the retreating young women.

He does not note the single female that awaits him within.

The lawman stands wet with towel in hand pondering the meaning of the departing images before him.

"Excuse me mister." A feminine voice asks for his attention.

The marshal turns to see a young woman standing to greet him.

Her hands are tightly folded together with fingers interlocked.

The woman's expression is one of distress.

The lady takes a deep breath, looks directly into the marshal's eyes as he begins to speak.

"You not supposed to be here. This place is for men only. None of them women belong here." He states with final masculine authority. "I'll have to inform Mr. Heberle of this intrusion!"

The woman is startled by the strength in the man's voice.

Her hands fold now as in prayer and her eyes close momentarily as if invoking divine guidance.

"The Heberles have invited us to use this facility!" Her voice carries some panic as she struggles to return to the unpleasant issue of his ruined vestments.

The marshal observes the lady's eyes as open full wide and filled with anxiety and despair.

The woman's back stiffens.

Her eyes close again.

Her hands are clasped in small grips as her arms lower to her side.

"We spoiled you cloths!" One hand rises to point to the bench where wet and dissolving materials rest.

The marshal's eyes follow her direction.

His boots drip and smoke rises with the work of the acidic secretion upon them.

His hat has collapsed into a pool of undistinguishable mess.

Large holes penetrate his trousers and shirt.

"My cloths! They are ruined!" Marshal Legs announces to him self. "I can't wear these!"

The marshal turns silent as he reflects upon his circumstances.

The lady near his side squints with her fists remains tightly gripped and lowered to her sides.

Her fears are being realized.

"It was a most unfortunate and regrettable accident. The ladies feel terrible and they wish for anything to take back our misadventure." Her voice trembles but it is forceful and sincere.

"I have no clothes! I have absolutely nothing to wear!" The tone of the marshal's voice is helpless.

A relief from the apprehension of her confession breaks the spell of fright that has held the woman. "You could wear that towel...at least for now."

The marshal looks to the lady.

She is bent forward with one hand jabbing at the long white towel in his hand.

The expression of her face petitions his civility.

He senses his nakedness.

His gaze returns to the scene of his distraction.

He casually wraps the towel around his thin waist and hips.

"I can't buy new duds till I get to a federal seat and draw some petty cash from the government."

The woman has watched the long lean hard body of the man.

She notes the small circular scars on his side and back.

Most are white with age.

One has much red as yet.

There seems to her to be the scars of stab wounds upon his abdomen.

"You've been shot!" She blurts out before she can hold her words.

"Been wounded by just about every kind of weapon a man ever carried...gun...knife...arrow. Just about everything I suppose!"

The marshal's hand rubs the small red circle on the back of his shoulder as he walks over and retrieves his holster for inspection.

"Well my gun belt survived the attack!"

The lady notices the U S Marshal's badge fixed upon the man's gun belt.

She is relieved.

"Let me see your feet!" She bends over for a best view. "They are the correct size."

Her attention moves upon the height and girth of the marshal. "Yep! The same!"

Her hands now rest upon her hips.

The marshal is captivated by the honesty and courage of the small female.

He notes the intellect in her expression as her eye measures him.

"Mr.Beaudreaux our guide has left some of his clothes behind...They will suit you right fine!"

A look of comfort fills the young woman's face.

"I'll fetch them right off the wagon outside. The gals will be thrilled that we can make up some for our mistake."

As the woman scampers outside the marshal notices her soft womanly form.

Her hair is light brown gathered at the back.

She wears a white cotton blouse that hangs loose about her thin waist.

The boat neckline of the blouse shows the pure soft skin of her long delicate neck.

The loose three quarter length sleeves reveal more sensuous soft flesh.

Her small hands hang beside a tight skirt of rose color that forms about most shapely hips.

"Right fine looking woman." Marshall Legs remarks.

In an instant the petit lady returns with her arms full.

A large round board rimmed hat is first to be handed to the marshal.

"This is the finest felt in a hat that can be purchased."

She states empathically. "Mr. Beaudreaux bought this when he was in Chicago"

Marshall Legs inspects the hat.

He places his nose close to it and sniffs.

"Ode Cologne! This man is a dandy for sure." He states as the chapeau rises to his brow.

Next a fine white shirt and black tie are passed over to the man.

"Silk! The finest you can get in New York."

Undergarments are passed as well.

"Shoot! This is woman's wear! I never wore nothing soft like on top or underneath."

His hands rub the material.

The woman notices that despite his reservation he enjoys the feel of the material.

"You will get use to them soon enough. Besides, it's better than riding in a bath towel." She smiles.

The marshal's disposition is not improved.

Dark slacks and dress jacket are turned over for inspection by the marshal.

"These are the finest linen made in San Francisco." The woman assures.

The cloths are inspected and again the marshal sniffs.

"More of the same cologne. Shoot! Even my own horse won't know me!"

The marshal's look is one of irritation. "I' look like a damn preacher."

Finally the best the woman has to offer.

She holds out for the man's inspecting gaze a pair of dark embroidered shinny boots with inlaid pearl covering the toes.

Marshall Legs' look is astonished.

"I can't wear them boots. The toes are white!"

The woman despairs.

"It's pearl. These boots are priceless out here."

She learns toward the marshal to insist in their acceptability.

"They came right from the French Quarter of New Orleans. They were made in Paris France!"

She cannot believe his reticence to accept her gift.

The marshal's hand searches the pockets of the coat.

"What did you say this Mr. Beaudreaux does for a living?"

"He's a guide...a scout. We hired him to lead us to California were we ladies will start a boarding school for young women." She states confidently.

The marshal produces a collection of cards from the one pocket of the coat.

"Seven aces! Seems Mr. Bueadreaux's deck is mighty short." The marshal says sarcastically.

"Well he does like to play cards with the boys now and then. Just for recreation he would say." The woman's face is sheepish in expression.

"What happened to this jasper?' The marshal asks authoritatively.

"He left us back a few days behind. Some men came to escort him to a wedding near where we were staying." Her heads hangs a bit low in reflection as she answers.

"We wanted to accompany him." She informs apologetically.

"He said it was too dangerous because otherwise the farmers wouldn't need to be carrying shotguns." She responds naively.

"Try these cloths on!" The lady begs.

The marshal's head lowers as he views the boots once again.

A sense of anguish and despair overpowers him.

"They'll call me a sissy in these damn things." He says as he takes the boots into his hands.

The woman views the man acting like a little boy about to be trussed up for his first trip to Sunday school.

"Your long trousers will cover most of the boot. You can hardly notice the pearl then." She states with disbelief in her own words.

"Just try them...I'll wait to see how everything looks."

She stands with hands on hips while leaning backwards adding to her feminist persuasion.

"Turn your head...please." The marshal is embarrassed as to what his appearance shall become.

"I don't know if I can do this!" He declares as he dresses.

"You don't really have a choice at the moment. Perhaps there is to be another choice once you can get out of this cellar."

She waits with her arms folded at her waist and tapping the one foot nervously.

The struggle at the new fancy duds and the stiff boots make the woman's stay less than brief.

As the marshal reaches for his gun belt the lady turns to take view of her effort.

The vision of a most virile man so splendidly dressed surprises her.

The lady's mouth droops open.

Wide eyed and mesmerized at the beautiful site her breath is stilled.

Unconsciously her two hands rise with fingers open in a desire to grab hold of the man. The urge to be held in his hard long arms surprises her.

She stands petrified at her feelings for the marshal.

The marshal finishes his dress and looks to the woman for her impression.

He finds her in shock and presently spell bound.

"Something wrong?" He asks, as he looks himself over carefully.

"You are perfectly gorgeous!" She utters. "I mean you look great."

She struggles to control her emotions.

"I look like a sissy!" The man frowns.

"Oh marshal there's not a woman made what would ever have that notion pass through her head."

She is about to squeal with delight at her creation.

Her eyes smile brightly at the most handsome man she has ever seen.

She needs to touch him.

"Women folk don't matter none when I'm chasing a bad man. Shoot! If I walk up to a desperado he'll think I've come to ask him to dance!"

The marshal continues to observe the disturbed state of the woman.

He further brushes his duds and sets the hat to his satisfaction.

"Shoot! It'll have to do! Guess I should be thanking you... ah...what is your name?"

"Bennet...MISS BENNET." She advertises.

"Call me Ali." A sublime smile fills her face.

"Call me Marshal Legs." This seems a proper response by the man.

The lady is desperate for the man to notice her as a woman.

"You'll have to come to dinner tonight with us girls over to the school house. That's where we are staying." Her best smile is unending.

"Miss, I can't be any more bother to ya." The marshal is delighted at the notion.

"The girls will love to have the chance to apologize first hand. We're having fried green tomatoes with purple onions, roasted link sausage, and pork gravy on hot bits of sweet potatoes."

She studies the marshal's response to her words. "Hot cobbler made from Montgomery Cherries for dessert." The confused look on the marshal's face causes her to speak further. "Wild cherries!" She clarifies.

"Oh my! Ali."

His use of her name warms her.

"I haven't had wild cherries since I was riding down around San Jacinto way." His appetite soars. "I wouldn't be no bother?"

"No bother at all. Turn around and let me see your back." She requests.

Her hands move over his shoulder and down his back as she pretends to brush up the jacket he wears. She could not leave without feeling the hardness of so tempting a man.

"Perfect...just perfect." She sighs.

She dreams.

"What time?" The marshal asks.

"Oh...any time." She muses then awakens to the invitation to dinner. "Any time well before sunset that is...I'll trim your hair after dinner if you please."

Delight over powers Miss Bennet.

"Do I have to call you Marshal?" Ali asks disappointedly.

"Legs isn't better either." Her eyes are cheerless.

"Just what is your given name?' She insists.

"My Sioux grandpa called me Chicha Mandoa...Wooden Legs!" The marshal answers proudly.

"My family calls me Cha. I prefer my acquaintances use the name...Woody."

"Then I'll call you Woody...for now!" She answers in an amiable but sassy manner.

As she turns to leave, Ali believes she notices Woody looking at her as a woman.

She is very pleased.

Fresh from the privy and dressed anew the marshal seeks Mr. Herberle.

Albert is within his store concluding a purchase of venison for the restaurant by the owner Mrs. Ruthy Chadwell.

The large woman has her hands filled with goods needed for the evening meals.

She notices the approach of a tall man dressed in a fine black linen suit.

Marshal Legs approaches the pair at the butcher's counter. He tips his hat to the madam.

"Good Day!"

"Are you a preacher?" She asks the stranger in reply.

Albert is arrested for a moment at the change in appearance of the marshal.

"No mam. Just a traveler passing through." Another nod by the marshal is added for politeness.

"He'll be in need of dining Ruthy." Albert adds.

"Venison stew tonight for two bits. All the coffee you can drink." The woman bows slightly then turns to leave.

"Ruth Chadwell this here is..."

"Mr. Legs!" The marshal interrupts.

"Please to meet you!" A slight curtsey is made as she begins to leave.

"We stay open till an hour past dark this time of year. Coffee's always hot and we sell tobacco." She calls from the doorway.

"Fine woman the Chadwell lady." Albert smiles. "Her husband was one of the best frontiersmen in the area."

"How did he die?"

"He was so drunk one night that he walked right into the river there below and was washed away in the quick flowing water!" Albert states sadly.

"The natives themselves had such respect for his fighting ability that they returned his body. They came with full ceremonial dress, just as a great chief had died. They said the spirit of the great warrior was joined to the stream. It was for them a great happening."

The marshal appreciates the sentiment of the natives.

"It was most unfortunate for Mrs. Chadwell as well" Hesitation, then the marshal asks

"I'm after a small man with tiny features. Talks good Texican. Goes by the name of Otter or Ott. Have ya seen anyone about like that?"

"Ott is a good German name. There was one small fellow here in the store what had boyish size...petite hands, legs, and feet. He said very little. His head was mostly bald but for a rim of shaggy hair above the ears. Yes! His eyes were very dull... lifeless...unhealthy."

"Was he alone?" This is the man the marshal is sure.

"No he was with the large heavy mountain man with hairs every where about his face and he dressed in only animal hides."

"How long ago did they pass here?"

"Maybe five days ago. They buy the whiskey from me. I make whiskey like the Germans very pure, very strong, very good and very expensive. They buy several bottles and they stay outside of the village and drink for one maybe two days then they are gone."

"It's good whiskey. Mr. Chadwell drank my whiskey when he is to die. Ruth is not mad with me. It's business to sell to drink. I'm am always sorry for hurt that comes from too much drink." Albert is sincere.

"I drink a glass of my whiskey every night. It brings fire to me for my woman but I don't ever go for to be drunk. It's no good!" Albert continues.

"I don't drink much myself. Just a glass when the soreness in the body gets too much. Whiskey takes the swelling away. Other wise I don't have need for it." The marshal adds.

Albert nods in understanding.

"A week maybe a day more would you say that the little fella left? Any idea, which way they'd go?"

"Yah! They buy goods to go to mountains by way of road to Fargo. There is well known trail to mountains from there. It's the fastest way. You go to way of Fargo the path to mountains is easy to recognize because most folks not go that way ever."

"I need to see a Mr. Roy Bowler. Can you tell me where he's to be found?" Marshal Legs inquires

"Yah! East of the village about three miles out you come to twin oaks. There is narrow path to left. There is the old farm house where does live Mrs. Ida Moore. There is cabin in very far end. This is where the Bowler man lives."

"Have you seen his wife recently?"

"No! Last fall at the apple fest she was there helping Ida sell goods. Since then no seeing of her." Albert obliges.

"What kind of fella is this Bowler?"

"I can not say much to that...he does no have the drink, he does no buy from my store." Albert ponders. "He is said to be honest, clean, and hard working but he has no friends here."

"Gambler?"

"No! He works then goes home only. Only business never the play or conversation for sport."

"Node him long?"

"Since he came. Just walked by foot one day to Sweet Creek. Ida hired him as hand on the farm. He stays now for 5 maybe 6 years in Sweet Creek."

"Has he had many wives?"

"Yes this is the third. All young girls from the mail he arranges the marriage. He has no luck with women. They do not stay with him. It's the way for some men to be alone even if they wish it not." Heberle asserts.

"Did he come asking about his present wife this spring?"

"This fellow has never inquired about any of his wives when they went missing." Albert is certain.

The marshal nods in thanks and leaves.

"Is Bowler in trouble?" Albert calls after the marshal.

"Every man is in trouble when his wife is missing." The marshal goes.

❧

A quick ride out of town brings the marshal to the twin oaks.

He examines the road to the Moore's ranch.

Tracts are days old.

The road is little used.

Rain and wind will not keep imprints in this pathway long.

"Any one afoot or riding out at night could do so easily and their trail would be easy to pick up the next day". The marshal concludes.

"If the woman ran to Sweet Creek then everyone would have known of it after the fact. Turning away from the village, a man would need several days ride or a week by foot to make off." The marshal knows that this didn't happen for Mrs. Bowler.

"His wife could make off with causal help. Her husband would have tracked her down easily. In either case Bowler knew she hadn't gone to Sweet Creek."

After several reflective moments pass the marshal concludes.

"The woman could not escape without premeditated assistance. The other wives would need the same just as well otherwise they do not escape!" The marshal thinks to himself.

The rest of the afternoon the marshal rides the country about the Moore's farm.

He looks for nearby residents and makes inquires as to those who knew the Bowler woman well.

The women who invaded the privy at Heberle's keep their wagon placed near to the church in Sweet Creek. Here there is a small corral where they stable and tend their animals.

A small tent serves their needs by day.

At night they retire within the church to sleep.

Provisions of the wagon make for cooking and serving of meals.

Much preparation is underway in anticipation of their dining guest.

The table is covered with special beige colored cloth used on holidays, birthdays and Sundays.

Buffet dining will permit the women to move about the marshal and engage him at one's convenience.

Seats will be carried out from the church.

The women have cleaned the privy of all signs of a disaster and enjoyed showers while the marshal is out and about the countryside.

Miss Bennet has acquired some sipping whiskey from Heberle for her guest.

She has chosen a white cotton skirt that is embroidered in panels all around. Tight at the hips the skirt broadens to flow into a full soft clean look.

Her blouse is a silk azure blue color. It again has a design that opens at the top to reveal bare shoulders and neck.

Her hair is pulled back to show the nape of the neck. It is tied and adorned with a fan of small cut flowers.

Upon his return, the marshal returns to the privy to wash up for dinner.

He wipes his boots clean then dusts his garments and hat.

He will leave his gun belt in his boarding room.

He will however take a small revolver strapped to one lower leg.

When the marshal arrives the girls stand in one line for greeting.

Ali steps out and takes the marshal's arm.

"Let me introduce you to Evelyn. A greatly admired cook and home decorator." Ali informs. "She hopes to start a bakery and bring her family along to California after her."

The marshal nods in greeting.

Evelyn is a thin wide eyed small mouthed beauty.

She is clumsy with cerebral tasks and prone to be contrary in her response to directives.

Her lips are thin and rose colored.

Her hair is a shade of light blond, and it hangs in tight ringlets down to the base of her neck.

Her waist is ultra thin.

Her mood is always happy and she is most energetic.

Evelyn comes from a large poor family that is hard working.

Ali introduces again.

"Layla is unparalleled in song and dance. Her voice is full and rich. She has a gift for teaching music." Ali smiles in approval at the introduction's end.

The marshal nods in greeting.

Layla is a small dark beauty with narrow shoulders and wide hips.

Her dark eyes sparkle with enthusiasm.

She speaks several languages.

Her parents are immigrants who support her in an effort to resettle the family to the west.

Ali moves to the third member.

"Michele is neat beyond the average and most capable with figures and keeps the financial records of our enterprise."

The marshal nods in greeting.

Michele is a tall lovely girl who is long in limbs and athletic.

She has a fetish for polka dots and much of her fashion is so adorned.

She is an orphan that has been raised by the nuns.

She wants to marry a banker, and live where the weather is always warm.

Lastly Ali presents.

"Judith is a passionate reader and author. Her poems have been printed in major journals and papers of the American Northeast." Ali comments.

The marshal nods in greeting.

Judith is a plain girl.

Stooped at the shoulders, and ordinary in dress and looks.

She has an invitation to visit and speak to literary societies all along the west coast.

Decidedly older than her peers, she is the resource for fact and information to the group.

Her mother has recently passed.

Her only brother is a missionary preacher in Mississippi.

"We are all so very, very sorry for the inconvenience caused by our foolish ways. " All the girls smile and stare into the marshal's eyes for forgiveness and acceptance.

"We hope this simple meal will show our sincerity and regret. We want you as our friend." Applause for the marshal comes warmly from all the girls.

"Let's eat!" Calls Michele.

The girls investigate the marshal's cloths while they eat.

Each in their time concludes that the fit and the look of the vestments of Mr. Beaudreaux are a perfect fit for the man.

Indeed they are decided that the wash time accident was a favor to his appearance.

The girls gather first and second helpings of food in competition to serve the marshal.

Ali is quick to see that his jar of fresh squeezed lemonade is not to go empty.

The girls' eyes are fixed on the countenances of the marshal and Ali.

Their ears are tuned to every word the pair pronounces.

All readily analyze the emotions exchanged in their conversation.

"Are you married?" Asks Michele.

Stark anticipation grips the face of Ali before his answer.

Her companions focus their senses upon her.

"Nope!" Answers the man.

Relief and joy surge through Ali reviving her enthusiasm for the moment.

"Got no reason to expect such ever!" The man adds.

Disappointment crushes Ali's ambition.

"You could marry if'n the right woman took your heart?" Evelyn asks.

"Maybe" Is his best response.

"You have been married before." Judith states.

The marshal nods yes.

"Lost your family? Disease most likely?" Judith consoles.

Ali listens with care.

The marshal nods yes. "Some time long ways back."

Ali shares the tenderness behind his words.

"Let's have some singing?" Layla offers.

Ali has clothed this man, fed him, prevented his thirst, made him comfortable in every circumstance, and has shared his feelings and personal pain.

She is bound to spend private time with the marshal so that he may have ample chance to discover her as a woman.

She wishes to see if he has feelings for her.

"Let's wait till after we have desert!" Ali begs. "I've promised the marshal a hair cut."

Judith is quick to understand Ali's plight. "Excellent idea! We'll clean from super while you tend our guest."

"The cobbler is best if it's reheated." Adds Evelyn.

"Yah! I'm stuffed. Let's reheat our appetites first!" Laughs Michele.

Ali leads the marshal out from the church to a small stand of yellow birch tress upon an open knoll that overlooks the western horizon and the river.

The marshal is walking just behind the girl.

Her scent stirs a youthful enthusiasm for the evening.

Her supple form and girlish gait produces a manly appreciation long missing from the marshal's life.

Miss Bennet is most aware that the marshal's eyes her.

He is seated upon a boulder in the shade of the trees.

Ali removes his jacket.

She places a large cloth around his wide and sturdy shoulders. She will let no loosed strain of hair spoil his appearance.

His attendant desires the marshal's closeness.

The woman's body brushes against his as she combs and parts his hair.

This proves to be an unexpected pleasure for the marshal.

He is forced to restrain his urges. This is the only path for behavior by a gentleman.

"You know the natives believe to cut one's hair is an act of deprivation, of penitence?" Woody smiles.

"Is being with me a punishment?" Ali barbs.

She will not divert from her hearts intention.

"No! I didn't mean it that away." He is embarrassed for his poor way with words.

Ali feels his discomfort from her remark.

"Are we savages?" She tries to recover his good humor.

"Depends on your point of view. Them natives feel cutting ones hair is the act of a savage." He responds.

"I cut my own hair. Am I a savage?" She asks with her hands upon his shoulders.

"Missy that's' for your husband to find out!"

Her back straightens at the thought of marital life.

She steps back and caresses the marshal's hair in both her hands.

"You look 10 years younger!" She giggles with delight of intimacy.

Ali stands with her back toward the setting sun.

The soft solar rays shroud her.

The fine hairs of her neck glisten with a golden hue.

Her face is young and pure.

Her eyes are soft and loving.

Her whole being is filled with care for the man before her.

The marshal rises to give thanks.

The vision of his companion holds his words.

At this moment he is overwhelmed by the radiance and wholesomeness of the woman.

If he holds her in his arms now, he would embrace the warmth of the sunset.

His eyes look to her lips.

If he kisses her now he would savor the sweetness of the evening breeze.

Her attention is posed to capture his every desire.

She yearns to be next to him.

Her hands burn to hold him.

The marshal's life is being transformed.

There is an ease and contentment present in him now.

This woman's goodness has moved his soul.

Ali dare not speak or move for the chance that the marshal's intention should become displaced.

The marshal must act.

He will not speak to have his malformed words dismiss her attention.

He cannot embrace or place his hands upon her for fear that all control should then be gone from him.

He steps close to her.

Her arms open to her side in permission of his intent.

He lowers to her lips.

Her head rises in greeting.

Softly and tenderly his lips hold hers.

For one moment of forever the pair is joined.

His mouth moves near to her ear.

"Forgive me." He whispers just above his breath.

So intense has the moment been that Ali's arms have never reached for him.

She is paralyzed by the passion of his kiss.

His words bring her eyes to heavy tears.

"I'll forgive you." Her trembling voice answers.

The next morning the marshal awakes hours before dawn.

He is to visit the Moore Farm long before first light.

Once arrived, he finds the farm house and cottage dark and yet asleep.

He will hide, watch and wait.

The dining, the music, and dance of his past evening with the girls at the church yet stir him.

His thoughts of Ali and their sublime embrace will not dismiss.

He must return to her soon.

The first tone of life is with the morning songs of the woodland birds, when the hens and roosters in the barn yard sound.

The large animals in the pens move to relieve the night's stiffness.

In the helper's cottage the first lamp is lit.

"Mr. Bowler begins his day." The marshal mutters.

The smell of coffee carries from the workman's lodge to try the marshal's patience.

In short time, a stocky man emerges.

His hair is orderly, and his dress neat.

His gate is short and lumbering.

The hired man begins the task of milking the cows within the barn.

Next the feeding of chickens, ducks, and other fowl begins.

Eggs are gathered into a pale and set before the door to Mrs. Moore's quarter for cleaning and inspection.

Milk cans that have been filled are set here as well.

"The old girl keeps watch on her daily produce." Woody notes.

By the time Bowler gets to tend the horses, mules, and cattle, light beams forth from Mrs. Moore's home.

Thoughts of Miss Bennet drive the marshal's want to be back in Sweet Creek.

"The girls will be going to Heberle's for a first wash up...my first shower there was the best I'll ever have. Made a damn new fellow out of me."

Near mid morning, the lady Moore emerges. She is a tiny woman little in weight but large in the number of her years.

At this time Bowler fills a handcart with tools and wood members. He waves to Mrs. Moore as he walks to a path that shall take him out into the meadows.

"Fence mending will keep him till noon when he's back for his lunch."

The man disappears over the way. The marshal walks to the door of Mrs. Moore.

As he approaches the woman steps out side with a shot gun in hand.

"Hold!" She declares in a determined voice.

The marshal waits as she nears.

"You a preacher?" She asks.

"Nope...U S Marshal."

"Don't dress like a marshal!"

He opens his coat to reveal the government badge fixed upon his gun belt.

"Come with warrants?" The woman has yet to drop the point of her gun.

"Come to find Mrs. Bowler!" His voice is official and imposing.

The old woman rests the shotgun to allow the marshal to advance.

"Have you seen Mrs. Bowler recently?" He asks

"Land sakes! She run off long before spring. Jenny, that's her name...she would come over and check on me during the dark days. We'd have tea and talk like women, not long mind you but just for a spell now and then."

"Any reason why she would run away?" The marshal asks.

"That man just doesn't understand women or canines for that matter...can't keep one of either kind. They all run off and leave him. Every puppy and every woman he brings here."

She pauses. "Call me Ida."

"Anyone from town or neighbors come to visit her ever?"

"Nary a one. Roy doesn't take to company and vice versa. She never went to town without her husband and for sure he would never stand for socializing. Just working that's all Roy does."

"He be mean or a drunkard?"

"No he's an honest enough man. Never saw him with drink let alone drunk. Jenny never carried any bruising at least ways that I could see. Roy never fails at his chores for one minute."

"There has to be a reason three wives run off?"

"Just one I can tell being a woman." Ida hesitates.

"It needs be told before another young girl shows up and then vanishes."

"Well marshal it's against me to be throwing stones at another, but the man just isn't capable of love. He's cold beyond toleration. No woman can take that for long."

"How easy is it for you to replace a hired hand?"

"Couple of weeks at the most. Put an add down at Heberle's is all."

Three wives missing.

Each was gone by early spring.

The one husband that seems indifferent to their loss.

The marshal has concluded his investigation.

He sits on the cottage 's porch and waits.

When Roy Bowler arrives for his midday meal he finds the marshal at his door.

"Who be you?" Roy asks. "Are you a gambler?"

"Roy Bowler, you are hereby under arrest for using the federal mail to perpetrate crimes, and for the murder of Jenny Bowler!"

The stunned hired hand rears back undecided as whether to run or attack.

"You'll be dead right off either way!" The marshal reads his mind.

"The woman ran off!" Roy protests.

The marshal knows that his wife didn't walk off in the dead of winter.

Roy killed her.

The only place he could have easily buried her at that time would be under the floor of his cabin where the dirt would not be hard frozen.

"Roy, I'm gone to send some men with dogs to search under your cabin floor. They'll find the body of your dead wife."

The farmer's head hangs low with exposed guilt.

He has no more words to say.

"I want you to help the men who will arrive to recover Jenny's body and the bodies of your other two wives. I mean to see they are buried Christian proper." The marshal waits for the notion to settle.

Roy Bowler does not respond.

"You'll continue to work here until Ida gets someone to replace you, even if it takes a couple of months. Then you get to Sweet Water, get on a stage to Fargo and turn your self in at the federal court there."

Roy Bowler does not respond

"Now if you run off, I'll come after you and shoot you dead where I find you. You do as I say and get them girls buried right and their families notified I'll see to it that after you're hanged, you'll get buried proper with your family."

"I'm sorry marshal! I didn't mean to hurt them women...I

deserve to die! I'd like to be buried with my mother back in Mingo, Ohio."

"It's done. God have mercy on your soul." The marshal walks off to mount and return to Sweet Creek.

The marshal stops at Heberle's to have a message sent to Sheriff Klinger to organize a recovery party for the bodies of the missing girls.

He rides to the church.

Ali has been at the watch since dawn.

Her mouth still savors the impression of the marshal's lips.

She recognizes his approach from afar.

"The marshals on his way!" She runs at the sprint past her companions towards the approaching shape.

The other girls know well the meaning in her actions.

"Best tell him were are leaving in the morning right off!" Calls Judith after her.

"Tell him the Fargo Road is open!" Shouts Michele as Ali distances her self from the camp.

As soon as Ali is aware that the marshal sees her, the woman comes to an abrupt stop.

She hopes the man has missed her.

She knows the man has missed her.

She wants to be in his arms.

"He'll want to be in my arms." She hopes to herself.

Marshal Legs moves directly to her.

"Yep just as pretty!" He announces to him self.

As he stops and dismounts, the girl moves to him.

His eyes devour her beauty.

Her joy shines from his presence. His look upon her confirms all his emotions of the past evening.

Ali recalls the pleasure of being in his arms.

The marshal's arms wish for her now more that ever.

He is afraid.

Ali feels his awkwardness.

"The road is clear from the flood." She hears herself say.

Her voice makes all correct for the marshal.

He takes her words in acceptance.

He reaches for her waist and in a swoop lifts her into a circular swirl.

She is ecstatic.

"I'm a gone to ride to Fargo with you tomorrow." He announces.

❧

The carriage used by the women is large with two forward looking rows of seats; the aft is covered with a large sturdy canvas.

Six mules of good worth form the team that pulls the load.

Woody appreciates the quality of the wagon and the animals gathered by their former guide.

Once shaped, loaded and his own fine horse strung behind, the transport makes good time as it moves out from Sweet Creek.

They follow the path of the swollen creek north along a wide and well traveled road.

Woody holds the horses' reins and drives the team.

Near sits Miss Bennet whom is desperate to remain at his side.

She takes pleasure in every jostle of the road that gives cause for her body to rub against that of the marshal.

"Are we making good time?" Ali asks.

The marshal nods positively.

"Good team. Good wagon. Good weather. Good company." Woody takes pleasure in her voice and her nearness.

"One time my family had to move our homestead when I was a young boy." Woody remarks to his friends.

"We loaded everything in one wagon with two old ponies. Started out a dawn. At sunset we had traveled just four miles. Took two and a half days to make the ten mile journey. All we did was rest them old animals and unload the wagon to get up every hill."

Woody shakes his side to side in remembrance.

The women are delighted to resume their voyage and elated by the presence of their new friend Marshal Legs.

For several hours they pass rural homes and farms separated by large agricultural plains and open grazing ranges.

Grazing horse, cattle and the occasional roaming deer are the only other travelers encountered.

Up and down the winding slopes the mule team moves on unimpeded.

The ladies make note of various wild flowers in bloom.

In among a stand of fir trees along a shady bank mixed with small fragile ferns Michele spies..."Painted Trillium."

"Trillium Undulatum." Echoes Judith. "It's a wild plant that can never be transplanted, the moisture, the type of soil, the temperatures are too delicate to reproduce."

To the left of the road near a small piece of wetland, Ali announces "Cattails...we always had some in our house."

"Typha Latifola. The brown cylinder is made of many small flowers." Judith informs.

"Fringed Gentian!" The marshal points out.

The ladies wait for Judith's pronouncement of the Latin name.

She is silent.

Stunned by the marshal's knowledge, they enjoy the contest of recognition and the challenge to Judith's vast knowledge

"Its root is used by the Sioux for medicine. That's how comes I know the name." He adds.

"Gentiana Crinita." Judith slowly responds correctly. "Some one should write a book of early American herbal remedies."

Layla spies a small gathering of buds.

"Stop...I believe these are the flowers called Fare Well to Spring. The scent is most unusual."

"I don't know of this flower." Declares Judith. "It must be vary rare."

Cheers and good fun raise the spirits of the girls to the delight of all for the stumping of their scholar.

The girls plead for the marshal to stop so they can pick several buds and collect flowers.

The marshal obliges.

As the girls move about the patch of wild flowers their mood and antics return to those of young girls.

They giggle at the simplest notion given from one to the other. Fingers are busy touching petals and stem. Noses sniff and scents are shared.

Laughter abounds with this simplest of pleasure.

"Mighty innocent gals." The marshal muses.

The girls break into dance as they sing together to the song of Ring Around the Roses.

The beauty of nature and the young women give great peace and comfort to the marshal.

His eyes hardly leave watch of the beautiful womanly form of Ali. She moves in a way most supple. She is alluring and sensuous at every turn and movement.

The marshal's caring for her grows.

With sufficient playtime enjoyed the marshal calls out.

"Get you flowers and lets be on our way. California is a long ways off."

"How far do you think we have gone so far?" Ali loves the manly tones of the marshal's voice. Especially so when his words are meant for her.

"We be making about 8 miles an hour maybe a bit more or less."

A long pause as the marshal calculates." "Should be nearing the river crossing soon."

The land begins a slow descent.

The stream nears in the distance.

Soon watermarks on trees and bush are to be seen.

Near the ground at first, then a bit higher up the trunks and branches, the dirty floodwater has stained.

The stone bridge that spans the water comes into view.

The road is yet damp.

The mules struggle but yield no loss in progress.

Tidal pools have been left behind from the flood in low spots on either side of the roadway.

"It stinks here." The girls call from behind the driver.

"What is that awful smell?" They ask.

"Dead and decaying matter. Fish stranded dry, drowned animals all about." Woody points to the swollen carcass of one sheep midway up a tree in the distance.

"This can't be healthy!" Ali states as she covers her mouth and nose with a kerchief.

Woody eyes study the bridge ahead.

He sees no cracks or leans to the stone structure.

"I'll cross straight off. You gals walk and follow after the wagon gets over to the other side. Then we'll hurry up the road on the other side till we are free of this flood zone."

The marshal strikes his whip out over the team of mules and calls out "Yeehah".

The team goes into a trot of quickened pace.

The animals are likewise disturbed by the stench and respond with eagerness to escape the present ground.

In a mile or two the signs of the flood are gone.

The air freshens and a normal pace returns.

The women are relieved to have passed trough the terrain that suffered the recent natural disaster.

The good mood of the female travelers is returned.

The marshal however is not so reassured.

Later the marshal observes one set of hoof prints that appears upon the road in advance. These lead onward for some time until another set of three horses joins the road in a similar manner.

All traffic is heading in the same direction away from the river.

The marshal is alarmed and brings the rig to a halt.

"Is there something wrong?" Ali asks sweetly of the marshal.

He knows that criminals are drawn to prey on the weak and abandoned in such times.

The highways become particular menacing

Woody does not answer.

His eyes drift across and behind to the horizon.

Instinctively his free hand searches and makes secure his firearms.

"Did you see something?" Ali becomes nervous at Woody's distractions.

"What is the matter?"

Woody places his hand over hers and squeezes.

Ali becomes still.

"Keep your eyes at the watch!" He answers her softly.

"Ladies! If for any reason I yell out...Stand to! I want each of you to immediately fall as low as you can get and as quickly as you can down on the ground."

"What about Evelyn?" Miss Bennet whispers.

"Grip her by the hair and yank her down straight off!" The marshal directs.

All the women take to an alerted state.

Onward and in short time, the wagon approaches a shape resting upon a rise in the road.

"There is some one in the way." Ali declares.

Woody has already come to this awareness and understands what the image portends.

Ali notices that Woody's eyes never rest upon the thoroughfare itself.

An unfamiliar frown appears over his countenance.

At the bottom of the rise just below where the motionless figure of a man rests sprawled upon the ground, the marshal brings the mule team to a halt.

He locks the wagon's brakes. "I'm going to get me a look about." He states.

"I'm coming with you!" Ali insists.

"Do you have any fire arms aboard?" Woody asks.

"A small derringer left by Mr. Bueadreaux." The girl does answer. "It's in my purse for safe keeping."

"Can ya use it?"

"I can fire the thing...don't know if I can hit anything." She responds coyly.

"Keep it in you pocket and fire it at close range from inside if'n ya have to." The marshal moves quickly to the fallen man with Ali following.

"Not much to guess at here." The marshal finds no signs of life in the deceased man.

"Three of them rode up behind and shot this fellow dead." The marshal's hands indicate the path of the horses used by the bandits.

"Then they rode off with his horse, his hat, any firearms and anything of worth." Again the Woody's extended arm shows the signs of egress from the scene of four horses.

"Why did they kill him?" Horror fills the voice of the young lady.

Her face shows terror

Woody shakes his head in disgust and states bitterly. "Just because they damn well could."

The marshal's eyes again scan the distance all around. "Them bastards think they can get away with this!"

Both of the marshal's side arms are removed and inspected for readiness.

"What are you going to do against three men?" Ali speaks in fear.

"Hell! They'll be four of them now. They've taken another horse." He pauses. "These are no men they be just wild animals. Shooting a lone rider in the back, they be cowards of the worse kind."

"What are you going to do?" Ali is anxious.

"I'm a gone to kill each one of them!" The marshal replaces his handguns into their holsters.

"Why kill them?" The girl cannot fathom the marshal's need for bloodshed.

"Cause they left a woman and children without a husband and a father most likely. This fellow was probably stranded by the flood and returning home as soon as he could pass over from the far side of the river."

The marshal pulls the body off to the side of the high way.

"I can't string four desperados for two days and two nights ride to put them in jail just so they can hang. Not to mention the constant worrying I would have to do while riding amongst them. Who knows what they might do to you women should they get a chance."

Ali stands silently.

She is misplaced in this brutal reality.

"Get them girls and cover this poor fellow with rocks. We get to the next town there we will inform the local sheriff. He'll send someone to fetch the remains back to his family. I'm a gone to step ahead just a bit and have a better look."

"Those men are going to come for us aren't they?" The girl ponders coldly.

"Yep...soon I expect!"

The marshal steps up to the highest point in the rise.

The girls are busy at covering the corpse when he returns.

He steps to the side and calls Ali to him. "We'll have one chance when these men stop us."

"Can't we just out run them or turn around?" Ali interrupts.

"They'll shoot the mules then they'll shoot me if'n we try to force our way out."

He takes her shoulders in his hands.

He looks with kind urgency into her eyes.

Ali looks up.

Her emotions surge in his grip.

Her eyes search and find his soul.

"I don't want to live without you." Tears accompany her words.

"I can't think of anything now but defeating them bandits other wise I'll fail and we will all be lost." Tenderness fills his voice.

Ali's heart cannot be stilled.

"I love you Cha. I never met anyone like you ever before."

The large hands of the marshal hold the small face of the despondent woman in promise.

"The most important thing is when we are stopped move as far away from me as possible. Remember get down when I shout Stand to!"

Quickly the wagon is again underway.

All are sober and filled with dread.

Every step of a hoof, every bump of on the road advances the mutual sense of coming peril.

The Marshall knows the highwaymen will appear quickly in a confined space that will permit no escape.

He is sure that their wagon has already been spotted from atop a high peak off on the horizon.

Ali's body presses fully against his.

Woody regrets the exploit that is destined to unfold.

It is to be one that he has faced upon many occasions.

Each time he has been prepared to face his own end in the pursuit of justice.

He is not ready to accept the loss of Ali or any of these innocent women.

Ali seizes from the immediate nearness to her marshal all the intimacy that can be shared.

These moments may be their last ever.

Her dreams of a life with the marshal cannot be hoped for past the present.

She cannot abide to see him die.

She wants this peril to pass.

The other ladies do not look ahead or afar.

They keep watch on the demeanor of the marshal and Ali for assurance and comfort.

The mules have taken the sent of death from the highway.

They are jittery and ready to panic.

The marshal has a difficult task to keep his team calm and under control.

As the road drops into a narrow gully, four men on horseback stand to close the way ahead.

The front mules rear upward and the last mules kick out from behind as Woody strains to bring the team to a halt.

Four riders all poorly attired and riding on mostly worn, aged animals stare down at Woody and his company.

The marshal inspects the tattered and dirty forms of the men before him.

Their side weapons are poorly holstered.

They are not handy with guns. He is sure they are not efficient with them at a distance.

He knows that his chances are good if he can separate himself from the women.

"Hey there!"

One man in the middle shouts.

This one wears a hat that seems a bit loose of fit to Woody.

The marshal puts one hand out to instruct the highwaymen to keep back.

"These mules are terrible skittish." He informs.

The spokesman for the bandits leans high in the saddle to inspect the wagon's cargo.

"Got a mess of women folk with you." His smile is mocking.

"He gots lots of pretty ones" The call is made from the big fellow next to the leader. He is the filthiest of the bunch.

The others laugh and slap at one another in expectant pleasure.

"Get'em on down Jed and lets have a see!" The tall thin one to the far left yells.

"Yah lets have at'em." Others call out.

"What'er we a waiting fur?" The big man pokes at his friend.

"Shut up!" The leader shouts out. "I'm going to try to think."

He is uncertain as to what risk he faces from the wagon.

"Say friend how about you locking them wheels and stepping down from up there so's we can make sure all's proper."

The four men on horseback assume a serious demeanor as if they are prepared for the final action that is to come.

The marshal observes that their leader's words are formed by broken thoughts.

Woody is sure that this one wears the hat from the dead man from back down the road.

This is the criminal that did the recent shooting that killed the lone traveler.

The marshal intends to kill this one first.

“"What say fellas that you just lets us pass in peace?” The marshal asks politely.

This brings a roar of laughter and delight from the treacherous band ahead of the wagon.

“I don't think so. We boys intend to see that this here road be kept safe for travels.”

A large smirk fills the leaders face. “You can help us by stepping down...and let them women get down so'd we can have a look...for well beings sake.” His fingers move to direct

More cheers from the bandits.

The marshal steps down from the wagon.

“Looky here at this big sissy.”

The large brut exclaims as his eyes look over the marshal's cloths. "His boots have white toes.”

The band of desperados shares much laughter.

Ali sees the rage in Woody's eyes at these comments.

She now fears for the life of these fools for taunting the marshal.

“Yah I can wear them.” States the tall bandit.

“Get them women down.” The leader is emboldened by the marshals' cooperation.

As Ali descends, the marshal assists and whispers.

“Get these girls down to the far end of the wagon well away from me.”

As Evelyn and the others off board, the attention of the four men becomes solely on the figures of the young women.

The robbers move to the side of the wagon.

Their lust for flesh distracts them from the marshals who steps farther away from the women.

Here he stands with his hands crossed under his coat each holding the handle to a revolver.

In the next moment the leader of the thugs realizes their mistake.

He turns to see the marshal with his hands at the ready.

He views the US Marshal's badge upon the gun belt.

He is about to call out in alarm.

"Stand to!" Roars the marshal as he draws his weapons.

Immediately Ali grasps Evelyn's hair with both hands and pulls her to the ground with the other women instantly obliging the marshal's command.

The leader reaches for his side arm just as the marshal's guns discharge.

One round from each of Woody's hand guns strike.

The leader and the big brut are hit center of their chests.

Each outlaw dies immediately.

The large bully descends side ways as in the manner of falling timber while the leader's body is flung in the air backwards to land and remain as in the form of a restful sleep.

The remaining two crooks ineptly reach for their weapons and turn to escape.

The marshals fires two rounds from each revolver in the directions of the two opponents.

The nearer outlaw is struck twice, once in the side of the head and once in the chest.

He tumbles dead to the ground.

The left most bandit is struck twice as well once in the shoulder and once in the neck.

None of the women have ever been in the presence of a shoot out.

None have ever witnessed a violent death.

None have ever watched as one man kills another.

They tremble uncontrollably at the instantaneous furry and death.

They view the marshal as he moves toward the lone surviving outlaw.

The girls are seized with panic.

Smoke pours from both revolvers as the marshal leans over the stricken bandit.

He kicks the wounded man in the thigh.

The outlaw replies with a moan. "I'm wounded!"

"You're dying!" Replies the marshal. "Are you holding any captives?"

The outlaw does not respond.

A more violent kick is given from the marshal.

"Boy you're going now to meet your maker. Best help your self by telling if you hold any one hostage!"

"Yes!" He moans, "A young girl."

"Nearby?" Persists the marshal.

"Up the next draw...in a miner's shed."

The marshal steps back away towards the wagon.

"Get on board right off." His words are stern and final.

"You were awful brave." Ali declares as she hugs him tightly.

"Them fools were evil and dumb. Just about any honest man would have done the same."

"No ordinary man could have saved us." Ali understands.

"Guess the Good Lord made some of us able to deal with this kind of wickedness."

Without further to do, the marshal collects the women, strings the outlaws' horses and gets the wagon under way.

"What about those men back there?" Asks Ali as the wagon makes haste toward the first canyon.

"They be the devil's own breed. Let Satan take care of his own." The marshal will speak no other words on this episode.

"Let's find that little girl what's a prisoner...perhaps will be able to save another innocent life today." The marshal pronounces.

Ali holds his arm in her one hand and Evelyn's hand in the other.

"I need to see some goodness being done!" She yet trembles over the bloodshed just passed.

Chapter 3

A Jail House

The ensemble of wagon, horses, mules, women, and marshal restart the trip north for the distance to the first draw to be encountered.

Just a mile or two more finds the narrow side road which forks away and up into the hills. It is a wide path but unused and very ruff.

"This won't do!"

The marshal informs his companion. "The ruts and holes in this road will damage the wheels and then we'll be stranded."

Ali looks with confusion. "Leave the wagon and let's walk up the hill. Can't be too far up to top."

"This here road could wind a couple miles before it comes to its end."

He looks about. "We'll hide the wagon in that piece of a canyon."

He points over to a retreating gap in a high wall of stone. "We'll ride the horses and mules."

A cavalcade of six mules, five horses, five women and one man begins a slow trot up the hill.

Past slips in the roadbed, around loosed boulders that have come to rest in the level terrain of the thoroughfare the marshal leads his column.

The sun is quite high dispelling shadows from the entire landscape.

This pleases the marshal as concealment for a waiting ambush is much reduced. He is sure that other outlaws may be encountered at the cabin.

Just as soon as the ladies are becoming accustomed to the motion of a large animal under them, the procession is brought to a halt.

The marshal has all dismount.

The animal's forelegs are tied together. He does not want the beasts to run off in the event there is to be any shooting.

"Other side of this bend is a cabin." The marshal informs the ladies. "Be where the hostage is likely held."

"What shall we do?" Asks Ali.

The marshal removes a single load army style carbine from his own horse's saddle.

He inspects and makes ready the weapon.

The serious look upon his brow disturbs Ali. "You are going to walk straight up there in the open view from that cabin?"

The marshal recognizes that this scenario is the most dangerous for any lawmen.

Injury is the least worry.

"You might get killed going up for that girl!" Ali understands the man's thoughts. "You're not afraid!" She stands near to view the response in his countenance to her words.

Her face is expressionless as she waits.

Her arms reach toward him with hands and fingers ready to grip.

"That child don't have no chance if'n I don't go up there now!" The finality of tone and resolve in his stare chills her.

She grasps the marshal in terror. "Let me go! They won't shoot a woman. They'll want me as a captive. I'll find out whom and what is in that cabin."

The marshal is surprised by her strength and her courage. "Can't rightly. It's my duty!"

"Why can't I help save some innocent child? This is everyone's duty." Ali does not ease her hold.

"Let me go with her." Judith steps forth. "If anyone else is there with that child, then I'll drop my kerchief outside as signal."

The marshal is forced to consider the wisdom of the scholar.

The plan of the ladies increases the chance of saving the captive child.

The peril to the girls is not lessened.

"I am not best with a rifle, but this here carbine is a powerful weapon. It's hard to miss with this here cannon." He deliberates.

The ladies remain silent for his reflection.

They are not anxious to face danger.

They are frantic to save a child and the marshal.

"When you get up there, throw open the cabin door. Wait till the light fills the place. Have a good look inside before entering. Judith you wait outside where's I can see ya at all times."

The marshal studies the faces of the two women.

They consume his every word.

"If'n there's someone guarding that cabin, they'll want to take you prisoner. Tell them there's a dozen riders down below with a marshal. If'n you get forced out drop down when I yell Stand To."

"You're going to kill them as well!" Ali is distressed.

Marshal Legs is aware of the atrocious character of any criminal to be found up there.

"I won't shoot unless in self defense."

He intends to kill the person as soon as he has a chance.

"I won't let them destroy that child now or anyone else later."

He looks longing into Ali's eyes.

His apprehension is unmistakable to her.

Her clutch becomes tender.

She pulls his face to her. "I believe in you."

She kisses his cheek.

"I'll be moving up that hill as soon as Judith gives a sign." His words break in emotion.

His sentiment is more commanding than he has felt in many lonely years.

He strains as his eyes water.

His free hand has to feel her waist.

His devotion veils her from all menace for this moment.

She must quit him.

Her need to save a lost child ends her desire for his embrace.

Slowly the two girls step out on the path toward the shed.

Ali's thoughts of the marshal compel her to time and again glance backward.

Her thoughts of the despicable bandits left dead on the road earlier in the day draw her to peek ahead to the fate approaching.

With every step that she advances in approach, her approval

for the marshal increases. For these seconds she shares the peril of his world.

Her death could come at any moment.

She has no heart for the violence that may be needed.

The shack ahead is in ruins from years of abandonment.

It is now only slack and leaning.

As the pair advances to the door, a noise from within calls them to a stop.

The marshal comes to alert.

Judith waits as Ali opens the door.

There stands a young girl just within.

The child is in the grasp of a large woman who holds a knife.

Judith kerchief falls.

Instinctively the two teachers step backward.

The woman within is dressed in manly cloths, dirty and shabby in the manner of her comrades. This scoundrel threatens the life of the child.

The captor and the youngster advance to the door while pointing for the visitors to retreat.

As the confronting ladies clear to the front of the shack, the marshal views the scene.

"Just a knife! Them boys didn't trust her with a gun." He remarks as he makes forward at a run with his carbine sighted on the hag who intimidates.

"There's a posse down below!" Ali calls.

Yet to speak a word, the witch from the ruin turns to gauge the threat.

The view of a man hurrying onward seizes her attention.

The fancy cloths of the marshal distract her.

Ali and Judith do not fail to seize the advantage.

Simultaneously, each snatches one arm of the murderous wench.

The child falls free from her captive's hold.

The struggling trio turns round about.

One pulls as the other pushes while the third yanks.

Thrust and parry the efforts go on furiously.

Screams and threats exchange.

Unable to free her self, the desperate waif tries to stab the delicate women who bind her.

She hurls Ali off to one side.

Her free hand clasps Judith firmly about the neck. The knife is raised to strike.

Ali screams!

The marshal is swift to their side.

One slam of the carbine's armrest strikes the female assailant at the base of her neck.

The blow is fatal.

The injured woman falls dead to the ground.

Judith and Ali are fatigued by the strength of the mad woman.

Both were moments from being pierced by the attacker's knife.

Their thoughts recover to the needs of the child.

They rush to her.

Ali looks to the marshal to depart so they may examine the native girl.

Judith has been trained in basic nursing.

The two women comfort and look over the body of the young girl.

The marshal steps lively to collect transportation.

The young girl is the child of natives.

She has been a captive for several days.

The women do not understand her words.

Ali greets the marshal upon his return.

"They have hurt this child! She needs a doctor at once!" Resentment fills her voice. "Animals don't harm their young like this!"

No thoughts are given to their fallen foe as the ladies ride off with the girl.

The wagon is reshaped for travel.

Judith attends the young native child. The girl has attached to Judith and will not leave her side.

The marshal walks toward the child.

He is to question her.

Ali observes the marshal as he signs with his hands to communicate with the recovered child. She stands with her hands upon her hip. Her eyebrows are lifted and her brow furrows in intense study.

A short inquiry ends as the marshal turns to Ali. "She been with them for three or four days. The girl is in shock."

"She needs to be cleaned and fed something warm. She needs rest. She needs a doctor." Ali instructs

Marshal Legs nods in agreement.

"How did you make your hands act as words?" Ali mimics some of his motions. "I want to be able to use sign language! Teach me...please?"

The marshal's one hand moves to point to one of his eyes.

Then the same hand drops to point to the center of his chest.

Lastly the pointing finger directs straight toward Ali.

The woman contemplates. "I understand!"

There is a pause then her face brightens with joyous eyes and smiling lips.

She blushes as her hands fold to her bosom.

Ali is much satisfied.

She moves to the native child.

Awkwardly but persistently her hands articulate her meaning.

The child responds. Despite much confusion the girl answers.

The marshal is surprised at the accomplishment of Ali, but not at the extended length of time consumed in the feminine exchange.

The two women involved in the pantomime share tears.

Ali hugs the child caringly for several minutes.

She pats the youth's head and face maternally.

"Her parents and brother were slaughtered by the band

that stopped us on the road. She is lost from her tribe now. They will not accept her as she is no longer clean."

Ali's words grieve her.

"I'll have to leave her with the sheriff of this jurisdiction." The marshal responds.

"No! Judith and the others all agree. We will keep her. She'll be our first student. We shall learn sign language and the child will learn English as we travel."

The decision is made.

"A doctor! Now!" Ali orders.

It is late afternoon.

The wagon moves toward Fargo when a road sign appears at a right fork.

West Liberty 9 miles

"Where there's a road sign there's a doctor!" The marshal states as he turns the wagon off from the Fargo Road. "As soon as we find water and a safe place, we'll make camp and get into West Liberty in the morning."

In an hour or two a large pond is approached.

Shade and meadow here adjoin.

Camp is pitched; animals graze, water boils, and women clean and dress anew the native girl.

By dusk all are fed and ready to retire.

The fatigue from the fright of the day dispels.

The marshal shall keep watch through the night.

All shall rest secured by his presence.

The sky is clear and cool.

The breeze is slight.

Sounds of this night are ordinary and they console those who slumber.

The hardship and cruelty absorbed in the day have worn man and beast.

On guard the marshal moves about the camp's perimeter throughout the time of dark.

The marshal will share the occasional whimper of the child.

He will witness the tossing of a sleeping lady enduring a moment of unconscious distress.

The animals settle, as they accustom to his roaming sent.

Marshal Legs has always taken pleasure in the night.

His Sioux grand father trained him in the skill of quiet steps and silent movement.

His vision in the dark has always been acute.

Living upon the open ground for many years has increased the sensitivity of his hearing.

He is a superb sentry.

The call of the child awakes Ali to comfort her.

A drink of water for the child then exhaustion moves Little Owl again into a deep sleep.

Ali observes the marshal's silhouette against the full moon.

She does not fully understand this man. He places his life before the danger to save others. Yet his violence is terrible and final.

She moves to speak with him.

The marshal cannot but enjoy the womanly saunter that approaches.

The moonlight illuminates the delicate features and shape of the young schoolteacher.

"Can we talk?" She asks.

The marshal responds by placing one finger over his lips to still her voice.

He signs. "Words travel further at night!"

The pair takes seat upon a fallen log.

Her shoulders lean towards him.

Her eyes open to the full.

Ali is delighted to encounter the man is this way." You never sleep. You never tire."

A masculine nod answers.

The marshal's eyes continue to search out and away.

"Tell me about you!"

"The marshal scratches his head.

"My father." He signs.

"English gentleman." He whispers.

"My mother" He signs.

"Daughter of a Sioux war chief." He whispers.

"So you are a warrior and a lord." She whispers.

"The two are much the same." He signs

"How did you become a marshal...a law man?" Her hands gesture with her words.

The thoughts and hands of the marshal are slow to recall and explain.

"As a young man on my own, I was in a trading post one day. An acquaintance of my childhood days entered the store at the same time."

"A close friend?" Ali signs.

A shake of the head gives a no.

"He pulls a gun and shoots the owner and the owner's wife dead." The marshal responds.

"What was the owner's name?" Ali questions in sign

"Jenashek" The marshal whispers.

"My friend instructed me to go and collect the money from the register."

Ali's hand interrupts. "Where there others in the store at this time?"

"Yes! The others in the store did not know the robber. They thought we were together. Robbing together!"

Her eyes inquire for the truth.

"As he took the money from my hand his eyes rose with a cold final stare toward mine. I knew he was not going to let me live."

Ali can't imagine such a circumstance.

"As he looked again at the cash...I drew my knife from its scabbard on my waist."

Ali's eyes close in fright.

The marshal pauses.

His hands rest.

"Was that the only way? To kill the man?" Hers hands beg.

The look of inevitability in the marshal's face is his only

answer. "My only regret is that I didn't have the chance to save them Janasheks."

She searches deeply into his soul.

Her hands and fingers move slowly.

"How did you feel at this man's death? Was this the first man you killed?"

"When the deer's path crossed my arrow for the first time. I cried for the loss of its life. My grandfather and I prayed for the deer's forgiveness. We asked the deer to understand that his life gives life to our family. Each deer I have taken for food saddens me." His hands are strong in their words.

"This man was not to be honored as the spirit of the deer?"

"Yes." He answers to her second question.

Ali yet attends his words.

"My life honors all that has been given to me from the beginning to my end." His eyes question her.

"I am grateful too!" Her hands respond.

"I have no need to kill a man!" She is confused by his lack of choice. "What about the pain and agony of his dying?"

"What of the pain and agony of birth? Should no one then be a mother?"

"It is not the same!" Ali maintains.

"If I kill a bear that stalks the children from a village...this act preserves life."

She waits for more understanding.

"The taking of the Janashek's lives did not give life. This crime violated nature. The taking of the life of their killer preserves that life that he shall never be able to take." He is quiet.

"So you are glad to kill these men because of the innocent life that shall not be lost."

His arm fully extends for his hand to open and firmly grasp and pull at the air in great strength.

"You give strength to life in the killing of evil ones!" She signs in question.

His arm makes salute. He affirms her understanding.

"This is the way your native soul directs you?"

Again his salute is given in confirmation.

She puzzles yet.

"To wound a bear is bad. To kill a bear is better" He signs.

"This is an old Sioux saying", he whispers.

"So you decided to become a marshal?"

"The job came to me! Came to me cause I could stop them bad men quick and easy like." He shrugs his shoulders.

Ali's knees knock about. She is restless as she sits watching the marshal.

She is anxious to fully understand this man.

She ponders why she fully loves him.

She fully accepts him.

"Life can never be measured in death." She signs as she departs.

"It is the maternal instinct that directs you?" He poses to her.

She nods to verify.

Her head is high and her nose is lifted in satisfaction as she returns to her bedding.

"He needs more life in its softer form." She considers.

West liberty is a prosperous small town of ranchers, farmers, and miners.

The territorial seat in early times, the larger Fargo has surpassed it in population several generations back.

The town sits in an open meadow that is rimmed with woodland.

One road passes through.

It is busy as the wagon enters under the marshal's command.

In the front of a low wide building hangs the sign ***J D Sumner Sheriff.*** Here the marshal brings the wagon to a halt.

Out from the entrance of the building steps a pudgy man

wearing a gray suit and black derby hat. A sheriff's badge hangs from his chest.

His face and neck are heavy with flesh.

His lips are full and hold a long burning cigar.

His white tight curly hair protrudes from under his cap.

His legs are short and his hands small. His abdomen is bulbous.

The sheriff approaches the gathering of strangers aboard the marshal's carriage.

His eyes scan the scene of mules, cart, women, and driver.

The fancy dress and boots of the man holding the reins determines his attitude.

"J D Sumner...Sheriff of West Liberty." He says before turning his large cigar about in his mouth.

The appearance of the bulging sheriff is more that of a chef then a lawman.

The marshal's gaze is confounded.

"You're a gambler!" The fat sheriff utters contemptuously. "No gamblers allowed in West Liberty!"

His plump eyes cast a vulgar glance over the forms of the women.

The teachers are uncomfortable.

Judith is insulted.

"Them prostitutes you're hauling are illegal in West Liberty!" J D Sumner stammers.

The marshal notes that several men wearing badges have come to occupy the porch to either side of Sheriff Sumner.

"These folk's under arrest J D?" Calls one deputy.

The marshal begins to step down from the wagon.

"Hold on there!" The sheriff announces as he spies the native child.

"That there native girl is illegal in town as well. Ordinances s don't allow natives inside the city limits."

"The child is injured and needs a doctor." Ali fires in response.

"That be so?" The ponderous sheriff eyes the maiden who speaks out disrespectfully with some irritation.

"No natives! The doc can see her out outside of town."

"So there is a doctor here." Marshal Legs prods.

"Doc Bayfield has a place just down the way." A fleshy finger of the sheriff points the way. "But you won't be stopping there! One of my deputies will show you folks outa West Liberty straight off."

The marshal opens his waistcoat to show his official emblem.

"U S Marshal Legs! This here child is a federal witness and under the protection of the US Government."

J D's cigar loosens in his mouth as the sight of the marshal's authority.

"I'll be taking this child directly for medical attention... without interference." Marshal Legs' voice is authoritative.

He steps down.

Judith and the native girl follow.

The stout sheriff is silent.

"I'll deliver this child to the doctor and return straight off." Marshal Legs informs.

Judith walks beside the marshal who carries the child in his arms.

Dr Bayfield's office is in the first floor of his spacious home.

There is a wide wrap around porch with railing that greets the visitor.

At the sound of the doorbell, a middle aged man untidy in cloths and hair opens the door to the sight of a homely young woman with a well dressed man holding a native child.

"You a preacher or something like that?" Greets the doctor.

"This child has been attacked!" Judith pushes inward taking the child into the first examination room to come to her view.

"This place is filthy!" She declares as she begins to clear space.

"I've had a tough time keeping up since my wife passed away." The Doctor apologizes.

"Being out on call at all hours. Mrs. Bayfield used to see to the place and help with the medical practice. God keep her."

The pain in the doctor's words gives Judith regret for her harsh words. "I've had some medical training Let me assist you."

Engrossed in the health needs of the child, Judith does not notice that the marshal returns to the wagon. He finds it abandoned.

The sheriff with all his deputies stands in front of the jailhouse.

A chubby hand pulls a cigar in and out of the sheriff's mouth. The puffs of his smoke match the pace of the approaching marshal.

Expressionless the marshal looks long and straight at the sheriff.

"Them girls are locked up inside!" J D Sumner informs.

"They been arrested for vagrancy, intent to commit prostitution, assembly without a permit, and a bunch of other violations that I haven't had time to write up yet."

The smirk of satisfaction looms large on the sheriff's face.

There is no change in the demeanor of Marshal Legs.

A placid gaze remains on the face of the sheriff.

"They'll be tried at the end of the month when court convenes." States the town sheriff.

Nearly thirty days according to Marshal Legs reckoning.

"Fine and penalties to accrue daily. There is no federal jurisdiction that'll be overriding these cases." His jowls shake empathically.

The marshal nods once defining his understanding.

He returns to Dr Bayfield's home.

The doctor is just finishing his work with the damaged child.

"Your friends have been arrested by the sheriff and they are in jail till the end of the month when the judge arrives." The marshal informs Judith.

The doctor shakes his head in disgust. "You know who the judge be? The sheriff is the judge as well!"

His pause gives ample time for the marshal's consideration.

"That Sumner is a cheating scoundrel, a lying thief, and a despicable coward." More anguish and loathing pours from the doctor.

"He's done this to other travelers?" Judith asks.

"Regular like. The folks here detest the man but we can't get him unselected as sheriff. As judge he rules delays or voids elections. His band of relatives intimidates us."

Marshal Legs is silent.

Judith finds the doctor sincere and most caring. "How did he get the job as sheriff?"

"The man came to town and put up the a saloon. Bought votes with free drinks. When the old judge passed on he got himself appointed in his place. Then it was too late. He cancels or postpones the elections as he sees fit.

We are supposed to reelect officials in a week but that'll never happen."

"Has he killed anyone?"

Judith looks to the marshal's eyes as the doctor answers.

"Not likely. He's a parasite but he won't do anything to lose the golden goose."

Judith questions the marshal with her gaze.

The marshal shakes his head no to indicate the absence of violence as a solution.

"Let me go and talk to the girls?" Judith begs.

"The sheriff will arrest you as well." Bayfield sees the strength of his departed wife in the woman.

He likes the courage and intelligence of Judith.

"Stay here and I'll visit the women." The doctor takes his medical bag and coat in order to leave.

"Both of you stay here and watch this child...no telling what mischief that overgrown rodent might stir up if he gets a chance." The physician leaves.

Marshal Legs steps on to the porch.

He sits and lights a small black cigar.

Puffs of gray smoke lift about his head.

He drifts deeply into thought. "There is little my authority can do here under these circumstances."

He cannot provoke violence this would be an abuse of his office.

"There must be some way to undo this sheriff." The marshal mutters.

Judith brings the young native girl to the porch. "Watch her while I clean about the house." She instructs the marshal.

The child sits to his side.

She stares at the mature warrior.

She recognizes the Sioux in his features.

The dark eyes of the child remain sad.

The marshal looks to her comfort. "Do you need drink?" He signs.

"No." She replies.

"Are you cold? He notes the long dark shiny hair that folds over her shoulder to the front.

"No." She replies.

"How are you called?" He waits.

"I' am called Little Owl?" She signs. "You slew those who took the lives of my family!"

He signs. "The great spirit has spared you. He has brought you here among the medicine people of the homesteaders."

The child nods in agreement.

"The woman Judith has great medicine. She will teach you much." The marshal adds.

"My heart has joined hers." Answers the child." My father was a great consul to our people. He wished to learn from the settlers. This I shall do for him."

The marshal does not reply.

"You come as a great warrior of the Sioux." She affirms. "There is no arrow with the power to kill such a one as you in battle!"

The marshal does not respond.

The jailhouse was originally a two room cabin.

The inner room was held by lock and key for the occasional rogue.

The present sheriff has had several expansions added with bars on the door and windows. It's holding capacity has been greatly increased.

The four school teachers have ample but confining space.

Doctor Bayfield has permission to visit the ladies inside the jailhouse.

"Miss Bennet." He calls quietly as he approaches their cage.

"James Bayfield here...Dr Bayfield."

"How is the child?" Ali's worry for the girl is first in her thoughts.

"She will mend in time. The shock will last outlast the pain." He nods in consolation.

"Judith, and Marshal Legs?" Her eyes strain in concern.

"All three are safe at my place for now. You girls are safe as well."

"Why are we here? Why are we in jail?" Ali is confused.

"JD Sumner cheats at cards and anything else he can get away with. That rascal has put you're in here to scalp your cash. He'll let you go for a fine now or bigger fine later."

Ali's face reddens in anger.

"What is the marshal going to do about this?" She fumes.

"Nothing at the moment. He has no jurisdiction in these matters. His hands are tied for the present." Bayfield regrets.

"You mean the people of this town let their sheriff conduct crimes like this?"

Bayfield is embarrassed.

"The marshal wants me to let you know that he's working on an idea. He'll get you free soon enough. Be patient he says."

Ali stomps with hands on hips and puffs at the doctor. "You tell that so called marshal if he can rid the road of all those killers then one overweight slow sheriff should be easy enough. If he cares anything at all for me...us then he best get over here now and open up these bars. It smells like whiskey in here!"

"Before I have to leave, let me say again be enduring in your faith for the marshal. Are you ladies well enough?"

"Under the circumstance well enough I suppose." She ponders then adds. "Remind Judith of a lady named Sally Wiggns."

Judith has joined the sitters on the doctor's porch.

"I love this house!" She sighs.

She holds the child.

The marshal has noticed how the child and Judith have become like mother and daughter.

"You're a fine mother. You'll make a fine wife." He adds.

"Men never look at me. Not the way a woman wishes." Her head droops in disappointment.

"Shoot! I've seen that physician look at you real manly like...more than once!"

Her mood alters to one of excitement.

"I could settle here with a man like Dr Bayfield. If he'd have me."

The last statement is intended as a question to the marshal who does not oblige in response.

"What does a man seek in a woman...a wife?" She perseveres.

"Clean...wholesome...man doesn't want to hear about his failings all the time. Woman is to make life happy. A man is to make life proceed." The marshal directs.

"I could make a man.... a home happy." She convinces.

"You brought a lot of happiness and goodness to your comrades that's for sure." The marshal assures.

Judith is certain.

She'll speak with the doctor.

She sees no success in remaining shy.

"What do you see that is special in Ali?" Judith questions.

The marshal is not comfortable about discussing his sentiments.

He flushes slightly.

"Can't say right out...I'm not good with words. She is special alright."

He can't express how this woman brings comfort and joy into his heart.

Nor can he speak of the warm purity that he shares when she is in his arms.

He wishes that he could speak these emotions so that he may gain the pleasure from hearing them said out loud.

"If you stay, Little Owl must return to visit her people before she becomes a woman. It's their custom!" The marshal instructs. "She may then return freely to you."

James Bayfield returns to his home.

"Them female companions of yours are waiting for relief and they want it soon."

The marshal puzzles.

"She asked me to remind you of a Miss Sally Wiggns." The physician turns to a nervous Judith.

Lost in the hope of an inviting look from the doctor, the message does not register.

The surgeon notes the maternal care by Judith to the child.

"You're a fine mother."

Judith's face erupts in a glow of hopefulness.

The doctor notes the change in the order and cleanliness of his dwelling since his departure.

"This house could use a woman just like you."

"Whose Sally Wiggins?" Interrupts the marshal.

"A girl back east!" Judith does not want the doctor's attention to fade from her aspirations.

"Helping you is a pleasure. The house is beautiful." She smiles.

It is clear to all the thoughts that pass the doctor's mind.

He has want for Judith.

"Why would she be thinking of an old acquaintance at a time like this?" The marshal is perturbed.

"Sally Wiggins!" Judith gasps. "I know why she brings that girl to mind."

It is just before the dinner hour when the marshal walks out to the jailhouse.

His saunter is not threatening.

His pace is relaxed.

The sheriff and several deputies await him at the front door of the jailhouse.

They observe a sign being carried under the arm of the marshal.

"Now don't start no trouble marshal. We know your reputation with a gun. Matters here are all legal."

The marshal moves past the local men to the door.

He produces a sign, which he hangs over the door.

It reads **Quarantined**.

"What's the meaning of this? You can't do this!" The pompous sheriff declares.

Marshal Legs produces a document signed by the doctor declaring a possible spotted fever epidemic among the woman in the jail and those who have been in contact with them.

He hands it to the sheriff.

"That means you and all the deputies at this point are hereby confined to the jail under federal order. Marshal Law has been declared in West liberty as of now and until the doctor announces the emergency over!"

The marshal produces two guns.

"Gentlemen you are to be held in confinement."

The local law officers are relieved of their weapons and locked into unoccupied cells.

In moments, Ali and her companions are released from the jail and ordered to stay under house arrest at Dr. Bayfield's residence until Marshal Law is lifted.

This is done upon the medical advice and order of Dr Bayfield.

Ali is quick to hug Judith and the native child.

"I wasn't sure you would understand my message?" Ali states.

"Not at first! The marshal kept asking me why you would speak of a Miss Wiggins." Judith responds.

"That Marshal Legs sure is curious." Ali squeezes Judith tightly just as she would the marshal.

"Lucky for you. I almost forgot about Sally the Carrier." Both girls laugh.

"Never heard of a case of measles that looked so much like small pox that an entire city shut down." The doctor inserts.

"Her daddy was the mayor. He took his little girl around to all the socials in the town. Sally was so cute the women folk adored her and Mr. Wiggins for being her daddy." Ali responds.

"Mayor Wiggins was afraid the city would blame an epidemic on him. He would then loose the next election." Judith recalls. "So he quarantined an entire city of 20,000 people."

"Yes when they found out the child just had only measles they voted out Wiggins in the subsequent election." Ali adds.

"Well Judith here made the suggestion right off. Spotted fever is to be had here abouts."

The doctor bows to Judith. "Dam smartest woman I ever meet."

Ali is quick to sense the feelings being exchanged between the physician and Judith.

"I thought the marshal was mad at me because he didn't even give me a notice when he was sending us off." Ali lips frown.

"What's the plan?" Ali questions.

"It's up to the marshal now." Dr. Bayfield shakes his head in respect. "He'll send word soon."

The marshal has taken a seat on the porch at the entrance to the jail.

His carbine rests at his side.

A small black cigar is being employed to pass the time.

He wishes all assignments were this easy.

Two riders are approaching.

Both wear deputy badges.

Both seem capable with their weapons.

The tall rider stops at the front. "Who be you mister? You be a preacher?"

"Marshal Legs! U S Marshal Legs!" The answer is given.

The riders note the quarantined sign.

"What's this all about?" The smaller rider barks.

"Spotted fever in the jailhouse! Dr Bayfield has ordered it closed."

The tall rider laughs slightly at the circumstance. "We come to see J D."

"If'n you go in you'll have to stay till the quarantine ends." The marshal informs.

"Hell we just came to turn our badges in cause we quit." The rider says in disgust.

"What be your names?" The marshal inquires.

"This here's my little brother Frank. I'm Jessie Coulter!" The tall rider divulges.

"You have a problem?" The marshal continues.

"Need the work but we can't stomach J D's ways. We just came back from a homestead of two old folks. We were supposed to serve foreclosure papers on their property. Them folks paid their taxes to the sheriff. He never sent a receipt over to them. He's a cheating them good people." Jessie shakes his head in disgust.

"Any man in this town or near about that you boys can't handle?" Marshal Legs requests.

The two riders look one to the other in a manner of reflecting. "Nope not really. Some means types but there be no fast guns here."

"Jessie, I'm a gone to deputize you and your brother. You'll both circulate the declaration of quarantine at the jailhouse to all the citizens. Further, you'll circulate a sample ballot for the general election coming in tomorrow's day."

Jessie and Frank nod agreeably.

Who's getting elected?" Frank asks.

"Jessie you are a going to run against J D Sumner for sheriff." The marshal pauses for objection.

The riders produce none.

"Who is a gone to run for judge against J D?" Jessie asks.

"Mrs. Judith Bayfield" Again the marshal waits for a complaint.

"Women can't hold office!" Frank blurts.

"They can't vote in this here territory as yet. But there be no federal law against them holding an elected office!" These words are final from the marshal.

"Yeah Boy! Let's get at it." Shouts Frank.

"I wouldn't miss this for the world. Dang! J D's going to be mad!" Jessie hoots.

"I'll take care of J D. You boys get the voters to arrive here tomorrow."

It's late afternoon.

The federal marshal awaits the return of his new deputies.

Sheriff Sumner is escorted to sit with the Marshal on the porch.

Cigars are enjoyed.

"J D tell me about Doc Bayfield. Is he as good a man as he seems?"

"Doc is about the only man I've ever had respect for. When my wife was dying he was at her side every minute he could spare." The confined sheriff recounts. "His wife was just as thoughtful as the doc. The entire community has suffered the loss with her passing."

Marshal Legs nods acceptingly. "How old be you J D?"

"Be seventy eight this fall!" The sheriff's eyes sparkle with health.

Lots of smoke plumes during their conversation.

"About time to retire? You got money put back J D?"

"Got lots of cash. Just feel too good to stop. Shucks got to have something to do."

"How did you get into this side of the law?" The marshal asks.

"My daddy was a tobacco sales man. He hustled all over the Mississippi dealing here and there."

The sheriff sighs for the affections of his youth. "He was so damn honest many took unfair advantage of him. My daddy died broke. Left us broke."

The flesh on his face and neck flaps with resentment. "Let me tell you no one has ever got the chance to cheat me. Just hustled my way in to being a sheriff."

"J D I'm looking for a man, smallish, young but balding real bad. Traveling with a large mountain type fellow."

"Seen'm...less than a week back. Didn't like the looks, the smell or the taste their presence. Run'm off straight away." A large cigar points in the direction away from town in emphasis.

"They be dangerous be they?"

Marshal Legs nods affirmatively.

He respects the proper concern of the heavy sheriff for the welfare of his citizens.

"Marshal your reputation precedes you. Heard tales of the Marshal Legs from Texas-Oklahoma way. Always hunting down killers."

"Call me Woody, J D." A small cigar salutes the sheriff.

"Woody! It's an honor."

Frank Coulter arrives at Dr Bayfield's house.

"I need to see a Miss Bennet. Have a message from the marshal for her!" He shouts as he dismounts.

Ali emerges uncertain.

"I'm Miss Bennet!" She replies

A ballot is handed to her.

"Voting tomorrow." He tips his hat to the teacher. "Marshal wants everyone here over to the jailhouse as soon as possible."

Ali reads the ballot.

Office of municipal judge J D Sumner ______ or Judith Bayfield ______

She laughs with delight at the pluck of Marshal Legs.

"How did he manage this?" She ponders.

Below he has written.

The wedding of Judith and James is to be performed at the jailhouse as soon as possible.

Ali marches straight to Judith who is cleaning medical instruments.

The message from the marshal is handed to her for inspection.

The intended bride is dumb struck.

"Do you want to marry the doctor?" Ali asks knowing full well the woman's desire.

Judith can only nod her head timidly.

"Do you want to be the judge in West Liberty?" Ali is unsure.

Judith's mouth hangs open.

She cannot speak as many thoughts fly.

"Do you know anything about the law?" Ali continues.

"I worked at the court house back home for Judge Elbridge as a law clerk." She manages.

"I know a good deal about the law actually." Judith holds the marshal's note against her breast.

She lowers it and reads aloud. "The wedding of Judith and James..."

"Do you want me to show this to Doctor Bayfield?" Ali asks.

Judith deliberates in deep thought.

She bobs her head side to side indicating no as her answer.

She walks away oblivious to all.

Dr. Bayfield is in his study.

He is browsing a medical journal when Judith arrives.

Judith will not delay.

Her dreams are to be settled at this hour. "I'm going to run for judge in tomorrows elections."

"Elections? What elections?" He inquires.

"The office of sheriff and judge are to be voted upon tomorrow in a special election." She moves close to the doctor.

She inspects his countenance.

She fumbles at the marshal's note that she holds in both hands.

She awaits his look.

The doctor's attention is given to her hands and their contents.

He peeks to see her face.

The stare of each questions the other.

It is a moment of deepest sharing by their spirits.

He beholds a woman who is offering her devotion.

She sees a man who desires, wants and needs her.

The power of the moment brings Judith to tears.

Doctor Bayfield rises to embrace and console her.

His arms tenderly surround her shoulders. They seize her.

She does not struggle against the tide of her emotion.

Her head falls upon his chest.

She sobs.

Compassion, caring and love surge through the man who tends her.

"I do not want you to leave me." He whispers prayerfully.

Her upper body heaves in longing.

"Stay and be my wife?" His words are filled with love.

Judith recovers stability and consciousness.

"Marry me? I worship you! I can not be without you!" He continues to plead.

Her face rises into his glance.

"We will go now." She presents him with the marshal's written declarations.

Judith's ensemble is a modest dress of white cotton with a silk veil.

Little Owl is wearing a shift in white as well.

Garnishes of flowers adorn both the bride and her juvenile bridesmaid.

Dr. James Bayfield has had his hair trimmed by Ali.

His clothes have been washed and pressed by Michele and Layla.

His youthful appearance is retuned.

The sheriff is astounded by the arrival of a wedding party.

"How did this happen?" He snorts as he gropes for belief in the visions before him.

"Need your help J D. These folks want hitched". The marshal makes a request. "You'll have to perform the service."

"That woman isn't in town twelve hours!" The sheriff is in denial.

"Love don't take but a moment to get going for some." The marshal gives note.

"I see the bride, the groom and the bridesmaid. Who's the best man?" Judge Sumner searches.

"That would be me!" Marshal Legs takes his place aside Dr. Bayfield

Ali is flushed with anticipation.

Her eyes follow the emotions from bride to groom during every part of the wedding service

Her ears filter all but the sacred rites being uttered.

However she sees at the altar her self beside the marshal.

"This should convince him." Ali tells her self.

"How could he not want to marry?" She looks at the marshal with agitation.

Afterwards, the wedding party returns to the doctor's home

"Hell of a way to run a quarantine, Woody", J D states.

"It's not over yet, J D. tomorrow the town holds an election."

The wedding feast is made at Dr Bayfield's residence.

Lot's of old family dinning recipes are prepared by Evelyn.

Breaded chicken breast served with light gravy, hot rolls and cornbread. Fried green tomatoes, cabbage fried in butter with sliced onions and seasoned with brown sugar is prepared.

Baked beef steak in thick gravy mixed with green peas, baked potatoes stuffed with grated cheese and diced fresh red tomatoes, eggplant fried with a covering of a lightly seasoned batter, tossed salad with a red wine vinaigrette and croutons are all served on a large table under the shade of a tall walnut tree.

Sliced red beats served with onions in vinegar, sausages boiled in a barbecue and beer sauce, fired ham with mustard, and pork roasted with apples, sliced cucumbers in a mayonnaise sauce, sweet potato pie, strawberry pie, chocolate pie, all land upon the dinner table.

Heaps of left overs will be sent to the jailhouse for all restrained there to enjoy.

Whiskey, beer, and cider will be sent to the sheriff, his deputies and the marshal as well.

The first night of the quarantine in the jail will be spent in the best of humor and comfort.

In the morning the marshal and all his jailhouse guests take porch seats to watch the activities of the town as the election proceeds.

"Who'll be counting all them votes? Mighty heavy turn out." J D asks.

"You and your deputies will tally up the results. Yours will be the last votes to be cast." The marshal points to the heavy sheriff.

"Woody, you're not in town twenty four hours and you'll have me out of public office."

The marshal nods in agreement.

"J D here's the deal. The new sheriff and judge are going to investigate all your financial dealings while you were sheriff and judge. You make good any cash shortcomings or irregularities and we'll let you run your saloon in peace. Otherwise, any crimes committed by a sitting judge are a federal offense and you'll serve time in federal prison."

"Hell Woody any time in a prison for a man my age is a death sentence. I don't rightly have no choice but to oblige!" The sheriff's large cigar is bitten.

"The new judge and sheriff will keep me informed as to your word."

A warning is given. "Won't be no second peace offer."

"What offended you so much that you took to such measures against me?" J D asks.

"J D you messed with my women folk. The only senior offense is messing with my horse...men have been died for less."

At the day's end, ballots have been counted. J D Sumner has sworn Sheriff Coulter and Judge Judith Bayfield into duty.

The quarantine has been declared lifted by Dr Bayfield.

A new age has come to the town of West Liberty.

Early in the morning after Election Day, goodbyes are made to Judith.

The marshal wishes Little Owl to continue to travel with Ali until a proper visit the people of her tribe can be made. The natives may take a notion that their child is being held against her will. The peace may not be kept.

The spare horses taken from the outlaws are left here to await Little Owl's return.

The wagon and remaining travelers return to the highway that leads to Fargo.

There was rain over night.

The cover of the wagon is full over.

The first of day is gray. The mood of the teachers matches the gloom of nature. Frowns, yawns, and desires for the gala of yesterday to continue band the onset of enthusiasm for the renewed journey.

The road to Fargo begins in a slow accent to higher elevations.

The muddy puddles conceal pothole and exposed rock.

The sun finds room to show between dispersing clouds.

Cheer is not part of the present mood of the group despite several hours of travel.

As the wagon is pulled along a winding meadow, Evelyn raises from her seat.

"There's a dog over there!" She points to a patch of golden rod. "It's hurt"

Evelyn bounds off the moving wagon and onto the side of the road.

The thin blond girl moves directly toward a chosen mark in the field.

"Wait!" Calls Ali in fright.

The marshal halts the progress of the carriage.

He is quick to grab his carbine and follow.

The caravan has recessed off the road to a scrap of bush to find Evelyn comforting a large yellow dog.

The canine has been injured and has taken an ending pause in its travel.

Evelyn is in tears for the beast grievous wounds. She sobs bitterly while petting the animal, which reposes nearing death.

Ali is fleet afoot and has arrived just behind Evelyn at the scene. She finds the dog wounded in the right back leg. Another wound is found at the joining of the shoulders behind the neck.

Blood stains the foliage in which the damaged hound has taken refuge.

As the marshal arrives, Ali stands silent with her hands held against her hips in utter despair.

He recognizes the gash upon the neck of the dog as a bullet wound.

The hole in the hind leg is the result of a shooting also.

The female animal is dying.

Ali looks hopelessly toward the marshal.

Her look seeks his opinion.

The marshal answers her silently with a shake of his head in inevitability.

Evelyn's large eyes do not smile.

The marshal has never seen such sadness expressed in a gaze.

He stands helpless before the scene of care.

"I can't let her die." Evelyn speaks.

"She's hurt awful bad." Ali informs her. "She's lost a lot of blood"

"Her heart is strong and she's warm." Evelyn refuses to let loose of her charge.

"That animal is suffering...best to put her down." The marshal states as he pulls one handgun free.

"No!" Evelyn screams, "I won't let you. I won't let any one hurt her."

"Don't Woody!" Ali whispers.

"Get the girls back to the wagon. I'll see to this!" She begs.

As the others return to the cart, Ali bends to hold Evelyn in her arms.

"We'll try! Let's carry her to the wagon and make her comfortable in the rear."

Evelyn's eyes smile once again. "I'll stay with her and watch her. Some water, some warmth may be all this dog needs."

The two girls port the harmed dog to the carriage.

A place is made at the back. Here Evelyn will stay while carrying for the animal.

The voyage resumes.

Mounting sunshine lifts the sprits.

All in the wagon share hope for the canine.

Miles pass.

Time does pass.

"Seems one of them wheels in the back is a might wobbly.

"The marshal informs the ladies. "Best we have a stop and a look"

The back right wagon wheel shows some cracks and a loss of shape.

"How good is your spare?" The marshal asks.

"It was fixed some weeks back by Mr. Beaudreaux." Ali returns.

The marshal examines the emergency wheel. "Could be better! Best to replace this extra wheel and have the one going bad fixed and then set aside as a standby."

"Should we change it now?" The lady asks.

"Seems the axel has a bit of wear and could use some bracing sooner than later." Marshal Legs notes as he recovers from an inspection underneath the wagon.

"Can we still drive the wagon?" Ali wants advice.

"The axel will keep to Fargo if the road maintains a good surface. This here bad wheel can split long before then". A thought filled moment passes across the marshal's countenance.

"Will go onward as we are just now. Keep a sharp watch on road hazards. Go a bit slower until we come to a wayside where a repair can be done. Get better prices in Fargo on wagon parts though."

Ali feels guilty that she did not have the spare rim check and replaced in Sweet Creek. "It's my fault. I should have paid more attention to the condition of the wagon."

"Wagons, and other things go bad natural like. One does their best then just deals with trouble when it comes." He consoles Ali with a smile.

"Be more of this kind of difficulty coming Ali. We'll get through it all."

Ali is thankful to be able to rely on the marshal.

A team of large horses is pulling a wagon laden with goods from the direction that leads to Fargo. An older man with long white whiskers drives the approaching cart.

The approaching freight wagon stops.

"Hello Parson!" He calls out.

Ali turns sheepish as she notes the marshal's grimace at the salutation.

The old driver views their present dilemma. "Need a hand?"

"Got a bad wheel and weakened axel." Replies the marshal.

"Well reverend..."

Ali cringes further.

"Got no extra wheel to lend but there's a road house back yonder a piece. They have wagon parts and the man there does some fine repairs." The old man notifies.

"Can we make it there do ya think?" Asks the marshal.

The old man drops down to inspect the damage.

"Yep! Take'er slow and gentle. You'll be there before lunch."

A hand of greeting extends to the marshal. "Dave Chorba! I drive freight along these roads for nearly 40 years now."

"Howdy!" The marshal shakes his hand. "These here gals be heading out to California to teach school."

Each lady gives a warm welcome.

"A long ways off, California. Got a cousin what married a dentist. They moved out there years ago...Got a big family now. They want me to come for a visit. I'm a going one of these days. If'n I can get the time and money together. Mighty pretty gals you got here preacher."

"Just riding along for a spell. Got business this side of Fargo." Interrupts the marshal.

Ali withdraws.

"Best be careful! Here there's been some robberies and some murders in these parts lately." Warns Dave "People getting mighty jittery."

"Close by?" Inquires Marshal Legs.

"Close enough! Got my double barrel shotgun primed and at the ready. Won't sleep out on the road." Dave has been through many dangerous times.

"These crimes be real recent be they?"

"Just the last couple of days, it's been peaceful for a good long spell."

Seen any unusual characters on the road ahead the past few days?"

"Well vicar, there's a lot of traffic closer to Fargo with the coming of spring. Hard to say. Lot's of strangers on the road now a days."

"Will be careful and thanks for the help and information." The marshal acknowledges.

Dave returns to his wagon. "Haven't helped a might. Be careful. Be alert!"

The marshal gives a salute.

Dave begins to climb his cargo wagon when he spies the wounded dog.

He pauses.

"That there looks like Curly's hound Bessie." He returns and moves to the wagons' rear.

He nods respectfully toward Evelyn then he looks down into the wagon's bed at the dog.

"Sure is! That's old Bessie!" He inspects. "She's been shot!"

"Hunter's mostly likely. Dogs that run free will upset serious hunters." The marshal supposes.

"Not Bessie! She never leaves Curly 's side. Never!" He shakes his head no to the marshal's notion.

"Find one you'll find the other. Something's got to be mighty wrong". Dave insists.

The marshal's eyes scan the horizon.

His hand finds the handles of his handguns at the ready.

Ali catches the steel glint in his eyes.

Her heart feels the coldness in his gaze.

He has left her.

He is returned to duty as a lawman.

"His place be near?" Asks the marshal.

"Curly Adams has a small spread back other side of that ridge yonder. Along side a wide stream. Raises horse and mules mostly." Dave informs.

"I have to ride over there." The marshal recovers his own mount.

"Dave, I'll ask you to turn your wagon around and see these gals safely on to the road house ahead."

"Be happy to oblige! This is no job for a preacher." Chorba cautions.

"That there be Marshal Legs." Evelyn states.

As the marshal is about to depart he looks to Dave and Evelyn.

"Don't mention that Bessie is in that wagon when you get to that road house. Keep that dog outsight." He orders.

The blood trail of the wounded dog is easy for the marshal's horse to follow.

Across the meadow, up the hillside, and along an old path used by migrating animals the marshal rides.

Down rocky ridge and long a steam the trail is pursued.

The marshal wonders why the inseparable dog was found so far from near her master.

His horse strolls onto a shady farm lane.

Old trees, and sunken road give tell of a road worn with much use.

After a long slow turn, the marshal comes upon a scene of violence.

An old cart, loaded with fence materials is held at the still by a horse fallen lifeless while still in harness.

A second tethered animal stands trapped.

The body of a man slumps across the front of the carriage.

He is dead as well.

The marshal inspects the landscape.

One attacker from ambush the signs read.

He shot the lead horse.

An intense fuselage followed.

Slugs have struck the fallen man several times.

The wagon has been raked with holes from the attacker's weapon.

There is no sign of robbery.

The man's property is intact.

He is dead from about first light.

The attacker knew of his victim's routine and waited perhaps through the night for a chance to strike.

The marshal shrouds the fallen man in a large piece of canvas.

The lone workhorse is freed.

The carcass of the rancher is secured upon this animal.

Following tracks of the rancher's wagon, the marshal is quick to arrive at a small home tucked in a hillside that overlooks a wide slow stream of water.

About the barnyard, a young man toils at the chores of a horse ranch.

He comes to alert at the approaching rider.

The young rancher recognizes his father's horse.

He does not understand the nature of the load it bears.

The marshal stops at the front of the workman.

He removes his hat in greeting.

"Who be you mister?" The ranch hand inquires. "Might fancy dress."

The man looks over the nature of the arrival with confusion.

"That horse you be a stringing belongs to this here ranch. She's carrying the Curly A-brand." He points to the insignia burnt in to the horses hide.

"Found this man shot back a ways." The marshal points to the shroud.

The young rancher lifts the cover to find the body of his dear farther.

"My God! Dad!" He calls.

There is no answer.

The man hugs his fallen father as tears find place in the boy's sorrow.

"How did this happen? Who?" Bitterness and sorrow take his voice away.

The marshal allows the shock and anguish of sudden death to be realized.

"Ambush early light...followed a blood trail from a yellow hound near the Fargo Road." The marshal informs.

The young man waits for his father to stir, perchance to show a sign of life.

"Dad, I love you". Holding his father as never again, the young rancher abandons any composure as his tears and moans pour over his beloved father.

"No one has a reason to do this to my dad. Everyone likes him." Bitter reality drives the boy to speak.

"I can't! My dad was my best friend." The youth's loss is crushing.

"You need to see to your dad buried now proper like." The marshal speaks with consummate compassion.

The boy sobs with respect for his father's remains.

He nods weakly at the solemn task he faces.

"Your dad have any visitors recently?" The marshal asks.

The boy nods no.

"He done any business recently...carrying any sums of cash?" The marshal knows time is pressing.

The man begins to say no.

He falters.

"Dad would play cards every so often at the road house. He was there the other night. He never wins much."

"Any place else your daddy been recently?" The marshal presses on.

No, we've been doing the spring work steady with no break.

Dad brought some whiskey back from the road house but it's in the house yonder."

"I'll send some help back right off. I've need to get to that road house now." The marshal speeds off.

Chapter 4

A Road house

Along any primary road way there is available way stops for coach and wagon. Rest and food are offered for both man and animal.

Here a shop or two will be found that sell sundry hardware and dry goods.

A large stable with a smithy is also likely to be found.

Occasionally even needed craftsmen are to be had.

Such a place lies ahead.

The name of the way side rest is Eighty Eight's.

A large gentle man of great girth has over many years built a thriving business from regular commercial freight haulers and coaches.

Log and wooden structures have been added with prosperity.

Hair cuts, sleeping rooms, beer parlor, stable, dining hall, and repair shop are to be hand at a fair price.

The owner and his family do most of the work.

To this way side the marshal speeds his mount.

Dave Chorba is moments returned to his original intent upon the road when the marshal arrives at the full gallop.

The marshal brings to a halt his steed.

"The ladies are just now at the road house." Dave shouts as they pass along the Fargo Road...

"Seen anyone arrive or depart that place?" The marshal inquires.

"Nope! Everyone is slow staring with the dampness this morning." Dave replies. "How's Curly?"

"He's been shot! Died early this morning."

"Dead! Who would shoot a good man like that?" Dave's head hangs low for moment. "Does his boy know?"

"Took Curly's remains straight to his family."

"That boy of Curly's...Seth...he will take this real hard. Seth was devoted to his dad. Curly's son will never stay on that ranch by himself. Most likely he'll abandon it and move off somewhere's he has relations." The old man mutters.

"That boy needs help with the burying." Notes the marshal.

"I'll stop there right off and help out." The driver nods.

The marshal kicks his horse back to a dash.

There is a stagecoach just loading when the marshal enters the compound of the road house.

The driver halts his efforts at departure as the marshal holds his team before him.

"No one leaves here unless I say so!" The marshal directs.

"Listen here. I've got a schedule. No gambler gives me orders." The driver is objecting.

The marshal opens his waistcoat to show his badge. "How long have you been staying here?"

"Since late afternoon yesterday. Rested the ponies extra while it rained. Why?" The driver informs.

"Get your passengers back into the residence there." The marshal points to the entrance of the road house." This is an order of the federal government."

Ali and her companions are just collecting themselves from their wagon when the marshal strides to their side.

"Woody! What's the matter?" She reads his concern.

He steps close to her. "Found the owner of that dog ambushed. He's dead. Took his body over to his home."

Ali is astonished and frightened. "Why aren't you going after his killer?"

"I am. His trail leads right here. Have you seen any one leave or arrive?"

"No one. We just arrived." She pauses. "What shall we do?"

"Best if you and the girls don't mention our acquaintance for now." The marshal spies the corral. "I'm going to find that shooter."

"I'll get the owner to look at this wheel. We'll stay put for now." Ali obliges.

The marshal walks his horse towards the corral.

A large man with heavy hands and arms is leaving the smithy. He moves toward the marshal. "Reverend can I help you?"

The marshal comes to a stop.

"You new in these parts." The large man speaks in a pleasant tone.

His eyes beam happily.

"I'm gone to have a look at your horses to see if any been rode lately!" The marshal instructs.

"What does a man of the cloth need to know that for?" The blacksmith asks.

"Was Curly Adams here last evening?" The marshal questions as he steps into the corral.

"Yes! We played cards for a spell. What's all this investigation about?"

"Did you leave this road house anytime this morning?" The marshal is pressing.

He moves about feeling the body temperature of each horse.

"No I was helping my wife with heavy chores at first light."

"Would you see any one leave or enter this stable earlier today?"

"Most likely! Can't say for exact that every one would be seen if'n they didn't want to."

"What's your name?" The marshal asks.

"Bill Freedman...my friends call me Eighty Eight. That's the number of acres I own around here. It's my lucky number." The big man muses. "What be your mane?"

"U S Marshal Legs!" The badge is shown. "This here compound is under house arrest. No one in or out unless I say so!"

"What's the matter? There's been no problem here. It was just a friendly game. Small stakes! No one ever loses big." The giant is upset.

"Any person about the place now that would not have been here when Curly was at the road house?'

"No sir?" The owner considers.

"Dave Chorba stop here recently?" Questions the marshal.

"Not this day! He does sometimes but not if'n he's in a hurry."

"Where can I find your wife?"

"Mary be over to the cook house. She's there most of the day usual like."

The road house is L-shaped.

Stores set to one side.

Guest dining is found in the center near the main entrance.

Guest sleeping quarters are to the other side.

As the marshal strides through the eating section of the road house, he notes several men and women quietly at the wait.

Some are smoking.

Some are sipping coffee.

Most are engaged in conversation.

All eye the marshal as he passes.

Mary Freedman and one helper are busy preparing a luncheon menu.

"Howdy stranger!" Mary calls in a good mood.

She enjoys the kitchen and loves cooking. "What can I do you for?"

"Just a question or two."

"You be the marshal? Them duds you are a wearing make you look like an eastern dandy." Her eyes linger at the toes of his boots.

"That's pearl on them boots!" She hoots." Never seen anything like'm."

The marshal ignores the issue of his apparel.

"Anyone in or out of the road house late last night or early today?"

"Not sure marshal. Bill and I do lots of morning chores. Never heard anyone moving about least ways. Never heard a horse." She smiles as bread dough is being rolled out.

"How about some breakfast? Some hot coffee?"

Mary is a remarkably tiny woman.

Her small frame surges with instant energy at every motion.

Her hair is reddish brown and moves in large glorious waves.

Her dress remains neat amidst heavy labor.

Mary is an attractive woman.

Her husband is oafish. His apparel collects much of the

dirt from his labors. His brown hair is course and untidy. He is not clean-shaven.

"How did you ever get hitched up with ole Eighty Eight?" The marshal blurts out before thinking.

Mary laughs.

"My dad's carriage broken down here some years back. I liked the place. So I stayed on as hired help. Things just happened I guess as in seven children under the age of twelve." She giggles as a young girl.

"Marshal what do you need? Why's the stage coach being held here?"

"Won't be long? Got some business with folks here."

"We are good people marshal. The community here abouts are God fearing hard working. Can't recall last time we had trouble." The petite woman's concern removes the carefree smile from her happy face.

The marshal nods as he begins to withdraw. "Dave Chorba... he been around here lately?

"Not recent, he stops in often enough."

"He play cards with the boys in the evenings?"

"Occasional. Usually stops for some of my ham and bean soup."

The marshal steps out the back doorway.

Mr. Freedman appears.

He is speaking with the school teachers.

The marshal approaches as the damaged wheel is being removed from the wagon.

Ali intercepts. "He is going to replace the bad wheel with an old one he has about the place."

"Your spare wheel is not trustworthy even for a day's ride." The large man announces.

"This here axel can be braced in Fargo right inexpensive like. Then it'll last you to the Pacific Ocean and back." The big owner asserts." You best start out from Fargo with two new quality wheels. Get rid of the damaged one and your old spare, neither is worth much!"

Thank you Mr. Freedman. "Ali comments.

"We will be ready to travel soon. What do you want us to do?" Ali asks the marshal.

"Wait!" He replies.

"Big man with a small sickly side kick! They be seen here?" The marshal directs his question to the owner.

"Couple days back. They ate then rode." The owner is confident.

"Curly Adams here abouts at the same time?" The marshal continues.

"Could have been don't rightly remember."

The marshal walks to the front of the road house.

The stage driver sits just outside smoking a pipe.

"Marshal how much longer before we can go? Like to be at the next stop before dark. Roads are too dangerous these days." He greets the marshal.

"Which way you headed?" The marshal asks.

"Left Fargo two days ago." The driver informs.

"Seen many on the road?"

"Some...busy time spring." The driver spits juice from his pipe

"Notice anybody in or out of the place this morning?"

"Just Dave Chorba, and that wagon full of women." More juice is released.

"You been with someone all night and this morning?"

"Slept in the stage...saved money...just by myself."

"Driving this stage long?"

"Marshal, I've been hauling folks here's about for nearly twenty years."

"Play poker here?"

"Every chance I get. Born loser that's me." Pipe is puffed for a long draw of heavy smoke.

"Where do you keep your weapons?"

"Atop the stage! Folks don't bother things here at Eighty Eight's. Never been trouble that I can remember."

"I'm gone to inspect them guns on the stage."

The marshal finds a Winchester rifle and one old hand gun. Neither has been fired recently. He returns to the driver.

"Seen a big ruff man with a frail boyish man traveling together?"

"Strange pair! Nothing like that the last two days for sure." Answers the driver.

The marshal knows his main quarry is now traveling off the Fargo road.

"Any reason a body would want to get hold of some land here's about?" He asks the stage driver.

"Some say the rail road is a coming for sure. Land be worth bit more in some places." More tobacco added to the pipe.

"How many of them guests in there are with your stage coach?"

"All of'em! Mr. and Mrs. Palmer. He's a dentist. They be heading back to bury her dad. The old man passed mid winter. Grounds too cold back there for digging a grave until spring come." The pipe shakes toward the east.

"Either of them ride?" The driver is asked.

"Difficult to say. Them eastern folks can get a buggy down a good road on a niece day. But haven't seen one family yet that can ride bare back off trail for hundred feet before getting themselves throde." The driver laughs heartily at his own words.

"What about the others?"

The driver considers. "Mr. and Mrs. Builderback, they be getting on in years. His rumatiz be too bad for setting up in a saddle now a days. His misses'll get lost a walking to church." More chuckles.

"And that young man in there?"

The driver considers the boots worn by the marshal. "That fella is a real dandy. Stays with the woman folks, he does. Doesn't carry no gun. Wouldn't know how to shoot one either ways!"

The driver's head shakes in revulsion. "Wears a lot of perfume he do...likes smelling good. That kind don't go near a horse barn let alone a horse!" The driver giggles.

The marshal nods in gratitude.

He has his man.

The marshal and his horse move to Ali and the wagon.

"How's Bessie?"

"The dog's been awake. Had a small bite and some water." She answers hopefully.

"You're going out after that murderer?" She grows tense with the recognition that another criminal waits for the marshal's justice.

"When I return will be departing!"

Ali senses the marshal certainty. "Who killed that poor man and shot that sweet dog?"

"Dave Chorba!" Answers the marshal. "I'm sure he's on his way to kill Curly's boy next.

"Why?"

"He's after their land most likely. Got no money to buy it." The man mounts his horse. "I'm a damn fool! Sent Chorba onto help the Adam's boy."

His eyes search Ali's face.

He wishes he might kiss her soft lips.

Ali's stare upon the marshal lingers.

She searches for tenderness in his face.

"He should kiss me goodbye." She believes.

On the way out of the compound, the marshal seeks Eighty Eight.

"What's the fastest way to Curly's spread?"

"Drop down the hill in the back. Pick up the big creek and follow the water down hill. It'll come out right beside Curly's." The large man answers assuredly.

"Regular road take's a whole lot more time. Longer than that if'n your hauling goods."

Ali watches the marshal ride off in great haste.

Danger awaits him.

She wants him safe.

She wants the dog's present owner safe.

"I'll place this old wheel on your axel for now." Bill Freeman announces upon his return. "Take but a moment."

"Mr. Freeman how many children do you have?" Ali asks.

"Six boys and a girl." The man answers proudly. "The middle child is a girl. Ann is small like her mother and busy as a bee all day."

"Who teaches your children school work?"

"Well the Mrs. do. The older boys right now...Ann begins this year. The older ones help the younger."

"No public school in the area?"

"Nope! Not till you're just about in Fargo." Bill replies. "School teacher and all is expensive. Homes be spread out. Plus there's more demand on chores. Mary insists our children learn reading and writing though."

"How about the law? Is there a sheriff nearby?" Ali strains to catch the owner's response.

"Be the same for law officers. Got's to go a ways toward Fargo. A deputy sheriff might pass by once a month. Mighty rare to have a U S Marshal visiting."

"So you protect your family!"

"That be a man's business for sure. Most folks are law abiding and down right helpful."

"What makes a man turn killer?" Ali hopes for understanding.

"Well a child reared with no comfort...no love makes a young'en grow up mean and angry. There is a family by name of Banfield back up in them hills." Bill points up toward the white peaks the distance.

"Had a mess of kids what them two parents raised'em like chickens from scraps and no tenderness. See one of them Banfields every once and a while. They always be in trouble. None a killer yet though."

"A killer enjoys what he does?" Ali ponders.

"Must missy else he wouldn't do it. Some say all killers want to get caught." Bill offers.

"What kind of man goes after killers? What kind of man does it take to be a sheriff or marshal?" Her hands open and stretch with her anxiety. "Family man?"

"All kinds! That there marshal what has the place here

tied down. He be just like every other man you would know. Excepting he has a job to do to bring killers to justice. If he weren't no good at it then he'd be a shop keeper like me." Booms of the man's laughter fill the yard.

Mary is quick to seek her husband to join in the frivolity.

"Ladies let us have some tea while the wagon gets fixed." Mary invites the four women inside to the family kitchen area.

"The dog here is hurt real bad." Evelyn utters with the sound of depression.

"Let me see here!" Mary hands search the dog's hide. "This be Curly's pup Bessie. That man goes no wheres without her."

Mary looks sternly towards Ali.

"Mr. Adams was killed this morning." Ali whispers. "Marshal does not want anything said on account."

"On account the murder might get away?" Mary concludes.

Ali nods in agreement.

"Marshal knows who did it?"

Ali dips her head in affirmation. "Dave Chorba!"

"That scoundrel! My husband never cared much for the man. He looses heavy when he plays card games. The men have to give him back most of his lost money. The marshal say why?"

Ali whispers to emphasize secrecy. "Land grabbing most likely!"

"Shoot that land of Adams isn't worth anyone's life. Plenty of land is waiting for homesteading here. Doesn't figure." Mary is unsettled by the account as she examines the dog.

"This pup just needs some good healing ointment. Them wounds be flesh only. She'll live. Her appetite will return right proper in a day or two."

Mary takes the dog in her arms. "Best she lay warm near a fire."

The women folk take to comfort of tea, and cookies in Mary's private dining hutch set off the large cooking area

Evelyn remains aside with the dog off near the wood burning stove.

Her devotion to the injured Bessie does not pale with the prospect for personal indulgence.

The enjoyment of fresh brewed tea and the welcome of the indoor relax the ladies.

Banter follows with their growing ease.

After many enjoyable minutes Mary and Ali clear the table.

Michele and Layla excuse themselves to view and question the stagecoach passengers.

"You ladies are school teachers?"

"All except Evelyn. She's our chef." Ali smiles.

"Lord didn't make everyone to be mightily educated." Mary nods. "I teach the children to read and write from the bible. Trade now and then for a printed book they can read about the world. I have a hard time finding something to teach numbers. Counting and ciphering is a big part of running a business."

I have an extra book on computation in the wagon I'll let you have it for being so hospitable."

Mary hugs the lady. "You've made my dream come true. It there anything I can help you with in return?"

Ali pauses to consider the appropriateness of her thoughts. "Mary how did you get your husband to ask you to be his wife?" Ali is hopeless.

"Who might be your interest?" Mary asks.

"That marshal?" She guesses. "He's a fine looking and a strong man."

Ali smiles as she ponders.

"When I arrived here years back the road house was a mess." Mary laughs at her recollections. "That big giant off a man can do anything but domestic work. He doesn't rightly know the meaning of those words."

"Did he look at you right away?"

"Not in a special way." Mary recalls. "I didn't notice anything particular about him either."

Ali is confused. "Well?" She prompts.

"That big man is so gentle, so kind, and so sweet. His heart is just as big." The more I saw his qualities the more I grew to love him...to want him." Love fills Mary's face.

"How long did that take?"

"Minutes maybe an hour! "Mary declares. "This place, this man...I knew that I would be his wife. I knew I wouldn't ever leave here."

"How?"

"Can't be said Ali. Just felt it deep and natural." Mary's eyes sparkle as she reclaims the very first monuments of her earliest revelations.

"So how did Eighty Eight get involved in your dreams?"

"No word had to be spoken. No act had to be preformed. No involvement by another to assist. Becoming partners was as natural as breathing. We just began to speak in the way married folks talk. We just began to act towards one another the way married folks consider their spouses."

Mary's explanation is too simple believes Ali. "How did you get him to change his life?"

"Ali! His life, my life changed when we met. The world changed for both of us. We just didn't know how to leave each other. We didn't want to seek any presence without each other. Still don't!"

"So you stayed! And married just when it was time?"

"Yes! When Preacher Doyle arrived on his rounds we wed."

"Your husband didn't have to change jobs. If he were a marshal would you have gone on with him as a deputy?"

Mary laughs at Ali's suggestion. "No! I can't fire a gun."

"Well then how would you stay together if he would ride off after bad men all the time?"

"First things first! You have time with your marshal now. The course of nature makes all roads turn. Your marshal isn't any more exempt from change than any highway."

Ali is delighted.

"If you know the man is going to be your husband then he will. Let nature deal with his disposition about marshalling."

"What work can a man do if all he has ever done is law work? So he can raise and protect his family."

"If he can ride then he can ranch! There's the whole empty territory about us with meadows and running water. Horses will always be in demand."

"I could start a school right around these parts!" Ali loves the scenery, the beauty and freedom of the land here. "You say that Eighty Eight was changed in a few hours after you two met?"

"Less!" Mary assures her.

"What about children?"

"That's the best part of a new life as a married woman. The children are all yours until the boys turn to be eight years old then they go with their dad for rearing as a man." Mary tells. "Your babies will be beautiful and intelligent and good natured."

Ali agrees. "I just need this marshal to ask me to be his wife."

"That's a wish that you already know if it'll ever be true." Mary prophesizes.

"Yes, I do. I'm just not a patient woman." Ali moans.

The marshal's horse moves through the stream in shallows, along the banks that rise near deep pools. The pair trod and prances about the obstacles before them.

Where the water flows in wide bends, the marshal navigates across the open field.

Hurried and direct the path reaches the Adams ranch ahead of Chorba's wagon.

Under a sprawling oak that overlooks the farm, Seth has dug a fresh grave beside that of his mother.

Here his father will be laid for eternity.

In a patch of elm tress the marshal hides his horse.

He steps by foot to Seth's side.

"Dave Chorba is on his way here. He'll arrive in just a few minutes from now."

"Marshal! My dad is ready for to be put under. Maybe you'll say a few words over him?"

"It'll have to keep! Chorba is the gun hand that killed your dad."

Seth is speechless.

His face reddens with rage. "What for did he killed my dad?"

"I'm guessing he wants your land. Maybe he was just jealous of your dad?"

"You going to arrest him marshal?"

"If he sees me he'll run. If he doesn't see me he'll try to kill you most likely."

"What do you want me to do?"

"Seth, act natural. Let the man ride on in to your place. Keep your eye on his hands. Don't turn your back to him. I'll keep off. When he's comfortable, I'll step out an arrest him."

"Hanging is too good for him marshal. That's a bad man coming here!" Anger fills Seth.

Among a gathering of tall bushes the marshal takes watch.

Seth continues his chores in and about the house.

Both men wait.

The wagon road to Adam's ranch is not wide but it is in good condition.

The experienced driver, Dave Chorba moves his team with ease.

He makes no rush.

He yet hopes to be well on his original tract after this present detour.

Seth hears the thuds of the heavy wagon approaching well before it becomes visible.

Dave brings his cart into the yard before the Adam's home.

Marshal Legs removes one handgun from its holster.

Seth is not to be seen.

"Hello!" Calls the driver.

There is no answer.

The marshal struggles to see Seth.

There is no sign of the young man.

Chorba and his wagon are in the marshal's unobstructed view.

"Hello in the house!" Calls Chorba.

All is quiet in the ranch yard.

Dave Chorba stands to look about.

His silhouette becomes tall.

Instantly, Seth rushes toward the wagon.

His gun is in his hand and pointed at the freight hauler.

The marshal realizes the deed that is to unfold.

Dave turns to view an approaching someone.

Seth's arm extends and rises to sight his weapon upon Chorba's outline.

The marshal breaks from his cover and dashes toward the scene at the wagon.

Seth's gun discharges once.

There is a pause.

The driver reaches down for his shotgun.

Seth fries a second shot as he closes the distance to his target.

Unscathed, Dave Chorba pulls his shotgun up and into his hands.

A third and forth shot are loosed form Seth.

One strikes Dave in the chest.

The old driver stumbles upon the bullet's impact.

He falls.

The marshal calls out. "Seth No!"

Seth strides over the injured wagon master. Their eyes meet.

He lowers his weapon to point at close range to the head of Dave Chorba.

A single shot from Seth's revolver brings the struggle to an end.

Dave Chorba is dead.

"I wanted him to die like he made my daddy die. I wanted him to experience the same terror." The young man states to the marshal.

The marshal inspects the body of Chorba and he picks up the driver's shotgun and smells the barrel's end. "It's been fired recently."

He climbs upon the wagon and examines the handgun and rifle stored in the boot section under the driver's seat. All have been freshly used.

"This man fired every one of his weapons." The marshal tells Seth.

The marshal climbs down from the wagon and moves to Seth's side. "I'll take your pistol."

The marshal holds out his hand.

Seth is exhausted.

He responds without emotion. "You're going to arrest me?"

The marshal collects Seth's weapon. "You are under arrest for the shooing and death of one David Chorba!"

"What will you do with me marshal?"

The marshal points to the freight wagon. "Presently you and I are going to take this here corpse and that wagon full of freight back to the road house."

He pauses. "You drive the wagon!"

Mary attends the injured dog. "Bessie is a might old but she sure is a strong animal."

Evelyn devours every word. "She'll live?" Dread fills the young woman.

"Expect she might." Ointment is applied and gently rubbed. ""No dog will keep a bandage. They know how to clean the wounds them selves once they are able. You place this ointment on her just as I showed you every time her wounds get a might dry."

Evelyn's face brightens. "You trust me?"

Mary pats the head of Evelyn just as she would for one of her own babies.

"How old are you?" Mary asks.

"I don't know for sure maybe twenty? My folks didn't hold with birthdays and such but I'm third oldest and the first girl child. My older brothers are both in the army for a couple of years now. So I'm legal age for marrying."

"Miss your parents?"

"Yes'm and the baby. My sister's just two now. When I get enough income, they are all coming out to live with me." Her eyes water as pride emerges in her voice.

"Times be hard back at your family's home." Mary inquires.

"My dad's not good at finding work, some odd jobs and such mostly. We'd keep a farm if we could get money to buy transportation for all of us to come out here and get a homestead."

"I'm sure you'll be able to help your family out. Hard workers are always needed in the west."

Mary takes her leave, and returns to the work in the kitchen.

Ali is just outside.

She wants to speak with Eighty Eight.

Mr. Freeman is pumping water into the troughs for the horses at the corral.

"Mr. Freeman?" Ali announces.

"Call me Eighty Eight. Everyone does even the kids on occasion." The large man is cheerful at his chores.

"You wife was telling me about the time you two first met and how you became married."

"Seems like yesterday. Quite a woman is my Mary. She's a small package but loaded with vigor. No one can keep up with her."

"Mind if I ask you about Mary?"

A roar of happiness comes from the brawny man. "My favorite topic be Mary."

"How did you come to ask her to marry you? What made you decide to?" Ali is thrilled.

"Never asked her! Never made no kind of decision!" The huge shoulders of the man heave in a mighty shrug.

"Just did it."

Puzzlement reigns over Ali. "You never felt your life change so you wanted her for a wife?"

"Nope! Never felt a change." He states calmly.

"But you changed? Your life, I mean changed?" Puzzlement continues for Ali.

"The large head of the owner moves side to side thoughtfully. "Nope. Not one bit."

"Your children? Your wife? Aren't these changes?"

"Yes mam. They be changes but I'm still the same man."

"Would you change jobs if you'd have to keep Mary and the children?"

"Yep! Don't know what I'd do. Not good at much else than running a road house."

She stunned in disbelief.

Ali wonders what if any emotions men feel.

"Marshal Legs can't possibly be that blind." She mutters under her breath as she departs Eighty Eight's company.

Evelyn is much pleased with the dog Bessie's recovery.

Yet unable to rise from her bed near the wood stove the animal is alert.

The dog's thirst and need for application of ointment occupy the young woman...

Mary watches Evelyn as the kitchen chores are attended.

Mary notes that this young girl is special, and she has a natural way with animals. "Be a good wife to a rancher." She muses.

"Evelyn! If you'd like you can help me a spell with the fixings for lunch." Mary offers.

"I love kitchen work. Could live in the kitchen!" The girl is all smiles with the invitation. "What you be a fixing?"

Mary is stimulated by the question. "Bread is rising! I'm thinking a chicken soup heavy with meat and vegetables, slices of cheese and apple salad, and hot cinnamon crisps for desert."

Mary awaits a response.

"How about serving the noodles separately. Warm and mixed with butter and lightly flavored with sprinkles of tangy cheese?" Evelyn suggests.

"Oooh! That sounds wonderful! I've never served the noodles separately. There's some extra sharp cheddar that I save for spicing up my sauces. You want to help prepare?"

The chance to work in the large well-provisioned kitchen of the road house is an unexpected opportunity for Evelyn.

She finds this as her element...

"Will make some English pudding as well." Mary notes. "The preacher Doyle is due to pass by."

"The reverend has a congregation around here?"

"He doesn't keep a church building proper. He travels a circuit between here and Fargo. He'll preach to anyone anywhere what will let him. He's converted lots of folks to religion even some native families. Powerful good man!"

"He takes his living off the hospitality of the people?"

"Every day, every meal, every night. If there's no one here to listen then he'll ride off until he finds some folks."

"He keeps no family?"

"Not one we know about." She stops.

Her look turns to ponder. "Nobody knows anything about him, or anything of his personality. We only see him when he is preaching."

As all in the dinning area of the road house are enjoying lunch, the marshal returns.

The stagecoach driver has again taken a seat in front of the road house and is smoking.

"We need to move right after lunch." He hails the marshal's arrival.

"You can leave directly!" Answers the marshal.

"I want you to stop at the freight office in Fargo and tell'm their driver Chorba is dead. His body, their wagon, animals and freight are impounded here at the road house. They are compelled to remove all before five days pass. They' re to pay the owners of the road house for storage and care of their properties." He orders.

The driver tips his head in acknowledgement.

"If they are not here in 30 days then the properties will have to be dispersed through the federal court after costs are paid." The marshal affirms.

At this moment Eighty Eight emerges from the road house.

"Marshal I see justice has been done for old Curly." The owner spies the remains of Chorba.

"Can you hold this body until the freight company comes to collect it?" The marshal inquires.

"He'll keep in the spring house. Will have to bury him if'n the temperatures get up to summer time levels though."

The marshal nods in agreement.

"You be leaving soon marshal?" Asks the owner.

"Not sure as yet!"

"You best you get some food. Seth, you take the marshal around to the back and have Mary fix you up with a plate of bittles. I'll be by as soon as the stage gets off and Mr. Chorba gets placed."

Ali joins the marshal and Seth at the kitchen's hutch.

The men indulge their appetites.

The ladies serve and tend their table.

Coffee is enjoyed at the dining's end.

The marshal lights a small black cigar.

Ali sits along side the marshal.

Bill Freeman enters. "Got the body of that Chorba safe away." He informs the marshal.

Ali looks with concern.

The marshal shrugs no and looks toward Seth.

Ali does not understand.

"I guess you'll be taking me to Fargo now?" Asks Seth.

"Why?" Responds Ali.

"I killed Chorba for killing my dad!" Seth answers.

Ali's confusion is reflected in her head's turn to question the marshal.

"He shot the man before it could be shown that Chorba shot Curly." The marshal answers her look.

Ali is astounded at his fate. "How can you arrest him after all the shooting you did on the road the past few days?"

"It's different I'm the law. The legal right law!"

"So! Did Chorba shoot his father?" Ali asks.

"Yes!" Answers the marshal.

"Isn't he dead like all the other killer outlaws you've encountered recently?" Ali asks.

"Yes!" Answers the marshal.

"If Seth were a law man he'd not be arrested?" Ali asks.

"Yes!" Answers the marshal.

"So why don't you make Seth your deputy and let him go?" Ali asks.

The marshal is stunned.

The woman is right.

If he'd had deputized Seth when he arrived at the ranch the boy would have had the authority to stop Chorba.

"That's the second mistake I have to correct today. Seth I here by give you the authority of a U S Deputy Marshal effective from the time I reached your ranch this morning. You promise to uphold the law of this here federal jurisdiction?"

"I do so help me God!" Seth answers.

"Well your first act as my deputy is to assure the proper impounding of the freight company's property"

"Congratulations Seth!" Ali asserts.

"Well marshal, I'll begin my duties right off. I'll see Eighty Eight about the freight storage." Seth heads out of the kitchen.

"He reminds me of you somehow." Ali indicates as she watches Seth leave.

"He's smaller than me, a bit too pudgy, 20 years younger and he is a red head." Woody is puzzled. "He looks nothing like me."

"It's his manly way. He also shares that look of yours that

cuts right through a person's soul." Her eyes gleam as she searches the marshal's face.

"He has the temperament to be a good law man. The way this section of the territory is growing, he may be asked to stay on permanent in the job."

On the way out Seth notices his dog Bessie.

The injured animal is awake but yet weak.

She hardly wags her tail but her response is familiar enough for Evelyn to realize the special relationship to the young man who approaches.

"That's my dog Bessie." He calls to Evelyn.

"She's been shot but she's doing well." The girl is timid before the burly man.

Seth pets the animal in the most tender and caring way.

His gentleness toward the canine does not escape Evelyn.

"My dad loved this animal like no other. He was her devoted companion." Seth notices the big blue eyes and slender form of the lady.

His stare causes Evelyn to lower her head and divert her eyes.

Her long ringlets hide her cheeks.

The near presence of this man compels her to consent.

She does not understand why.

The beauty and the coyness of Bessie's attendant attract Seth. "I'm Seth Adams...deputy U S Marshal." He does want his introduction to be lacking.

"I'm Evelyn...I'm with the group of teachers...heading west to start our own school." She desires his appreciation.

"I'm the just the cook." Her honesty prevails.

The modesty of the young woman is alluring.

"I'm just a temporary deputy." He smiles in relief. "I'm a rancher...Curly Adam's son."

"I'm sorry about your father being killed."

"Can't never replace a good man like my dad." His expression shows a deep loss.

"You seem to be a very good man too." Evelyn's look into Seth's eyes is lengthy and thought filled.

"I hope to be as much like my dad as possible."

Her long thin arms cradle Bessie. "Suppose you'll have to take her home soon."

"There is much goodness to the girl. She is perfect in her manners and appearance." He thinks to himself.

"You will take your dog home?" Her eyes shine with wholesomeness.

"Would you like to help bring Bessie back to the ranch. You could have a look about and see how we live?"

Seth is excited.

"I don't get invitations like this." Evelyn feels wanted and needed.

"Maybe you'll stay...settle here I mean." This notion is a grand dream to Seth.

"I'm supposed to go to California and work so I can pay for the cost of my family to come and live with me." She seems unsure.

"Well you can get a paying job and have your family come here. Lot's of work and land and all!"

The man's presence dominates her.

Thoughts of disappointing him make her feel guilty.

She cannot speak her feelings in words.

Hope and happiness brings one set of tears to track down her cheeks. So soft are they that their presence is not felt.

Seth understands her emotion. "Stay till Bessie is all better. If you decide to rejoin your companions I'll pay your coach fare to rejoin them lady teachers. You can raise chickens and eggs to sell to the road house while you wait."

"Where will I stay? Where will I live? Who will help me?" The change is imposing for Evelyn.

"I'll see to your needs. The Freemans will help you too I'm sure."

The exhilaration of the moment weakens her knees such that she cannot rise without help.

No place or no one has ever contested for her presence.

Always she has felt herself as inadequate and a burden upon others.

In this instant her being is transformed forever from insubstantial to significant. This gentleman has altered her life by his temptation.

"Do you mean I'm really desired?" Lost is her present facial expression.

"You are truly wanted and necessary for Bessie's sake...and my own." Seth's hands reach to take her arms so that she that may stand.

Her touch in his hold ends the loneliness brought by his father's death.

Her warmth brings him hope.

Her voice brings life.

She gives him courage to face the heartbreak of the loss of his dearest father.

"You help more than you can know." He whispers.

A surge of sympathy seizes her.

Caring, compassion, want, and submission swirl her emotions. They are centered on Seth.

Her childlike dependence on him causes Seth to caress her shoulders in support. "It is alright. Shall we go and speak to the Freemans?"

She is quiet and does not desist in his grasp.

Out front of the road house the coach is ready to depart.

Passengers, cargo and driver are in place.

The team of horses has been made ready by Eighty Eight, and his two oldest sons.

Mary has prepared some food stored in a basket to be carried within the coach.

The marshal watches as the coach departs.

He also spies a lone rider arriving slowly upon a large older mule.

Dressed in a black rim hat and a black suit, a middle age rider moves comfortably in the direction of the road house.

"That be Reverend Doyle." The owner informs the marshal. "He passes this way once a week usual like."

Mary Freeman is a rush to set the dining table special to receive the man of God that arrives.

Ali assists her new friend Mary. "What will the reverend do upon his arrival?"

"He'll be hungry. If he does not get offered food for a spell he just makes it a fast to offer to the Lord. Most of the time he arrives to ask the folks about what they might need in a spiritual way. Baptisms, weddings, funerals maybe just giving over the word of God to us sinners." Mary responds.

"How long will he stay?"

"Till God's work be done here I suppose. He speaks with the Lord!" Mary whispers in order to caution Ali.

"He can read the soul of any person. He tell them their sins if they be in serious need of repenting."

"He is a holy man?"

"Doing only the work of the Savior makes a person holy... as much holiness as a body can get. If the good Lord him self was arriving He wouldn't get no better reception." Mary nods in assurance.

Seth and Evelyn arrive at the front of the road house just as the preacher stops.

"God be with you all." The reverend sings in a joyful tone.

His gray eyes smile broadly.

"Welcome! You look well for all your traveling." Greets Eighty Eight.

"The Lord be mighty fond of you and your family." The vicar says as his eyes scan the building and the folks present to him. "The blessings of God show all about."

"We are most grateful." Responds Eighty Eight.

"The Lord sees to his own!" The cleric announces as his eyes look upon the marshal.

The eyes of the two men look one over the other.

Neither smiles nor frowns.

They search.

At the preacher's satisfaction in, the moment of inspection ends. "You be Cesar's man." The vicar declares.

The marshal does not respond.

"Your cloths speak of sin but your soul is clean!' Describes the rector.

The marshal does not respond.

"You are a man of the sword." The reverend pauses. "The sword of justice!"

The marshal does not respond.

"This be U S Marshal Legs." Introduces Eighty Eight.

"I am God's servant and your servant in the Lord, Rev. E J Doyle." Responds the preacher.

The marshal tips his hat respectfully.

"There is death and there is joy come to your road house this day." Instructs the man of God. "Death is an act of sin. Joy is act of God. Sorrow is come from the work of the devil. Love is acceptance of the will of God. There is much for me to do here."

Mary and Ali emerge. "Reverend sit a spell and have something to eat?"

The beam of goodness does not quit the preacher's face.

His face radiates endless joy. "The want of God's creatures is to be served first. Who is dead here?"

The marshal is surprised by this revelation. "Dave Chorba was killed this morning while being apprehended."

Who else?" Asks the preacher.

"My father was shot to death early this morning!" Seth replies.

Marshal let's us gather over the body of this Mr. Chorba.

'That's the man what killed my father."

The bitterness in Seth's words does not escape the reverend.

"We'll pray to God for the soul of this dead man and ask forgiveness of his sins. We will ask the Father to forgive us our sins. Thus shall we be able to pass on to our Father's house if called soon."

The bible is removed from the preacher's bag.

The procession of adults follows Eighty Eight to the spring house.

The small cellar underground does not permit all to enter.

The preacher steps down inside next to the shrouded remains of the man.

He removes his hat.

His head is large and shiny bald.

The other men remove their hats and bow their heads.

"Lord your child...Mr. Chorba has come to you this day." The parson's eyes look to a present figure not seen by others. "He has sinned grievously this day."

Pain returns to Seth as he recalls the morning view of his murdered father.

"Man's justice has been done this day Lord. We now ask for your divine justice and heavenly forgiveness to follow this day. Heal the wounds of this mortal loss with the grace of divine forgiveness."

The preacher's words are not shouted to a distant deity but are as spoken tenderly as to a nearing companion.

"Let us all entreat His pardon not only for our sins but for those of our dead brother."

The pastor looks upon the faces of all attending.

He notes the anger that Seth yet bares.

"Lord through the death of your child Chorba let there be peace in our hearts and pardon in our souls."

The rector reaches down and takes a handful of dirt. "Remember thou are dust and unto dust thou shalt return."

The dirt is poured over the man's remains.

"Let us remember that sin is cause of our death. Sin is the cause of our illness. Sin is the cause that makes us old. Only in the presence of the Lord is their peace joy and eternal life."

The preacher looks directly into the eyes of Seth. "Unless we absolve those who offend us then we can not ask God to excuse our offenses. Unless we love others then we can not expect another's love."

The preacher's hat is returned upon his head as he states. "Amen. Now lets us unto our brother Curly."

A caravan has made way from the road house to the Adam's ranch.

The marshal and Mr. Freeman have entombed Curly's remains.

Seth and Evelyn have fashioned a suitable head marker for the fresh grave.

Again Reverend Doyle leads the ceremony.

"The Lord is with me I shall not want. He leadth me to rest in green pastures. These words from the bible are meant for us here today."

All are listening

"Sin evicts us from life mortal" The preacher observes the response of each in his audience.

"Here lies a good man, good father, and good husband whom we trust is in God's presence."

The preacher looks only to Seth.

"All of us, every man be he king or pauper will die from sin. None of us is fee from sin or death."

Another pause is made for examination.

"Yet I tell you Curly lives. His soul attends us now. His spirit will remain near to his son, his home, and his family to come. He has joined his beloved wife in the house of the Lord. He has not abandoned the ones he loves."

The preacher hands rise above his head.

"Let the blessings of God and his saints and Mr. And Mrs. Adams be upon us all at this time. Let us ask our departed friends and parents to give us strength to live forever by forgiving."

Another stare is made at Seth.

"Curly Adams is at peace in heaven at this time because he has shared in the Redemption of the Lord. We here must prepare for life everlasting."

Tears flow from Seth.

"Our Heavenly Father commands us to love despite mortal pain. To pardon is to love and to live forever...Amen!"

All have taken ease in the parson's message.

Seth senses the sound of his own father's voice in the preacher's words. He is much comforted.

"At last! The vicar's words boom large for all mortals to

hear. "Let's us to the road house to dine and to prepare the coming marriage."

Only Ali has taken note of the parson's last phrase.

She scans the crowd for indicators of a wedding intent. Evelyn's arms taking hold of Seth reveal to her the coming nuptial.

❧

At the road house the famished man of the cloth ends his fast.

Ali is quick to seek the marshal. "I think the Adam's boy is going to marry Evelyn." She states.

"No word has been spoken about any wedding." He responds.

"I can sense it even if those two birds don't know as yet that preacher does." Her look is incredulous that so obvious a need is seen by no other.

The preacher emerges from his buffet.

He seeks Seth.

Evelyn and Seth have returned to the kitchen area to tend Bessie.

Here the preacher arrives.

"Brother and sister what plans have you?" He asks.

"I'm going to take Evelyn and my dog back to the ranch. I want Evelyn to stay…want her to make a home among us." Seth replies.

Evelyn's head rests upon her chest.

Her face conceals.

She speaks not.

"What would you do with Miss Evelyn?" Challenges the parson.

"I want to see her provided for so she can make a home and have her family back east join her. I want to see her happy."

Evelyn cowers.

She does not speak.

"What do you think God may have intended for her?" The question is gently placed.

"To find a husband that will be good to her...for her to have children and make a happy home."

"From where will this husband arrive?" Yet another tender question is asked.

Seth contemplates but he cannot answer.

"Young woman has God called you to a husband?" The preacher looks at the veiled girl.

Her head shakes yes.

Seth's mouth droops in surprise.

"Have you accepted the Lord's wish?" The vicar asks.

Her head shakes yes.

"Are you prepared to enter a marriage tomorrow?" The parson asks.

Her head shakes yes.

Seth's confusion is absolute.

The communication from woman to preacher is totally cryptic to Seth's mind.

"Well Seth do you agree?" Asks the parson.

Only his blank expression returns an answer.

"I'm talking about marriage to Evelyn." Reverend Doyle remarks.

"Who? Marriage? Evelyn!" Seth's confusion does not dispel.

"Evelyn whom are you prepared to marry?" Queries the parson.

With head yet drooped full down, the thin arm of the girl rises with thin hand and long thin finger to point straight on to Seth.

Realization brings Seth to the impending arrangement.

His words are not yet to come.

"Did you not ask this woman to remain, to take up a life, and begin her home here?" Asks the reverend.

Seth nods in affirmation.

"Do you think any woman can achieve this honorably without a husband?"

Evelyn is frozen but her attention is intense.

Seth shakes in negation.

"Is this not the work of God to have placed you two together?"

Both silent heads nod in consent.

"Is it not then the will of God for you two to be joined in holy matrimony?"

Both silent heads nod in consent then both silent faces turn slowly one to the other with approving inspection.

"The wedding will be tomorrow after this day of morning I'll have Mary Freeman make all the arrangements." The parson instructs as he departs to secure the owner.

News of the marriage excites the female population of the road house.

The ladies delve into preparations and niceties that can only be had for such an occasion.

The place of the men is pushed far to the side.

They are blatantly ignored.

Evening approaches.

Left over foods is set forth with instructions for the men to help themselves. Interruptions of the groundwork being undertaken for the next day's nuptial will not be tolerated.

Even the parson is abandoned.

The men find solace together at the fireside in the main hall of the road house.

The owner produces a bottle of brandy.

The marshal shares his supply of small black cigars.

The men sip sweet liquor and puff smoke.

"Do you taste brandy parson?" Asks the marshal.

"Brandy is made from wine. Our Lord Himself partook of wine at the last supper. The bible tells us the fruit of the vine is acceptable." The preacher sips with enjoyment. "In all things, excess brings opportunity for the work of the devil."

"How are the roads these days?" The marshal asks the preacher.

"Difficulty among men hides the devil's presence." The preacher notes.

"The flooding has been wide spread this spring!" The traveling coach drivers have informed Bill Freeman

"The creeks are returning to normal depths now." Adds Seth.

"There been much trouble back Fargo way?" Inquires the marshal.

"Always much need for healing and forgiveness at the end of winter. Every life that is lost is sad. Illness, accidents, and crime are found everywhere especially now a days. Only with the presence of the Lord brought through out the land will needless death end."

"If a body wants to ride up into them mountains where will he find the most direct route?" The marshal seeks assistance.

"Rourke's Bend!" States the parson.

"Yes Rourke's Turn is the easiest for wagon and horse. Them natives here about steer clear of that trodden way. They don't take much part of that high country." Bill Freeman informs.

"This here Rourke's Place is up ahead a piece?" The marshal pulls a deep puff from his cigar.

"A days ride toward Fargo." The preacher proffers.

"More like about 6 to7 hours normal ride parson...not everyone sits atop a slow mule." Chides the owner.

The marshal calculates the men he chases are two days ahead and that they are moving without haste. If he rides out in the middle of the night he might well close a days ride on his prey.

"Seth I'm going a ride out early. You'll have to tell Ali and the girls to wait here until my return. Keep a hand ready for them."

"Will be proud to assist you marshal."

"Don't worry a might. Mary and I will keep them busy for a good spell if necessary." Promises Eighty Eight.

"After Cesar's work?" The preacher inquires.

"Justice is every one's work reverend. I just deliver it to those who are most deserving." Answers the marshal.

"Give to Cesar that which is Cesar's...give unto God that

which is His." Instructs the cleric. "God's justice is everyone's work as well!"

The men will keep company until the women retire late in the night.

The reverend will decline a second helping of the brandy.

He will not share any tobacco.

Seth does not smoke but he enjoys the relief of drink.

The marshal will sip little brandy and smoke but one cigar.

The owner with his large appetite will consume most of the liquid and enjoy several cigars.

All the men observe the intense efforts and enduring pleasures the women share in the wedding preparations this night.

Early the marshal enters the corral of the road house and prepares his mount for the ride to come.

He intends to conclude his federal mission then return to Ali and see the school teachers safely on their way west.

His attention is now upon the search for his outlaw as he mounts his horse. He turns to ride past the road house.

There he finds Ali at the entrance.

The light of the moon shows the figure of a beautiful woman at the wait.

She stays to see him.

Her shoulders are covered in a shawl.

The marshal sees the bright eyes of the woman shining straight at him. He is compiled by his need. He stops before her.

"Will I see you again?" Sadness fills her words.

"I don't enjoy leaving you!" Truth fills his speech.

"You're going after some really bad people?" Tears are held back.

"Doing my job Ali." Pain surges in the marshal's chest for the agony his leaving brings to the woman for which he has much feeling.

"I'll wait for you for as long as it takes. I don't want to be without you Cha." Tears cannot be held back.

"You have a grand wedding to enjoy tomorrow. You'll be busy." The marshal hopes to ease her pain.

"Wedding! All the other girls seem to be marrying at a dizzying pace." Her words tell of her loss.

"None of the gals be as desirable as you!"

Her heart lightens with his notice of her.

"Hope that parson doesn't get you hitched before I make it back here!"

A smile lifts her frown. Her tears still fall.

"Never node a prettier, more caring lady than your self. Any man would be proud to be your husband."

She is moved with desire.

She wants to be held.

She needs to hold him close to her.

"Never met a man as powerful good and courageous as you. Don't want...don't need any other man. When you return we'll talk." Strength fills her resolve.

Her hand gives sign.

Her finger points from her one eye to the center of her chest then straight at him.

"Will talk!" He returns the signs to Ali.

The marshal rides away.

Ali watches as long as sight and sounds tell of his being.

The motion of his mount along the road returns the marshal's attention to the business of the long trek he has commissioned.

Each sound of his horse's hoof upon the road dims the sentiment of the past days.

Renewed is the hardness of a marshal upon the chase.

Soft memories fail to remain.

Desire to present justice dominates.

His senses reach into the distance. They reach not for pleasures but for dangers.

Hours of midnight follow in short measure compared to the demand of the manhunt that is extending.

Darkness is a time of comfort for horse and marshal.

Want for sleep is not a deterrent for either.

The present night air is uplifting.

The moon gives adequate light.

The road is easy.

Much time of pursuit is being gained.

The first sounds that announce dawn's approach come from the trees laden with berries or fruit.

Cooing birds awake upon the branch and begin song toward the place where the sun will first break. This vigil with chorus marks the compass.

The mountains are found to the northeast of the road house.

The birds' melody arrives from due west.

Celestial bearings confirm the current path as faithful.

The first light of dawn comes in splendor. "Ali's face and form measure to this beauty. Her soul could hold all the magnificence the morning sun and earth can design." His thoughts remain of her.

A small stream nears the road.

First glow and early mist call for a moment of refreshment.

His horse will drink in the stream.

The marshal shall enjoy a small cigar.

The fork of the road that will lead into mountains is soon to be found.

The marshal notices the white toes of his boots.

"Can't pay a man enough to have him to dress up like this. What it takes just to get this job done!"

The marshal is embarrassed by the realization that he has become comfortable in Boudreaux's clothes.

Chapter 5

A Log House

A spell of time passes after first light, the desired fork in the Fargo Road is reached.

A less used, narrower run moves to the right and slowly winds upon a rising meadow of large distance.

The marshal hopes at this trail's end he shall collect the fugitive that he has been chasing across the wide western territories.

If the way is unimpeded, the marshal should likely close his time behind the outlaw to within an hour or so by midday tomorrow.

❧

The first range of hills that separate the highlands from the flatlands is home to a small town.

The road to be followed by the marshal here makes a sharp turn with a raised inside bank.

The slope of the road falls dramatically from the inside edge to the outside edge of this near ninety degree curve.

This bend is an engineering failure.

At other then slow speeds, and under conditions that lack a dry surface, the unwary wagon will experience an immense loss of its stability and tilt upon its side.

The resulting shift is most abrupt and irreversible.

The only conclusion is the wagon will role over as it is literally thrown out of the corner.

This town is aptly named Wagon Spill.

As inferred, the town came into being as a result of recurring cart accidents and the business of cargo salvage.

There are a few dozen homes, several commercial buildings, and one tiny church.

The graveyard is crowded and placed just aside of the defective curve. Most of the graves have been provided for the fatalities due to this road's extreme hazard.

Here the marshal shall arrive near midway.

Here he will seek information on his fugitives.

He will inquire as to the location of the residence of the well known guide Pauli.

The vicinity of Wagon Spill has many families dispersed near and not very near.

The town's prosperity is from tumbled goods that have been left damaged, or stolen.

Over the years transients have found their stay profitable.

The people of Wagon Spill are more pugilistic and less encumbered by honesty than most.

Their industry is superior as they make difficult and successful efforts to preserve their sole sponsor, which is the highway's danger.

There are a number of bullies that pass their time in the town's midst.

Presently there are three young adults that take sport in the physical intimidation, and the personal degradation of their neighbors. Billy Lewis and his two companions, the Neville brothers are ill bred, loud, poorly mannered, and mean tempered.

The Neville boys are manifestly bad. They are large, strong, and dumb. Their facial expressions are dull and their clothes soiled.

Billy Lewis is bright by comparison.

He is aggressive.

His stature is short, and stocky.

The want of a sense of guilt in his character along with his dire conduct makes him a most dangerous fellow.

The community is much afraid of Billy Lewis.

His companionship with the Neville boys sanctions much misbehavior by the trio at Billy's direction.

The main commercial site in the center of town is the country store of Homer Bodley. "All goods at all times," is the store's motto. In fact few goods are to be had and the prices tend to the unreasonable.

Mr. Bodley is not a well man.

He is also not a well-liked man.

He survives in the midst of ruffians as an accomplished diplomat.

His served favors are intended to cultivate the obligation of others.

In this capacity, Homer has accrued a vast knowledge of the people and their private business.

It is said that his wife died from the depression that must only come of being his spouse.

There is no school.

There is no teacher, cleric or other professional that lives or comes to the area.

The only symbol of decency in the town is a miniature church. This was in fact built solely as a distraction.

The church rests at the inside of the perilous bend opposite the cemetery.

Its novel features capture the eyes of the traveler at the unsafe moment.

It is rarely used for any social event.

❧

Near midday, the marshal is riding through the infamous curve.

As he approaches Homer's store, the malevolent trio is exhilarated by the arrival of a stranger.

They have never seen a person attired in a fashion such as the marshal now wears.

The sight of the pearl toed boots rouses their malicious natures.

The marshal dismounts in front of Homer's.

He ties his horse to a rail.

A young woman is exiting Homer's store as the marshal arrives at the entrance.

The marshal is tipping his hat toward to the lady, when Billy Lewis runs past the marshal and shouts loudly. "Hey you big sissy look out!"

The suddenness and the amplitude of the message compel the woman into embarrassment as she looks upon the marshal.

The marshal does not flinch.

He casts one glance at the man as he hurries past.

He spies the two cohorts waiting and watching the scene.

His gaze returns to the discomforted woman who awaits a response by the marshal.

"Do not worry about that kind missy." The marshal reassures calmly.

At these words the woman relaxes and smiles in her retreat.

Upon entering the store, the marshal is greeted by Homer Bodley.

Hearing the Lewis' shout, Homer's curiosity is peaked.

"You're a gambler!" He states in a rude tone.

"Gamblers are not allowed in Wagon Spill." The store man's tenor remains insulting.

The marshal is again unshaken.

He is not pleased with the town's incivility.

"Best you just get on your horse and keep riding." Homer orders.

A long searching stare upon Homer gives the store owner a sense of concern. His mood is changed.

"If you need some goods to help you get on your way...I'll be glad to sell you some supplies."

"Need some...." The marshal's words are interrupted by a commotion near his horse.

The marshal steps out on the store's veranda.

His faithful mount has kicked and pulled.

His horse's eyes are wide with panic.

"Easy now!" The marshal sings calmly to his horse.

The sound and sight of the marshal quiets the beast.

The marshal looks about for some one or some cause for his mount's distress. There is none to be seen.

In unhurried fashion the marshal enters the store and resumes.

"Need some information. Looking for a big man riding with a small fella what looks undernourished real bad."

"Wade Fite was here yesterday about this time...he is heading back up into the mountains. Had a companion with him but the little guy was no trapper." Homer informs.

The marshal knows he will close upon his chase tomorrow.

Again the marshal's horse erupts in snorts and pounds of panic.

Outside the marshal walks to the horse's side.

He pats and speaks calmly until the animal's composure returns.

The source of the mischief is found.

Several rocks have been thrown at the horse.

They have struck the animal.

The rocks have fallen on the ground near the mount.

The marshal is filler with angrier.

He steps into the storefront's door but turns aside after entering. Here he can watch the horse and the street.

The marshal points to Homer as instruction for no words or motion.

Homer's eyes are fixed upon the marshal. This piece of mischief is not new for him.

The marshal's hands slide under his waistcoat and secure his weapons.

Homer spies the handguns and the marshal's badge.

He begins to speak.

As soon as Homer's mouth opens, a burning stare of rage chills the older man into stillness.

A motion across the avenue turns the marshal's head.

Billy Lewis is lifting his arm with stone in hand to punish the horse yet again.

Before the stone can be loosed, the marshal steps into Billy's view.

There are giggles to the far side from the Neville boys at the antics of the brazen Billy Lewis. These chuckles draw the marshal's attention.

His observation of the Nevilles gives cause for their retreat.

In this moment of distraction the Lewis boy disappears.

Homer steps outside to join the marshal.

"Need to find a tracker named Pauli." The marshal poses

"Lots of Pauli's about. They be like goblins though. Moving about in shadows and places most folks shun." Homer responds. "Most can track better than the natives."

"Need the one Pauli that hunts big bear in the high country." The marshal wants results.

"That be Pauli they call Pelts...He lives down Shadow Lane somewheres. That woman that was leaving my store when you arrived is a Pauli. She'll know the right way to Pelts home."

"Where can I find her?"

"Three doors down on the right." Homer answers

"What's the name of that boy what hit my horse with stones?"

Homer hesitates.

"Billy Lewis! He's a bit ruff around the edges but he don't intend no wrong marshal."

Without further comment the marshal leads his horse to the home designated.

Here while yet holding the horse's reigns he knocks upon the door.

The woman of earlier acquaintance appears.

"Hello! You a preacher?" The woman asks.

"Looking to find a Pauli they call Pelts."

"He's my cousin on my father's side. His wife be named Tessie. They live way down Shadow Lane." The woman points toward the end of town opposite the marshal's entrance.

"How do I find this place?"

"No way to give directions but just follow the lane until someone stops you. Then ask to see Pelts. They don't take to strangers down that hollow. Can be dangerous for a body what makes them Pauli folks upset!"

The woman holds in her hand a large spread of cloth upon which she has been stitching. Various forms of small flowers are embroidered in different pastel colors on a white cloth.

These designs catch the marshal's eyes.

"Do you like this?" The woman asks. "I make these for sale over to Homer's store. My husband takes some of my work with him when he is hauling commercial freight and sells them in Fargo. They be right popular with the ladies."

"Them flowers are cute like." The marshal finds the artwork attractive.

"I do all kinds of needle work. My best products are the rolls of cloth that can be used for making dresses, and such. Would you like to see some others of my creations? I have sheep and rabbit patterns." She senses a sale.

"Just why be they liked so much by the woman folk?" The marshal favors the material but sees no reason for it to be purchased.

"These embroidered flowers make a woman feel good. Every time her eyes catch sight of something sweet like this she has a moment of pleasure. The women don't pay for only the material they be purchasing, they are acquiring the good feeling it provides as well." The lady frowns on his lack of understanding.

"Do you make things with badges and guns and such on'em?"

The woman is speechless.

She shakes her head no.

The marshal knows that Ali would make a nice social dress up gown from this. "I'd like to buy this. Is it finished?"

"Sure is! Just now was folding it up to put away. Six bits!" The woman is thrilled for an unexpected transaction. "You got a sweet heart waiting?"

The marshal is stunned by the woman's realization.

He is a might embarrassed.

He makes no response.

The marshal nods in thanks.

He turns to take his leave.

"That Lewis boy is an awful bad man. He can be hurtful." The lady warns.

"He hurt anybody serious like?" The marshal asks.

The lady shows much wavering.

"The Jones boy, Carl Ray. He was always being picked on by those thugs cause he was sissy like. We found him hung from a tree down to the swimming hole one night. Everybody knows that Lewis boy was responsible."

The marshal scans the village for signs of the man.

"Carl Ray was a very nice boy. No man in this here town would do one thing to bring justice for that poor child." The woman's disgust and remorse is complete.

"Them fools aren't done with you until you get well out of Wagon Spill."

"Let me keep my horse out the way for a spell here and I'll see some justice gets down for your Carl Ray."

With the procured material under arm, the marshal returns to Homer's storefront to await his tormentors.

Unintentionally, the flowered textile he carries has been noticed. This fabric he protects for Ali removes all hesitation from the bullies might.

As the marshal arrives at the store the trio affronts him.

"Nice dress sissy. It'll look real pretty with them white toe boots of yours." Billy Lewis shouts.

The Neville brothers roar in approval.

Undisturbed, and indifferent the marshal continues his march to the store's veranda.

The lack of response by the marshal unsettles the bullies.

"I'm taking to you sissy!" Threatens Lewis.

Carefully Ali's fabric is laid to wait.

The marshal turns to face the trio.

All three are gathered.

Lewis steps closer to the marshal. His fists are rolled tight as he prepares to strike his victim.

The marshal looks upon his attackers.

None are his equal with guns.

None are his equal with wits.

Billy Lewis closes quickly to within a half a dozen steps of the marshal. His face is distorted in wickedness.

In this instant the marshal pulls his waist coat to reveal his two handguns and his marshal's badge.

Both of his hands hold the grips of his six shooters.

At the sight of newfound authority and the deadly threat unveiled before them, the trio freezes.

Their expressions blanch.

The Neville brothers begin to turn for escape.

Billy Lewis is too near to flee.

The marshal pulls a gun with his left hand and points toward the Nevilles. "Get on the ground face down with arms and legs stretched out"

So forceful is the marshal's command the pair obey at once.

"If either of you twitch, I'll shoot you dead."

Billy Lewis is now abandoned.

His protectors are ineffective.

His victim is more dangerous than any man he has ever bothered.

He is rendered meek.

The marshal's long strides put him atop the boy at once.

One kick of a pearl toed boot lands into Billy Lewis' ankle.

The man hops on one leg while holding the injured foot.

A second strike from the marshal's boot is given. It hits upon the good ankle of the hopping villain.

Billy Lewis spills to the ground.

The marshal stands to the side.

His one boot steps down hard on the right forearm of Billy Lewis breaking the bones above the wrist.

"That's for my horse!"

Billy Lewis wriggles and wines in pain.

"My folks will get..."

The words of Billy Lewis are interrupted and the boot of the marshal slams into his midriff expelling air from his lungs.

"That's from me!"

The marshal calls to the Neville boys. "Leave them guns on the ground and get over here."

The large trolls slowly gather themselves before the marshal.

"You two and this here scoundrel are under arrest for the killing of one Carl Ray Jones." The marshal now holds both weapons in his hands.

The Nevilles do not reply.

"I'm agoing to deputize both of you."

The Nevilles smile.

"Get you horses. You two escort Billy Lewis to the U S Marshal's office in Fargo. Tell them that Marshal Legs wants all three of you held until I arrive."

He pauses for his instructions to be understood.

"When you get there you tell them all about Carl Ray and how he died. When I get there I'll see you two get proper consideration for helping the law."

The Nevilles still smile.

"It's a day and half's ride. You get going and don't stop for nothing till Fargo. I'll be there in a couple of days. If I don't find neither of you or Billy Lewis in the federal jail when I get there I'll hunt you all down as escapees and kill you dead where I find you."

The chill of his words ends the Nevilles' smiles.

"Get now!"

The brutes scurry to collect three horses.

They mount.

Billy Lewis is unable to control his horse.

His reigns are held by one of the Nevilles.

They speed off toward Fargo.

"That Lewis' boy's daddy is Willard Lewis." Homer Bodley interrupts. "He and his kin are dangerous."

"You tell all them Lewis that any interruption of a federal marshal in his duty will bring the U S Calvary in what ever numbers be needed."

The marshal holsters his guns.

"Now how do I get down Shadow Lane?"

❧

Moving briskly out of Wagon Spill, the marshal goes on toward the highlands.

A couple miles out of town a rabbit sized trail drops off into a tree filled hollow.

It is a way that shows forbidding little use.

Bracken fills in between sections of sand and stone.

It is a ruff and an obscure path compared to the road through Wagon Spill.

The marshal finds Shadow Lane lonely and covered over with growth.

His horse is disquieted by the choice of path.

In nature there are sounds and odors that warn and tell.

Wetlands and ponds though hidden by a natural screen reveal by aroma and flutter the presence of fowl and fish.

Musk and urine fragrances and the rustles of the bush can expose the home of many varmints.

The scent of manure and the moan of the cow is the unfailing revelation of a nearing barn.

Held by loss of air currents along the sunken trail, animal odors linger.

Some are weak.

Some are quite strong.

The stilled breeze cannot mask the sound of a snapping twig upon the ground. These omens also tell of the attendance of human inhabitants aside the trail.

Slow steps of the horse make short progress.

The deeper in to the hollow the more certain the marshal is that he is under constant observation.

No sign of home or dwelling is yet to be seen.

"Where there are people they'll be dogs," the marshal notes.

"Our first acquaintance will be canine mostly likely." He tells his horse. "Then someone will have to show themselves."

Into a widen glen the marshal emerges from the compacted trail.

Tree covered but clear of brush this open ground is used by several families. Pieces of sunlight passing down through the canopy above flicker about the ground.

Three shabby homes of wood stand along the side of a shallow brook.

Campfires burn.

Loose chickens strut to evade.

Blue gray smoke of several fires rise but have difficulty to penetrate up through the overburden.

There is no sound of dog but tracks in the stream say they should be near.

There are no people to see but tracks in the mud show the bare feet of children present.

"Here! This is the place!" He whispers to his horse.

Both travelers seek to end their thirst at a near flowing spring.

Both travelers sense the eyes of the hidden are upon them.

The marshal notices the white toes of his boots.

"I'm no preacher!" He calls about into the woods.

There is no response.

"I'm no gambler!"

There is no response.

"I'm a US Marshal."

Tension fills the air.

"I'm here to hire a tracker to take me up into the high ground."

The air turns relaxed.

"I want to hire a man for several days. I'll pay a month's wage."

Excitement permeates.

"How much you pay mister?" A thin woman asks as she steps out from behind a shack.

"Three dollars! Five if I'm back in less than two days."

The woman closes.

She likes the tone of the marshal's price.

"My husband is a tracker but he be gone to the high country for some time. Don't know when he'll return."

"Your husband go by the name of Pelts?"

"Yes sir! You after Pelts for some crime?"

The marshal shakes his head no.

"After a man what has killed men, women, and children back in the Oklahoma." The marshal exposes his badge.

The lady studies the marshal's appearance. "Don't dress like any law man I ever node."

"I need a good tracker for them high ridges. Any here be near as good as Pelts?"

"They be one who's better than my husband up in them rocky slopes. Cost you five dollars for one week, ten for anytime more days up to a month."

"Won't need no month." The marshal assures.

The woman ponders. "Peaches, come over here...bring you rifle."

A thin adolescence girl steps out of the cabin holding a one shot long riffle.

"You lead this here marshal up into the rock country and find him the man he's a looking for." The mother instructs.

The form of the child stuns the marshal. "It's awful dangerous", he blurts in objection. "They may be shooting and killing."

"This here girl can shoot better than most and that there rifle of hers will shoot accurately at distance greater than anything you're carrying."

'That's ruff territory up there!" The marshal yet objects.

"She's been going all over them rocks with her daddy since she was three. Going hunting by herself up there since she was nine." The woman has no understanding for any uncertainty by the marshal.

"She don't talk much. Named her Peaches cause that was the first word she ever spoke."

The marshal scratches the back of his head.

"She can trail, shoot, and skin any critter what walks, flies or crawls in these here mountains marshal. In almost all types of weather besides."

"I don't know if I can protect her up there?"

The woman laughs heartily. "Protect her?" More laughter is given. "She'll be protecting you!"

"I'll take her along for a spell. If'n she can't keep up or gets in the way, then she'll have to come back but with no pay! That's my final offer."

The woman spits on the ground. "Done! If you quit and come back then the girl gets a month' s pay."

The marshal spits upon the ground in a like manner. "Done!"

He looks awkwardly at the girl. "Girl get you ride and let's be off."

Peaches runs off and returns riding a small donkey.

Again the marshal is shaken. "That animal's too slow!"

"Marshal, next to a goat that's the best critter you can

ride to climb up in them rocks. You'll abandon your horse long before that there donkey."

The marshal turns to head back the way from which he arrived.

"This here ways!" The slender mother points for the marshal to follow her daughter in continuance of the same direction that led into the homestead.

"You'll save half a day's ride that a way." The lady assures.

The marshal hopes now that he will be upon his prey by morning.

The path from Pauli's home continues to be remote. In deed it becomes more diffuse and tortuous with time.

Several small gatherings of hut and shed are passed, as their travel grows long.

Each settlement is disturbed by the incidence of the tall man with black fancy clothes.

The presence of Peaches Pauli serves to gain safe passage.

In all instances the men are absent from view and the women seek to hide their small children.

The dogs are permitted to bark and the older children given leave to approach.

"Peaches and the marshal sitting in a tree..." Calls out one adolescent boy in tease.

The girl ignores the offense.

The news of his business passes faster along the way then the progress of marshal's mount.

They pass one lone cabin upon which an old man sits rocking and coughs in a weak voice. "Good day marshal!"

He waves to girl on the donkey. "Take care of my granddaughter now."

"The whole lane must be related by blood." Whispers the marshal. He nods to the aged figure.

At the end of Shadow Lane any sense of pathway is lost.

The travelers trod out into a rising field laden with heavy shrub. The girl finds the marks of the fleeting deer with which to navigate.

For many hours, horse and donkey tread casually.

Up along a ridge and across a gorge they move toward the higher ground.

Into a long forested mountain valley the pursuers arrive.

Here the higher air is filled with a sweet pine scent that gives pleasure to rider and animal.

The girl has remained at the lead.

The marshal has been comfortable to follow.

He has gauged their progress and the stamina of his guide.

His instincts tell that camp should soon be made for the night. The tall fir trees will conceal their campfire.

To the left of their slim trail comes a slighter path used by only smaller animals.

"Will ride on yonder and find a place to camp." He calls to the girl.

He points toward a denser section of the forest.

The marshal takes the lead.

He comes upon a descending mountain brook with a span that is less than a foot at its widest.

The marshal and the girl follow the watery path in the direction from which they entered the valley.

In a short distance the creek widens in to a flat piece of ground.

Before them appears a log hut made in native fashion. It consists of a large pile of tall wood branches standing end on end and braced with stone.

The entrance is a crawl way of wood pieces of lesser height.

There are little signs of life about the shelter.

"You know this place?" Asks the marshal.

No responds the girl in silence.

"See any signs?"

The girl dismounts and walks about.

She points to one slight mark then to another.

The girl points into the woods in a direction that the marshal has been observing for a time.

The marshal is a much practiced tracker. He has read the signs before the girl. He is pleased with her skill.

The girl's motion seizes at a sound unheard by the marshal.

She raises her rifle but does not point.

The marshal's hands do not seek a weapon. He remains silent upon his horse. His sense tells of an onlooker within the thicket.

Silent moments pass as all seek a conclusion.

Suddenly from behind a womanly figure emerges without notice.

The ghostly vision carries no weapon.

She shows no fear.

"Why is this child here?" The gray lady speaks.

Surprised by her flanking move the marshal turns abruptly.

He sees a small woman of considerable age.

She is dressed in skin boots, an animal hide dress of native fashion with a fur cap.

An elderly white female stands in charge.

The marshal does not answer.

"You are a girl!" Remarks the woods woman.

The marshal and the girl remain silent as they study the apparition.

Her voice is gentle and soft.

Despite the age the woman is nimble. She steps to one side to gain a better view.

The pearl toed boots gain her attention.

"Seen boots like them in New Orleans when I was a child. You're a long way from home." The woman gains some distance toward the girl. "This girl not be yours!"

As civility begins, the marshal introduces. "That is the Pauli girl from down near Wagon Spill."

"Who be you?"

"Federal Marshal Wooden Legs."

"Knew you had a child with you. Didn't expect no girl."

"You knew we were coming?"

The marshal is surprised.

"Heard ya a bit ago. Smelled your animals a good while back."

"You could have run off. Why did you stay?" The marshal remains confused.

"I haven't seen no child since forever. I should not want to die without the chance to see another one maybe hold one in my arms." The woman strides up next to the girl and holds the child's head with her hands.

The lady of the forest melts in maternal response. Her form softens.

"This child don't speak." The woman states as her hands feel about the child. "She has no ills. It just be personality."

The woman signs to the child to suggest some dinner.

The girl signs back in agreement.

"Use of words don't always fit some people." The woman tells the child.

"Get down marshal! I'll fix some supper. I haven't had a guest here for years. Haven't had spoken conversations in near that long." She adds.

A fire is started.

Bits of dried meat are placed on a spit to warm.

A crude crock is set upon the coals.

Water is added with legumes and dried seasoning to make a stew.

"Got no bread or dried biscuits. My teeth are too old for hard chewing any more. Could use some whiskey if'n you got any." The matriarch poses.

The marshal recovers a bottle of brandy to his guest's delight.

A cordial taste of the distilled liquid is shared.

The little girl enjoys a sip.

"Can I ask your name?" The marshal is anxious.

"Verna Cox...maiden name is Elroy. My folks hail from back east. Came out years back. Hardly remember why. Met my husband, he was a trapper. Handsome man...older than me by good bit but never made any difference."

The woman hesitates and takes another measured look upon the girl. "Not a whole lot older than this her child when my family stared out here to the west."

"Family in these parts?" The marshal inquires.

"All dead now...dead for more years than I can remember. I'll be passing on soon. Sleep with the departed every night now. Dreams of my husband, my mother, my family fills the evenings and night...most of the days too."

"How did you come to live by your lonesome for so long?"

"My husband taught me all I need for to survive up here. He was a good man. Love the woods and the mountains. Here you can touch the horizon. No place else to be going. Time was right to stop moving on."

The young girl consumes every word from the lady.

"Never get lonesome?"

"Feel the presence of my man here's about. He died long time ago. We were...we still are happy together. Just don't need more marshal!"

The marshal understands the love of freedom in the open land.

The Pauli girl understands as well.

"Why the child?"

"She's my guide for up them rocks."

The woman eyes the child in a questioning way. "Spend a lot of time up her do ya?"

The child nods yes.

The woman removes from her neck a rawhide string holding a small pointed piece of a heavy stone.

She places it over the girl's head while giving the child a kiss on her cheek.

"My husband give me this here stone pendant. I don't have much time for use of it." The old woman makes a sign with her one finger in finding direction.

"Float this stone on a piece of wood in a bowl of water and it'll always move to point north. Besides you can strike it against a stone and make fire. Used it plenty over the years. Glad to leave it with a girl like this one."

Peaches smiles in return for the prized possession.

"Any other folks been up this away early on?" Inquires the marshal.

"Not for a good spell?" Verna answers.

"Get many trappers through here?"

"Nope! Trapping is best west where the water runs more deeply and more gentle. Get some hunters for elk but they pass through to the higher meadows only."

"No one but us here then?"

"Nope! Smelled a native pony following you two for sure." The lady begins to serve the stew.

The marshal is surprised.

He looks to Peaches who indicates no knowledge of another rider on the trail.

"Any idea who trails us?"

"Hasna Gova most likely. He be a warrior of the Black Bear Tribe. He always hoped to be chief one day. He's partial to passing this way up towards the peaks. Making a journey for his vision to begin the warm season. Some natives hold the Great Spirit resides on them snow caps.

"He's a regular then in these parts?"

"Most natives are a feared they will trespass and offend the Great Spirit by getting too close. This warrior is a might aggressive. He'll stay out of the rocks but camp right on the last of the tree line."

"Be he dangerous?"

"He be! He is curious about you two just for now." The meat is sliced and served.

The marshal is disturbed that he failed to sense another behind.

He ponders what course of action to undertake.

"Don't fret. Hasna Gova is an honorable warrior. If he means to make fight with you he'll give sign of his challenge first. Them Black Bear peopled don't take children from homesteaders. The girl is safe I'm sure. However it's best you both make night camp here while you search above during the day. Stay on the rocks and outside of the tree line as much as possible."

The marshal wonders what might occur should the native cut the trail of the outlaws he now pursues.

"You're not afraid of this warrior."

The old woman gives a smile. "There be no boon to the warrior what harms a crazy old woman soon to pass away."

Her eyes search the heavens. "My only fear is in the dying. Don't know what to expect."

The marshal lights a small black cigar.

He offers one to Verna.

She accepts. "Tobacco! Not had any since before my husband Luke passed."

Peaches looks disappointed.

"You smoke tobacco as well?" The marshal notices the child's expression.

"Just a bite then!" The marshal cuts a small piece of one cigar and hands it to the girl.

"Don't rightly have anything to fear when it comes to dying." States the marshal.

The old woman looks inquiringly.

"When I was just staring out as a marshal, had occasion to pursue three bank robbers along the Red River back in Texas. They shot me up in an ambush and left me bleeding real bad." The marshal rubs his body in a place where those early wounds were made.

Both women listen to his words intensely.

"Lay there a dying. Then a boy of about ten years in age came running up to me from no wheres. Hey Woody Legs, he says, I've been a waiting for you. Hey Jimmy Doyle, I says in return. I'm too busy to go with you now. I've got to catch these men what tried to kill me."

The marshal's eyes swell with water.

His expression is turned solemn.

"Jimmy Doyle was my best friend. We were in fourth grade together. When school started again the next year Jimmy wasn't there. I was told that during the summer recess Jimmy got tetanus on the Fourth of July and died."

One tear sneaks softly down the cheek of the marshal. "I

couldn't remember his name for all those years. I was afeard to hurt his mother by asking when I saw her."

He wipes the stain of the water from his face.

"Jimmy was just as I knew him back in my childhood. Thick red curly hair, black eyes, ready to run off and make fun. His name just came back when I saw him on the Red River just as I see you both now."

Both females share tears.

"So dying just be going home to were you want most to be." The marshal stands and moves off to be alone.

This night Marshal Legs will not sleep.

He will watch the camp.

After the woman have reclined and slumber, the marshal will walk back on the trail towards the direction that the warrior Hasna Gova is to be found.

Upon a pole top he'll wrap in a scarf holding two cigars to be left as a gift to the warrior. This is a custom of his grandfather's tribe as welcome to an unseen visitor.

The women will sleep in the log house with a small fire to keep the chill away.

The marshal will stay near the animals and watch the camp.

He is disturbed by a notion that he may not see Ali in the next life.

❧

After first light, the marshal moves to inspect the pole with the offering to Hasna Gova.

The scarf and its contents are gone.

"This native knows that we have manners." The marshal gives a sigh. "If he means trouble then he knows it'll not be easy to surprise us."

Dealing with rogue warriors is an early lesson for all inhabitants in the territories of the west.

"This here native will have to return favor or he'll not be

able to stand tall when we meet." The marshal ponders what possibilities may unfold.

"It is more important to keep the business at hand, and not borrow more trouble." He decides.

At sunrise the women are at the ready to start the day.

"Will head up this valley and turn west when the country opens." The marshal instructs the guide. "We should cut the trail of them we are after by midday and have them in sight not long after wards."

"Mind what I say about them rocks. Most warriors will not trek up on them least they loose favor with the Great Spirit." The old hostess warns.

"If'n there's shooting...if'n I'm wounded you get back to here pronto! "The marshal gives command to the young girl.

Peaches nods in acceptance of his terms.

"I mean to see the end of my chase today!" His words are final.

"Move quickly! If Hasna Gova follows for any time he intends to have dealings with you." Verna gives a final caution.

The pair rides off.

They make quick time up through the covered valley onto a sweeping meadow.

A herd of elk grazes peacefully in the far reaches.

The marshal knows that as they approach the trapping territory used paths shall be found for travelers. Here he expects to find fresh sign of two riders he shadows.

The wind bows stiffly across the wide rolling mountain meadow making scent or sound easy to spread.

For several miles good time is made.

The marshal will call a stop upon a rise that permits a full view of the trail back across the section of the long field through which they have passed.

"If'n that warrior appears then we'll have to deal with him straight away. If he doesn't then we will keep our appointment with the outlaws "He tells Peaches as he removes a small telescope from his travel bag.

"That warrior can't flank us and gain any time. So nows when we find out if'n he means to show his intentions."

Over several minutes he scans for a visual sign of the native.

None is found.

'This Hasna Gova is more interested in discovering our reason to be up here."

The telescope is retuned to storage.

"He's no friend of that trapper Fite otherwise he'd be ahead of us and they be sign of the native's pony." The marshal inquires to his guide.

The girl indicates no sign of the presence of another rider.

An hour or more passes upon the plain when atop an apex the view ahead shows down into a mountain basin swollen with stream and small lakes.

Here the marshal halts their progress.

"If'n you were going to hide for a spell to make sure no one was heading after you where would you make camp?"

The Paula girl answers without hesitation.

She points to the rocky ridges above the verdant landscape.

Her hands clasp together in the form of a recess.

"Caves be up there?"

She nods yes.

"If'n we ride down into that basin we may miss them yahoos I'm a chasing. Can we ride up above and descend down to them caves?"

The girl acknowledges affirmatively.

"We'd be there before anyone else most likely?"

The girl nods yes again and points to a pass that they need to make through.

The marshal pulls his army carbine.

It now lays in his lap ready for use.

It's possible that the native warrior or the fugitives might now have taken sight of him and Peaches.

A deadly trap might wait in the pass ahead.

The superior crest of the meadow runs straight up passed the tree line into the rock formation.

Grassy cover gives way to gravel and shell then to small stone then to boulder then to rock wall.

All the while, the ascent increases in steepness.

Between the boulders horse and donkey are stepping with care.

The diameter of the obstructions is increasing and the width of passageway through the labyrinth is decreasing.

Finally the horse's girth will not permit advance.

Peaches' donkey remains able.

"I'll leave my horse." The marshal goes afoot.

His mount is secured.

He walks behind.

Later at the foot of a high wall the donkey is tied and abandoned.

Climbing by foot and hand will end at the summit of a lesser peak whose view dominates the valley of the trappers.

The thin girl finds the needed crack and crevasse to maintain progress to the top.

The reach and strength of the marshal's limbs propels both around and upward.

At the top they rest.

The spyglass is employed to the fore then the aft view.

A rise of dust in the distance draws focus.

Two riders; one large one small are advancing.

The caves are just below.

A worn trail up from the wetlands tells of much occupation of the caves in the past.

The place of the caverns is slightly recessed. Any one closing upon them will be seen at the distance.

"I'm going down there before they arrive."

He realizes the bandits could unexpectedly trap him inside one of the caves.

"When them two riders get well into the fissure that holds them caves I want you to fire a couple of rounds behind their horses. Drive them towards the caves where I'll be a waiting."

The girl nods in understanding.

"Can you make way back to your home by riding around and down through the wetlands?"

The girl signifies yes.

"Don't make tracks back the way we came!" They marshal points toward Verna's roost. "My guess is that warrior is closing from that direction now. You'll just have time to get back to your donkey and scat."

The course is set as the marshal moves to the front.

Agilely he descends to the canyon's floor.

Here three caves dot the face of a rising rock fortification.

The largest is just a ground level.

Two lesser ones are found to one side and a bit off the level earth.

Into the most distant he takes refuge. His view is set upon the road ahead.

Minutes pass.

Peaches above and the marshal below have taken place and set their sights on the road.

The cloud of dust moves toward them.

The forms of two horses with rider become visible to the eye.

The marshal with telescopic aid identifies the pair arriving.

The hulk that looms to his left wears a beard and long scraggly hair. A beaver cap sits upon his head.

His leggings are dark elk hide.

His jumper is rawhide with fur collar.

He carries a heavy rifle tied to the side of his steed.

The smaller form he recognizes his wanted outlaw, Van Lemmon.

He is raggedly dressed.

He carries a handgun and knife.

His mount is quick and agile.

Just as the riders enter the mouth of the recess that holds the caves, he expects the girl to fire her long rifle.

The carbine is set to rest upon a flat rock to steady the shots to be made.

The desired distance to the target is estimated at less than a hundred yards.

The pace of the coming rider is at a trot. They close at a yard every second or so.

They are marked now at 500 yards.

Hence in minutes the marshal shall conclude the capture of one of the most murderous villains of his career.

At the girl's first shot the riders will seize, stop for a moment to gauge the direction of the threat and then they shall close to the caves at full speed.

The marshal calculates he has time to fire two rounds.

He ponders how to best make use of his advantage.

His expectations rely on the girl's ability.

A low profile is maintained with in the rocky recess so as to give no indication of a waiting presence for the fugitives.

Peaches is an experienced hunter.

The marshal knows that her rounds will come quickly and then she will move out of danger.

The mark of the approaching outlaws is now 300 yards.

The marshal inspects his weapon and lifts the safety in order to fire.

Simultaneously the girl readies her long rifle to action.

The mark is now 200 yards.

Both waiting snipers take aim.

Both their firing hammers are at the same time pulled back to the set.

The 100-yard mark approaches.

The final aims are taken.

The marshal looks down the barrel of his carbine as the sound of the Pauli girl's rife is heard and a round thuds in the dust several yards behind the pair of riders.

The criminals' horses come to a sudden stand as the pair looks about.

Immediately a second round from above strikes yet closer to the murders.

The horsemen abandon all hesitation.

In a few gallops both horses are at full pace heading directly toward the large cave.

The marshal squeezes the trigger of his carbine.

A loud roar and plume of smoke head toward the renegades.

The horse under Van Lemmon is hit square on. It stutters then falls abruptly spilling its small human load forcefully upon the dirt ahead.

The carbine shifts.

A second aim is made.

The gun discharges a second time.

At the 80th yard mark, Wade Fite is struck in the chest.

His bulk lifts off his mount, as he is held motionless in the air.

Fite's horse races off alone.

The body of Fite drops straight to the ground.

With a thud he lands to rest is a slumped sitting position.

The marshal aims now at the form of Van Lemmon upon the ground. It does not move. The blackheart's neck has broken in the fall.

Both villains have died instantaneously.

Neither assassin saw their slayer.

Fite's horse will permit the marshal to make at full speed around the parapet to recover his own mount and see that Peaches has gotten on her way home.

❧

In his haste to end his pursuit of Van Lemmon, the marshal did not plan his own exodus from the cave area.

Fite's horse is recovered.

The marshal rides around the base of the escarpment to collect his own horse. This will take much longer than the climb with the girl and his descent to the caves.

Afterward he approaches the location where his horse

was tethered to wait. He discovers the trail of two horses and a donkey exiting the area.

His own mount makes one set of the tracts of the missing horses.

A native's pony makes the second.

Hasna Gova has closed much more quickly than expected. He has taken captive the Pauli girl and their animals.

The tracks show no haste but they are unmistakable in their direction.

Hasna Gova, and his party move back toward Verna's log house.

It will be just dark when the marshal may arrive there if he moves at the present.

He is uncertain as to the reliability of Fite's horse.

He wishes that he also had Van Lemmon's horse so that he might ride faster with an available spare.

Even with the donkey's lesser pace the marshal cannot over run Hasna Gova.

He's only option is to keep his present mount fresh and sustain his march.

He will ride directly to Verna's camp.

Hasna Gova is expected to travel directly to his tribal village.

At dusk, the marshal is departing the extended mountain pasture into the pine valley where Verna dwells.

At dark he is entering her camp.

'Thought you'd be here sooner." Calls Verna toward the shadow with the reflective toed shoes.

Upon the fire roasts a large section of venison.

The figure of a slender child stands to greet the marshal.

"You're in good time for a special meal. Fresh venison!" Verna is excited at the festive dinning.

Peaches stands smiling at her reunion with the marshal.

The women are happy.

The feast must be a gift.

The marshal walks straight to the girl and embraces her joyously.

"You did real fine up on that peak today." His hug does not end.

"She just rode in to camp late this afternoon." Verna informs.

"That native brung you back here close by did he?" The marshal is sure of her answer.

Peaches nods yes.

The girl is relaxed.

She is relieved.

"That native didn't say why he wanted the girl to return with him. Just give her that beautiful hunk of meat! Don't get fresh meat unless the animal dies from injury right close by. Let her on her own real close to here." Verna cuts a slice of the roast to hand to the girl.

The child is eager.

The marshal releases her from his grip.

"That native give over as a favor the meat and the release of this here child. He is grateful" Verna surmises.

The distant warrior can now stand tall before the marshal.

"That native got my horse!" He is perturbed.

"You'll have to ride into his camp marshal to get that pony of yours back." A large chunk of cooked venison now enters Verna's mouth.

"I expects that is his intention after all today's goings on." The marshal responds.

The girl points for the marshal to join the eating.

"That native was waiting for you when you got back to your donkey?"

Peaches nods yes.

She chews enthusiastically.

"He gave you a scare did he?"

The child is embarrassed.

"Can 't be no worse then stirring up a big old grizzly bear!" The marshal is smiling with relief.

The ladies get to serious dining. The marshal joins the feasting.

He eats. He wonders how long it will take his horse to break free.

The marshal will wait here at Verna's.

The night is gone dark early with arriving heavy clouds.

There is a light fog in the morning.

The weather is changing.

The marshal has started a campfire.

The ladies emerge but drowsiness lingers.

"Rain will come by night." Verna foretells.

"We had company last night." The marshal points to the one side.

Here stand his horse, Fite's horse, Peaches' donkey, and a native pony painted with many spiritual markings.

"That be Hasna Gova's pony. How did it get here? How did your horse get here?"

'That horse of mine don't like to be without me. Got a whole lotta smarts too."

"Some one will need a ride!" Verna warns.

"I'll take his pony back as soon as the fog lifts. Will be heading back to Wagon Spill at the same time."

"Hard to stand tall when another man has to return your pony." The old woman tells.

"You want Fite's horse?" The marshal asks Verna.

"No need. Won't be walking the Earth next spring."

"You take that horse then." The marshal is pointing at Peaches. "It be part of your pay for the bother that native caused you."

The girl has received a fortune.

"I can hitch him to a cart and make runs for goods at a price into Wagon Spill for folks." The girl speaks in excitement.

Their hostess is delighted to hear the child's delicate voice.

The marshal is dumbfounded. "You probably haven't said that many words at one time to anyone since you was born!"

The girl moves to her new ride for an inspection. "He's a big strong one."

The marshal's mouth droops for a moment. "Seems you saved all your conversation for the time you be getting rich."

"I can afford to get me another horse before long." The child is dreaming out loud.

"What about all the hunting up in them hills?"

"Make money faster hauling hides then hunting'em." Peaches responds.

"Seems that animal you took from Mr. Fite has changed the world." Laughs Verna.

"Let's get on our way. There's one disappointed native out there what will be happy to see his mount."

The trail of the marshal's horse into camp is now retraced.

The morning fog has risen only partially.

The tops of trees may not yet be measured.

A distance from Verna's cabin the trail moves into thick fir tree stands. Under large boughs, around flush evergreens, between narrow gaps the marshal and Peaches track.

The native has used the terrain to obscure his retreat.

The dampness lingers.

"Weather's a changing?" The marshal calls to the Pauli girl.

The girl signs with one hand to tell that when the winds begin then rain shall come.

"We get this here pony back to that native then we make quick retreat to Wagon Spill." Orders the marshal.

The camp of Hasna Gova should not be far in this rugged landscape reasons the marshal. "Just a couple of miles and handful of minutes." He utters out loud.

Emerging from the pine needle covered ground; the trackers enter a grassy opening that flows between pine ridges, and about isolated evergreens.

Here the trail of the escaping horses is easily read.

The marshal is cautious.

The horses' pathway through openings in the forest makes all riders simple targets.

Perhaps the native, Hasna Gova has freed the marshal's horse in hopes of staging a surprise attack.

These concerns mount as they clear the dense firs.

Near the end of the willowy meadow the tracks of several native ponies are found.

They move in the same direction as the marshal's cavalcade. They head toward the start of the previous night's escape by the marshal's horse.

The joined trails empty into the thickest stand of pine yet encountered.

The marshal and the girl must dismount in order to traverse through the natural blind before them.

Inside the deep hedge of evergreens is a small clearing adjacent to which is found a native's lodge.

Boughs have been covered with hide.

Log and stone mound in a circular fashion.

Half a dozen trees standing in a circle have had their trunks partially cleared from the ground upward.

These have been fashioned into supports for roof and wall.

Signs of bear and eagle are drawn and painted upon the structure.

"It is the counsel lodge of a bear hunter's society from a near by native village." Signs the marshal.

The young girl returns in sign. "Three riders...two are children."

'That leaves one other adult bedsides Hasna Gova inside." Answers the marshal.

The side arms of the marshal are inspected. "They'll come after their lost pony before long."

"Can you get home without me?"

The girl indicates the way toward the nearest mountain peak is short.

Her signs tell. "Once upon the rocks I'll make my way on the high ground where the natives will not follow. By the time they make my trail I'll be past any danger."

"Go now! More natives may be arriving. I shall follow your trail if possible."

Peaches and her animals force their departure through unyielding boughs, the marshal leads horse and pony into the clearing.

He comes to stand at the lodge's entrance.

His cloths are dusted by hand and made tidy.

The scent of the natives' ponies stalled behind tells the lodge is indeed occupied. "Hasna Gova." He calls.

There is no reply.

"Hasna Gova. I return your pony!"

There is no reply.

The marshal's arms are raised to his sides with open hands.

"I shall tie your mount and depart." The marshal knows his gift of tobacco must be answered.

There is no reply, but a gentle stir comes from within the lodge.

The entrance to the cabin is made from heavy bear hide.

The slender figure of a young native maiden partially emerges. "Hasna Gova welcomes you to enter our lodge."

The marshal speaks their tongue.

He nods in accord.

Upon entering, the sight of two children huddled in one corner, and an old man that reclines beside a small fire greets him.

The maiden hands a small black cigar to the old one.

The maiden then hands a second cigar to the marshal. She indicates for the marshal to sit beside Hasna Gova.

On the far side of the fire, opposite to the marshal rests a man of advanced years. He is injured.

The men inspect one another. The maiden provides a burning twig upon which the cigars are to be lit.

"I share my gift with the one who makes the offering." The old man speaks in a weakened voice.

The marshal is impressed.

The old one has made an acceptable gift of tobacco with his hospitality.

The marshal does not speak but his eyes shine with respect for the old warrior.

The old warrior recognizes that he now stands tall in the marshal's sight.

"It is good! We both have our mounts. We both have tobacco. We both share the company of another warrior."

"You returned the girl to Verna's camp?"

"The mother spirit of the high woods, she has want to spend more time with the girl child of her own people." His voice lacks strength but holds excitement. "It was in my vision to lead the child back to the place of the mother spirit."

"What of my horse?"

The old man smiles in his accomplishments. "It was in my dream that a warrior dressed in black with white feet should visit my lodge."

"Did you not ask Verna of our business?"

"I may see the mother spirit only in my dreams. The mother spirit appears to see the child in your presence."

"She lives in the log house?" Questions the marshal.

"The home of the mother spirit has been empty for many generations of my tribe. My people do not disturb her spirit. We go to leave offerings, to repair her cabin. Her spirit does not greet our presence."

The injured warrior makes long drafts on the fuming cigar.

The marshal understands not all the meanings in the words spoken by Hasna Gova.

The nature of the lady with whom he has camped is a mystery.

There are many mysteries in life not to be understood.

The ever greens thrives in the harshest winter upon the mountains. This is a mystery to all.

The native blood of the marshal accepts such a mystery as part of the living world.

"You followed us into the high ground? This is much a feat for a warrior of any age." Notes the marshal.

"I do not fear the great spirit now. My time comes to the finish." The face of the old warrior shows much contentment.

"I saw your fight at the caves. You fight as the native warrior."

The marshal gives sign of the Sioux.

"I thought you must be of native blood. No settler would fight in such a way. It is good."

"Only a warrior of strength and courage would have followed." The marshal compliments the old one.

The marshal moves to the side of the stricken elder.

He feels the pulse of the ancient warrior.

It is week and irregular.

The old one is dying.

The old man sees in the marshal's eyes the lawman's thoughts. "It is good. My visions have told me that I am soon to be with my father and my mother. My ancestors are waiting now."

The old face glows in happiness. "I have made the good life and I have helped to hold up the earth."

The marshal recalls the passing of his own grandfather.

Tears water the marshal's eyes. His heart enters his throat. "The earth has been made better for your steps upon it."

"How have you come to be injured?"

"Your horse broke loose. He is a great animal to be so devoted to his warrior." The old one sighs with regret

"My pony does not have such good sense or good character. He broke to run as well. I tried to hold him. He knocked me to the ground awkwardly. My injuries are deep. They will not be healed."

The marshal is ridden with guilt.

The old one sees his discomfort.

"The ponies today are not like the ponies of old. In my youth a pony would die with it's warrior before it would abandon him. I wear shame when I ride this pony, but I fear more to be without him." This irony delights the old man.

He laughs.

"I cannot stand tall before you." The marshal confesses.

The old warrior waves this notion away as one would send off a pesky fly.

"You are the great warrior. I was a great warrior." He pauses.

He speaks reluctantly." There are few great warriors now."

"What of your people?" The marshal inquires.

"They do not seek visions. They do not want to learn how to seek visions. How can they hold up the earth? Only with the signs from the spirits can nature be maintained."

The marshal listens.

"The young ones of the tribes seek coins for use at the trading posts. They hunger for marriage with the sons and daughters of the homesteaders. They desert their duty as the people of the earth."

"It is a good way, the way of our ancestors!" The marshal confirms.

"When the peoples of the earth do not hold it up then troubles come to our land." The old man's head dips in great discontent.

"What does your vision tell of me?" The marshal is curious.

"Your are to marry the oldest daughter of my youngest brother."

Chapter 6

A Lodge House

Hasna Gova consumes the acrid smoke of his cigar.

He drifts into a daze.

The marshal waits politely.

The small children, a young girl and a younger boy sit wide-eyed at the form of the tall marshal. They strain to look over his cloths and especially his fancy boots.

Closer but also retired is the form of the young woman of whom Hasna Gova refers.

The room is poorly lit.

The dull moon does not brighten the lodge.

The maiden's gaze diverts.

"When my eyes close for sleep this day they shall never more open." Foretells Hasna Gova. "The spirits of my parents are here."

The marshal relives the moments in the passing of his own grandfather.

He speaks not.

"Mother! My duties are now done. Let me go into the fields?" The old one's mind enters another world.

The maiden begins to sob.

The marshal does not speak.

The old one eyes turn to the marshal.

Yet bewildered, the sight of the marshal gives pleasure to the old warrior.

"You must accept the betrothal of my niece, Inot Mai." Insists the old warrior.

The marshal turns to view the maiden whose name means Soft Winds.

She wipes tears from her face as her smile greets her intended husband.

The marshal's thoughts remember Ali. He feels such an arrangement would deceive the beautiful schoolteacher who waits faithfully upon his return.

Again Hasna Gova reads the mind of the marshal.

"Soon Inot Mai will reach the age of woman full grown. It is time for her betrothal." He pauses to ensure the marshal attends his words. "Inot Mai is to be yours...to marry or to be given to another for marriage as you decide."

"Why me?" The marshal sees some relief in the words of the old one.

"It is a time of strife for my people. In our village and between villages our people argue and fight with one another. Brothers hold anger in their hearts, one against the other. The parents of Inot Mai are dead. Her father was chief. There is a contest to become the new chief. If I die before her betrothal our law allows any man to make marriage with her if he is strong enough. Those who would be chief will force her marriage to gain stature in our tribe."

"So once betrothed she is by your law spared?" Reasons the marshal.

"Only a strong warrior can survive such as task. There will be danger from rogue warriors to end your betrothal."

"By my death?"

The old one nods yes.

The thoughts of the marshal are influenced by his native heritage. "The ways of the native is not the way of the settler."

Honor and duty among the natives marks the warrior.

"You wish me to hold up the earth?"

The old one nods yes.

"What would the great warrior Hasna Gova have me do?"

"My vision tells that you shall take my brother's children to a place of my nation in the west. Beyond this you shall have to seek a vision from the girl's ancestors."

"What time for travel is needed?"

The old one holds up two fingers to sign two days of riding.

If his Sioux grandfather had asked such a chore, the marshal should have obliged.

The marshal must stand tall to hold up the earth.

He turns to view Inot Mai. She is small and slender.

Her long black hair flows aside her beautiful face.

Her black eyes shine with purity.

The maiden listens intently to her grandfather's words.

Her face shows surprise.

Her eyes search the warrior dressed in black.

She wonders if this man is to be her husband.

"In the village of the west, the descendants of my mother's sister dwell. Here my shared blood shall be welcomed. Here the natives yet keep life by the visions of the spirits. Here there is yet peace." The eyes of the old one wait upon the marshal's decision.

"I have no authority of law in the nation of your ancestors." The marshal informs.

"The spirits have chosen. You shall have their authority as needed."

"I do not wish to kill any of your people."

"If one wishes to take your betrothal he must face you. It is our law. Once in the western village Inot Mai shall be free to select your replacement should you permit. She is much desired. Some warriors will follow and make challenge for her."

Two days will be needed after the old one is passed.

Moving with small children will not out run the hurried pony of a determined warrior.

He will have to make contest if he accepts.

"My death blanket is here." The old one points to a heavy hide fashioned with signs of the important events of his life.

"Wrap me in this and take me to the village in the west. Death songs and burial with my ancestors will be made there." His eyes plead for assistance from the marshal. "It is not for us to decide who shall die. This is the business of the spirits."

The marshal eyes tell that he has accepted the wish of the old one.

He will take possession of Inot Mai in the matter of her marriage.

"You must show sign of betrothal. Personal objects must be exchanged and worn to show this betrothal." The old one instructs.

He motions for Inot Mai to approach.

The girl arrives with much shyness.

She kneels.

Hasna Gova removes a pendant from her neck. It is made from the teeth and claws of a bear.

"This necklace is known to all as belonging to the daughter of my brother." It is placed about the marshal's neck.

The old one examines the marshal's dress.

A stick pen with pearl tip is stitched into the marshal's lapel.

He asks for the adornment to be handed to him.

The stick pen is ceremoniously placed in the garment above the heart of the maiden.

"It is good." He looks to Inot Mai. "This warrior now commands you as husband to be."

The young woman looks up into the marshal's eyes.

She shows no fear.

She shows obedience.

She stands tall before her intended husband.

Hasna Gova looks to the marshal. "This is your accepted woman to be. She will obey you as a wife to be. It is done!

The marshal looks into her eyes to show his sincerity.

He stands tall before her.

The old warrior enjoys the last bit of his cigar.

He smiles at the marshal.

He opens one arm to Inot Mai.

The maiden rushes to close to his side.

The hand of Hasna Gova holds her face lovingly.

He whispers to her.

The girl's head falls upon Hasna Gova 's chest amidst bitter sobs.

One last caress then the warriors arm falls to his side.

His eyes close.

They shall not reopen.

This poignant moment of the passing of the old warrior swells tears in the marshal's eyes.

The winds arrive.

Rain blusters.

The old warrior's absence from his village will not be of concern. The disappearance of his brother's children shall cause alarm.

Rogue warriors may already be pursuing Inot Mai.

At the end of the day the rain has halted.

Hasna Gova is dead.

His body has been washed and anointed by his niece, Inot Mai.

The marshal has shrouded him in his death blanket.

There are several hours of light remaining in the day.

The cloaked corpse of Hasna Gova is secured upon his pony for the several days journey to come.

The marshal shall lead the children and horses from the lodge house immediately.

He again follows the trail to Verna's camp.

"Each trip increases the number of people and animals in my charge." He mutters lowly.

The rain has washed much sign from the ground.

The marshal takes care to choose a path that shall leave little new sign for others to stumble upon.

He will avoid soft ground.

Pine covered ground will be best for hoofs to step upon.

Tall grass once bent will remain deformed for days. This is avoided.

The boughs of fir do not snap or break easily.

His chosen path will be covered by evergreen.

The experienced eye will always be capable to follow.

The lazy and careless will not.

Arriving at Verna's, the camp is found deserted.

Inot Mai is neverous.

"Do not worry! I know this spirit. You and the other children are welcomed."

Inot Mai is offended by the inclusion of her as child.

"Does this spirit welcome a woman?" The maiden is bold.

"Yes! It is better if the woman is a princess."

Thus is taken by the maiden as the marshal's apology. "It is good." She smiles.

"Do you have other wives?" The maiden wishes to know of her intended.

"Looks like you may be the only one." He has no need to discuss his past with a child. "You and the small ones keep inside that log cabin there. Get as much sleep as you can. We'll leave early."

"It is my duty to sleep beside my betrothed." She is confused.

"I shall not sleep this night." The marshal expects a visitor.

The owl will perch atop a tree that looks out upon a clearing.

There is little visual aid to this hunter of night.

Sounds that emanate from the dark ground below are the only guide to the bird's prey.

The marshal has chosen an elevated roost from which to keep guard.

The horses have been tethered and corralled near heavy brush.

The entranceway to the log house of Verna has been stacked with loose logs.

There is no easy approach from the rear of the marshal's position.

All will enter Verna's camp before him.

The sounds of the night are many.

The breeze will cause branch and limb to rub and create unusual squeaks and moans.

The dew drips to ground and recreates the rustle and tapping of motion.

The wind pulses past one's own head to howl just in the lone ear.

Creatures that travel at night are skilled at keeping silence. Yet the occasional twig or loosed stone may meter the progress of any wandering nocturnal being.

Some signs of position are given by the course of living.

It is these that are attended by the skilled hunter.

The mammal must breath. The heat from breath causes the serpent to strike.

Scent deposited upon the trial leads the fox to dine.

The rodent must chew to eat. This sound once located puts the owl to directed flight.

The human form concealed and kept in stealth is held by nature as well to be revealed.

As a child Marshal Legs would play games at night with his Sioux grandfather.

One would try to close upon the other unseen in the dark.

Roles would be reversed, the boy staking the man, and then the man to stalk the boy.

The Sioux train their young to listen as the owl.

The scent of the horses in the camp will draw much attention from large roaming predators.

The raccoon, the fox, the wild cat shall seek examination about the camp.

Each horse shall keep a safe watch and announce any new presence with distress.

Should the human visitor seek the livestock, his approach shall differ from those who seek the maiden.

Only if the keeper's guard should dull with need for sleep shall nature's warnings be missed. The marshal shall not fail to receive the first alert.

The first native to come will be much experienced.

He shall recognize the destination of the maiden's trail early on.

He should be familiar with the home of Verna. This one will violate the sacred place of the Mother Spirit. This one does not seek the visions of his ancestors.

He is to be a scoundrel planning to slay Hasna Gova and to capture Inot Mai.

He is to be most dangerous.

The assassin will choose the darkest time of the night when sleep is most dear.

So reasons the sentinel.

The marshal does not want to harm the ones who come.

No crime has occurred.

Darkest hour is at hand.

The lawman assays every whimper, click, swoosh, and clack heard.

All is well to now.

Abruptly a shrub is brushed.

The whole of the night is seized on this singular natural instant.

A heavy shove has pressed against a sizable piece of leafy plant.

Bear?

No the rustle was short and unrepeated.

Deer? Elk?

No, there is no continuance of browsing or meander.

It is a large creature.

The marshal locates the direction of the alarm along the entrance path followed earlier by his own horse.

A twig upon the ground snaps softly.

The footfall has closed in the direction of the log house.

A flash of light issues from a vague form in the dark.

A reflection of the moon identifies the creature as human.

If the marshal fires his weapon at this close range into the general shape that moves, the intruder will fall.

The scruff of knees sliding upon the ground is heard at the edge of the opening of the camp. The villain is crawling toward the entrance of the Mother Spirit's cabin.

His knife is in his hand.

Midway through the clearing the marshal steps quickly toward the executioner.

In an instant the muzzle of the carbine rests against the back of the head of the native who is prone upon the ground.

"Do not speak. Do not move." Whispers the marshal in the native's tongue.

Surprised the rogue warrior is stunned into submission.

He is a large thick man.

The visitor is bound gagged and placed near the camp's fire in middle of the clearing.

The marshal returns to his watch.

The captured one is the most aggressive of those that may follow after Inot Mai. He may not be the most clever to come.

The marshal expects the next culprit to be more deceitful and less of age.

The bulky captive may sit or recline but his straps will not permit him to stand or walk. His disposition is agreeable, as he fears his life belongs to the stranger with the white marks upon his shoes.

A horse snorts from the camp's coral.

The animal has taken strong scent from the wind nearby.

The breeze is slight but irregular.

The corral is opposite the log house and the worn path of approach.

The captive native warrior discerns the presence of another in the same instant as the marshal.

He ponders if he should give attempt at warning.

His eyes seek sight of the marshal's location.

The marshal is already moving.

He is rounding the clearing about the camp opposite to the horse's corral.

He moves to wait aside the entrance of the log hut.

He has the captive native within reach.

The captive's head turns from his left than to his right. His interest is split between the missing marshal and the third man who draws near.

The second stalker has made his way to the far side of the log house.

The squirms of the captive have been noticed.

The stalker will round the hut and strike the form that sits upon the ground. He assumes this to be Hasna Gova.

The marshal has anticipated the risk to his captive and is ready.

From behind the hut steps a tall thin warrior with hatchet in hand.

As soon as the sitting captive comes into his full view, the second attacker runs with ax raised to fall upon his victim.

The marshal is hiding just out of the attacker's view at the near side of the hut. The assailant is to pass the marshal on his way to strike his prey.

The long leg of the marshal sweeps toward the lanky form making charge, tripping the warrior to land flat upon the ground.

Similarly the second native is placed and secured adjacent to the first.

The two captives know each other.

They wear the same village signs as Hasna Gova.

Again the marshal resumes his sentry.

There is yet much darkness to pass before dawn.

Time advances.

The captives grow still.

The marshal does not tire.

It is now the period of deepest slumber.

By and by the two captives give way to the fatigue of the day and lie down.

They now sleep.

The flutter of a screech owl from a low perch near to the marshal reveals the approach of a third thief immediately to his left.

It is a small muscular warrior with bow and arrow in hand. So close is the nearing wrongdoer that his breath warms the marshal's face.

Instantly the carbine is pressed up under the chin of the culprit.

As the sun rises, three native combatants sleep in their restraints.

The marshal begins a morning fire.

Corn fritters and dried meat are warming upon heated stones.

Water is warming for an herbal tea.

The children will wake to nourishment before the most dangerous part of their trek begins.

Inot Mai exits the log house with her two siblings. She is stunned to find three men from her village eating at the campfire.

She is shocked to see their restraints.

The captives eat with relish.

They ignore all else but their food and drink.

The marshal indicates for his charges to join him at the other side of the fire.

He watches his prisoners.

"Do you know these men?"

"They are of my village." The maiden is not pleased to see them.

She is pleased to see them confined. “They are not honorable. They do not hold the earth.”

“They came to take you?”

She nods in agreement. “They came to kill my uncle, as well.”

The marshal nods in agreement.

“The heavy one is Mukjee. The tall one is Samjee his brother. The smallest one is Tahmuh.” Informs the maiden.

“Does their word hold?”

The maiden shakes her head no. “Mukjee has always been a bully. Only the children carry admiration for him due to his great strength.”

“Do they keep the law of your people?”

Inot Mai answers. ”Yes...if watched by all others of the tribe.”

“What of the tall warrior?”

“Samjee is dull of wit but his brother is more dim. Samjee holds avarice in his heart.“

“The two brothers are ambitious, dumb and lacking in character.” The marshal says. “Settlers of this kind often end up being hung by a rope.”

“The smallest warrior is bright. He is young and given to mischief. I am surprised he would consider harming my uncle.”

After all have eaten the time for departure has arrived.

The marshal stands before the three captives.

He calls Inot Mai to his side.

“Hasna Gova has made marriage contract for his niece Inot Mai to be my wife.”

The three prisoners study the marshal and the maiden. They observe Inot Mai’s necklace about the marshal’s neck.

Inot Mai fingers the ornate stickpin that has been added to the front of her deerskin dress.

All the captives watch and understand her meaning.

All the captives watch to understand the marshal’s intent.

The marshal looks into each captive’s eyes.

The smallest warrior shows shame.

"Release Tahmuh!" The marshal instructs the maiden to loose his bonds.

"Take the mounts of these warriors and ride east toward the sun." Tahmuh is ordered. "When the sun is overhead then return here. Leave the horses of the other two nearby then depart back to your village." The marshal instructs the small warrior.

Tahmuh understands." I came to protect Hasna Gova, not to do harm. Others like these pursue Inot Mai." The small warrior points to the confined brothers.

"Are you not afraid he will betray us?" The maiden whispers.

"He may remove his disgrace if he acts tall before the others. Otherwise I shall have to kill him." The marshal wishes better for the willing warrior.

"What of the brothers?" Inot Mai asks.

"They will attack us as soon as they possible. If Tahmuh does as asked we shall gain a day's ride in advance. These two cannot close before we arrive at the western village of your people."

"Others will yet come!" The maiden assures.

"They shall be watching as we march today. Once our final destination is obvious we will be in much trouble." The marshal knows that others warriors shall go ahead and make ambush.

The maiden, Tahmuh and the small children collect the horses and the body of Hasna Gova.

Tahmuh leaves on his east ward mission.

The convoy of the maiden departs west ward out from the camp

The marshal waits, and then releases the two brutish brothers to wait for the return of Tahmuh near day's end.

He follows after Inot Mai.

The caravan moves north first as in the manner of the Pauli

girl to gain ground toward the rocky slopes near the mountain peaks.

The marshal hopes to dissuade the causal pursuer.

Much time cannot be lost in the making of this ploy.

An hour is spent grinding upward in difficult terrain. The path is then turned west.

Quick time must be made on their journey.

The marshal hopes to move stepwise west by south west. Dropping southward down the previously encountered mountain valley for a short spell then again to run west.

Each step to the south is taking the horses toward flat land and speedier navigation.

Avoiding terrain that is open over wide areas, he hopes to blind any who chase within the tree cluttered trail. Thus is reduced the risk of a speedy pursuer gaining a flanking maneuver.

Near late afternoon, the marshal is confident that his party has not been overtaken.

However his escaping party is now forced to more open ground.

Here a band of Sioux would choose to split trails to confuse and distract their trackers. Well before dark the marshal will have the two small native children share one mount.

The weakest animal shall be loosed and left to drift.

Moving into topography mixed with open ridge, bushy ravines, and winding gullies, the marshal will choose pathways that keep the lowest profiles and enhance the pace of traverse. Here the risk of attack is the greatest since departing the log house of Hasna Gova.

The spirits of the ancestors of Inot Mai are soon to offer protection. Before the immediate path of the maiden's entourage lays a heavily traveled passageway.

Descending from the top of a grassy knoll, the marshal's mount brakes abruptly.

The horse's head rises.

His nostrils flare.

A heavy snort blares followed with repeated sniffing of the upper air.

"What are you searching after?" The marshal asks as he pats the neck of his ride.

The lawman's horse is much agitated.

He steps repeatedly without advance.

The animal leans to one side of the trail.

"Something over the ridge there?" The marshal stands in the saddle to gain view. "Don't expect no barns in these parts... could be a horse nearby."

He gestures by hands for Inot Mai to close with him.

Upon her arrival, the marshal nods in the direction of the wind that roused his steed's interest.

He makes hand signs. "I'm going to search over this rise. Wait here. Keep me in sight. If my horse breaks into a sprint gets your ponies racing with me."

Inot Mai nods her head in understanding.

Once atop the ridge of contention, the sight of the ditch below reveals a heavily trodden way.

"You're worth your weight in apples if not gold." The peace officer pats his horse's neck.

Uncovered by the equestrian sensibility is the recent passage of many horses.

"Must be at least a dozen foals in the string of horses that moved through here." He tells his stallion. "Heading in the same direction...not far ahead it seems. Traders must have colleted them young mavericks off them high meadows."

The marshal is quick to have his associates join onto this trail.

The marks of their animals mix with the many moving before them. The large number of hoof marks will end any threat in daylight from native hunters that shadow.

The assortment of voyagers joined by the compass progress expeditiously through the land of the ravines. Near dusk the marshal's force is close to the slower moving pack of young horses before them.

The land here turns to forested hill and flourishing dale.

"He'll make camp near water." He signs to Inot Mai.

Thirst will keep a herd of new born horses restless.

A small stream makes a wide bend about a high shoulder of steep boulders and thorny bush.

"Likely a deep recess up that a ways to pen them foals up for the night." Whispers the officer to his mount.

Inot Mai signals in panic "The notice of the bear."

She points to a large paw mark near the stream.

"After them foals! He'll keep off down wind most likely until dark then he'll move after them young horses." He responds.

The marshal removes one of his side arms.

He passes it handle first to Inot Mai.

The maiden looks upon the handgun and the marshal with confusion.

"Can you shoot one of these?" He inquires.

Inot Mai signs yes.

"Keep them little ones near your side at all times. Empty that there six shooter into any thing what moves after you in the dark tonight."

He pauses. "Anything except what wears white markings on its toes."

Inot Mai laughs at the notion.

The marshal's gaze turns stiff to warn of his concern. "Hungry bear will take a woman or man child just as quickly as not."

The maiden becomes frightened.

"I'm a going to ride right into that camp!" The marshal prepares his second handgun.

"Follow a couple ten paces behind me. Leave that there handgun where you can get it busy quick if needed."

At a slow trot, a line of riders enters the camp of the horse trader.

A large fire roars in an opening.

To the one side away from the stream is corralled several horses and large gathering of foals of every color and shape and all just separated from their mothers.

There is no sign of any other person.

"U S Marshall Legs!" The lawman calls out loud as he looks about the site.

"Need to share your camp!" His hands remain open and visible.

"Got some children what need protection."

The marshal waits.

A young man steps from the bracken with rifle in hand." You look more like a preacher! Need to see your badge if you please."

The lad is lean and straight with long arms and legs.

The rifle hangs comfortably in his grip.

Boy's demeanor and his authority impress the marshal.

"Just under my coat on my gun belt." The marshal lifts his waistcoat away from his side.

The lad gradually gauges the marshal's intent.

He steps closer.

"Where for you be bound?"

"Taking these native children to their people in the west." Replies the marshal.

The lad studies the signs and dress of the three natives. "They belong to the Big Bear Tribe."

The marshal nods yes.

"You be a bit south if you're heading to their villages on the west side of their nation." Informs the boy.

"There be trouble in the east of their nation." The marshal informs.

"You being chased are you?"

"Most likely." Answers the marshal.

The boy steps closer yet.

He drops the muzzle of his rifle towards he ground.

His eyes are fixed on Inot Mai.

His eyes search the marshal. "You two betrothed?"

The boy is confused.

The marshal nods yes.

"She be a princess then!"

Inot Mai smiles at the handsome youth's remark.

The marshal waits.

"I'm heading to the Nez Perce village of Chief Many Horns." The boy points to the south...half a day's ride."

He turns toward the north. "You're at least another day's ride to her people."

The boy turns and walks toward the campfire. "Dinner is about to get underway. Best you all get down and eat! Pancakes and roast mountain goat is all I can offer."

Inot Mai loves to cook.

She is quick to get to the spit on the campfire and inspect the preparations.

She assumes all cooking duties. To the pancake mixture the maiden ads fat from the goat. Available herbs are gathered from her pack and employed.

Large biscuits shall be quickly heated.

The flesh of the goat is cut in strips and wrapped on sticks and these are set over the fire to roast.

To the fire selected leaves are tossed to smoke and flavor the meat.

Inot Mai is inspired to give a demonstration of good eating this night.

The boy assists the marshal in stabling his troop's animals.

The smaller children enjoy visiting the many newborn horses.

"We have seen sign of a large bear stalking your train."

"Yep!" The boy points to a collection of fresh bear hides. "These will fetch a good price when I get back to Sweet Creek."

"You know Sheriff Klinger then?"

"Ought to right enough...I'm her son, Joe."

"Spent the night at your folks' place back a few days...right hospitable people!"

"You had business in Sweet Creek marshal?'

"Business is over." The marshal looks at the topography about the camp. "That bear will come in from down wind at dark."

"Most come just after the camp settles for the night marshal."

"Well from them hides you seem to know what you're about."

"This here be Nez Perce land. The Fargo Road separates the Nez Perce from the Black Bear Nation." Joe informs.

"Didn't take any note that we crossed that there highway." The marshal replies.

"You did back when you picked up my trail. That there section be an old desolate stretch. You are west of the Fargo Road now." The lad identifies.

"Taking these ponies to Fargo then?" The marshal guesses

"A share of them foals and them bear hides belong to them local natives."

"You not afraid of the Nez Perce?" Asks the marshal.

"Shoot! My grandmother was full-blooded Nez Perce. Our ranch be part of the Nez Perce Nation."

"No wonder that princess has eyes for you."

"More than bear worry you!" The boy notes.

"Could have an ambitious Black Bear warrior or two after that princess maiden cooking up a storm over there on your behave."

The boy laughs at the idea.

"Them native women will win your appetite first before they own your heart." The marshal warns. "That princess has eyes for you."

"She be big magic?" Joe questions.

"Her father passed. Seems some warriors think forcing her to be their bride gives them the inheritance needed to declare themselves as the new chief."

"That's a powerful incentive. Don't that mean they have to kill you first?"

Yes is in the marshal's stare.

He nods affirmatively.

"If I shoot that bear then all them scoundrels will be arriving." The lad suggests. "They won't spend daylight in the Nez Perce land"

"I've got her uncle's bow and arrow." The marshal acknowledges

"Takes more than one well place shaft to fell a large bear." Informs Joe.

"Sioux can kill a bear with one arrow, or one long sharpened pole." The marshal states.

"You going to have a try at that bear with a bow?"

"I'll use your repeater rifle with the muzzle wrapped several times in a horse blanket to muffle the sound of its shot. We get through the night then the children be safe. " Woody determines.

"Next time you and I will do this in the way of the Sioux... with no gun powder." The marshal smiles as he baits the youth.

"Best I keep watch with the camp? Let's have some eats first!" The boy is quite hungry.

"When you take the first bite of that native woman's fixings best you look her in the eye real hard. Grin like you never tasted anything as good in you life else you'll insult her entire nation." The marshal is smiling at the boy's predicament.

At dark the marshal moves to hide near the stable of foals.

Inot Mai and her siblings take rest some distance from a small fire.

Joe Klinger sits close to the maiden and keeps watch.

"My mother was the fifth wife to the chief of my people." She has want for her guardian to appreciate her status.

The boy understands much of her tongue and is attentive.

"She died during birth. My father was quite old. His heart burst with the fullness of life lived as a great warrior."

The maiden keeps watch on the boy's eyes as she speaks.

"My mother was a much respected cook." She would like a compliment.

"Was the food not to your liking?" She will help bring the needed words from the lad.

Joe is uncomfortable.

He has never sat in a remote night camp alone with any female yet a comely native maiden.

"It was good."

Joy fills the maiden's heart with his words.

"Many warriors wish my hand in marriage." Self advertisement is appropriate.

"You are too young!"

The maiden is shocked. "All the girls in my village marry before another year at my age. I could marry any I choose."

"I thought you were going to become the marshal's woman?"

"He is my betrothed by arrangement from my uncle's death bed." She waits for his understanding.

"Any may trade in honor for my hand from the marshal."

"Why? Do you not wish someone to kill the marshal and steal you away?

"These are thieves who carry no strength in their heart."

"You do not wish to marry the marshal?"

"His eyes show no desire for me. Another woman holds his heart."

"Just what kind of man does a princess like you desire?"

Such questions are not asked among her people.

The maiden is uncomfortable to speak of such feelings.

Joe senses his mistake. "I mean...do native girls have preferences for marriage?"

This question is better asked.

The maiden is eager to respond.

"Most girls want a brave warrior whose heart is good and kind. They wish to replace our ancestors by bearing strong children. The husband must hold up the world in which his family must survive."

"Age is not a concern?" Joe inquiries.

"A bad marriage is with a man who is too weak to embrace the earth."

"Does the man who will marry you have to be a native?"

The girl wags her head no.

"So if I offered the marshal half them foals over there for your hand then I could marry you?'

She is delighted with this question. "To bring a foal from the high meadows is a gift of favor from the Great Spirit. Any maiden would welcome such a marriage?"

"You like the high mountain meadows?" The lad is curious.

"My father and uncle kept a hunting lodge in an evergreen valley high up near the peaks. Since my birth I have ridden that range with my family."

"I would like to spend more time in the high range of the Nez Perce. One man cannot handle more of a load than I bring now."

"A good woman would more than multiply such rewards." The maiden promises.

The night is in full measure.

The sound of a muffled shot collects the attention of Joe and Inot Mai.

The marshal has charged an approaching grizzly bear. As the great predator rose, the marshal sent one high-powered round straight through the heart of the animal killing it instantly.

Inot Mai and Joe stand and face the direction of the marshal's hunt.

Without warning, a warrior in hiding surges from behind.

His war club strikes.

The blow glances from the side of Joe's head to stop upon his shoulder.

Joe is hurled unconscious to the ground in front of Inot Mai.

A large hand grasps the hair of Inot Mai from behind.

A warrior has penetrated the camp.

He pulls Inot Mai back to him.

His retreat will be made to the stream with the girl as his captive.

The preparations of the encampment were observed.

The villain has staged his attack precisely.

The attacker will use the time the marshal is dealing with the bear to disappear into the night with Inot Mai.

Griping the maiden tightly the assassin pulls her away from the camp.

Reaching with a free hand the maiden gathers the marshal's handgun, places the barrel tightly against her captor's chest, and squeezes trigger.

The explosion of the weapon upon the warrior's torso hurls the native's body into the air.

So forcibly is the impact that Inot Mai is thrown as well.

She is still in the man's grasp.

The entangled pair crumples together to the ground. The dead warrior yet binds her with his arm.

The marshal arrives immediately.

He finds Joe yet collapsed.

The maiden struggles and is freed.

A rogue warrior is dead.

Inot Mai darts to Joe's side.

His head is cradled in her lap. Her hands feel for injury. She presses her finger against his scalp to stem his bleeding.

She is distraught.

She instructs her siblings to gather bandages.

Her anxious gaze questions the marshal.

"He'll live." The marshal surmises. "But he can't ride. He needs to hold up for a good spell till these wounds heal."

"I will sow the gash. I have ointment to stop fever." The girl announces.

"He'll need to rest and stay quiet till the fog clears his mind." Experience of the lawman determines.

"I will tend him until he can return to his people." The maiden replies.

The marshal is pleased.

"Do you know the warrior that attacked you?"

The maiden glances at the face and the signs worn by the dead native. "He is not from my village. He is not from the people near to my village but he is of my nation."

"There must be a ransom put out on you. The way back into you nation will be heavy with warriors seeking. We must look for refuge in the Nez Perce village of Many Horns."

At daybreak all are ready to travel.

The two native children will drive the tethered string of foals.

The marshal will string the spare horses, which are packed with goods, hides, and the body of Hasna Gova.

Inot Mai will share a horse with the injured lad.

Joe will have his waist bound to the maiden so that the dazed lad will not fall.

The band will ride south deeper into Nez Perce country and away from Black Bear pursuers.

The village of Chief Many Herons is large.

There are many trails to follow. Those that show much wear are chosen.

Into a wide opened valley the trail leads.

A distance plain shows much sign of rising plumes of campfires.

Remote drums beat.

"It seems we arrive at the time of a village celebration." The marshal tells the maiden. "We be interrupting a big Pow Wow."

Spring brings forth the first of several major festivals for most native tribes. Fertility and the renewal of the earth are celebrated in song, dance, and feast. Marriages are arranged and newborn children are named. The dead of winter are remembered.

All participate in such village festivals.

The lands under Many Horns' rule are prosperous.

The people under Many Horns law are healthy and content.

Many Horns has always listened to the spirits.

The appearance of a dark rider wearing moccasins of toes marked white, leading a large band of mountain foals, and possessing children from the Black Bear Nation creates a consuming stir.

Children of the village race to see and touch the newborn ponies.

Women pack to see the stranger who arrives with bounteous treasures.

Warriors step forth to show their collective might and to estimate the strength of the man who enters.

The medicine men of the tribe react with a stirring of shaking rattles and fluttering of gathered feathers to remove any evil spirits that may be involved in the marshal's visit.

The posture and demeanor of the marshal emanates enormous authority, and much experienced in battle.

So impressive is the marshal's appearance that the women of the village break into a traditional song of greeting for the return of a champion from fight.

Each refrain of the chorus builds in volume.

Drums begin to reinforce the melody.

Uncontrollably the men of the tribe assume an appropriate dance of celebration for visiting spirits.

The emotions of all are peaked by the glorious vocal union of a thousand voices.

The complete eruption of the entire village into a rousing gala ends the counsel of elders with the chief.

An opening is made among the throng to invite the marshal and his troop to the front of the lodge of seniors.

Many Horns is dressed in a brilliant red tunic adorned with gold, and a headdress made from several pristine eagle fathers is tied to one side of his skull.

He stands to greet the marshal.

Coming to a stop the marshal waits upon the words of Many Horns.

Many Horns looks over those who arrive.

The frantic dancing and singing do not abate.

Once the composition of the arrivals is ascertained, Many Horns eyes fix upon the marshal. For several moments his mind searches for meaning to his appearance, and to his presence among his people. The answers are not clear.

Many Horns raises one hand to call to silence his tribe.

The people of the village regain quiet at once.

They are intent on hearing the words to be spoken.

Many Horns holds out one hand to invite the marshal to make words.

In the language of the Sioux, the marshal calls aloud.

"I am Chicha Mandoa of the Sioux nation. I return your injured youth." He points to Joe bound to the maiden on horsed back.

"I return the children of the great warrior Hasna Gova to his people." He points to the siblings of Inot Mai tending the foals.

None in the village understand the tongue of the Sioux. All recognize the marshal as a native from a distance nation.

Many Horns look is of confusion.

The marshal signs by hand.

"The youth of your nation was injured in battle with a rogue Black Bear Warrior. I bring him here to recover from his serious wounds"

Many Horns has the son of his friend taken into his lodge to be attended.

"The maiden is to be my wife. She must keep watch on the lad as he is bound to me forever in spirit. This maiden slew his attacker."

Permission is given for Inot Mai to accompany Joe to the chief's lodge.

"There are many warriors pursuing from the land of the Black Bear. They now search in the lands of the Nez Perce."

The marshal is pointing in the direction from whence he arrived.

The chief looks into the soul of the marshal.

It is true.

Only one who travels with the guidance of the spirits could make such passage.

Many Horns makes a sequence of shrill calls. Immediately one hundred Nez Perce warriors rush to their mounts and speed off in the advised direction.

"The two children must be taken to the Black Bear Village. They are children of their chief." The marshal is pointing due north.

A second array of calls from Many Horns is given.

His words are soft and filled with compassion.

Several dozens of warriors collect to escort the children to their intended destination. "It shall be done in one day's time." Signs Many Horns to the marshal.

"The body of my friend Hasna Gova is to accompany the children for burial among his family."

The chief adds instructions.

The two children and the shrouded warrior are lead away as requested.

"The young horse foals and the bear's hides belong to the people of the Nez Perce." The marshal has no more to say.

Many Horns is pleased.

❧

In the evening the marshal accepts a social invitation from the chief.

The domicile of the great chief of the Nez Perce is spacious. Made from wood and hide it's ceiling is high and vented in several places to accommodate more than one fire when needed. Tribal matters are dispensed within during harsh weather.

The marshal is to dine with Many Horns and his closest counsel before the great spring festivities consume the night.

The war chief, Bog Don sits to the right of Many Horns.

To the left of the chief sits the head medicine man, Sewa Kac.

A young strong brave, Mara Nar has been invited to complete the dinning. He is the grandson of the chief and he sits with Marshal Legs across from Many Horns.

Odd numbers attending the meal are considered to favor the spirits.

Women serve the diners.

Bowls of an alcoholic brew made from honey and yeast is provided.

"Let the fire from the drink bring health." The chief's words tell that the meal begins.

Young maidens hand to each man a bowl of porridge made from crushed wild roots, dried berries, and select green leaves.

This traditional appetizer is held by the tribe to be a remedy for colds and intestinal complaints.

The appetite of the chief is large and the sampling is quickly consumed.

Next large bowls are served of a chili made with black and white beans. It is heavily seasoned.

Chunks of spring fowl are cut and nixed within. It is served in a warp of large thin round bread fried in oil.

This dish is intended to feed the amorous desires of men.

The women who serve offer second helpings to the men

The native ale is consumed freely.

The supply is bounteous and will outlast all demand.

Lastly comes the main fare. A young wild pig has been roasted over flames.

A large flat wooden slate carries a hundred pounds of succulent pork.

The offering is set in the midst of the diners.

The eyes of the chief bulge with anticipated delight as he shreds a large strip of the soft flesh. With his hands dripping of fat, Many Horns chews large bits to be quickly swallowed.

The others share the eagerness of the chief.

No words are spoken but many grunts and smacks from the lips fill this corner of the lodge.

Eating is the primary task.

Fingers are licked clean of the precious juice of the pig.

Gulps of drink make fresh the palate before new charges of warm pork are taken.

The appetites of the natives are prodigious.

Pieces of unwanted flesh are tossed to the sides for the dogs to pick from the floor.

The women stand in silence, watch, and fill the drinking bowls as needed.

Eating is held as a private experience.

Social banter comes after the passing of hunger.

When the chief ends his dining, then all end.

Bowls of water for cleansing of the hands are brought forward.

It is time for tobacco.

The marshal produces a supply of thin dark cigars.

The first is offered to the chief.

Then next is handed to Bog Don.

Finally, Sewa Kac, and Mara Nar receive one each.

The men sniff and touch the small sticks of tobacco.

Their lips wet the outside to enjoy the fresh flavor.

"Such tobacco comes not from lands nearby." States the chief.

"These here cigars come from down the gulf coast in the great southwest. Many weeks travel from here." Informs the marshal.

The chief gives sign to an older woman.

She arrives with a firebrand in hand.

The first to smoke is the chief.

The order of service is repeated.

The marshal is the last to light his cigar.

The woman's face and forehead is smeared with ash.

She mourns.

"It is good!" Begins the chief. "The spirits have sent you."

The chief's hand calls for Bog Don to speak.

"There is trouble." He makes sign directly to the marshal. "Some homesteaders come onto the land of the Nez Perce to dig for yellow rocks. They ruin the land and foul the water." Informs the war chief.

Bog Don is an older warrior.

He wears many heavy scars from battles upon his face and arms.

His chest is covered with booty taken from fallen opponents. Necklaces recovered from the dead enemies have been made into a chest plate.

The feathers in his headdress are notched many times to record the killings in battle from his knife and bow.

"To slay the enemy is easy. To make peace with one's enemy takes much work." Bog Don becomes quiet.

The chief calls the medicine man to speak.

"The settlers that enter our lands bring much sickness.

These spirits are not of our calling. They do not depart when compelled to leave. Many are sick with out help from our medicine." Sewa Kac now becomes silent.

The chief's look invites the marshal to answer.

"The soldiers of the fort are here to keep unwanted visitors from your nation. The fort has medicines for sickness of the settlers. When I arrive at Fargo, I shall order federal deputies and doctors to arrive. Peace will be kept!"

The marshal nods in assurance of his message.

"You are war chief among the nation of homesteaders?" The chief's fingers ask.

"I carry the badge of U S Marshal. Any settler who breaks the code of law of their government will meet me or one of my kind for justice." The marshal's coat is pulled aside to show his badge.

Many Horns wears an expression of determination.

He calls the older woman wearing ashes.

"This is my sister. Her youngest son and his family was slain by settlers on the way south from Fargo several days back. All were found but a young girl is missing. We fear she was taken captive. We fear she is now dead. My sister, my people want to close their pain with the proper burial of the girl. Justice is needed. The spirits are greatly troubled."

The marshal ponders.

He looks upon each face that watches upon him.

The old woman is close to tears.

Bog Don holds much anger.

Sewa Kac is sullen.

Many Horns reaches for hope and trust.

"Is the child's name Little Owl?" The marshal signs.

All the natives are struck with surprise, and disbelief over the marshal's naming of their lost daughter. Shock gives way to respect.

The woman cannot hold her emotions. "Little Owl is my only granddaughter. Does she live?"

The chief forgives her breach of etiquette.

His hand calls softly for her stillness.

"The child is being tended near Fargo." He fears to name the exact location for fear of hostility due to the natives' grief. "She is being treated by our medicine people. She is well."

Great sighs of relief by all show in the marshal's audience.

"What of the her attackers?" Bog Don is quick to petition.

Many Horns shares the need for justice. "Can they be found?"

The marshal gathers his thoughts.

"Four men and one woman...outlaws...murders all...I killed each one where I found them. Left their bones to rot on the spot where they fell." There is cold finality is the marshal's signs.

The native leaders observe afresh the marshal. They conclude this man is appointed by the spirits to choose the soon to be dead.

His calling is greater than any that has been received in their camp.

"Only the Sioux have such warriors." Bog Don testifies. "It is why they are a great nation."

"What of Joe Klinger's condition?" The marshal says to Sewa Kac.

"His wounds heal. His mind will be clear in the morning. His shoulder needs several days before the soreness will permit safe travel." The medicine man assures.

"In the morning I must return to my duties. I shall depart as soon as I talk with the injured lad. I wish Inot Mai to remain with him until he may join his family." Says the marshal.

"Come! We go to the dance and song. In the morning we shall make more thought on this matter." Many Horns gives order.

The old woman caresses the hand of the marshal in appreciation as he departs the lodge of the chief. Then she signs. "Return our child!"

The marshal halts close to the old woman.

His gingers move gently. "The girl fears that the harm she has suffered will make her unwelcome to return to her family."

The old woman understands.

She removes a ring from her finger. "Ask that she returns this to her grandmother. Let Little Owl come back. Mara Nar will ride with you to escort her."

"I can not compel her. She must search her heart and seek a vision from the spirits." Answers the marshal.

The fires will burn long this night in the village of Many Horns.

The energy stored through the winter will vent the passions, sorrows, and wishes of spring.

The youth will purge their inhibitions in song and dance.

The elders will renew passions that rested in deep winter.

The recent dead will be praised in tales.

The ancestors will be invited by name to participate in the celebrations and their favors will be invoked.

The camp will sleep late this morning.

Marshal Legs rests little.

He appears near Joe and Inot Mai at first sun.

Inot Mai has watched through the night. "There has been no fever." She says as she greets the marshal.

"You need rest." Responds the marshal.

"I'm fine." Injects Joe. "Awful sore shoulder though."

"Joe I must ride out soon. May not get back to your family's ranch. Need to settle the issue of Inot Mai." The marshal must come directly to the point.

The boy is confused.

"This here maiden is powerful fond of you. Kept the fever off you...maybe even saved your life."

Inot Mai bows her head in modesty as she follows the marshal's words.

"I may not get to her people's village. Can't let the matter of her coming marriage be left to chance. I owe Hasna Gova my word."

The boy listens. He does not yet comprehend.

"I want you to marry Inot Mai!"

The native maiden brightens.

Joe's eyes dance. "Never give thoughts to taking a wife

marshal. Inot Mai is right pretty enough. Likes the high lands too."

Inot Mai takes pride in her importance to Joe.

"Inot Mai...you be satisfied with Joe here as your man?"

The maiden nods yes emphatically.

"Joe I'll give you my stick pin the maiden wears on her breast. Inot Mai will offer to you her bear claw necklace."

Inot Mai hands the pin to the marshal who presents it to Joe.

The marshal hands the necklace to Inot Mai.

"If'n you two exchange pin for necklace directly then you be betrothed. Into Mai will return to her people until she comes of age for a wedding..."

"The time of the next sprouting leaves!" The maiden informs.

All are silent.

The maiden keeps her necklace in hand.

Her eyes divert Joe's respectfully as he makes his decision.

The boy fingers the stick pin.

He muses.

"Couldn't find a better woman than Inot Mai." He mutters.

The head and shoulders of the maiden stiffen with the consequence of his words.

"I'm a bit young just now...my folks might be upset."

The head and shoulders of the maiden sag with the disinclination in his words.

"I'm going to have to be a man some day. There's plenty of room for another family on the ranch. Hell could be the times come to settle up in that high ground."

The head and shoulders of the maiden wait to move.

"Seems proper enough...easy enough." The boy looks upon the maiden as only a man can measure a woman.

The eyes of the maiden give answer.

The marshal knows the final reply.

"Where would we have to go to be married?"

"She is daughter to a chief. She must marry in her village. You will become a member of the Black Bear family and entitled to hunt their high meadows." The marshal gives answer. "Marriage is the business of family."

"I'll do it!"

The head and shoulders of the maiden swell to the zenith.

Her eyes open in joy.

She is ready to receive his stickpin

Joe hesitates

"It's done once you exchange gifts." The marshal reads the boy's confusion. "Give her the pin!"

Inot Mai receives her adornment.

Her eyes water in happiness.

She thrusts her necklace for his acceptance.

Joe receives the necklace and again he hesitates.

Inot Mai is agitated.

"Best put that on right away." The marshal warns.

The necklace finds a place about Joe's neck.

❧

Mara Nar and the marshal ride out from Many Horns' village before the breakfast fires are warm.

The locations of the sites where the dead outlaws that slew Little Owl's family were described to the Many Horns and his war chief Bog Don.

Mara Nar is dispatched to inspect these sites and report to Many Horns. Souvenirs of these dead will be collected.

These inanimate bits will be tried under the law of the Nez Perce.

The spirits of Little Owl's ancestors will be made content.

Mara Nar leads the path south back toward Eighty Eight's roadhouse using many native shortcuts. Near the day's end they are leaving the nation of the Nez Perce and heading southeast ward toward Ali.

The native trail opens nearby into narrow a wagon road.

The land rolls gently between meadows and tree stands.

Here homesteaders work and live.

Approaching the first fork of the highway, the pair of riders finds the intersecting lanes alive with hundreds of roaming chickens.

Large, and small fowl strut in confusion.

Many bands of chickens are eagerly merging to immediately dispel in aimlessly purpose.

Peeps, hens, and roosters scurry to follow, chase, or flee.

None move with purpose or intention in direction.

Red, white, spotted chickens, chickens with long necks, chickens with short wide heads, chickens with assorted dimensions of feet and legs have dispersed over the terrain along the lanes.

Clucking and pecking at hidden treasures a dissonance of lost poultry covers the landscape.

Mixed with this horde are wild ducks and turkeys invited by the sheer number of their domestic relations.

Never have the marshal or his native guide encountered such a panoramic scattering of fowl.

Down they lane the two trod.

With each step feathers are ruffling as chickens scramble to rush clear.

Over nearly a mile the chicken pageant persists.

The view ahead shows no loss in chicken population.

Under a weeping willow sits an old man in baggy cloths.

His chin rests upon his knees.

Unshaven, dirty, and forlorn the elderly man seems to have been abandoned by the entire world.

"Say old timer whose chickens are these?" The marshal is confused and annoyed.

The disheveled man sadly answers. "Any one what wants them!"

"How many be they all together?" The marshal asks as he looks about.

""More then ten thousand!"

"You after collecting these chickens?"

"Tried all morning! My body done give out from fatigue.

I'm just sitting here wondering if I'm gone to watch them die or will they watch me die first."

"They be yours!"

"Was mine till last night. Came home and found my ranch all tore up and buildings damaged. All my live stock run off."

"What be your name?" Asks the marshal.

"Jeremiah Cloug...my wife Nancy been passed on better than ten years back. My sons are all grown and have moved up to Fargo. Doing real good in the grocery business. They buy lots of my chickens and eggs. Them hens are all the family I have left."

"Some one threaten you recently, did they Jeremiah?" The marshal asks.

"Don't rightly have any enemies. The natives have always been more than peaceable."

"How far to you homestead?"

"A mile back up the lane yonder maybe a bit more." The old guy answers despairingly.

"Mara Nar here and my self can help you round them up and shove them back to you ranch?"

"Them birds going to roost anytime now. First light we can give it a try. I'll need help getting them back to my farm. Pay you in all the chickens you can take away with you." Jeremiah's cheer rises.

"How about we have a chicken dinner tonight to settle the account?" The marshal likes the spirit of the old man.

"Done! Ill clean a few if you boys get a fire up."

As the chickens fly up into the trees for their night's slumber, a fire begins near to the willow.

The marshal makes a roasting pit.

Jeremiah prepares three good sized hens for cooking.

The moon is full.

The sky is clear.

"You'll have to excuse my cooking...just roasted chicken with no fixings for now. You gents stay tomorrow night I'll make a feast with all the trimmings."

"How did you get into the chicken ranching?' The marshal questions.

"Came out to the northern side of these mountains from Canada in a gold rush quite a while back. Dug in that there ground till I was afeard to stop and look up cause I might miss out on finding a gold nugget. Had me gold fever. Wouldn't eat. Hardly took time for a drink. Just dug myself sick. Dropped unconscious. Some natives found me. Took me to their village. Treated me right fine. Healed me. Never dug another shovel full of dirt."

"So how do the chickens come in?"

"Started raising me chickens in them gold fields, cooking, and selling them to the miners. Made a mess of money. Moved to Fargo. Got married. Moved down this way. Been here with my chickens ever since."

Chapter 7

A Chicken House

In the morning the marshal, Mara Nar, and Jeremiah Cloug form a triangle to push the roaming flocks of thoroughly puzzled fowl towards the old man's ranch.

Progress is made not in horse strides, or footfalls but chicken scratches.

"Keep them roosters moving toward the lane and down?" Jeremiah calls.

Mara Nar has only herded horses.

The marshal has driven just about every other animal there is to be found but chicken herding is new. "You ever rounded up chickens like this before?"

"Well actually I did once. Not as many as these. Just several hundred down Texas way when I was in the army." Clough responds.

"Didn't know the army raised chickens Jeremiah!" Replies the marshal.

"They don't. Was visiting my relatives' ranch down Galveston way. They had one of them big storms with heavy rains and mighty strong winds. Drowned every turkey on my cousin's farm. Blew chickens over dozens of acres.

The marshal reflects.

"Leave them stragglers. Some will wonder back by and by." Jeremiah instructs.

Mara Nar takes sport of riding fast around the perimeter of the fowl to insight pandemonium with individual birds lifting in the air to sweep distances out and away.

"That native has a powerful lot of energy." The old man testifies.

"What be your family's name down to Galveston?" The marshal conjures.

"Autry...on my mother's side...used to be a good number of them back 10-20 years ago living around them parts. Most moved closer to Houston I expect."

"Met some Autrys a few years back down that a ways." The marshal is surprised by the possible relationship.

"Them birds be getting thirsty soon. They'll get the smell of the pond water from my ranch. Moving them will become easier like." Jeremiah points off to the distance.

"How many do you think you'll lose?"

"Them birds be tough to kill during the day. Predators will be busy at night out here. Some will wonder farther off then most. I guess 2 or 3 out of every ten will be lost one way or the other." The old fellow calculates.

"They navigate pretty good do they?"

"Not for great distances. Ones that get loose on the ranch keep themselves around an acre or so about. Close enough for getting at the supply of the grain and salt."

"What's the expense of raising all them birds? Grain?"

"Grow plenty of grain about the farm. Lot's of insects for eating near the water by them birds. Grain can be cheap and local. No! Biggest cost is salt. Have to haul a good bit in from Fargo. There be some beds of rock salt about but gathering up time makes it impracticable."

"You haul live chickens up to Fargo?"

"Yep about once a week. Damn near 1 in 5 birds sold in Fargo goes to buy salt that has to be hauled back here."

"Get a good price up there do ya?" Wonders the marshal.

"A fine healthy bird what's been raised on plenty of water and adequate salt brings a real good price. My boys sell them live or butchered."

"You keep as many birds as when your wife and the boys worked the farm?"

"A good hand can raise about 10, 000 birds alone. At one time we hand 24, 000 birds on this here ranch. Liked to get up to that number again If'n I could find the help."

"You could marry again?"

"Some times I think about taking me another woman. Just don't know how. Seems natural now to be alone. Had me a good dog. Someone shot him recently...Miss my dog. Will get me another one. He was the best at killing critters what wanted to get at the chickens"

"Any other problems about your ranch recent like?" The marshal is suspicious.

"Lots of damage to the fences. Had one horse run off or was stolen. He was an old sick one though."

At the end of the day the Cloug Ranch comes into view.

It is a flat spread with one log cabin and small barn.

A long narrow pond sits at the center.

The entering wagon road passes along one lengthy side. A U-shaped wooden structure that stands about three feet in height spans the long axis of the pond on the other.

This low long structure is the chicken house. I was built to pen the birds in a vast yard on three sides with the pond as the fourth boundary of the perimeter.

Large swing gates open for access.

The gates have been sprung open and damaged.

Driven by thirst, and a recovered sense of home, the chickens are eager to be returned into the poultry yard of the ranch.

The marshal and Mara Nar continue to circle the end of the flock to drive fowl homewards.

Jeremiah makes temporary repairs to make the gates. They will be operational soon.

Most of the birds are again in their pen.

The marshal and Mara Nar watch as vagrant chickens take to the wing to fly over the chicken house and into the poultry compound.

"If it's that easy to get out by flying why do you need a gate?" The marshal asks.

"Only the rambunctious birds have the gumption to fly. Once out most chickens will miss eating the easy way and fly back in. If'n the gate's open they'll wander in a bunch like today far enough to get lost without knowing it. No one raises birds for their brains."

"When will you feed them?"

"They go to roost at dark. I'll fill the troughs with feed and salt at night. That's all there is to it. I'll round up another thousand, or so birds what will be looking for grain in the morning."

"Get many visitors out this way?" The marshal continues his investigation.

"Occasionally folks will come to barter for chicken with pork or beef. Sometimes folks will loose their whole flock and come out here to acquire a set of hens and roosters for restarting. Some have their children collect buckets of salt rock for trading."

"Any strangers recently?"

"Well just some gals from over Eighty Eight's Road House. Some school teachers wanting a few hens for eggs and meat."

"Real pretty petite sandy haired gal goes by the name Ali?" The marshal guesses.

"Can't rightly recall her name but the description fits.

Comes with a pretty dark haired gal name Layla. Mighty fine looking woman." The old guy declares.

"Any one unusual in the last year or two come a visiting?"

"Let me see. My cousin Luke, and Jed Autry came up this way on business and paid me a visit. Paid a visit to my boy in Fargo too."

"They be from down Texas way?"

"Yep the same bunch." Jeremiah testifies.

Without the old man noticing the marshal makes hand signs to Mara Nar.

The native is asked to ride the outside of the ranch to look for marks of any rider making camp over the past weeks.

The native is also asked to keep watch on the road that approaches the Clump Ranch through the night.

The marshal will carry his carbine and watch the compound for a human visitor this night.

He will keep safe an enormous number of poultry, and protect the old man.

His thoughts will be filled with remembrances of Ali.

Again and again he will relive his first meeting with Ali in the bath house in Sweet Creek.

He needs to be with her.

The first rays of the sun return Mara Nar to the Cloug Compound.

Thousand of chickens emerge into the yard. Hundreds of roosters begin to crow. The volume of noise makes speaking unheard.

"One rider. Comes from the south. Spends the night than departs as he came." The native gives signs than points to the precise direction.

"That be someone from the Sweet Creek local." The marshal signs then ponders.

"What kind of horse be he riding?"

"Light...fast...strong." Mara Nar replies.

"Sure it's no rogue native warrior?"

"No native harms the earth." Mara Nar is insulted at the suggestion.

The marshal nods in acceptance. He signs an apology.

"It's time you make visit to the graves of those what killed you kin." Directs the marshal.

"I'll speak with Jeremiah then ride over to the east and see about them school teachers and Little Owl. I'll return here after midday." The marshal concludes.

"It is good! It shall be as Chicha Mandoa says." The young warrior is anxious to keep the wish of his chief. He is happy to be free and on his own. He is happier to leave behind the roar of the waking multitude of birds.

"One never gets use to the racket." Jeremiah shouts. "This is about the time I get to the planting fields for solace."

"You have business in Sweet Creek? The marshal calls out loudly.

"Sell some fowl to a German butcher over that away every once and a while."

"Have any family thereabouts?'

"Nope! Don't know too many people. The sheriff Ann Klinger, been to her ranch a couple times trading for horses. But not in the last 4 or 5 years."

"I'm gone over to Eighty Eight's Road house. Be back midday. Think someone is stalking your place. It could be dangerous for you here by yourself."

"Thanks marshal. I'm too old to worry about hauling a gun everywheres."

"Keep near your cabin and have a gun handy in case shooting starts." The marshal departs.

The marshal resumes his ride to the road house.

Retuning to the wagon road where he first encountered Jeremiah and his lost flock, he will follow the wagon tracks due east heading for the busy Fargo road.

This section of the country has long been settled and the roads have all sunken with wear over the years.

The lanes are tree line.

Large bush and shrub line the road's edges

Traffic moves quickly past the farms and homesteads.

The land provides bounteously. The domestic animals are strong and active. The pastures are large and lush. Streams and ponds are abundant

Buildings stand erect and are well maintained.

"Fine living in this here stretch." He shares his thought with his steed. "Plenty of barns for you to get inside and be chummy."

The scents from farm animals are heavy in the breeze.

"Wonder what kind of living I could make out this a way. No chicken work that's for sure. Mighty pretty country!"

The solace of travel in the open country has always appealed to the marshal. His heart and mind are at ease.

His anticipation of being with Ali makes the journey's end welcomed.

Sooner or later all roads directed east to west shall cross the main corridor to Fargo. These minor intersections are mostly hidden from those moving on the main highway.

The hurried travelers on the Fargo Road take no note of these slim access ways.

Today the marshal shall find the entrance to the Fargo Road congested.

A stagecoach heading north has had an accident. The coach is found at a complete stop in the midst of the highway.

The driver is tending one of the horses that pull the coach.

He is a round thick man of medium size.

His bulbous torso leans over a fallen animal.

The solid arms of the driver tug at the horse's reins but the animal will not rise.

"Can I be of assistance?" The marshal calls as he approaches.

The full bodied driver shakes his head in disbelief. "Can't figure what has this critter down!"

The marshal notes the swollen abdomen of the stricken

animal. The legs of the horse are stretched full out and frozen. The animal shivers uncontrollably.

'That there horse is dying!" The marshal informs the attendant.

The chunky form of the driver straightens.

His hat is removed.

His pudgy hand rubs the long threads of wet red hair upon his head.

"He was fine yesterday. No sign of him feeling poorly." The driver takes guilt. "Didn't mean to work this creature to death but he's my lead horse. Can't rightly move this coach without him."

"He's been poisoned!" The marshal is certain.

"Poisoned!" The driver is shocked.

"They all have the same feed?" Asks the marshal.

"I reckon. Ride together, stable together. Heck they always be together. Can't figure how one get poisoned without the other's going the same way." The driver holds the small of his back with both hands as he stretches.

"This here job has ruined my back! Made me heavy as well! Sit and eat...eat and sit. If'n it didn't pay awful good I'd quit right here on the spot." The fellow is agitated and depressed by the present circumstances.

"You bound for Fargo?" The marshal assumes.

"Yep! Gots me a stop at the road house up ahead first." The driver studies the scene of the dying animal.

His head turns side to side. He is disheartened.

"Best to unhook that critter and move your team and coach clear." Advises the marshal.

"I just can't leave him a dying by himself. Seems cruel to continue with him sick this a way."

"Could be hours before his ends comes. Best to put him down and end his suffering." The marshal is reluctant.

"I can't do that to him. No way! He's my best friend. Have him for a good number of years now." Tears are ready to fall.

"I'll sit with him to the end. Least way's he knows someone cares. He won't have to be sacred cause he was left here weak on the ground". The driver cannot bind his emotion. His heavy shoulders tremble as he cries.

The marshal sympathizes. "I'll wait with your animal."

"No sir! He'd knowd the team was gone. It's our duty to see him to the last."

"Sorry I can't wait for you. Best get to my business ahead." Announces the marshal.

"You a preacher or something?" Asks the driver.

The marshal shakes his head no.

"You look like a gambler!" Calls a man stepping down from the coach.

The marshal turns.

A small thin man approaches.

He has the form and face of an adolescent. His appearance tells something else.

A black fine tailored suit covers him. A black-rimmed hat with a silver band covers a clean shaven face.

His hair is neat and trimmed.

His shirt is ruffled silk with cufflinks of a gold and silver mix.

Several large rings are viewed on his hands. They are made from gold and jewels.

His boots are shiny black with the coverings of the toes inlaid with silver and trimmed in gold.

The driver stares at the two men. Their style of dress makes them twins of unequal proportions.

The marshal is speechless at the vision of the stranger.

The visitor grins at the marshal.

The smallish passenger smokes a tiny cigar.

He waits for the marshal to complete his inspection as plumes of smoke exhale.

"From the way you ride that horse, and talk you have to be a lawman." The little man announces. "My name is John Bryant Ledford."

"I see you've been down to New Orleans." Responds the marshal.

The passenger nods in agreement. “Been just about every where...sheriff.”

“U S Marshal Legs.”

“Damn, you are Wooden Legs! Heard tell of you. Never thought we would meet up. Just call me J. B.”

The small delicate hands of the passenger tell the marshal this man is a gambler. His jewelry tells the marshal he is a very successful gambler.

“How could you tell that I am officer of the law?” Asks the marshal.

“It’s my business to know about others. Got to be able to read a man’s character in my line of work.” Responds J. B.

“You carry money?” The marshal asks the driver.

“No valuables marshal!”

The marshal looks to the gambler for his response.

“Just a small traveling sum.” Ledford responds.

“No valuables inside one of them travel bags?”

“Nope! You can look if you wish.” The gambler offers.

The thin waist of the small man hides no weapons. Yet the marshal holds the man to be dangerous. “What weapons be you carrying?”

Ledford produces a small pearl handled derringer for inspection.

The marshal suspects a delicate knife to be hidden in the fancy boot of the gambler.

“Any reason someone might be following you?” The marshal looks to the driver.

“No problems recently.” The driver is alarmed.

“Folks expecting you up ahead?” The marshal asks the gambler.

“Got business ahead.” The little man is hesitant.

“Fargo?”

“I’ll be staying at the road house nearby for a few days.”

“Then where to?”

“Not sure at this moment marshal.”

“You been to Baytown Texas a gambling have you?” The marshal is suspicious.

"Gambled there a time of two."

"You hired by a syndicate?"

The small man is taken back at the marshal's words.

He does not respond.

"You here for a high stakes poker game?"

"What makes you think so marshal?"

"It's my business to know a man's character and what doings a man is about!"

The hesitancy of the gambler convinces the marshal.

"There is an extra large poker game to be held at the road house in the next coming days." Defines the marshal.

"Yes sir...it's supposed to be held a secret for security sake."

"How many gamblers? Where from?"

"Usually 6 or 8...from all over. Won't know for sure until the cards are dealt"

The marshal looks to the driver. "Cut me one out of them horses. I'm taking your passenger on head. I'll send some help from the road house." He orders.

"Think some robbers are following?" The small passenger asks. "Some one wants to rob me?"

"They are after robbing you...want to kill you first! They'll be here before long I expect." The marshal understands that a major crime is under way and someone wants Ledford out of the contest. "How large is the table stakes?"

"One hundred thousand dollars each. No law against a private game here abouts."

"Who hired you? Where's the money being kept now?"

"I live in Tennessee. Got an invitation in the mail plus a bank draft for expenses. A fellow named Ron Baker hails from Denver is sending the cash."

"Work for him before?"

"Yes sir. Done right well for him. I keep 50 percent of the profits plus my expenses."

"Ever hear of a fellar named Beaudreaux?"

"Well marshal I have played cards with him a couple of times. Why do you ask?"

"He be a loser?"

"Small stakes winner. Likes women too much. He's the type that gambles for money. They never win big."

"Oh! What keeps you in the game?'

"Winning! Just like the winning...beating all the others that is." The small man smiles impishly.

"We'll J. B. looks like there's some looking to join uninvited like into your game."

The horse from the coach's team is ready for riding. The marshal and the small gambler race off to the road house.

❧

Bill Freeman is busy as usual about his road house as the marshal and J B arrive.

The similar clothing has Mr. Freeman confused. "Hi marshal!" He looks to the small rider. "You a marshal as well?"

The marshal shakes his head in frustration. 'This here be Mr. Ledford. He's a guest of yours."

"Come for the game I suppose." Bill does not yet understand choice of the marshal's dress style.

"Who's responsible for arranging this poker game?" The marshal asks.

"Fella arrived here some weeks back. Gave me a large sum for holding some rooms. Said he wants to have some friends over for a private game of poker." The owner replies.

"Others arrived yet for the game? Asks the marshal.

"Two fellows and one lady."

The marshal nods in appreciation. "The stage is broke down a few miles back. Lost their lead animal."

"I'll get help right off marshal."

"Ali near by?" The marshal asks.

There she is now!"

Ali has just exited the main door of the road house carrying a bundle of wash.

She catches sight the marshal.

Her eyes are fixed upon him.

She sees none other.

As the marshal's eyes met hers. Ali's face erupts in surprise and sheer delight. She wants to rush to him.

She is uncertain as to how to make her greeting.

The marshal eyes are also dedicated. The fragile shape and inviting form of the lady revives his desire.

He stands to fill his senses with her being.

Ali makes a timid step.

Her heart beats rapidly.

Her eyes devour him. She is reassured. She is thankful to have his return.

The marshal is tempted to hurry. The smile that erupts upon her face calls him irrevocably to her.

There is no more invitation needed.

The approach of the marshal brings Ali to her tiptoes. Her hands fumble about her package.

The height of the marshal comes to tower over the fine woman.

Ali lifts her head to greet.

The softness of her skin and the glow of sunlight through the strands of hair about Ali's neck end all formality.

His hands grip her shoulders.

His face closes to hers.

Tears release her unspent passion. "I didn't know if you would ever return." Her eyes search.

"You never left my thoughts." He hugs her tenderly.

His lips briefly caress her cheek.

The strength of his body reassures. The meaning of her life, the hopes of her future replenish.

"I looked every day for your horse in the distance. I prayed for your safe return." She presses close.

The pleasure of his arrival ends all matters before her.

The pleasure of watching Ali move and speak before him is the only substance for the marshal.

"I want us to go some place together. A special place just near here." Her eyes beg.

"I have to see to this fellar there. Where do you want us to go?"

"There's a place nearby you have to see. We have to see together. We can walk there. It's very close."

Ali turns to gauge the man of the marshal's interest.

Her look turns to disbelief.

The apparition of the smaller form dressed as the marshal bewilders her. "Who is that sissy?"

Her words give sting.

The mortification by his material condition is refreshed.

Ali recognizes her mistake instantly. "I mean that little man is dressed like ah...you." Proper words fail her.

"He's a friend of Mr. Beaudreaux."

"Oh! How nice! Is he a guide as well?"

"He's a gambler."

"Gambler? Why is he here?"

"Let me put my horse up and then you and I shall have some private time."

The woman smiles warmly.

"Mr. Freeman?" The marshal calls the owner. "I'll need to get over to the Cloug Ranch midday."

"Jeremiah's on old timer in theses parts." The owner replies.

"You do business with him?"

"Trade for chicken and such when we have the need."

"You know his boys?"

"Yes sir. Those boys own most of Fargo by now. It's been rightly said them Clougs can make money falling down. One of'em fell in the snow as a boy, when he got up there was a 20 dollar gold piece stuck to his one hand." The owner laughs with the irony.

"They have relatives here abouts?"

"None here but they be some in Fargo I understand."

"The name Autry mean anything to you?"

"Sure do! Autry is the name of the fellow what made all the arrangements for the poker game fixing to start up soon."

The marshal is surprised.

"That fellar to return here soon is he?"

"Suppose! He didn't say. Paid in advance though." The owner responds. "Best I get on to that coach marshal."

The marshal retraces his steps. "J. B. best you keep about the road house. Don't wander off."

"You staying for the game marshal?"

"Be back and forth but I'll be around that's for sure."

"That be you lady?" The small guest asks nodding toward the waiting Ali.

"Keep you eyes out for her J. B. She's awful innocent." The marshal can only smile.

"Be my pleasure marshal."

"Call me Woody!"

The tiny gambler makes a large grin. "Woody!"

Ali is impatient.

Her toe taps.

She watches for the marshal to end his present affairs.

She skips toward him as he breaks his conversation.

"This way." She leads along a path from the road house. "I found this place picking flowers the other day. You just have to see it"

"What kind of place?" The marshal wishes to perpetuate the woman's glee.

"Seems years ago some homesteaders lived back here. One day they just packed up and left the place to whom ever wants it."

The path turns slowly.

It is over grown yet navigable.

The two march while holding hands. The marshal carries her package.

Ali talks and turns incessantly. She consumes every moment of his presence.

Their trudge ends in front of a log and stone house.

Large oak trees shade the front.

The windows have been boarded.

Dust covers the flooring of the wrap around porch.

"This is the front." Ali shows.

"The door opens to a large room with a big fireplace. The main bedroom sits off to the right. A second room sits off to the left. It could be a work space or a bedroom for children." She giggles at these words.

The marshal notes the structure is dry and standing straight.

He is unmoved.

Ali leads around to the side of the covered porch. "Put the wash down here for the time being."

"In the back is a spacious kitchen with a huge wood stove and fireplace. They spent some money on their kitchen."

At this side Ali stops.

"The best is yet to come." Her hands clap in excitement.

They step to the rear.

Ali holds the marshals arms.

She turns him to look away from the distance and to watch her.

She positions the marshal. "Turn around! Look!" She instructs.

The rear of the house sits atop s a ridge that overlooks a long open valley.

The marshal turns to view the white capped gray mountain range rising into an azure sky.

Toward the distance flows a lush golden meadow with flowing water. Dark green woods rim the valley.

Eagles soar above the clouds.

The air is crisp and fresh.

Spring flowers of various sizes and colors spot across the floor of the valley.

Meadowlarks scatter about.

Songs of mating blue birds accompany the visitors.

"I've never have seen such a beautiful view." The marshal gasps at the vistas before him.

Ali arms and hands press against her chest.

She eagerly waits for the marshal's decision.

"That meadow is natural for raising horse and beef."

Ali anticipates his every word.

"It's perfect...absolutely perfect." Confirms the marshal

With these words Ali leaps against his chest and enwraps him with her arms.

"I knew you would love it. I knew it." She squeals in ecstasy. "As soon as I saw it I knew it was made for us."

"Those gorgeous mountains, that beautiful valley, the freedom one has here...is wonderful." He looks into her loving face.

He whispers as in a prayer. "It's heaven because we are here together."

Their embrace continues in a kiss.

This kiss begins their eternal sharing.

A kiss only made possible by the truest deepest love.

They return hand in hand.

"What will you call this place?" He asks.

"The Hideaway! What else?" Ali responds with happiness.

Woody enjoys the satire.

"What marshal's work are you doing now?" Asks Ali.

"I have the companionship of a young warrior from Little Owl's village. He is to invite Little Owl to return to her people. I have to meet him at the Cloug Ranch."

"The place with the biggest chicken house I've ever seen?"

"The same! There's more than that happening there."

Ali is alarmed. "You have to shoot some more bad guys?" She is displeased.

"Some outlaws are headed this way. Not sure what their plan is about. There's a high takes poker game to be played at the road house soon."

"How come there's always some crime that comes between us. Don't people live without fighting desperados?" Her need for civility dominates her emotions. "I never saw a murderer until I met you!"

"I never met an angel until I met you! Seems there ought to be a way to live peaceful like."

Ali is comforted by his words. "It is just whenever there is a really bad person around you turn into this possessed avenger. The look, the stare upon your face...it frightens me."

"Being a marshal is about beating the bad guy."

"Do you have to ride across the entire country after any bad man that you hear tell about?"

"If he's wanted in my jurisdiction...I have to chase him down."

"Then get a smaller jurisdiction!"

"I'm gone to ride back to the Cloug Place, collect Mara Nar and return. We'll all have diner together." Suggests the marshal.

"We'll have a meal here at our future home. We ladies can keep fine here with a bit of work." She pauses for his approval.

"Get busy!" He comments. "Get Bill Freeman to move your wagon and all your goods. I'll return to this house...ah the Hideaway. Collect all the girls and get my deputy here as well."

"Supper will be a waiting Woody!"

❧

Mara Nar has made his visit to the graves of the outlaws.

He has collected bits of exposed material, small stones, samples of dirt, even tuffs of hair from the place where the murderers' bodies repose. These he has placed in to one small deer skin pouch to be returned to the tribal counsel for trial.

They will be burned as sacrifice to the ancestors of those killed.

He waits upon the marshal to conclude his mission and return Little Owl to her grandmother.

Directly, the marshal rides into the Cloug Ranch at a full gallop.

Mara Nar greets him. 'The one you seek is again in the hills above. He makes watch upon us now."

"So we are just in time!"

"Hello marshal!" Calls Jeremiah from his front door.

"How long can you leave them birds on their own?" Returns the marshal.

"Plenty of water...just mound the feed up...they be fine for 3 or 4 days. Why?"

The marshal is stepping next to the old rancher. "There's a man watching us. I believe he is very dangerous."

"What does he want with me?"

"I'm afraid he wants the use of your ranch. He'll likely kill you if he has to."

The fright caused by the marshal warnings causes the old man to freeze.

"I want you to load your wagon with all the goods you can get out quickly. Cloths, food, bedding, pans and such, just like you was quitting this place."

The old man remains confused.

"Put you guns on first. Mara Nar and I will put the food out for the chickens. Then we'll get you loaded and your team ready."

"My guns...how long am I to be gone? Heck where am I a going?" Jeremiah's replies.

"You'll stay with me until I say otherwise." The marshal gives order.

Deputy Seth Adams and his wife Evelyn arrive late in afternoon.

They find Ali, Little Owl, Michele, and Layla cleaning and preparing supper. Evelyn has already composed some dishes for the evening meal.

Seth gets busy clearing, cleaning and hauling water.

Mr. Freeman has unloaded the wagon and stabled the mules for the ladies at the Hideaway. He will return soon with spare items from the road house needed to setup house for the gals.

His older sons will help Ali with a variety of the chores.

Diner will be set upon the porch.

The rooms will be clean and tidy for sleeping tonight.

Plenty of fresh water will be available.

The windows and doors will be unbarred.

Lights will shine from every room.

Temporary curtains of old linen will be hung.

Table and chairs will be placed for eating and sitting out after dark.

A small supply of animal feed will be gathered.

Several vases of fresh flowers will be placed about inside to aide the removal of stale odors.

All this plus a warm meal is to at the ready for the marshal at dusk.

Only a maiden energized by romance could manage such a task in a short period.

The menu for dinner is collected from various sources.

Mrs. Freeman has sent several baked breads and a large pan of apple dumplings from the road house's kitchen.

Evelyn Adams contributes a pork and large noodle casserole, a large hunk of cold ham for slicing and frying with onions and bits of potatoes, fresh churned butter, baked sweet potatoes, and jug of sweet cider from their cold cellar.

Layla has hot coffee, and hot tea being made on the stove.

Bacon is frying, and cheese melts in a pan of cream in preparation to be served on slices of warm toast.

Michele is mixing flower, eggs, and milk to make dough for deep frying. Some fried cakes with be served sweetened for desert, some will be seasoned for use with gravy.

Little Owl gathers wood and tends the stove while assisting the cleaning efforts in the food area.

Ali has little time left from her duties as head of the household.

She will collect some whiskey and wine from the road house.

One dish she will prepare is baked stuffing made from stale pieces of bread mixed with bits of onion, chicken fat and seasoned with sage...just as the marshal loves.

The Hideaway will be as lovely, and gracious, and appetizing a home as Ali is capable of making.

There will be no excuse for the marshal not enjoying the home for which he is intended.

The center of activity in the Hideaway is the kitchen.

Here Evelyn assumes command with her superb home making abilities.

"Ali, I've sent my Seth to the road house for some lumber to make saw horses and set planks for serving tables."

Ali knows better than to try to sway the stubborn girl. Besides Evelyn's judgments in matters of home are appreciated by all who know her.

"The house desperately needs proper furniture." This problem will have to wait as Ali has too much to do and too much about which to think.

"My Seth tells me there is a old man that lives just this side of Fargo who is a master craftsman. He builds everything one can imagine for inside and outside of the home."

Ali sighs. "It's got to be pricy?"

"The best part is that he will trade for almost anything. He loves trading as much as woodworking. My Seth says that if people visit him they can arrange a piece of furniture for a deerskin or whatever."

"Is he married?" Ali ponders.

"I think his wife is as craft worthy as he. She has a small gift shop."

"Evelyn I spoke with Mrs. Freeman about starting a gift shop at the road house. I think we girls could make some crafts and souvenirs to sell to the people that stop there with the coaches."

"Oh! I would love to make some money. My home needs lots of small things but there 's not a lot of cash. If my Seth can keep his deputy's job even part time it would help."

"If the Freemans can find the space then we girls would have to share the time required to be at the shop." Ali asserts.

"One day a week is no problem for me besides I could make some items while I'm there. We should a least try it."

Ali is encouraged. "We could trade crafts for furniture items to sell here."

"This cooking stove is marvelous. It's better than the one in the road house kitchen. Why would any one leave something this expensive?" Evelyn begins to fry ham slices.

"I understand the people that lived here had money. The woman's moved out here from back east after her mother passed away. The father died recently. The woman inherited a vast amount of cash and land." Ali informs

"So it's yours for the taking?"

"Squatters rights and I aim to squat!" Ali declares.

Both ladies burst into laughter.

"You're going to marry the marshal?"

"Yes!"

"When?"

"As soon as that traveling preacher returns."

Evelyn understands Ali. "He asked you yet?"

"He doesn't have to because he understands we are going to be man and wife. He just doesn't know how soon."

More cheer from the ladies.

"What's it like...how is it to be a wife?" Ali wonders if her dreams are to become real.

"It's wonderful. To have someone close and tender, to share plans, to work together. I've never been so happy. My Seth treats me good."

"What's the best part of having a husband?"

"You may think me daft but cooking for him! My Seth loves to eat. I cook a heavy breakfast, a heavy lunch, a heavy supper, and before we retire my Seth will have a big piece of pie or cake. He just eats up everything and anything I can make."

"No problems?"

"Well my Seth is a heavy snorer. He wakes me up once or twice in the night. He works so hard I just don't wan to be a nag!"

"Does he taste a bit of hard liquor before he sleeps?" Ali questions.

"No he hardly ever mentions a drink of whiskey before bed."

"Try a small serving of wine or brandy to open his breathing pipes. They say it can help people who snore. I have some wine. Take a bottle home and let me know if it does any good."

Michele runs into the kitchen. "You have to see this."

The girls scurry into the front room of the house.

"I was cleaning in this corner. Look what I found under some rubbish."

A large oak chest opens to show its contents.

"Everything you need to decorate the house. Candle holders, candles, small mirrors, lace covers, table linen, it's a treasure chest."

The girls squeal with delight as they touch, smell, open, unfold, weight and measure all the goods contained within the chest.

"What are these? Asks Ali as she holds a pair of silver bells up for inspection.

"Christmas decorations!" The other two girls answer together.

"Why would she leave these beautiful things?" Asks Evelyn.

"Just had too much stuff I expect!" Ali answers.

"I wonder if there are any other storage places." Michele wonders.

"Ladies will have plenty of time tomorrow to poke about. Let's get ready for this evening." Directs Ali.

The fireplace in the main room of the house is aglow.

The windows have been cleaned, the rooms dusted.

Flowers are placed about.

"Which room for the newly weds, which for us gals?" Asks Michele.

"Newlyweds? Would that be I or the marshal?" Teases Evelyn.

Ali blushes. "For now...the small room for Mr. and Mrs. Adams. The larger side room for Little Owl, Layla, Michele and myself...unless any of you girls has any surprises." All the ladies laugh at the possibility of an impish option.

"Where is Layla and Little Owl? Ask Michele.

"Outside sweeping and cleaning last I looked." Answers Ali.

"I'll need some help getting the side rooms set for the

night." Replies Michele. "I guess it'll be just Layla and myself heading out to the west before long."

The mood saddens with impending separation.

"Don't fuss! That decision doesn't have to be made soon." Ali begs.

"I'm so happy for you and Evelyn. Your both have your own lives, homes. You both have found the right man." Michele feels deserted.

"If we have found the proper man to share our lives out here close to nowhere, then you'll be finding one soon as well." Evelyn offers solace.

"Can't be any bankers here about. Maybe Fargo? Layla and I will have to find paying work to buy tickets to the west." Michele worries.

"After my wedding is settled, we will all ride up to Fargo and see about starting your future." Ali insists.

"What about Little Owl? She's attached to Layla now" Asks Michele.

"She needs to be near to her people for a spell. I'll keep her, and school her here until ready to return to live with Judith in West Liberty should she wish. The future is good for that poor child either way." Ali will not see the child tossed about.

Layla and Little Owl share the joy of song and music. Both females have a gift for language.

They talk as they make the porch ready for dinning this evening.

"My father's people are chiefs." Little Owl tells.

"My father's people are musicians who entertained chiefs." Answers Layla. "Do you have musicians in your village?"

"There are those who beat the drums. Everyone sings together." Answers Little Owl.

"Well if you wish I can teach you to make music from strings."

"I shall have to know how this music sounds." Answer the native child.

"Tonight you shall see how we settlers make song, music and dance. Then you shall see the soul of the homestead people."

"I saw the spirit of Ali when she came to my rescue. She wore much courage. Ali has the heart of a warrior."

"That doesn't seem like the sweet girl that I know. Perhaps you saw something of her that lies deeply hidden." Layla has never considered Ali as a combatant.

"Well, how comes the effort on the veranda?" Ali asks as she appears.

"Done! Little Owl and I shall prepare some music for afterwards."

"Play something romantic...please?"

Layla smiles at her friend's suggestion.

"The night is to be special is it?" Layla beams with anticipation.

"Well...maybe...I hope so!" Ali is most anxious.

"Ali you will make a great wife. That marshal will never let you slip away."

"It just that everything is perfect right now and I don't want anything done wrong to ruin it."

"We all will be ideal...at least for tonight." Layla laughs at her silliness.

"You have helped me so much I can never repay your kindness." Ali hugs her friend.

"I prefer not to move, leave either I love it here. I want to be with you girls." Layla is also sad.

"Can't you stay? We can have a small school to begin." Ali is hopeful.

"Michele really wants us to go further west. I kind of do as well. I'll miss you and Evelyn so much. Judith is close enough to visit often." Tears of contest swell in Layla's eyes.

"Let's all say our prayers that we can settle here together. This night...every night should be a beginning. With every change that seems to turn bad there is good that must come as well." Ali's spirit is contagious.

Layla takes hope for tomorrow.

"I'll have to get Woody something different to wear. I can't let my husband walk around in fancy cloths like Beaudreaux! It just wouldn't do for a married man." Ali tells herself as she heads back to the kitchen.

Mr. Freeman and Seth arrive with a wagon full of supplies.

Lumber, a number of unused chairs, a small barrel of beer, jugs of milk, cartoons of eggs, sugar, spices and sundries for cooking and cleaning, and some bedding.

"Mary says if you need anything send Seth to the road house." Bill thunders as the wagon stops.

"Tell Mary we have more than I had hoped for...you best get back to your work." All the unexpected help overwhelms Ali.

"Mary says you are to wed the marshal?" The big man roars with happiness.

"It's what Marshal Legs says that counts...so far he hasn't said anything to me."

"He will by golly...he has eyes too you know."

Ali remembers the first time she noticed the marshal seeing her as a woman.

Her spirit brightens.

"Mary also says the boys can stay till you have enough wood and water in the house. They can walk home together after dark."

"Your sons have done enough. We have all we need for several days."

"Are you ready for the marshal's return?" Asks the owner of the road house.

"In the next hour we set the table. The marshal should be here by then...thank you!"

"I must tell Mary. She will want to see the place all fixed up for living here." Joy is in every word from Mr. Freeman.

"Tell her to stop by midday for tea!" Ali cheers.

The Freeman boys have found a trap door entrance into the loft of the house. Little Owl has joined the band of half grown explorers.

The crawl way above is crammed with wooden boxes.

Some containing books, some with discarded leather goods

such as shoe and purse, and others with collected items ported from a previous home but never put to use.

"We'll use the day tomorrow to haul everything down and rummage to our hearts content." Ali advises the ladies.

"Is there a cold storage cellar about the place?" Asks Evelyn.

"Don't rightly know. Haven't searched the entire grounds." Ali answers.

"Best put them boys to work in the morning. They seem to be natural explorers." Michele advises.

The evening preparations at the Hideaway have escalated from a simple meal to a house warming to a community gathering. Living has returned to this dwelling in a most glorious manner.

The marshal arrives just as the sun is low on the horizon. Mara Nar sits in the wagon with Jeremiah. None are prepared for the ovation to greet them.

As the marshal's horse comes to a halt. The occupants of the house emerge with an eruption of cheer and welcome. Applause, whistles, and laughter fill the veranda at the front door.

Jeremiah is delighted with the assortment of young women to be entertained.

The serving tables have been loaded with the cuisine prepared for the night. Although food items are covered with linen, the aromas of cooling pies and warm meats permeate the air.

Mara Nar does not understand the significance of the salutations.

Marshal Legs is content to be with Ali. However he is little more perceptive than his native companion for the reason of the ready welcome.

"Welcome home." Shouts the waiting throng.

Little Owl immediately recognizes her fellow tribesman

and relation, Mara Nar. She is anxious for the meaning of his presence and moves to stand behind Layla.

The native notices Little Owl but his gaze fixes on the attractive woman with dark hair.

The virile muscular form of the native immediately moves Layla. Her attention to his presence will not abate. His dark eyes, and striking features are unlike any man she has ever seen.

The crowd of animals stabled about the Hideaway excites the marshal's horse.

"Looks like we have found the right place." The marshal announces. "This here is Jeremiah Cloug. He'll be staying for a few days. Next to him is the ambassador from Chief Many Horns of the Nez Perce. Mara Nar is also our guest."

"Jeremiah we meet again!" Ali greets. "Let me introduce you to the place."

The marshal calls Mara Nar to his side.

They move toward Layla.

Little Owl peeks from behind her friend.

Layla is thrilled by the men's approach. "Hello marshal... nice house."

"Layla, Mara Nar needs to speak with Little Owl."

The native warrior is without ceremony.

He pushes the ring he carries toward the young native girl. "It is from your grandmother who says to Little Owl, return to your village."

Eagerly the ring is taken.

Little Owl holds the ring close to her heart.

Her eyes water but tears are not permitted.

The native child looks to Layla.

Layla has learned many words of the native language from Little Owl

"Your family wants to see you. They wish to know that you are well." Layla advises.

"Many Horns ask that we return together." Mara Nar adds.

Little Owl is uncertain. She wants to see her village and morn the dead of her family. She fears punishment."

"I bring belongings of those who slew your parents. We shall hold counsel on their spirits and judge them so our ancestors will be pleased. It is good that you participate and give testimony to the great counsel." Mara Nar explains.

"My honor pledges me to the women of the homesteaders who saved me. I must learn to hear and make words from paper." The girl informs Mara Nar.

"Many Horns will hear your tale and keep the honor of our nation. Little Owl must speak before the counsel." The warrior replies.

"I'm sure that you may return." Layla states. She turns to look to the marshal.

"Many Horns is most honorable." The marshal cannot interfere with the law of the Nez Perce nation.

"It is best that this woman comes to speak with Many Horns." Mara Nar points to Layla.

Layla takes the invitation from the attractive warrior as personal. "How long will I be at your village?"

The marshal interrupts. "These affairs can be spread over many days even several weeks. Mara Nar must be your escort for all of this time. He will see to your needs, comfort, and safety. He represents their chief Many Horns. You will be well treated and most secure under his watch until you are returned."

"Little Owl, with Layla there to speak, the chief may well favor your return." The marshal knows the chief will be offended if the child is not returned.

Layla is a daring soul.

She is most curious to see the home of Little Owl.

The posing length of companionship of the stirring Mara Nar is irresistible. "Let us speak more on this tomorrow."

The lady holds the child's hand.

She looks into the warrior's dark eyes.

She has no fear of this man. "Partake of our hospitality. Eat! Enjoy our festivities. Many Horns may wish to hear your words on the things you shall see here."

"It is good to have Mara Nar as our guest. Let some time be

shared." The marshal wishes to have Mara Nar available. "Let Layla have time to consider your words."

"It is good!" Mara Nar will be patient.

"Take this warrior to his diner Layla and see that he is honored as our guest." The marshal needs to speak with Ali.

Ali has been watching the marshal.

She is nervous.

She wants this night to be special for him as well.

"Woody!" She beams with love as she nears. "Everyone is hungry. We have all been waiting for your return."

"Best the folks eat then. Right off!" The marshal agrees. "We need to have words!"

Ali is thrilled.

The guests commence dining.

All will sit out on the porch.

The men are first to take food.

Layla sees to Mara Nar's plate. She will serve him until his hunger is at an end.

Evelyn gathers heavy portions and takes a plate to Seth.

Ali prepares a plate of supper for the marshal.

Little Owl and the Freeman boys will be served next.

Ali will eat with the women while they watch over the needs of the men and the children.

The marshal moves at the conclusion of his meal into the fresh air.

He lights a small cigar.

Ali watches.

She quits her plate and joins him. "How do you find the house?"

"It's remarkable. How did you manage this transformation in half a day?"

"With lots of help. Wait till I get started. You have no idea what possibilities there are here." She is everlastingly content in his presence.

The marshal eyes fill with her lovely vision. "There lots of words needs be said to you. I don't have the gift to make them so my true feelings come out right."

He is embarrassed by his inadequacy before her. "Never could get out fine talk."

Ali sees the words that he needs to speak in the intention of his soul.

Her heart pounds just as if he had said everything she wanted to hear. "We have forever to share our feelings."

"You make me a new man...a new person." He pauses to let his thoughts clear.

These are the precise words for which she has prayed.

"I just don't know what to do with the old Wooden Legs. I just don't know how to change." He suffers.

Ali's heart hungrily embraces his pain. "Oh! Don't! You are perfect now. We'll change together. You and I together now! That' all we need! Not one tiny bit more."

Tears of joy flow, as her love grows greater.

"You mean that all I have to do is stay with you?"

"Yes! Yes! I'll take care of everything. Leave us to me!" Her arms spread out in emphasis.

"I haven't depended on anyone for a long time Ali."

"It's easy. All you have to do is listen to me!"

"What bout marshaling? It's all I know!"

"Do you know how to pray? To ask for help?"

"Course I do!"

"Well?"

"Okay! I'll pray on it but I got marshal duties coming right at us!"

Ali is confused in the switch of subjects from love to crime.

The marshal reads her thoughts.

"There's a big poker game with huge sums of money going to start any day here at this road house." He pauses.

"Yes that little dandy...I mean little gambler who arrived this morning."

"Well some mean desperados are coming to rob Eighty Eight's place".

"Are you going to kill them?"

"Yes if they're coming to kill people here. I have to."

This marshaling business is one of the things that must change by Ali's view of their future.

"Husbands and fathers just don't kill people as a way of making a living" She is compelled to answer.

"You can kill bad men for now but only if necessary. No riding away across the whole United States after anybody. Aren't there other marshals? Let some of them earn their keep for a change."

More contemplation on Woody's needs in becoming a husband. "I'm going to get you some suitable cloths."

"I'm used to these fancy duds now!" The marshal brushes his lapels.

"The hat and coat are acceptable. That silk shirt and those pearl inlaid boots...a woman could never feel like a spouse with a man dressed in this way!"

The marshal is stunned.

Jeremiah has a chance to speak with Michele.

It's a privilege to meet a young pretty gal like yourself. Glad to see the territory grow."

"Well Mr. Cloug, I'm here for a visit but I expect to be moving out to the far west soon. You're the first chicken king I ever met." Michele enjoys the jest.

The old man laughs at his new title. "Chicken king for sure! You know how much money a man can earn from a good year selling live chickens?"

Michele is inspired at the possibility of large commerce. "No idea."

"My two sons are both wealthy even if they never worked another day in their lives. I own the largest commerce building in Fargo. The rent from that one piece of property makes me richer than most folks in these parts." The old man spits to the outside side in emphasis.

"Why all the chickens? Why not enjoy your money?" Michele is bewildered.

"I love them damnable birds. They keep me young. Old men have no need for lots of money. Heck young folks need to hold one another more than holding big sums. There be no life inside a cash box."

Michele has never known a truly wealthy person. "How does one get rich like you?"

The old man laughs at the notion. "Getting rich just happened. Always made money on my work. It came natural like. Trick is not to spend it like a fool that gambles."

"How did you begin to save?" Michele is now totally captivated.

"When I made four pennies, I'd keep my costs at three pennies and put one penny away. Then when I had enough pennies saved I'd invest so I'd earn five pennies. The pennies add faster than you now."

"You liked saving?"

"A man can save just about anything he wants but no man can save time. The richest men aren't the ones that have the most money. The richest men are the ones that are satisfied with what they have."

"Liking business is no sin!" Michel defends her interest in money.

"As long as you like your family, friends and neighbors more than making money. When money comes first then it's a terrible sin." Jeremiah warns. "Remember raising a family is the most important business!"

"Well I'd like t see your business in Fargo before I go." Michele asks.

"There are lots to see. Lot's of young men in Fargo... bankers, lawyers, accountants. There are not as many women of marrying age as men up there now a days."

"Take me up for a visit?" Michel's interest heightens.

"Next load of chickens you'll be invited. Get my boys to keep a room at the main hotel. Got inside plumbing there and everything. We'll show you the town proper like. You'll get to meet plenty of folks." The old man is delighted for her company.

The marshal finds Mara Nar.

In sign language he asks the warrior to keep near the Hideaway this night and keep close watch.

"Some armed settlers are coming into the camp. There is danger soon. The women and Little Owl must be watched. I shall keep watch at the approach to the road house." The marshal makes a sign of the dagger next to his heart.

Mara Nar reads the threat as close enough to be a hand's length away. The warrior disappears into the trees.

"Where has he gone?" Layla is anxious for the return of the stunning warrior.

"He will be near your doors and windows all night to keep guard."

"Oh! You mean he'll see inside?" Layla's face flushes.

"Occasionally, if he needs."

The marshal senses her feminine worry. "There are some strangers heading this way. All need to be concerned."

"Were will you be?" Michele is alarmed.

"I'm going to the road house. Tell Ali I'll return before dawn. Keep them Freeman boys here."

It is quite dark when the marshal steps into the road house.

Mr. Freeman immediately greets him.

"Most of the visitors are here with the late stage from Fargo. The game will begin tomorrow for sure." He informs.

"I want you to get your wife and children over to Ali's tomorrow at first light!"

The owner is concerned. "It there danger?"

"Plenty! Is there a place close by where you can hide all your horses for a few days?"

"There's a small cattle pen down behind the place. It's well out of sight. Hasn't been used since I bought the place. Why?" Freeman worries.

"I don't want any one stealing fresh horses. I want all your doors and windows barred form the inside when not is use!" Orders the marshal.

"Haven't had needs for such security here marshal."

"You do now! At least till all them gamblers depart."

"Mary won't leave the kitchen without help...I can't cook none."

"I'll get Jeremiah Cloug to come over and cook chickens" The marshal lightens the moment.

"The humor is not shared by the owner. I hate to carry a gun around marshal. Makes me feel like a jail keeper."

"There been unusual strangers around the road house lately?"

"There always a lone rider what don't seem to belong nowheres what stops for a coffee or such."

"When do you lock up tight for the night?"

"Right after the night stage."

"Is Mr. Leford about?" Inquires the marshal.

"He be near the bar! That little man sure can drink whiskey!"

The small gambler sits at a table.

A half empty bottle of whiskey sits before him.

A large cigar fumes from his hand. "Good evening marshal... game of cards?"

"Never gamble J. B. Weakens a man's resolve...one starts to think about luck too much and ignores ability." The marshal sits.

"Luck is all a small fellow like me has to help win. It's everything to a gambler."

"Game starts soon does it?" The marshal asks.

"Marshal tomorrow night you'll see the biggest pot of cash on one table ever in your life." The small man sips a large glass of whiskey.

"That stuff part of your game?" The marshal points to the whiskey bottle.

"My nerves! They get mighty raw before the cards are dealt out. Whiskey don't bother me none. Settles me. I won't touch the stuff once the game starts."

"Any thing you do for superstition to help when the game is on?"

"Well since you are my friend I don't mind telling you Woody. Every hand I pick up I pretend, I'm going to play a hand of Old Maid with my mother. She was the best at hiding the loosing card I ever knew. As long as I think I have a chance to fool ma I usually win at poker."

"You mean that you're trying to win at Old Maid at the poker table?" The marshal is deflated.

"Yep! Seems there should be more to it. Confidence is all you need and a couple of the right cards. Fools think they can out smart ever one. The game is basically making illusions like in Old Maid."

Chapter 8

A Guest House

The Hideaway has grown into the local guest house.

Mary Freeman and all her children have taken refuge with Ali.

Jeremiah indeed provides his assistance at preparation for the meals to be served at the road house.

The marshal has seen to the fortification of the public house. All auxiliary access has been closed and locked.

Those who enter will do so only by the main entrance.

Obstructions to the field of fire in the front of Eight Eight's establishment have been removed.

The marshal takes a seat at the front of the entrance to the road house.

It is midday.

He props up his feet and lights a cigar.

There will be little work required until dark.

"Well marshal all the preparations are done. We are ready for the poker game to night. The last member of the players should be here anytime. Anything else you wish from me?" Bill Freeman asks.

"What's the weather to be like tonight?"

"No rain in sight, no winds. The sky will be mostly clear." The owner responds.

"The moon?"

"Won't be full for another couple of days."

"Well then Mr. Freeman those desperados will have light enough to travel easy like in the night. They'll be here long before midnight...before you lock up...before the night stage arrives."

"That be after dinner is served."

"Right after the game is started, I expect!" The marshal leans back upon in his chair to rest. "When the trouble starts you go to ground. Don't wait, just fall to the floor. After the robbers leave get to the front door and bolt it tight from within! I don't want any of them getting back inside."

"Sounds easy enough." The large fellow has lost his jovial mood.

"Where will you set the game?"

"We usually play near the liquor cabinet in the dining room."

"Lock the door to the kitchen. The only admittance to that game area is to be from the front door."

"Should I have my shot gun available in there?" Asks the owner.

"Not unless you want to get your self killed. I want no weapons. No one is to be armed. Isn't that the normal rule?" The marshal wonders.

"Yes. Card playing brings hot tempers."

"Then everything goes on as normal Just like you and your local friends at your weekly poker game." The marshal instructs.

"Well then we wait!" The owner replies.

"One last item, I want a list of the names of all the poker players."

"Mr. Autry gave over one when he was here." The owner recalls.

Ali has looked toward the direction of road house all day hoping to catch a glimpse of the marshal.

"You'll have to go over there yourself if you want to be with the marshal." Mary Freeman comments.

"When that man gets onto a crime he losses interest in everything else...everybody else." Ali sighs.

"These are important days for you Ali. Your man has a job to do. He's saving lives tonight."

"You worried about your husband Mary?"

"Yes. Not so much now the marshal is there. Otherwise I couldn't leave him alone to face the danger that's coming." Mary tells.

"I'm worried about all the folks there." Ali agrees.

"Come on Ali the boys are going up and clear the loft. We'll find out what stuff has been left up there."

The diversion is welcomed.

The house needs much attention.

There is plenty of time till dark.

"Did the people who gave up this place build it or did they buy it?" Ali questions.

"The place was left empty when they came through. They just occupied the house and staked out a mess of ground for homesteading. The whole valley clear to the mountains behind are yours now that you live here."

"Any idea who the owner was before them?"

"The place was lived in by an odd couple for years. They were from Europe somewhere. Both had passed on before I arrived. Bill wouldn't remember such details."

The two older boys have climbed above to rummage about the loft.

Soon a long slender chest made of rough oak planks is uncovered.

It is heavy.

Seth Adams assists in lowering it onto floor in the main room.

The women quickly wipe the accumulated layer of dust off the container.

"There's some kind of family crest here." Evelyn uncovers.

"Fancy enough design. Seems like a mighty impressive coat of arms." Ali notes.

"There is an emblem of a castle, crossed swords, and sailing ship inside the outline of a shield." Observes Michele.

"The whole thing is held by wooden dowels. Not an iron nail anywhere." Seth notices. "Must be mighty old."

Maybe we shouldn't disturb it." Worries Layla. "It could hold one of those ancient curses."

"Someone's has brought it a long way. If there was curse, can't imagine anyone wanting to keep it way out here." Mary remarks.

"Could be a body in there?" Michele fears.

'There's a small cross in the crest. This belonged to Christian folks. We bury our dead." Analyzes Ali.

"Must be valuable. It's heavy and old enough." Seth struggles to move the box into better light.

The children crowd about the adults.

They stand on chairs to peek over their elders.

"It has to be opened. I just can't have the thing about the place on its own." Ali decides.

"Can't promise that I can reseal this chest once it has been pried open." Seth scratches his head at the unusual task.

Mary agrees. "Open it.

"Get ride of it." Calls Layla.

"Open it then get ride of it." Echoes Michele.

"Open it, open it." Repeat the children.

"I'll get me a pry bar and have the top off it in a jiffy." Seth goes to his wagon.

Mary organizes her children to one side.

They are kept at a safe distance to view the ensuing effort to open the box

Seth returns and begins to work off the lid to the chest.

The women move to the other side to wait and watch the cover as it comes off the trunk.

Loud squeaks and groans emanate from the separating wooden members.

"I think this here lid has never been off since after it was put in place." Seth twists and struggles.

"Never been opened?" The women repeat together.

"I may have to damage the thing!" More intense work is needed from Seth.

"Don't fret about that. Do you want some help from the road house?" Ali comforts.

With one gigantic groan from the lumber the lid pops off.

All eyes freeze to watch Seth's hands lift away linens soaked with oil.

"Oh! My!" The man breathes. "Oh! Oh! My!"

"What is it?" Barks Evelyn.

"It's metal, heavy metal." Seth adds, as he pulls from the chest a shiny helmet wrapped in a soaked cloth.

All gasp at the sight of the trophy Seth holds above his head.

"What is it?" Ask the children.

"Quiet Please!" Demand the women together.

All inspect the object.

"It's some kind of head wear." Ali gasps.

Seth puts the object down over his head.

His face disappears behind a metal mask with slits for eyes to see and mouth to speak. His head is fiercely decorated in a protective iron head covering.

Ornately designed and engraved, the metal headdress astonishes all who look on.

The object is removed and handed to Mary.

Mary passes the helmet to Ali.

"I've never seen anything like it." Layla comments as she inspects the heavy object.

"I have in a museum." Decides Michele. She places the thing on the table just behind for the children to touch.

The business of the road houses resumes as ordinary.

The daily chores compel normalcy.

The owner returns to the marshal who yet occupies a chair at the entrance. "Here's the list of invitees given to me."

Lucy Patterson
William McElroy
R D Weir
Rainer Johnsen
J B Ledford
Averill Alderdyce
Clive Ferguson

The marshal reads over the note handed to him. "Who's not yet arrived?"

"Rainer Johnsen is not yet here maybe delayed."

"I believe I'll ask you to send Lucy Patterson out here for a talk. If'n you please!"

"Right away marshal." The owner disappears into his establishment.

In moments an attractive middle aged lady emerges.

She is elegantly dressed.

Her manners are refined.

The marshal rises to greet the woman. "U S Marshal Legs, mam." He invites her to take a seat.

"Mrs. Patterson here! You wish to speak with me?" The lady greets.

"There's a high stakes poker game here tonight?"

"It's supposed to be kept a secret. Yes there is certainly a grand game of chance." She is undisturbed.

"You were invited?"

"Yes, I get several such invitations a year. However, I choose just one in which to participate."

"Who invited you?"

"A Mr. Autry."

"You know this man?"

"No! I have never met the man. Most such invitations are made by mail. I received a letter from Mr. Autry."

"Why did you choose this particular invitation?"

"Marshal I wanted to see this part of the country, to play a different group of gamblers...a kind of vacation if you will."

"It's a bit of a lark. Isn't it?"

"Yes! Mr. Autry provided adequate references. Apparently he is known in high stakes circles."

"Do you expect to see Mr. Autry here?"

"Not necessarily. He will receive a handsome commission from the winner. Protocol is to leave this sum at the establishment unless collected in person."

The marshal muses.

"You look like a gambler! Are you entering the game tonight?" The woman finds the marshal's eyes most catching. Her eyes enjoy the man's fancy boots.

"I'm afraid I don't have near the table stakes required." The marshal is delighted by the invitation. "Love to see how the big gamblers handle their cards."

"Just like anybody else. It's all about luck! If one draws the right cards one can't lose." She relaxes. "You are a very attractive man marshal I can finance your stakes if you like."

"That's a lot of money. What about your stakes?" The marshal grows uncomfortable with the aggressive beauty.

"I have plenty of money...plenty!" She replies with ease.

"How are you transporting all that wealth?"

"In my hat boxes! No man ever looks inside one of those." Again this is said in a most nonchalant manner.

"You're not sponsored by some cartel?"

The woman laughs vigorously. "My dear marshal I am a cartel. I own numerous hotels all along the California coast."

"You just came out from California?" The marshal is astounded.

"Why not?"

"You enjoy poker that much?"

"Not at all. I enjoy showing those bilious bastards that a mere woman is capable of taking their money."

"You're not a compulsive gambler?'

"I learned to play card games with my husband when he became ill. He was bound to his bed and unable to venture out of our home." She observes the marshal. "I was a loving wife all the days we were married. He just happened to be very wealthy."

"Where you happy...married I mean?"

The woman understands the marshal's interest. "I married for money! My husband had enormous wealth. I was very happily married to Carl. People marry for many reasons, some for companionship, some for security, some to have children, and some for just love. If your marriage works then both are happy. I have no guilt!"

"No children then?"

"No! Just step children who hate me. I won't deny them their inheritance but I don't intend to save it either."

"I'll take you upon that offer to be my sponsor. Share my profits?" He accepts her financial backing.

The lady eyes the marshal devouringly. "It will be a pleasure."

❧

Seth searches the chest.

A large section of formed metal is recovered from it storage.

He holds it up for all to see.

"Breast plate!" Announces Michele. "Saw it in the museum as well."

"Try it on!" Mary instructs. "Let the kids see how it looks."

The straps are tried and the chest of Seth is covered in protective metal that is lavishly engraved.

"That's the same crescent on the front of the body plate as is on the box." Layla recognizes.

"Put the helmet on as well?" Evelyn asks.

Seth again wears the headgear.

He is transformed into a medieval knight.

The children are mesmerized by his fierce look.

Michele peeks inside the box.

"Well! How did you miss this Sir Seth?" She states .The older Freeman boy is asked to pull out of the chest a large board blade.

"This sword is a tall as I am. "The muffled words ring from underneath his metal mask.

All are now frightened by the deadly image presented.

"Who would own such gruesome items?" Layla is repulsed.

"Family heirlooms...valued for their heritage...perhaps quite precious?" Mary concludes.

"Anything else in side the box?" Evelyn asks as her hands search about the bottom inside the chest.

"Wait! There's more." She produces a small plaque.

She reads. "Presented to the Royal Knight of Wigan for out standing service to His Royal Majesty Henry, King of England."

The room is silent.

One lady looks to the other.

The children attend their mother's amazed countenance.

Ali receives the award.

It's has the same family crest. "The High Lord of Wigan! What else could this crest mean?"

"It means those folks that lived here where royalty...English Royalty!" Mary stutters.

"Hold on! There seems to be a small box within the chest?" Calls one of the Freeman Boys.

Mary is directed into one corner of the chest.

A small wooden container hides under the last of the rags. Mary lifts the object. It is the size of a shoebox.

The lid opens easily.

Held in velvet lining is a pair of golden goblets.

Mary presents the box to Ali for inspection.

Everyone's attention is on the items, which are now lifted by Ali.

Two identical chalices of the purest gold emblazoned with the royal seal of King Henry sparkle and gleam in the dim light.

Elaborately engraved, and studded with small jewels, the pair of noble cups illuminates the faces of the mesmerized crowd.

"You're rich!" Seth babbles through his iron mask.

Moments pass in awe.

Ali awakens slightly from her awe. "Together we a found this chest. Together we discovered the contents. We have acquired this wealth together. The Freemans, the Adams, Layla, Michele, Little Owl, and my family will share all."

The room is suddenly interrupted by the arrival of Mr. Freeman. "Sorry to interrupt but the lady at the road house wants tea to be served for her and the marshal."

Mary is not yet recovered from her dreams of the royal court of early England. "What lady? Tea?"

"There is a beautiful rich lady from San Francisco who has come to gamble. She has been talking to the marshal for a long time. She wants to serve tea to him." The owner insists.

"Beautiful? Rich? My marshal?" Ali responds.

Mr. Freeman nods his head affirmatively.

The marshal and the affluent lady gambler share much banter.

There is much for the marshal to learn of the far west.

There is much for the madam to understand of the wilder west.

"You not a feared of being robbed?" The marshal asks.

"Gambling is thievery! I steal your money if I win, or you steal mine if I don't." The lady retorts. "Call me Lucy."

"Fine Lucy! There be some mean men after that cash in your poker game!"

"There are mean men everywhere after everything. I know men and how to handle them...mean or otherwise."

"I have to protect you...it's my duty." The marshal asserts.

"There's much more to protection than a hand gun marshal." The comely woman insinuates.

"Call me Woody!" The aggressive nature of the Mrs. Patterson keeps the marshal uncomfortable.

"Well now that we are friends, I think you should come to my room before dinner. We can discuss the poker game and what may happen when it's all over and done."

At this instant, Mr. Freeman arrives to place a small serving tray near Mrs. Patterson.

Ali Bennet carries the pot of tea and immediately follows him.

The wealthy woman ignores the servants. Her attention does not abandon the marshal.

The marshal is shaken by the appearance of Ali.

Ali does not note the surprise of the marshal.

She does note his sense of guilt.

"Let me pour you tea while you consider my request for you to attend me in my chamber." Lucy busies with the teacups.

Ali's stare questions the marshal.

The marshal is unable to respond.

He seals his lips.

His glance to Ali is for understanding.

"Cream? Sugar?"

"Just plain mam...Lucy" The marshal answers.

Ali is uncomfortable with the marshal's familiarity the female gambler.

"Lucy this here is Ali...our school teacher" He introduces.

"Oh how nice!" The woman is polite but uninterested. "Earning some extra income?"

"I own the guest house!" Ali responds coldly. "I'm helping the Freeman's because they're so busy."

"You are a friend of Woody?" Lucy asks.

"Oh my yes! We thought the marshal was busy shooting robbers all day!"

"I'm in his protection...gratefully." Lucy's eyes smile at the marshal.

"Looks like the marshal is grateful as well!" Ali's glances harshly as she steps away.

"Pretty thing! She isn't married is she?" Lucy asks the marshal.

"Not as yet! She and her companions are just settling in." The marshal is reluctant.

"Let's enjoy our tea then I have to freshen. We will talk more at dinner.

Later the marshal walks Ali back to the Hideaway.

Ali is silent.

She is hurt by the marshal's enjoyment of that woman's attention.

"Ali are you angry for some reason with me?"

"I saw you flirting with that hussy!"

"She's an interesting woman...very rich!"

"Interesting? Is she the only interest you can find here?" Ali is wounded.

"No it's just she has a great wealth."

"Money! Is that what interests you in a woman?"

"I didn't mean that! I am interested in how she came to be rich and how she handles all that money." The marshal tries." She just happens to be a woman."

"So you'd smile like that at a rich man?"

"Didn't mean anything...I just was enjoying her way of

talking and the unusual things that happened to folks what are rich."

"How do you find all that time for entertainment when you marshaling after desperados?"

"Well I asked her to answer questions on the game. The conversation just got carried away is all." He is apologetic.

"Where you just going to converse in her room later?"

"That's her way. I'm going to get in that game tonight. That lady is advancing me the sums to enter."

Ali calms. "And what do you have to give her in return?"

"A share of my winnings if they be any. These gamblers are out of my league. If I can buy some cards then I'll be inside and the robbers won't know I'm marshaling. Beside Lucy was jealous of your looks."

Ali blushes at the marshal's observation. "Did she say so?"

Her hands tend loose strains of her hair. "I see you got to first names with a strange woman soon enough."

"Ali that woman knows she faces being shot tonight but she has the courage not to let some evil men change her way of living. I respect her strength. She deserves to be treated as a friend."

Ali is embarrassed.

"Marshaling has its moments of danger...it has its light frilly moments as well. If that woman weren't part of the poker game then I won't give her a moment's notice. It's only you that consumes my private time...and my horse." He searches her face for softness to return.

His last words heal.

She smiles. "I forgive you!"

It seems that everything has returned to the correct now. The marshal is not sure what all the fuss was about but he's grateful. "Thank you!"

"I'd ask you to stay!" Ali comments as they near the guest house. "But you've had tea already! "

The marshal misses the remnant of vinegar in Ali's disposition. "I have more gamblers to question before dusk. I'll pass by a bit later."

"Good...I have something to show you that I'll bet that floozy doesn't own.... There really is no good reason to visit her room."

❧

Upon returning to the road house the marshal finds two horses just arrived and tied at the front.

Bill Freeman waits at the entrance.

"Two riders inside. I don't like their looks marshal." The owner greets.

The horses are in poor condition.

Their saddle gear is worn and shabby.

These are the animals of vagrants.

The body temperature of the pair of horses is not hot. They haven't been ridden fast or long.

Inside the marshal finds a pair of untidy looking men.

They are unshaven.

The marshal judges them as unskilled with side arms.

The one is of a thicker build and shorter than the second.

The taller man does most of the talking.

"Mind If I join you? Let me buy you both some whiskey." The marshal asks as he takes a seat with the pair.

"You a gambler?" Inquires the shorter man.

The marshal finds the eyes of the two dreary and lifeless.

He is sure they are dangerous.

"Like to ask a couple of questions?" Poses the marshal.

"Whiskey is welcomed. We don't know much to be answering no questions." Answers the taller rider.

"You boys just arrived?"

"Yes." They both respond.

"Come in from the north did ya?"

"Yes, came in directly from Fargo." The taller man answers quickly.

The whiskey arrives.

"You a gambler?" The taller man requests.

"I'll be a playing cards here tonight." Answers the marshal.

"You be inviting us to a hand of poker?" The taller man responds.

As the two visitors sip their whiskey, the marshal has quietly withdrawn one of his hand guns.

"Just what do you want from us?" The spokesman is annoyed.

The marshal's right hand lifts onto the table.

His hand is filled with his six shooter.

Both men are stunned at the presence of his weapon.

"I want to look at your boots." Smiles the marshal.

He raises the gun toward the pair.

"Boys place both of your hands flat on the table. Easy like! Spread all them fingers apart. Don't let any one of them flicker." Orders the marshal.

The pair slowly obeys the command.

"We don't have no money." The dumb one answers.

"Stick them legs out from under the table so's I can see the bottom of your boots."

The legs of the pair slide from beneath the table.

The marshal makes a thorough inspection.

"Now just what do you boys know of poisoning horses?"

"We didn't kill that stage horse!" Blurts the stocky one.

The taller one nudges him to be silent.

Immediately the marshal places the barrel of his gun onto the forehead of the tall drifter.

"Close your mouth and close your eyes!" Instructs the marshal to the leader.

The duller rider takes fright.

He is uncertain.

He is without direction.

"How did you poison that horse?" The tone of the marshal is final.

The shorter man looks to his companion.

There is no advice to be had.

"We gathered some fresh sweet grass. Mix in some sap with hot peppers. Then watered the horse with some poison mixed in."

The marshal is livid with rage. "Where I come from folks get hung for killing horses out of meanness."

"You two fellars get on your horses and ride west. Get yourself work with the railroad. Stay out of trouble."

With a thump the marshal pounds the edge of his gun on the shooting hand of the taller stranger breaking bones.

The rider winces in pain.

"If I hear of a pair of riders causing trouble, or a man with sore gun hand doing bad...I'm coming to get you two. I'll ride day and night. I' ride you both into the earth."

The pair is escorted out of the road house.

As they depart the marshal hears the shorter rider yell.

"You go get him by yourself. I'm going to work for the railroad. That fellar was fixing to kill us! You're going to get both of us dead!"

Inside the guest house the work continues in preparation of family living.

Mary has sent her children outside to play. Little Owl joins them.

Cleaning resumes with much intensity.

The medieval armor and crescent trophies are set upon a table for all to inspect and touch. Ownership is established as communal.

"I can't understand why anyone would abandon a treasure." Layla puzzles.

"Had to be left by no other choice. I don't intend to leave it idle in the loft!" Ali responds.

Mary is measuring the dimensions of the main room. "18 paces by 22 paces. It's large! What do you intend to do with all this space?"

"I'm not sure. How did you set your nursery?" Ali asks.

"Next to our bed...until the child was old enough to crawl out of the crib. Then we'd move the baby in another room with the other children."

"The other rooms here are large enough for our bed and a crib?" Ali responds.

"You could put your bed in that corner of this main room. There is still plenty of space." Michele suggests.

The options for the future needs of family dispel all of Ali's irritation with the marshal's flirtation.

During this instant, Jeremiah Cloug returns from cooking duties at the road house.

He enters the main room.

The knightly treasures capture his attention.

"These items are worth a small fortune!" He comments.

"Found a chest full of that stuff in the loft." Mary Freeman answers.

"We hope to sell these items." Ali adds.

"Write a letter to some museums in Chicago and New York. Include sketches, especially of the crescents and designs of the engravings." The chicken king advises.

"I can make those." Layla offers.

The old rancher inspects the plaque with the royal name. "Do you realize this tablet contains the mark of the royal seal? It alone could be priceless."

"Any idea of what some of these things can be worth?" Ali asks.

"It's worth more if it is undamaged! May be ten times that for pieces what be bent or scratched." Jeremiah offers.

The ladies are surprised and alarmed.

"The children will play with this stuff sooner than later." Mary states. "Best lock it away.

"Keep the chest and everything in it intact as well. Antiques like old wooden crates could be valuable as well." Cloug advises.

Hurriedly the iron and gold items are returned carefully into the original containers.

"Best to have Seth lift it back into the loft then seal the access way to keep everyone out." Evelyn warns.

Little Owl runs into the room excitedly.

She signs to Laya. "We found a hidden lodge under the ground outside."

The children scurrying about chasing and hiding from one another have found a cellar dug into a bank of earth.

The ladies, Jeremiah, and Seth arrive for inspection.

"It's an unused storage basement." Seth believes.

"Why would it have the entrance covered with shrubs?" Michele ponders.

"It's the original homestead. Folks lived here while they built up their home above ground." Cloug asserts.

"Why did they hide it?" Ali continues debate.

"Back a good while ago; they used this underground place as a hideout whenever they were fearful of being attacked." Jeremiah recalls.

"Is there anything stored inside?" Layla hopes for more treasure.

The sunlight passes into the interior of the cellar. Parts illuminated show the clutter of accumulated junk and discarded items.

"This place has been used to store items unwanted and unneeded." Michele blurts.

"Best to clean it out! It'll make a fine chicken house. Could easily stack a hundred birds in there safe and sound. Be happy to donate to the marshal his pick of fowl from my place to start up a hen house." Offers Jeremiah.

"Well! Thanks, however this is a job for another day."

"Shoot Ali. I can clean all the junk out in no time and we can burn it." Seth wishes.

"My boys will help. They need to use some of their energy up during chores." Mary adds.

"Never know what good can be made of this cellar." Michele advises.

"Looks like it could be made into a big wine cellar!" Evelyn comments.

"We would like to sell more wine at the road houses." Mary muses. "All you need is some grape harbors and a few barrels.

"Mary, we could make crafts to sell as well as bottled

wine, and maybe some furniture. We could store items here in the cellar. All we need is a small space at the road house." Ali asserts.

"Some extra poultry, dairy, beef could be sold as well." Mary suggests.

"The marshal can ranch horses. He can ride all day in the back meadow. Even teach his sons the business of horsemanship." Evelyn contributes.

"It's perfect!" Ali agrees.

R D Weir is a huge man.

It is not possible for him to mount let alone sit upon a horseback. He moves with great effort.

He must travel with his own personalized chair. Ordinary seats do hold his enormous waist.

"Marshal? Mr. Freeman told me to expect you." R D Weir greets from his repose.

"Mr. Weir, I'm expecting that some men will enter the road house tonight to rob all you gamblers."

"Been robbed before marshal. Glad you are here."

"How did you get an invite to this here game?"

"Letter! Actually a note to one of my brothers, Dale makes all my gambling arrangements."

"You have no knowledge of the person who is responsible for this poker game to night?"

"No sir!"

"You carrying cash on you person?"

"Yes of course. No one pays attention to what a big man is carrying. Always carry my money in a black satchel."

"Know the folks what come here to play?"

"Actually I've played with some of them one time or another. Most are new. It'll be a great game." The large man eyes shine.

"Your brothers provide you all financial backing?"

"My family is from Milwaukee. We brew a great deal of

beer. I don't need to work. My share of the business pays from my habits. My brothers make the needed arrangements through our corporate offices."

"You gamble a lot, Mr. Weir?"

"Call me R D. I gamble every chance I get...mostly cards. Own a couple of race horses."

"You be a winner?"

"Not at all. I'm lucky if I break even, but I gladly pay the price for the entertainment."

"You're not afeared of possible gun play?"

"No one shoots a fat man marshal...I pose no threat."

"With all the money you possess isn't gambling just giving it away?"

"I'm famous marshal. People want me from all over the world. I gamble in Europe, Mexico and South America. Royalty, politicians, criminals, famous names of the world have set down with me intimately over a hand of cards."

"Price be no object?"

"Marshal, I've played a hand of poker for prizes that were worth over a million dollars. Those sums remove all pretenses from folks. It comes down to one mind against another, one's own character against another. I learn about the other player deeper and truer than their mother or wife."

"You could write a book...about them famous folks?"

"Yes but I'd never be asked to another major poker game again. What happens here to night stays here. That's the first rule!"

"You've seen gunplay at some of these games?"

"It happens marshal. Most games like this are held without outsiders ever being aware. There's more danger that someone gets too depressed form losing and might try to kill themselves."

"You've known a man to shoot himself after a game?'

"Yes! If we suspect a player has gone over board in losing, then we'll return most of his cash. This is why the players are supposed to be screened. Those persons playing to night can all afford the sums they may lose."

"You mind if I sit in the game for a spell tonight?"

"Delighted! Happy to ante up your table stakes marshal."

"You want to get into a law man's mind?"

"Never played poker with a famous marshal. It would be pure fascination!" The mound of a man laughs freely.

"Call me Woody. Think I have chance to win a hand tonight?"

"Could...if the sums don't bother you. Most men never see that amount of cash. Changes a man Woody. Doubts and fears emerge that most never experience. It's more paralyzing than having someone aiming a gun in your direction."

This notion excites the marshal. "I'm not addicted to the game. Play it occasionally."

"In that case Woody, you'll lose!"

"Still want to back me R D!"

"Oh yes!"

"I intend to play until the night coach passes then the game will be safe!"

It is late in the afternoon.

"I made a mess of boiled cabbage, baked potatoes, and ham for the guests at the road house." Jeremiah reports to Mary Freeman.

"There's plenty of cake and such left there for them gamblers to have eats later." Mary adds. "I'm grateful to you, Jeremiah for helping out during this crisis."

"The marshal feels all will be safe come daylight." The old man assures. "He wants everyone inside the guest house and all the doors and windows locked before dark. No one is to go in or out until morning."

"What about that warrior, Mara Nar?"

"That native is to stay and watch Little Owl here. Them's the marshal's words" Jeremiah responds. "Oh! Seth, Mara Nar, and I have to gather all the horses about the guest house and hide them out of sight."

The men depart on their final mission.

The ladies continue unabated on their preparations for the night.

"The men will watch from the main room tonight. The children and little Owl will take the larger side room. All the ladies will keep to the smaller room." Ali directs.

"Let the boys get the fire in the main room going. Then after dinner the children can make popcorn." Mary suggests.

"While the boys are popping corn I'll help the girls pull taffy!" Evelyn offers.

"Let's have stories before bed?" Michele pipes.

"We can sing some sweet songs?" Layla hopes.

'"Lets do some lullabies after stories to help the little ones settle for sleep." Ali compromises.

"There's a good wash up needed while dinner is being prepared." Mary demands.

A tub is placed on the deck outside of the kitchen and filled with warm water.

Under Mary's eye one child at a time undresses, and stands into the tub and washes.

Mary provides a good rinse by heated water from a bucket.

Layla provides Little Owl with her first experience in this settlers' nightly ritual.

Eight children are purged from the grime accumulated through the day.

Each then returns into the guest house in fresh slumber garments.

Each is handed a plate of super and directed into the main room to take a seat near the fireplace.

"Seth do you have a favorite children's tale?" Ali asks.

"In deed! My grandpa use to tell me a tale from the old country about an old woman what use to steal children." He replies.

"Sounds scary! You go first." Ali orders.

"Jeremiah, how about a good night story for the little ones?"

"Well Ali...I have true story about an eagle that my boys use to ask me to tell over and over again."

"Is it scary?

"Nope! Got a real happy ending."

"Wonderful you go last."

"Latyla do you think Mara Nar has a tale to tell the children before bed?"

Layla signs the question to the warrior.

He ponders than makes a suggestion.

Layla rejects. "No stories of war."

The native makes a second suggestion.

"Marvelous!" Layla applauds.

"Mara Nar will tell the tale of the princess who fooled the man who brings winter."

❧

A handsome well groomed Negro sits at the corner table of the road house.

He is elegantly dressed in the style found in the business districts of any large eastern metropolis.

His appearance is neat and spotless.

He sips a brandy and smokes a long slender cigar as he reads.

"That is Clive Ferguson." Bill Freeman informs the marshal.

"Best send another drink over to that gentleman on me. He appears to be the type what likes not to be disturbed." The marshal asks as he moves to the table.

"Mr. Ferguson. May I interrupt?" The marshal greets.

"Must you? I am bloody well into this novel." The man is irritated.

"Must! I'm U S Marshal Legs."

"I'm a British subject marshal."

"Well if you want to gamble here tonight then you'll have to answer a few questions." The marshal sits. "I'll be as brief as possible."

"If I must then begin by all means...please." The dark reader marks the book's place then rests his book upon the table.

The requested glass of brandy arrives. "From the marshal." Bill Freeman announces.

Mr. Ferguson is delighted. "Cheers old boy."

The marshal nods to acknowledge the appreciation.

"You received an invitation by mail to participate in the large cash game tonight?"

"Not at all! I was introduced to a gentleman in Chicago. We played a few hands of cards. As we parted, he informed me of the game and directed me to this establishment. I have appeared at the required hour."

"The man's name?"

"Autry as I recall... William Autry!"

"You've seen this man here or about?"

"No! I don't really expect him necessarily."

"Why?"

"As he actually never stated his intention, I can only deduce that this theme was indeterminate at that time."

The black gentleman's speech is more articulate than the marshal can comprehend. The marshal takes these words to mean the gambler wasn't told.

"You take such invitations often?"

"Quite so! Jolly good luck, what?" The gambler smiles with enjoyment. "I started this sojourn in London where I won a handsome piece of real estate in New York City on a wager. Seems that I've arrived with the same good fortune as before I left."

"I'm not following all this." The marshal apologizes.

"I live in London...England. There I was involved in a game of cards with a wealthy American. To sustain his loses he wrote out a deed to a Manhattan residence worth a great deal."

"He's a heavy loser?"

"The more he lost, the more alcohol he consumed, and the more he would gamble. Truly I wanted to terminate the game and avoid his further fiscal decline. He became enraged. I had no choice but to continue."

"You arrived in America to cash in on the New York property?"

"Precisely! I never won so much money before in my life as that night. However I favored the place straight off and stayed."

"You continue to gamble in high stakes games?"

"It's my profession!"

"Just how did you come to be gambling in merry old England?'" The marshal is bemused.

The fancy man turns shy. "I was conscripted into his majesty's armed forces. My lessons were learned in his majesty's military barracks all over India."

"Just what was your profession before the army?"

"Please don't repeat this marshal but I unloaded sea food at the docks."

"You've come a long way! You be good at gambling?"

"A very long way! Never lose...maybe I just break even or win a mere pence but I never lose Marshal."

"Call me Woody?"

"Awfully fine of you old sport! Call me Mac. That's what me mates on the dock called me."

"Mac?"

"Short for mackerel old boy. Let's toast!"

The men lift their glasses.

"To America!" Calls the marshal.

"To America's money." Answers Mac.

"You carry your own cash? Not worried about robbers?"

"Black men are invisible in white society. Most never see my luggage either."

"You'll be seen tonight Mac and your money bags as well!"

"What ever do you mean old chap?"

"Several bad men will arrive tonight to confiscate your cash, and everyone else's."

"This is your reason for speaking with me? Real western highway men?"

"This is my profession Mac. Those men who are coming be dangerous as they come anywheres."

"Woody let me assure you that I can take care of myself. Ten years of fighting on his majesty's frontiers leaves me undaunted by a handful of miscreants."

"Well I promise that you'll have your chance after dark tonight."

❧

The children have bowls of popcorn, pieces of vanilla taffy, and mugs of warm milk mixed with honey.

The fire flickers brilliantly.

Embers burst.

Glowing logs crack upon occasion causing all heads to search the hearth.

The youth sit upon the floor rounded before the flames.

The older folks sit upon chair and bench in corner and side so to view the children's faces.

The women's hands stay idleness with knitting needle and yarn.

Smoke from pipe and cigar comfort the men at the day's finish.

Ali's first evening at her new home bodes of her family years to soon begin.

Her contentment fails only for the absence of her marshal.

Seth is called before the fire.

Here he is to sit and compose his tale.

All are alert.

Seth begins.

His voice is low.

Hi speech is slow.

"In years long ago, in a land far from here, a land beyond the great ocean, a land distant from any like unto our ways of living, there dwelled an evil woman. An old hag, her body curved with bend, she walked only with the help of a great uneven stick."

The children huddle close.

The smallest attach to their larger brothers.

"The weather had been cruel for several years all around the small

kingdom where the witch lived. The skies were gray and wet all year long even in the midst of summer. A cold settled over the land. A cool that can only be found in the deep of the grave held below the earth."

The youngest girl covers her head.

"Hunger and cold could not be moved from the kingdom. Men worked, women worked, children worked. None played or made merry. Animals and all the inhabitants were starving. The people in groups prayed for relief. Only one person lived well amidst all the hardship. The hag showed no hunger, she showed no cold, she showed only bitterness and resentment at her fellow countrymen."

Mary's very youngest child runs to gather in her lap.

"This old monster of a female had four small children that in later years would disappear. One at a time, in the middle of the night by torchlight the ugly prune of a woman took her child to be sold in the land beyond the mountains of her valley."

The children compress.

Arms and hands interlock.

They collectively slip nearer the fire.

"With each of her wicked crimes she became uglier and meaner. After each child disappeared her greed and avarice grew. Animals would not live with her. All ran from her presence. Birds would not near her house. Flowers would not grow aside her door. Her body began to give an odor that repulsed all whom she passed. An aroma that does not wash from flesh as it is comes from inside a rotting soul."

The grown women in Seth's audience become uncomfortable.

They squirm in their seats.

Each looks to another for assurance.

Seth breaks the dire moment as he sips his glass of whiskey.

The children recover bravery on the moment.

"Evil breeds evil. As the heart blackens, the need for wickedness becomes insatiable. Darkness of the soul brings one in malevolence to haunt the shadows of the night. The detestable old ghoul was hardly ever seen and never to come under human eye during the day. Only at night and more often only her putrid scent was left to tell of her passing."

Jeremiah is now scared.

He wants to shift toward the firelight but is seized.

Only Mara Nar remains composed. He is aware of the fright that gathers within the room.

Ali is anxious for Seth's tale to end.

"In the worst of those times, in the midst of the most severe want and need about the land, when hope had vanished from all hearts, when tomorrows came with more hardship than yesterdays, Children began to vanish from their homes. Mothers began to find the beds of the children empty at first light. Fathers' walked the day and the night to search in vain for their lost ones."

A small boy blurts. "Why don't they get ride of that witch?"

All laugh to relieve the dread.

Seth holds the moment.

"One night the men gathered with axes, shovels, pitch forks. With torch lights they mustered. Hounds were put to leash. Doors were barred with mothers and children kept inside. Blessed Water from the churches was bottled for mothers' use. All the graves were covered with crucifixes so no sprits could emerge or submerge under ground. The men dispersed in groups with canine to seek the trail left by the decomposing soul. The first parties to take scent sounded their horns. Across plowed field and wide meadow, along the bank of streams the host of men pursued."

The children's hearts and eyes beat in pace to Seth's words.

The feet of women in the main room tap in his spoken meter.

No pause comes.

"Out toward the mountains the hated hag made stride. The boom of the army in chase, the frenzy of the baying hounds drove the malicious wench into a rugged unused mountain pass. Her path is to end upon a ledge that over looks a deep rocky abyss. Here at the narrowest point of the broken trail the men halted. They collected boulders to block the footpath. So high and so deep is the obstruction that no one human can make way through. The devilish hag is forever held at the far side. A

wooden crucifix washed and blest by Holy Water was mounted to hold the witch's soul from returning."

The children applaud in release.

Smiles of reassurance that this creature may not visit nearby are undivided.

Ali and her companions laugh at the foreboding shared.

The older boys are skeptical of the tale's truth.

"To any who may dare, to those who chose to tread where angels shun, for living souls that keep no faith, the evil on that mountain yet stands. To the reckless who seek from near or far, there is dreadfulness that continues behind a stone façade below a wooden cross. In present days, upon the foulest nights, sounds not just from gales of wind but unnatural howls carry into the villages. The mothers still watch their children in the night and the fathers hitherto guard their doors."

Seth stands for uproarious cheer.

Sun light is fading.

In the road house the assembly of gamblers is soon to their super.

The marshal sits with his back to the entranceway.

He has joined Averill Alderdyce.

"Mr. Alderdyce you have been invited to this big poker game tonight?"

"Not really, Marshal. My wife's brother is the professional gambler in the family. He has given me his invitation to use."

"Have you any idea who is responsible for this here affair?"

"Not in the least!"

"You be carrying a large sum of money when you traveled here?"

"Yes! I wear a money belt."

Averill Alderdyce is an older man, modestly dressed wearing a gray beard.

"You sponsored by a syndicate Mr. Alderdyce?" The marshal asks.

"Call me Avy. Sponsored by my brother in law."

"You be a regular high stakes player are you?"

"No! This is my first professional game. Normally I play for fun with my wife's family."

"What is your regular job Avy?" The marshal likes the gentleness of this man's soul.

"Was a school teacher most of my life...mathematics. Love the problems in the law of probability of cards. I just can't afford to gamble for sums."

"You wife's people be rich be they? Call me Woody."

"Woody, my wife's family is in the insurance business back in Ohio. I came to work for them as actuarial some years ago."

"Avy why after all them years are you a taking your first money game in high stakes playing?"

The mature gentleman pauses.

The smile disappears from his eyes.

"Woody, I'm dying. I have only several months left. My dear wife wishes me to have one long time dream to come true."

The marshal is stunned.

He cannot speak.

"I have had a wonderful life with three children grown and all happy. My wife has been caring and loving all of our life together. I have no regrets."

"I admire you and your wife and her people Avy. If'n there's anything anyone or I can do for you to be of service please ask." The marshal extends his hand.

"I just want to have the chance to prove my calculations work. To this end I must win tonight." The man's eyes brighten. "To have this opportunity is marvelous. I shall report my results in the New England Journal of Statistics."

The marshal knows that there is no possible threat that may come tonight that shall worry Averill. "I'm going to set in for a few hands. Be my first high stakes game as well."

"Well Woody, we are members of the same novitiate. For the rest of our lives we will be classmates."

The bond between the two men is made.

“Tell me Avy about your wife.” The marshal is thinking of Ali. “How will she deal...later I mean?”

“You mean after I pass Woody?”

The marshal nods politely in affirmation.

“We’ve talked and cried together. She has our grandchildren for comfort. There is plenty of family about.” His eyes fill with water. “She will have to forgo intimacy. Women need that Woody. They are made to live so. That’s why it’s more difficult for a mother when the child grows up.”

“Nothing we can do for them is there?” The marshal shares his grief.

“Just to be considerate while they have us is all!”

“It’s sad Avy.”

“It’s life Woody. You married?”

“Once back a life time ago. My wife passed when we were young.”

”How did you deal with her loss?”

“Got on my horse and drifted!”

“Still drifting?” Averill senses the truth.

“More or less Avy. Never got back to married life. Thinking on it now though.”

“Is there a lady somewhere?”

“Yep! Worried that my marshalling will leave her a young widow.”

“Can’t be a marshal forever. Can’t be alive forever! Time may be here for a change Woody.”

“Seems like it...bit hard is all.”

“Shoot! It’s easier than you think. Take my advice and make life, make living, and leave dying for later.”

Mara Nar has moved to the front of the audience.

Layla sits to his front to interpret his account.

The warrior will make signs to speak his tale.

His body will make movements to enhance its description.

He begins.

Little Owl gives aide.

Layla speaks.

"When the earth was very young, the land and the seasons where much different than now. The early natives lived not as the natives today. There where great hairy beasts that ran the hills, some with great long horns upon their head, and some with great horns upon their face with noses longer than a man's arm. The skies were filled with birds of a size large enough to lift up a man full grown."

The children have never beheld a native making story.

The signs given are by an old form.

The signs are from an early native tradition no longer in use today.

Mara Nar has captivated the imagination of the children who observe.

"The medicines of the early people were not as many as the medicines of today. The trees and plants were young as the earth. The people were few. The villages were small and distant. Not as the great camp of Many Horns. So early was the time of the land that the horse was but the size of a large dog, none bigger."

"What did people ride?" Call the boys.

Layla signs the question to Mara Nar

"None rode any beast. All natives walked. In winter sleds were drawn by hand or packs of dogs upon the snow. It was very dangerous for all that lived. Great cats with teeth the length of a man's hand stalked the terrain. Great bears much larger than any bison to be found today strode the earth. Only by cunning and disguise could the natives hunt and live."

The women ponder the truth held in the tale from Mara Nar.

Seth and Jeremiah whisper to one another of other tales that contain such information.

The children have never had such ideas presented before now.

"In the hills near here a tribe of warriors dwelt long time ago. A small band of hunters moved after the great herds of hairy beast as they roamed after forage. In the middle of the year, when the earth warmed,

the beasts would settle in the open meadows of the forests. The natives could make long camp. In this time of the year, the women would give birth. During this period the newborn would have time to grow strong enough to make the difficult marches of winter."

The women understand the immense task of carrying for a new born while tramping in the deep snow.

The men have both hunted in deep snow.

Neither is easy.

The children revel in the play afforded by a snowfall.

"Among this tribe was an older woman that was to give birth before winter resumed. She had not carried an unborn child for 16 springs. Her last child, a daughter of the chief would come of age at the time of the coming birth. One by one the other pregnant women of the tribe gave birth. The maiden was having difficulty because of her advanced years. The medicine man told the chief's family that if the birth was late then the mother and the newborn child would not likely survive the first months of the new snows."

The ladies in the audience cry quietly.

The men understand.

The children are somber.

"The maiden's daughter was distraught. The princess sought the advice of all in the tribe. None could comfort her. There was no medicine, no practice, and no help that would come to save her mother. The daughter sought visions from the spirits. She slept little. She ate little. She held her mother's hand and prayed sacred chants to their ancestors. There must be a way to spare her mother's life."

All attending Mara Nar make a wish of hope for a happy ending to this tale.

"Late in the warm time no birth has arrived for the mature maiden. All in the tribe begin to prepare for the man who brings winter."

The children interrupt. "Who is this man?"

Layla signs to Mara Nar who answers.

"There is a spirit who brings winter and later he returns to take winter away. He comes in the form of an old man dressed in heavy hides."

The tale resumes.

"Here at the native's long camp the coming of winter is first seen along the trail that follows down through the high passes of the mountains. The maiden's daughter decides to make a camp in the midst of the trail to be used by the man who brings winter. So alone by herself away from the protection of the warriors' bow and spear the young girl resides."

This notion raises the excitement of the children and adults as well.

"Day after day the girl waits. Then at last came a tiny old man wearing a heavy bear hide walking along the trail.

"As one nears a native's camp it is the custom to ask permission to enter. It is also the custom to ask permission to leave a camp once entered, and it is the custom to offer assistance to the camp while there."

"The old man finds a beautiful young princess living alone. He is much taken by her comely looks and courage."

"The young native girl is busy crushing white hazel nuts between two stones. The old man offers to help. The princess sends him back up into the passes to gather more of the special nuts, which are just beginning to ripen. After many days the old man returns. "

"He again asks permission to enter. Again he finds the handsome young maiden alone and busy boiling herbal leaves from a red birch tree. The work is so consuming that he must offer assistance to his desirable host. Again the old man is asked to search the highlands but this time for the rare precious leaf. After several weeks he returns."

"The lovely young native girl is again busy. The old man is now late upon his journey and wishes to pass through her camp without further delay. He asks for such permission. The princess pauses to consider his request. There is just one more task that needs his assistance then he shall be permitted to pass. He agrees."

"The maiden produces a small white stone. It is perfectly round with a natural hole passing through its center. There are only a dozen such stones needed to complete the necklace that the maiden is making. The old man hurries off to seek the needed stones."

Mara Nar hesitates.

He seeks anticipation in his audience.

"Many months passed. So long delayed was the man who brings winter that the warm season had turned into the first season of heat

upon the earth. When the old man finally retuned from his task the young princess had long returned to her village with the birth of her sister."

"So impressed with the condition of the earth was the old spirit that he has delayed the bringing of winter each year since. This hot season upon the earth is named after that young princess who tricked the old man of winter."

"The maiden's native name means summer."

All applaud.

William McElroy enters the dinning room of the road house.

Mr. Freeman approaches and speaks to the thin stately gentleman of retired years. Refined in dress and manners, the gentleman is well groomed and energetic.

"Marshal Legs I presume." He greets as he nears the table where the marshal sits.

"Yes, please take a seat. I wish to ask all the participants of the game tonight some questions."

"Of course sir. What is your pleasure?"

"You have carried a large sum of cash here?"

"Yes I have a cash box well secured I assure you."

"You are financed by an alliance?"

"I am a member of a cartel. U S Calvary 3rd Army, Colonel William McElroy retired at your service. I have escorted sums much greater in my day."

"What cartel may I ask?"

"A group of retired officers. We play poker every week in Topica. We put sums aside and take turns going to a high stakes event. It happens to be my luck to participate here."

"You boys are successful at these events?"

"Quite! The winnings and stakes go back into a general kitty for further offerings...minus expenses of course."

"There will be some action tonight colonel. Men are heading this way to rob the stakes."

"I am at your service marshal. I can be ready to ride in a half an hour."

"I intend to let them arrive."

"A trapping ploy! Good idea! We will get them with the goods."

"I have a plan colonel. To save innocent folks from being hurt and isolate them varmints so I can arrest them easy like."

"So you wish us to proceed as usual? Bate the trap?" The man is excited. "Wait till those old troopers back home here about this engagement. How many of the enemy do you anticipate?"

"Could be half a dozen? Not sure but more than I want."

"You are seriously outnumbered marshal. Best let me sign on to improve the odds a might. A few of us could set up a cross fire at the entrance of the road house and cut them down as they charge."

"What about our losses?"

"One maybe two at the most. Reasonable!"

"Not colonel if you're a civilian with a home and family. What I want to do is run'em down. Keep their horses tired and pick'em off one at a time from a distance."

"You know civilian affairs best marshal. My offer remains. I can still outride most."

"I want your word as a gentleman that you will desist from all hostile action in or about this road house tonight?"

"Damn it sir I'm an officer! I'll agree as long as you have command."

"No weapons in the game room. That's the code I understand?"

"Proper it is and I'll carry no weapons."

"Oh! I'll be playing the first series of hands in the game."

"Undercover? Grand idea!"

"Do you know a William Autry?"

"Yes, he served with me in Texas years back. Our group received an invitation from him for this event. Why?"

"I expect that he be the ring leader of this gang of outlaws what be coming."

"Never thought of him as a criminal. Never liked the man personally."

Jeremiah Cloug replaces Mara Nar as the storyteller.

He eyes are fixed upon the children.

"In the spring time when families stroll to search for the first flowers, inevitably one comes upon a bird's egg laying abandoned upon the open ground. The lost egg is always found misplaced, broken and empty. Often it is a blue robin's egg."

All the children have shared such an experience.

"The robin is a bird that tends little its nest as it must dance from sun rise to sun set upon the earth that holds the worm. So then the birds that prey seek its nest unprotected. Without difficulty the robin's egg is carried away so that its contents may be eaten. Much practiced is the blue bird and raven in such tactics."

Ordinary is the tale to the adults but its freshness to the children is not lost to Jeremiah.

"In years past there was a ranch up toward the higher ground. It were a short flight by feathers from the tallest mountain peaks. This here homestead was set in a natural ravine with one narrow access way at each end. Wide enough it was that the family kept chicken, goose, and turkey easily. So bountiful was the ranch that the number of birds became sufficiently large that the long ravine was packed full."

The tale appears to be much like Jeremiah's chicken ranch to Ali.

"The raven is a bold intelligent rascal who is capable of stealing from any nest. They be grand fliers as good as any critter in the air. Seems that some ravens will try their thieving as far away as the mountaintops. One day a black bird was carrying an egg what it made off with from a distant nest. It wanted to take that egg to its own home for dinner. It weren't no ordinary egg from no ordinary nest."

The children are enthralled.

"Well sir, that raven was so anxious and in such a hurry to return with that egg to its neighborhood it just got right clumsy and dropped the thing. Down from above the egg tumbled with that crow a cawing

and fussing over the loss. That there one egg landed smack dab in the center of that old chicken ranch. Fell right into a pile of hay in the chicken yard. Landed safe and sound. Caused a mighty stir among them hens what feared for the welfare of that unborn bird that just arrived from the sky."

The children smile.

"There was one larger than normal female chicken what won out and toke to sitting on that newly arrived egg. Well by and by that egg took to hatching. Out came a bird what weren't no chicken, or duck, or turkey. It was a might good-sized critter and a mighty strange looking peep. In no time this here hatchling was a big as any rooster. In fact them roosters began at once to pick on the critter whilst it were still a baby."

None of the adults have ever heard this tale.

They are captivated along with the youngsters.

"Before them roosters could do any harm to that young bird it grew to be taller than any thing what was in the chicken yard. In a matter of a few weeks that there new hatched bird grew to stand over three feet tall. Believe it or not that ravine had stold an eagle egg. It weren't no small eagle but an egg from the largest eagle's nest. That eaglet thought it were as much a chicken as any other in the yard. It went about strutting and pecking just as the hen what hatched it. It's different size and color didn't make no mind for any critter on the ranch. That there young eagle was accepted as being as proper a chicken as any young chicken ever could be."

All in the audience laugh.

"So large was it's eagle beak and eagle claws that critters what normally would hunt for chickens got sacred off. No hawk, or falcon, or other eagle would swoop near the ranch. The weasel, the mink, the fox all feared to become dinner for the great eagle in the chicken yard. All the birds in the ranch hailed the wonderful changes the eaglet brought to their lives. That there eagle never had cause to learn to fly. It never left its chicken family. It lived its life out as a full grown chicken."

"To this day some say there are found up in them mountains chickens 3 to 4 feet in height with dark feathers like an eagle except for the chicken colored white heads and tails. Them mountain chickens are

fond of perching in the tallest trees and that's about the only place one can see'm."

The silliness of the tale delights the children.

The women are grateful for its simplicity.

Chapter 9

“A Covenant House

The night coach arrives early just as the road house’s occupants take to their dinner.

There is just one passenger.

An elderly woman Mrs. Beth Miller from Fargo is off to visit her son.

She will not leave with the stage tonight but will continue her journey the next day with the morning stage.

The marshal reposes with Lucy Patterson at a table not far from where Mrs. Miller has taken a seat.

The only fare on the menu is boiled cabbage and potatoes with ham

Mrs. Miller is 95 years old. She is in remarkably good health but given to periods of mental agitation.

"Woody, any suggestion of the coming of the outlaws?" Lucy asks between sips of a large glass of red wine.

"That night stage is early. The driver must have worked his horses hard. May be that something was spooking them." Answers the marshal.

"Your company of robbers following behind the stage?" The lady is worried.

"Them desperados will come in just as if they where going to rob a bank."

"Well we are a bank with over a half a million dollars in paper money."

"If'n I'm right the next man to come through that door will be the point man of the gang."

"Point man?" Lucy asks.

"They'll be sending in one man to see that all is well inside before they begin their theft. Lead man will make sure the game is commencing, that all the cash is at hand, and that there be no unexpected security."

"Soon?"

"Any time before the game commences. If"n that lead man stays content and happy then they'll ride in when they be sure the game is underway."

"Good! We can enjoy our meal." Lucy eyes devour the handsome marshal.

Suddenly a piece of warm cabbage lands upon the shoulder of the marshal.

A second piece falls to the floor at the marshal's side.

Anther piece of vegetable is hurled past the marshal's table over Lucy's head.

The marshal's back is to Mrs. Miller's table.

The elderly lady is disturbed.

It seems that she is not fond of cabbage. In anger she is

removing bits of the plant from her dinner plate by tossing them aimlessly away and over her shoulder.

The look of shock upon the marshal's face causes Lucy to burst into laughter. "Go get her marshal!" Her sides ache with amusement.

The elderly lady's peculiarity in her table manner has stunned all her fellow diners.

The marshal feels the obligation to assist Mrs. Miller.

"Can I help?" He walks to stand by her.

"I hate cabbage! I can't digest thus stuff. It makes me ill. Why do I have to eat this?" More slices of vegetable are made air borne.

"Madam! It's not needed to toss the bits away." The marshal understands.

"Rules! I'm tired of rules. Rules all my life and what has it gotten me. Let them who made the decree of cabbage in my dinner clean up after my ruling." Another hunk is sent aloft.

"I'll be happy to take your plate and return with a portion that has no cabbage." The marshal suggest patiently. "These folks may think you're..."

"Touched?" The elderly lady barks. "Let them get to my age and we'll see how touched they seem to be to others."

The woman reaches for her drinking glass. "I asked for a little milk not half a glass full this is too much!"

The marshal reaches the glass first and pulls it from her reach. "And what would you be doing with this?"

The old woman's face puckers in determination. "I'm going to remove the extra milk so I won't be forced to drink more than I wish"

"On the floor?"

"I don't care as long as I'm not bothered. Just who are you?" The woman demands.

"U S Marshal Legs mam."

"My God they've sent a marshal to correct me!"

By now all the dinning room community is attending the marshal's predicament.

Their glee is to continue.

"I'm not after you mam."

"They make everything hard for me marshal. I can't hear well. I can't see well. But they keep giving me orders. They must have something for me to worry about and keep me annoyed."

The marshal looks to Lucy who over hears all.

Lucy smiles and points to a third chair at her table.

She points for the marshal to invite Mrs. Miller.

"Madam please join us for dinner?"

Mrs. Miller inspects Lucy Patterson. "I'd be delighted to have a woman's company!"

"Excellent! While you join Mrs. Patterson I'll bring you a fresh serving of boiled ham with potatoes only."

As the marshal enters the kitchen, a rider has arrived at the road house.

"There's a stranger entering the dinning room." Mr. Freeman informs the marshal.

The marshal is busy at the supper's kettle pouring a serving for Mrs. Miller. "What's he look like?'

"Tall slim fella. Wearing a Texican style hat."

"Riding a Texan breed Quarter Horse I'll wager." The marshal gauges.

"You think he's one of the outlaws Marshal?"

"I'm fixing to find out straight off. Where is he taking a seat?"

"He's gone into an empty corner. He's all alone."

"Well Mr. Freeman best to request the guests to clear out of the room as soon as they finish their meals."

"And the game?"

"Starts as usual!"

The marshal is unnoticed by the newly arrived guest as he makes his way to rejoin the ladies."

"Woody this is Beth Miller." Lucy introduces.

"I'm starved marshal." The old lady begins to consume her dinner.

Lucy whispers. "Did you see that man who just entered?"

The marshal turns and glances at his suspect.

He recognizes the man as the helper from Klinger's Ranch.

"That man's up from Texas! Best you and Beth finish eating then get to your rooms."

"Where's my milk?" Beth asks.

"Here it is." The marshal hands the elderly woman a small glass with a couple of ounces of fluid.

'This isn't too much!" The woman holds the glass to measure its contents. "This is fine. I hope the owner doesn't charge me for a full glass. That's the way they force a profit from your pocket book...drowning you with an overpriced beverage!"

"Beth who are you going to visit?" Lucy hopes to continue the meal as civil.

"My son is the commander of Fort Meyers. He's going to retire. We will all return to the old family home in Fargo together." Beth informs.

"Was your husband in the military as well?" The marshal asks.

"No he was the sheriff of Fargo for many years. Got himself shot in the back while arresting a prostitute for murder. He always treated every woman like a lady. He paid for it with his life."

"You made out on your own?" The marshal inquires.

"Went to work as a law clerk in the circuit court for a judge. Took my law degree by mail study from Chicago. Practiced law until my sight failed."

The marshal has to laugh at the irony. "You got tired of the law?"

"Course not! Didn't want to stop working but they made me. It's not right marshal to be forced to retire. Damn rules!"

"How long ago did you have to give up your practice Beth?" Lucy asks.

"Six months ago! Hated every day since then!"

"Your son will be home with you soon. Life should be become more interesting?" Lucy supposes.

"My poor boy! That wife of his is as lazy as can be. She doesn't cook, and she doesn't clean. She's hasn't been a wife to my son for years."

"You'll have to get along Beth!" The marshal is worried. "You can't be throwing food and such in her presence."

"It's not food I'm worried about marshal...I'm a crack shot!"

"You carrying a hand gun are you?" The marshal asks.

"I always travel armed. I prefer a single action Colt- 45. Got the best stopping power."

"What about your vision?' Lucy asks.

"Can't hit anything with a rifle any more but something at ten paces directly in my front then I'm still dangerous."

"Does your daughter in law know about your ability with firearms?" Lucy is shocked.

"She will soon enough." The old girl bristles.

"Mrs. Miller, may I ask for your maiden name?" The marshal asks.

"Autry!"

"Have family down Texas way?"

"My first cousin way as seaman. He made a home and business down on Padre Island hauling goods around the gulf waters. There were rumors that some of his dealings were not all legal."

"Smuggling?" Lucy surmises.

"Running guns into Mexico?" The marshal adds.

"Every family has its black sheep marshal!" Beth confesses.

"See any of them Aurty boys from Texas up heres about?" The marshal continues.

"William T Aurty Esq. marshal is a lawyer from the Galveston area and he visits Fargo regularly."

"You play poker Beth?" The marshal responds.

"Damn fine player, if I say so myself." The elderly lady confirms.

"How about a couple of hands of poker after dinner tonight? Here in the salon?" The marshal makes the invitation.

"Just a few, I won't stay up late. Need to use cards with large face markings. My eyes won't like it otherwise."

"I'll see to it Beth." Lucy promises. "You can sit next to me during the game."

"You know Jeremiah Cloug?" Suspects the marshal.

"Yes he is my sister's boy. He is a very rich man marshal. Made his money from chickens."

"He prepared that dinner you just enjoyed!" Returns the marshal.

"Figures! He never was a cook!" Disgust reigns over the elderly woman's face. "What's he cooking for at this road house?"

"All the women folk and children are hold up at a guest house nearby! I had Jeremiah stay there as well. There's trouble about! Could be a robbery here tonight." The marshal does not tell all.

The eyes of Beth Miller brighten.

Her countenance rejuvenates. "Sounds like a lively time that I wouldn't miss for another ten years added on my life."

"Can't bring your hand gun Beth. I don't want shooting around all these folks."

"More dam rules!"

"All you need to do is hit the floor should there be any bullets flying."

The dark of night arrives at the guest house.

Mara Nar has exited the house. He will scout the grounds all about during the darkness.

Layla has taken charge of the main room.

With guitar in hand she sings lovely soft tunes. Her sweet voice fills the home with comfort and peace.

Ali has taken Mary's three-year old girl into her lap.

She cuddles the child's small feet and legs in her hand.

She pats the child's long flowing locks and strokes her head.

"How lucky you are...a house and soon a husband and a

family not far behind. Your existence is beginning." Michele whispers.

"I know! I can't believe that I'll finally have my own life... perhaps my own baby to dress up cute and cuddly. I am so very happy Michele."

"How does it feel? To be bound to a man."

"Love has ended all emptiness in my life. The presence, the nearness, the image of love makes sound my judgments, heals my injuries, holds me above despair, and prospers success from my efforts. He is my love! We are the companions of each other's soul. We are life complete together. He shall live life because of my love. Death may only part us on this earth."

Michele sighs as only a young woman complete with longing to give her love." I think I'm ready to start my own family."

"Michele! It would be wonderful if you could find someone nearby so we could visit, take the children on outings together."

"I'm going to take Jeremiah up on his offer and spend some time in Fargo. Maybe even find some work there."

"What about Layla? Will she join you?" Ali asks.

"Have you seen her with Mara Nar? She's has strong feelings for that warrior."

"Oh! Did she say so?"

"No! Her eyes ceaselessly follow him about." Michele testifies.

"What about the warrior? Does he notice her?"

"Well! Those natives hide their emotions. Even Little Owl is slow to express her personal preferences after all the time she has been with us. I've seen Mara Nar watch her the way a man does when he fancies a woman and more than once."

"I've noticed that he shows her a lot of patience when they are trying to converse. He is a considerate sensitive man. Can any thing come of it?" Ali wonders.

"Mary Freeman tells me that the young natives are more than anxious to take a homesteader as a spouse."

"Don't they have more than one wife? Layla would never

stand for that. I can't see her keeping a native lodge for a home."

"Mary tells me that a mixed marriage with the natives can make a wonderfully strong family." Michele responds.

"How would they make a living together? Layla is such a city girl!"

Mary Freeman arrives to collect her smallest child. "Time these little ones go to bed." The mother announces.

"Just a while longer Mary?' Ali pleads.

Mary takes a near seat.

She holds her second youngest child in her lap. "These older boys will have to keep quiet soon." She informs.

"No ruff play boys!" Mary instructs.

"Mary? Do you think Layla has an interest in Mara Nar?" Michele asks.

"Oh my yes...serious interest I'd say. Mara Nar is very handsome! I'd be guessing many a settler's daughter will have eyes for him." Mary counters.

"Would you let your girl marry a native? Or one of your boys?" Ali poses.

"If the natives consider the marriage to have worth then yes I would also consider it. My children have to share the land. The natives hold marrying as a way of making a strong bond. My grandchildren will be part of the native tribe of these parts. This gives the youth greater security."

"It's easy for boys to take a native wife. They can hunt and trap and live in the high lands. How about your daughter?" Michele questions.

"The native women make good wives. They are not quarrelsome. They are trained to work hard. They are not much interested in learning our language is the only real problem. Now taking a native warrior as a husband is a different matter. It takes a special warrior to take a settler woman for a spouse."

Michele and Ali are interested in her every word.

"Not a common event?" Asks Ali.

'The natives consider their woman as more suitable for intermarriage. The warrior has to make a more substantial change in his life. He has to learn to speak the tongue of his spouse's people in most cases. He has to adapt to the settler's society."

"Seems like it isn't easy for a settler to marry a native man." Michele observes.

"Some natives are interested in the homesteaders way of life...ranching especially. There was a young girl that worked for us here at the road house. She married a native. At first they keep a hut near the tribal lands. The woman took care of gardens and some livestock. After she had the second child the woman couldn't keep up the entire demand for the farm work yet take care of both children.'

"What did she do?" Ali asks.

"She talked her husband into moving to Fargo. I hear they are doing well. Her husband works for a trading company making good money." Mary tells.

"Layla could live in someplace like a road house but she needs more civilization than up in the mountains catching beaver." Ali is certain.

"The way this territory is growing we could have a town sprout up right here around the road house." Mary comments.

"A school will certainly be needed here in the future. Layla would be very happy." Ali determines.

"A trading post would be needed as well. Mara Nar could have a major role in its success." Mary knows business.

"We have to find Layla a home for her family...and Little Owl perhaps." Michele is excited.

"There's an old stone house down behind the road house. My Bill uses their corral and shed for storage occasionally.

"We could walk there tomorrow and have a look?" Mary offers.

Let's only tell Layla after we see if it's suitable. Any other places?" Michele asks.

"I'd stake some ground and look to build my own home in a prime spot before all the people begin arriving." Ali suggests.

"Will have my Bill show us around. He knows all the best places." Mary determines.

"Well have to plan a second wedding!" Ali laughs.

The diners at the road house are mostly retired to prepare for the beginning of tonight's poker game.

The marshal sits alone.

Beth and Lucy have retired to their rooms.

The marshal fears the outlaws will arrive soon.

He withdraws his handguns from their holsters.

The rider from the Klinger Ranch sits with a cup of coffee.

He shows no sign of intended exit.

This ranch hand seems comfortable with his weapons. The marshal suspects he is capable with a handgun.

The marshal slides his firearms into the side pockets of his coat. He stands and turns toward the corner of the room where his suspect remains.

No notice is made of the casual movement of the marshal.

With his hands inserted into his coat pockets both fists hold a weapon.

He approaches with his eyes fixed upon the hands of the lone rider.

Sheb Ledbetter does not recognize the nearing figure with the white toed boots and fancy dress as the marshal. He is unaware.

Feigning no interest, the marshal makes passage to one side of the table. Here he stops, turns, and produces his weapons.

Shocked by the threat, Ledbetter is roused from his indifference.

"Freeze!" The marshal instructs. "Place your hands flat on the table. Easy like. Spread them fingers wide apart." The marshal's eyes are strained upon Ledbetter's hands.

Ledbetter complies.

"Marshal Legs! Didn't make you out dressed up like a gambler." He speaks easily.

"You be a long way from the Klinger's Ranch."

"Running some long errands marshal. Why them guns?" His words are disarming.

The marshal makes steps to stand directly in front of the table.

His eyes do not leave the watch of the fingers upon the table. "I need to see the bottom of them boots you are wearing."

Ledbetter relaxes.

His hands become supple, unstrained.

They do not move.

"I can answer any questions you may have marshal. Be glad to oblige."

"Push them feet of yours out from under that table! Slow and easy."

"Just stopped for to rest my horse and have a bite. Not causing any trouble?" The man declares.

Ledbetter's feet move into the open at the floor of the table.

The marshal pulls back the firing hammers of both handguns.

Ledbetter tenses.

"If you move...if you flinch...if I think you'll flinch then I'll kill you right off." The marshal pauses.

The man under the marshal's guns is seized absolutely.

His face is blanched at the marshal's words.

One of the marshal's eyes is fixed upon the outlaw.

His other eye searches the bottom of Ledbetter's boots.

The marshal is satisfied.

"You doing any chicken work for the Klingers around here are you?"

"No! Just delivered some horses up Fargo way is all." Ledbetter responds.

This is a lie.

The souls and heels of Ledbetter's boots are stained with chicken droppings.

The marshal's gaze is hard and cold. He senses that he must keep complete advantage over the outlaw.

"You from East Texas maybe down south east way?"

"Lived there for some time. Why?"

"I know you be riding with Bill Autry!" The marshal declares.

Ledbetter flexes but his hands do not move.

He does not answer.

"I know that some of your acquaintances are coming into the road house tonight!"

The stare of the rider is now fierce. He does not speak.

"I know when you and friends leave here you all will ride to Cloug's chicken ranch."

The man wants to run.

He's mood is dangerous.

He does not speak.

"I know what is to be buried below the floor of that chicken house!"

"I am not here to rob no gamblers." Ledbetter's words are threatening.

The outlaw wants to clear his weapon and shoot the marshal.

"You have some choices." States the marshal.

The outlaw looks for an opportunity.

"You can cooperate with me before there is a crime committed and in a week or so I'll set you free."

The outlaw looks for an opportunity.

"Or you can remain silent and in a week or so I'll have you hanged most likely."

The outlaw looks for an opportunity.

"Or I can kill you right here."

"Won't turn on my kin marshal."

There is only the last option.

"I want to know how many men are coming with Autry. Four? Five?"

"Marshal..." Freeman calls as he enters the room.

The marshal's attention diverts.

In a fraction of the moment Ledbetter's hand moves below the table top and upon his handgun.

From the corner of his eye the marshal recognizes the movement.

Ledbetter's gun appears as the marshal discharges both of his weapons.

The roar of the gunfire hurls the body of Ledbetter back against the wall immediately behind his chair. This impact causes the dead man to rebound forward.

Ledbetter collapses in his seat with his head to rest upon the tabletop.

Mr. Freeman witnesses the violent instant.

He halts frozen before the scene.

There is disgust on the marshal's face.

"Mara Nar is outside and waits to speak with you." Freeman is uncertain in his delivery.

"I hated to kill this man. There was a better choice. His word was worth his life." The marshal shakes his head in regret. "Damn unnecessary!"

"What shall I do with this man's body?" The owner asks.

"We'll move it into the cold cellar and get this game started." Answers the marshal.

"What about his horse?"

"Leave it out front so the riders a coming won't take suspicion."

"These are very dangerous men coming?"

The marshal has always disliked unnecessary killing.

It is the one part of his profession that he will not miss when he retires. He replaces his handguns into their holsters. "Awful dangerous!"

Out front Mara Nar waits upon horseback.

"I'll ride a distance out and watch the approaches. When riders near I'll signal with the screech of the owl at the window." Mara Nar gives sign.

The marshal agrees.

He points to the dinning room in which he will be waiting.

The gamblers are assembled about a large round table in the dinning room.

"Let the marshal deal the first hand!" Lucy suggests.

"Happy to oblige. Woody is the only name I'll respond to while we're all gambling!" The marshal looks each player in the eye to ascertain the participation of all in his wish to be unofficial.

"Beth you can call dealer's choice." Woody offers.

"Three card draw aces high. Let the fat man cut." The old woman calls in a practiced manner.

R D Weir laughs at the woman's pugnacious tone.

All take ease with the game's commencing.

"Let's start small." Lucy advises. "Five hundred dollars per ante, one hundred dollar minimum raises."

All agree.

"I'm good for a few hands." Beth figures her cash. "$3500 dollar limit per game per player."

This bound is not to the liking of the professionals.

They accede however under the weight of the looming trouble.

The marshal's first hand draws A_8_5_5_2. The pair of fives offers a good chance for a winning draw.

The marshal's attention is on the players.

He searches for any sign of anxiety, for anyone who maybe unduly interested in the passing hour of the night. He is concerned that one of the players maybe a plant, a co-conspirator in the thieving to take place.

It costs the marshal another $500 dollars to draw three replacement cards.

He holds now J_5_5_5_5. Four 5's and a jack is a winning poker hand almost anywhere.

It is here tonight

The .beginning hand earns the marshal $15, 000. This is a sum greater than the combined wages from his years as a lawman.

"It starts as your night Woody!" Comments J. B. Ledford.

"Well played!" Lucy compliments.

"Beginners luck!" Barks old Mrs. Miller.

The marshal slides $2500 to Lucy.

Lucy sneaks this sum back into Mrs. Miller's pile of cash with out her notice.

After a number of games the marshal has accumulated over $50,000 dollars in winnings.

This is simply a fortune to the lawman.

His thoughts are of the many things he can now provide for Ali. He desires not to lose at poker tonight.

All have forgotten about the coming of the outlaws.

Mrs. Miller remains oblivious to the fact that she has yet to lose one dollar. All her bets have been returned to her surreptitiously.

She fatigues. "One more hand then I must retire. Have I won anything?"

The screech of the owl is heard.

None but the marshal pays heed.

The screech owl is heard again.

The marshal forgets his concern over acquired wealth.

He makes signal to Mr. Freeman.

The owner disappears into the kitchen and there bolts the door. He takes up his shotgun. He is prepared to confront the robbers should gunfire begin.

The players' cash stores are collected at their sides about the poker table.

The marshal calculates that at least four men are needed to carry off the booty.

Two additional men are needed to watch the gamblers at this time and at least one man outside to tend their horses.

He wonders with Ledbetter's absence how the gang of outlaws will change their plans.

At this time, Bill Autry and his accomplices are walking to the front of the road house. They lead their horses by hand.

Their approach is quiet.

Autry is a small man with shiny dark hair.

His fellow conspirators all stand above him.

At the entrance the band of outlaws halts.

Autry recognizes Ledbetter's horse. "Check your weapons!" He instructs.

All remove their side arms and make certain their weapons are ready.

"We go in fast. Spread out in front of the gaming table. Follow my command. No shooting unless someone pulls out a weapon. They should not be armed inside! This will go easy so don't panic." Autry commands.

"Masks on!" He whispers.

The men who will enter pull hoods over their heads.

They march inside.

"Lucy, I forget how to count. Will you help me?" Asks Mrs. Miller.

"Why..."

The bandits rush in to the dinning room causing a great commotion.

Their guns point at the sitting gamblers.

Stunned despite being forewarned the gamblers raise their hands instinctively.

Autry steps to the center of the gaming table.

He inspects the disposition of all those at the table.

He recognizes his elderly aunt.

He does not find Ledbetter's presence.

His words falter.

His assistants are confused by his hesitancy.

Autry regains his command. He faces no weapons or resistance.

He chooses not to speak.

His hand waves his comrades forward to gather the sums of cash.

The marshal is correct in his estimation of the number of outlaws.

With Ledbetter's absence only the leader is able to watch the behavior of those being robbed.

It is not enough.

Quickly boxes, bags, and money belts are confiscated.

The table stakes are swept into canvas bags.

None of the intruders identifies Marshal Legs.

Immediately upon the completion of the removal of the poker funds, the renegade band steps back to exit the room.

Mrs. Miller just begins to understand the nature of the event transpiring.

As the last of the robbers turns to exit, she produces her handgun and fires several times.

Her bullets strike no one.

This fusillade brings the owner quickly from out of the kitchen. He discharges both barrels of his shotgun toward the front door.

At once the last robber leaving drops dead.

The retreating highwaymen direct return gunfire randomly into the room.

R. D. Weir is struck in the abdomen. His great girth renders the wound as non-fatal.

Averill Alderdyce is shot fatally in the head.

He dies within minutes.

Lucy has taken hold of Mrs. Miller and guides her to safety upon the floor.

The marshal retrieves a small six-gun from inside his left boot.

His directed fire strikes the next to the last exiting criminal. The wounds are terminal.

The others at the gaming board remain stiffen.

They move to follow after the marshal and Mr. Freeman arrive to the front door.

The entrance door is barred from within.

The gamblers have recovered the weapons from the dead.

The ladies and Mr. Weir are attended.

As the desperados ride off they continue to fire at the road house to discourage any pursuit.

"Marshal this pouch has your winnings inside." William McElroy states as he inspects the treasure left behind by the dead outlaws.

"We've recovered about half of all the gaming funds." Clive Ferguson is calculating.

"Get those weapons at the ready! Forget the money till later. Them bad boys may return." The marshal instructs.

"I'm taking Beth up stairs." Lucy offers.

"Wait until Mara Nar signals the all clear. There may be other bandits approaching. Those bad men may have a back up plan to complete their theft."

Mr. Freeman scurries to gather more firearms.

The sound of running horses circling the road house brings the dining room to silence.

"They're after fresh horses." Announces Mr. Freeman.

Maybe we wounded another." Colonel McElroy considers.

The sound of thundering hoofs fades.

There is silence.

All listen to the outside.

Dark minutes pass.

The owl's screech is heard.

"Get Beth to her room. Best stay with her till light." The marshal suggest to Lucy.

"We need to make a litter to get Mr. Weir to his bed." Clive Ferguson mentions.

"Colonel McElroy will you take first watch at the door?" The marshal requests.

"Certainly!" The retired colonel takes the shotgun from the owner.

"I'm going over to see the folks at the guest house." The marshal advises.

"Take your earnings with you." Lucy demands. "They won't get misplaced with your lady watching over them."

As the marshal walks to the guest house he encounters Mara Nar.

"All riders are gone." The native informs the marshal.

"They will ride to the great chicken house. They will bury their loot and then disperse the gang to return later"

"I shall follow!" The warrior asserts.

"I will lead a posse and arrive there just before dawn. Their scout is dead. It won't be as easy for them to ride away as they had planned."

The native leaves.

His horse is fresh and will arrive at Cloug's ranch not long after Autry's gang.

Inside the guest house, the distant sound of many weapons discharging has put the men and women at the alert.

Ali holds a small handgun.

Michele has possession of a rifle.

Layla sits with Little Owl in a corner.

Evelyn and Mary attend the sleeping children.

Seth Adams is heavily armed at the front door.

Jeremiah Cloug holds a shotgun at the kitchen door.

The marshal offers a dark silhouette.

He is cautious at his approach.

Seth is alert.

The darkness hides all from sight at the distance but sound carries only from a directed place.

Seth hears the footfalls of a man's advance. His rifle takes aim in this direction. His vision is focused.

"Deputy Adams!" Calls the marshal.

"Marshal Legs." Seth responds as he cautiously opens the front door.

The marshal's first steps into the front room of the guest house bring the arms of a grateful Ali.

"I heard the gun fire and I was frightened for you." Her hands search the marshal's chest for any weakness. They measure the strength of his breath.

Her eyes look into his questioningly.

Relief fills the instant.

The two share the private moment where upon a husband returns to wife and home. Deep mutual care forecasts their future.

"People where hurt." The marshal announces. "Bill Freeman is fine. Two outlaws are dead. One gambler is dead, and one is wounded."

"They get away with any cash?" Seth asks.

"Most but not all of it. They be heading to your place Jeremiah. Their leader is William Autry!" The marshal informs.

"I'll be damned marshal! Most of them Autrys are good folks. There has always been a wild streak in the Texas side of the family." Jeremiah responds. "I'll have to get that money back from William is all."

"We won't have a problem getting the money back. Getting them boys into custody without getting a mess of people shot is the hard part." The marshal responds.

Ali is again concerned. "Don't go after them by your self Woody...Please?"

"I'm getting a posse together to head out a couple hours before light."

The marshal hugs Ali.

He turns to Seth." I want you and Jeremiah to leave for his chicken ranch with a wagon at the same time. Will haul them desperados back all trussed up."

"We'll get ready straight off." Seth responds.

The marshal hands a bag with poker winnings to Ali. "Won a good bit of money tonight! Seems that we have a home, a ranch, and a fortune." He is delighted to share.

"All we need is each other!" Ali is yet enthralled with the marshal's regained presence.

The federal officer insists upon Ali's inspection of the poker bag's contents.

The gathering of bills in denomination of one hundred mesmerizes the lovely young lady. Her eyes give notice to the marshal.

"I'm thinking that my marshaling days are just about over. If you can keep this stash safe!"

"Just wait till you return! I'm thinking my days as a single lady are over."

A posse has been formed from the road house.

Ledford, McElroy, Cloug, Adams and Ferguson ride with the marshal toward Cloug's chicken house.

They depart several hours before first light.

Their travel is easy as the light of the moon maintains its brightness.

The posse arrives before dawn.

At the entrance to Cloug's ranch the marshal makes conference with his posse.

"We don't want to be shooting up a bunch of chickens and horses and anything that moves." His eyes study the attention of his companions.

"The idea here is to get this gang of outlaws to move off in the direction they least desire." The marshal pauses.

'That would be into the nation of the Nez Perce." Jeremiah answers.

The marshal nods in agreement. "Them fellows will want to return to the Fargo rode and split up. Their guide was killed last night at the road house."

"So they have no choice in option for egress from pursuit." Colonel McElroy analyses.

The marshal nods in agreement.

"We set a defensive perimeter here at the ranch's entrance?" Clive Ferguson supposes.

The marshal nods in agreement.

"If'n I were with them fellows I'd get a moving just after sun up." Seth Adams predicts.

The marshal nods in agreement.

"Need a cross fire old chap!" Determines Clive Ferguson.

The marshal nods in agreement.

"Will use the wagon to block the road back this away!" Jeremiah suggests.

The marshal nods in agreement.

"What about the cash?" J B Ledford asks.

"Before them desperados depart they'll bury that money inside the chicken house." Answers the marshal.

"As soon as my birds get out into the yard!" Jeremiah is certain.

"Then they'll make to the highway but we will be here a waiting." Seth offers.

"You men hide in them trees. Just before they are in range begin firing your weapons as fast and as often as you can. Make it seem like there's a dozen armed men after them." Instructs the marshal.

"They'll turn immediately and head in another direction!" Determines Colonel McElroy.

"I'll be up on that ridge above with Mara Nar. As soon as they seem to be interested in our bearing will begin shooting at them." Answers the marshal.

"That leaves their only way out toward the native territory." Concludes Jeremiah.

"Then what?" Asks J. B.

"Mara Nar and I follow after them from the ridge. You boys follow us from here. Seth and Jeremiah get into that chicken house and recover the money." The marshal's plan is set.

"I'd like to help recover that money." J B Ledford offers. "I'll follow you marshal afterwards."

"Good idea! You best help guard the wagon as it gets the loot back to the road house." Answers the marshal. "Any questions?"

"When do we close upon our enemy?" Asks the colonel.

"Their horses are not refreshed. They'll tire up in them hills right quick. Them outlaws will have to push their mounts to get rid of us. So we trail behind. Let them bad boys make some mistakes then we'll pick'em off."

The marshal mounts his horse. "Colonel take charge here. J.B.L. you get this wagon returned straight away."

The marshal greets Mara Nar atop the land overlooking the chicken ranch. "As soon as them outlaws turn our way we ride straight at them and turn them deep into your land."

"When my people see so many men riding upon tired horses they will be troubled. Many eyes will follow after them. Their trail will be wide to follow."

The marshal nods in agreement.

The air this day is warm and sweet with fragrances of late spring.

There is much stirring within the chicken house just before the first light of day.

The birds have awakened.

They cluck and fuss gently.

They do not move but wait for the day's start.

The men and the wagon have moved into the trees for cover.

The marshal and his warrior companion hide under the ridge's edge and wait.

"Any time now." Jeremiah warns his cohorts.

At this instant, the edge of the eastern horizon brightens. Every male bird springs forth to the doorways of the chicken pen.

They strut in practiced order into the yard where an enormous cacophony of rooster calls erupts.

The competition among the many hundreds of male poultry to be heard and judged best fills the landscape with strained efforts.

No creature about is saved from this audition.

The outlaws emerge from Cloug's home as the many hens are quitting their roost.

The accumulation of newly gathered cackles raises the power of the noise over the ranch to unbearable.

The coming out in mass of thousands of fowls at the squawk is painful to all ears.

This dreadful clatter persists until the birds discover feed whereupon calm among the flock obtains.

William Autry instructs his nervous gang towards the hen house.

They carry bags, and boxes of plunder.

The distance is continuously scanned for a view of any arriving person as they make their way.

Only a few hurried moments are needed to accomplish the task of stashing the money stolen from the road house.

With dispatch the outlaws make to their horses.

They race toward the ranch's entrance.

Immediately upon site of the approaching riders the Colonel barks. "Get the wagon in place! Commence firing!"

Many rounds of gunfire arrive with the emergence of a wagon moving to block the pathway of the outlaws.

Startled by the posses' firing at their advance, William Autry turns his band and heads around behind the chicken house and up towards the ridge where the marshal is waiting.

The marshal and Mara Nar mount and strike at full speed towards the nearing outlaws.

The marshal rides with both handguns firing rapidly.

Autry is again displaced from his intended route. Only the way toward the native land is open. He leads his band with speed into the unknown native lands

The Colonel and Clive Ferguson mount and hurry after to regroup with the marshal.

The pursued and their pursuers disappear into the woods. The wagon heads toward the chicken yard to recover the gamblers' missing sums.

"We'll stay close and push the till midday, then will ease up and drift far behind them." The marshal instructs the posse as he calls them to a stop.

"You risk losing them all together." Remarks the colonel.

"They be a wanting to turn when they feel safe and they think we are misdirected. It'll be late afternoon or so when they make their break. They'll use as much dusk as they can to cover their exiting trail."

"If we are far aft how we will know which way they shall turn?" Asks Clive Ferguson.

The marshal speaks to Mara Nar who then races off alone.

"That native will swing around to the front of them scoundrels to watch them every step of the way. When Autry's gang turns back we will be notified."

"And we will be positioned to cut off their retreat." Agrees the Colonel.

The marshal nods in concurrence. "They have no way of knowing that we have a native guide what knows the territory quite well. My guess is they still hope to cross the Fargo Road sometime tomorrow and split up."

Autry and his men are experienced at misleading posses.

They choose a route that moves with ease.

Winding and falling trails through the tall brush and trees is preferred at the start.

High exposed ground is avoided.

Upon the encounter with stream and creek the outlaws move into the water and stride with the flow for a good distance to slip out where the ground is hardened.

For many hours the posse remains sufficiently close such that the outlaws hear the sounds of pursuit.

At midday the marshal calls his band to a halt. "We'll rest our horses for a spell and give those fellas up ahead a chance to be free."

"Just who are these men we are chasing." Inquires the Colonel.

"A gang of outlaws up from East Texas after mighty big stakes. William Autry has escaped capture for many a year as well as his kin what be riding with him."

"Desperate felons?" Asks Clive.

"Don't come no meaner or more dangerous. Hell, the entire west will be far safer after we ring them in to justice."

"The wagon should be back to the road house by now." Proffers the Colonel. "At least the folks back there will be safe."

"No one be safe until that cash moves out and away with you gamblers."

"After all this hard work I should hope we might continue and finish our poker game." Clive Ferguson speaks

The marshal is worried that others may yet arrive to the road house with villainy in mind.

The sun is lowering from its zenith when the posse prepares to resumes the chase.

They will trek slowly along the path left by the escaping road agents.

The marshal knows that Autry will make his final turn soon.

"Keep your weapons at the ready. If the men we are chasing get frantic they'll set an ambush for us. So string out single file, ride quiet, and leave separation between you and the horse in your front."

Causally the posse progresses with the intention to flank the band of outlaws later in the day.

Mara Nar has been at the distance in the front of the outlaws since morning. He has observed their maneuvers to confuse the pursuing marshal.

The horses of the bandits are nearing exhaustion.

It has been hours since the Autry Gang has realized any note of the posse's presence. Their procession has slowed.

The pursued have become relaxed.

Their hopes for escape increase.

In late afternoon the outlaw bunch comes upon a trail that moves off in the direction of Fargo and away from a deeper penetration into the natives' land.

The outlaws turn.

Mara Nar knows the path now chosen for their retreat.

He departs for reunion with the marshal.

"The men you seek head back toward the settlements." Mara Nar signs to the marshal.

"Is there a place for us to make a trap?"

"A narrow pass with rock to one side and gulch to the other." Answers the native.

"Can we reach this pass before Autry and his riders?"

The native makes signals with his arm along a path up over the hills to the side. "We must hurry!"

Dusk is forming when the marshal and his company arrives at the narrow divide chosen by the native.

At the entrance of the pass, Ferguson and McElroy dismount and take sniper's positions down along the falling embankment.

The marshal dismounts and takes position at the other end of the slip.

Here he waits to confront the band of desperados.

Within the hour the sound of approaching riders sends the posse into preparedness.

Autry has no alarm as he decides his pursuers are long lost from his present trail. However he is still watchful only for surprise by native warriors.

The path within the pass is wide enough for the riders to gather. Autry's thoughts are of making camp and resting his mounts for a successful completion of his plan.

Halfway through the narrows the marshal steps into view.

The approaching riders quickly come to a halt with surprise.

"U S Marshal Legs! You men are under arrest. Drop you weapons to the ground."

The outlaws look about one to the other.

All know of the marshal's reputation but none fear him.

Autry scans the landscape for any sign of a posse.

There is none.

"You are a brave man to try to stop us marshal. We be a might too much even for you." Autry replies.

The marshal pulls his waistcoat to the side.

His handguns are yet holstered.

His badge shines forth.

"You all are not leaving here as free. Your thieving days are ended."

"Better men than you have tried marshal." Autry replies.

"William Autry! I mean to see you hang later or die here today." The marshal stance is set for the confrontation to come.

Autry kicks his horse.

The animal lunges ahead toward the marshal.

The remaining raiders follow the attack.

The charging brigands pull their firearms

Two shots ring forth from below the embankment.

Two outlaws fall dead from their mounts.

The Colonel and Clive have fired instinctively.

Autry and one remaining accomplice discharge their weapons at the marshal.

The marshal is struck in the thigh and one shoulder.

He is thrown to the ground in front of Autry's racing steed. As the marshal falls he frees one gun from its holster.

He fires rapidly at his attackers.

One horse and rider collapse dead at once.

Autry is unscathed as he closes upon the form of the wounded marshal. His weapon points at close range upon the lawman.

In the final determining instant Autry prepares to escape over the soon to be dead body of the federal officer.

An arrow is loosed from Mara Nar's bow.

Before the passing of this desperate moment, it penetrates the center of Autry's chest.

The bandit's gun discharges wildly as he spills in death from his horse.

The posse rose late in the morning.

The marshal's wounds have been tended.

He is in much discomfort.

Their return has been slow and methodical.

It is just the start of night when the posse rides into the road house.

Bill Freeman rushes outside to greet the retuning men.

"Marshal we've been robbed!" The owner calls with agitation.

"What was stolen? By whom?" The marshal responds as he winces from the pain of his wounds.

"The gamblers' stakes! Everyone's money has been taken by the little man Ledford!" The owner imparts.

"What?" Puzzles the marshal.

"They took the cash returned from the chicken ranch and the cash saved during Autry's break-in?" The owner is stunned.

"When?" Demands the marshal.

"The wagon returned from Cloug's ranch. It held a wounded outlaw. The injured villain pulled a gun. Ledford pulled his derringer on us as well. He ordered us to collect all the money and put it into the wagon. We obliged."

"They made off with everything?" Questions the marshal.

"Every dollar was taken but your winnings from the table. That's still over to the guest house." Freeman becomes nervous. His eyes fall to avoid the marshal's look.

"Any shooting? Anyone hurt?" The marshal must ask.

"That Ledford got mean after the cash was placed in the cart and he was going to leave. Started yelling crazy like he wanted everyone afraid. The two men began shooting randomly. There was nothing anyone could do marshal."

"Mary and the children returned to the road house with the movement of Jeremiah's wagon at dawn. Ali and Evelyn accompanied them to the road house. Michele, Layla, and Little owl remained to keep the guest house." Seth adds to the tale. "There was no reason for them men to begin shooting at us."

The avoidance of his latter question has the marshal concerned. "Who got shot?" He despairs.

"It was a ricochet...extreme odds at best." Bill Freeman stumbles with his answer.

"Ali...she's hurt?" The marshal guesses.

"No one else! Piece of a bullet lodged in the back of her head just behind one ear." Freeman responds hesitantly.

"She's not dead!" The marshal would have sensed this.

"She's hurt marshal real bad!" The owner informs. "Mary is with her over to the guest house."

"Get me over there Eighty Eight?" The marshal is weak.

Jeremiah greets the marshal at the entrance of Ali's home. "She's not doing well marshal. I was able to get out the sliver of the bullet from the base of her skull. She lost some of blood. The swelling is modest. Had she been hit with a larger caliber slug she would have died at once. Her condition can go either way."

The marshal does not respond.

He must see Ali.

Mary steps from the side room in which Ali rests.

"She hasn't moved or been awake since she was wounded." Mary fights back her tears.

A single light shines near the bed where Ali lies.

A gaunt gray look covers the face of the beautiful young woman.

Her breath is shallow and not easy.

Her life wanes.

"Has she spoken?"

"Not one word to anyone." Mary answers.

"Has she called out to anyone...someone unknown?" The marshal is worried that her death angel may be coming.

"Her lips have not moved in my presence marshal." Mary notices the blood stains upon the marshal's wounds. "You need to rest. I'll have a bed ready for you at once."

"I want a bed near to Ali where I can watch her through the night." The marshal's eyes do not leave the injured woman.

The marshal's wounds are deep but not threatening.

His bed is placed next to Ali.

He lies within reach.

His hand holds hers.

"My Bill has sent a man to fetch the preacher. Reverend Doyle should be here tomorrow most likely."

The lawman feels for life in Ali.

He attends her very breath.

Her lips are dark and thin.

The flesh about her eyes is discolored.

"I'm here Ali." He whispers lovingly. "I'll stay till...as long as you need me with you." His heart aches.

There is no response from the woman.

Ali's bandage seeps little.

"I'll have to change this every so often marshal." Jeremiah informs.

"Where did you get your training in medicine?"

"Duty with the surgeon general in the army marshal. Learned a lot about wounds and healing."

"Does she have a chance Jeremiah?" Prays the marshal.

"The longer she fights the better her chance."

Through the night the marshal keeps talk at his love's side.

Despite little rest for several days and weakness from his wounds he struggles to stay alert.

In the darkest hour Ali's lips move.

The marshal hears no words.

He squeezes her hand tightly.

"Aunt Linda? Is that you?" She mumbles.

Alarm overpowers the marshal.

His heart races with anguish.

"We have been looking for you. Mother wants you to come for dinner. Where have you been all this time?"

Ali is being visited by her death angel. The marshal believes.

"Aunt Linda please do not take Ali with you? She is too fine a lady. She deserves a chance to live the life for which she has prayed." The marshal begs for mercy.

His touch senses that weakness grows in Ali.

He is desperate. "Jimmy Doyle! Jimmy! I need your help!"

His words break apart with unhappiness "Help me please?"

Ali hands are going cold.

"Jimmy! Get Aunt Linda to leave Ali with me?" Don't let her take away my love."

In the dimness of the room a boy appears.

"Woody I'm not supposed to be here. I still have to wait before you can come to play with me." The young lad answers with agitation.

"I want Ali to stay with me." He pleads to his childhood friend.

The lad looks over the dying woman.

"Her aunt is just going to walk with her to her mother's house." The boy does not understand the marshal's concern.

"I want her here with me. I need her with me Jimmy till we go off to play together "

"Okay Woody! When I come back the next time you have

to go with me." The lad points his finger at the marshal. "It'll be okay if this girl comes along with us."

The boy adds with a consolatory tone. "I have lots of fun places to show you."

The young lad moves away then turns. "You get the man who hurt your friend then put your guns away"

The boy waits for the marshal's response.

"I promise Jimmy. I'm just going to play here with Ali for now."

The little boy smiles as he dances off.

Ali's face is now relaxed.

Her breath is deep and easy.

Her lips are turning red and full.

Warmth returns into her hands.

The marshal slides into a deep sleep.

In the morning Mary, and Jeremiah find Ali awake and alert.

She holds the marshal's sleeping hand.

"You're up!" Mary remarks in disbelief.

"Let me see that wound?" Asks Mr. Cloug. "How do you feel Ali?"

"I had a long dream. I was back in my mother's house as a young child. It was so peaceful. I was so happy there. I didn't want to leave but the marshal's voice kept calling. I had to see what he wanted."

"Ali you were wounded during the robbery yesterday. The marshal was wounded the day before while chasing the Autry Gang. He asked to rest near you." Mary informs.

"When I awakened from my dream the marshal was here asleep. I have never seen the marshal sleep. He is just like a little boy so dear and so sweet." Ali sighs.

"Well, you're healing right fine. You gave us a mighty scare last night." Jeremiah tells.

"How is the marshal?" Ali responds.

"He's fine! Just collected a pair of new scars for the marshal." Mary replies. "He'll be up and about in no time."

"I'm tired now." Ali immediately slips back into a deep slumber.

"What is her chance now Jeremiah?" Mary asks.

"You get this child to eat some chicken soup when she wakes next. Her wound is doing nicely but she has lost much strength. Fever might get her if'n she doesn't eat proper."

Through the day the marshal sleeps.

Ali wakes on and off.

She has taken some food.

Her hands never leave the touch of her marshal.

Late in the day, the marshal is conscious when Ali awakens.

The two look to one another.

Their eyes search.

No words are spoken for several minutes.

"Why were you in my dreams? Did you see my Aunt Linda? I've never been shot before. Does it always feel like this?" Ali is eager for his voice.

Much strength has returned to the marshal.

"I didn't want you to leave with you aunt. I felt her presence but I could not see her." The marshal answers. "Being shot is simply a major hurt. You've have a mighty seriously wound."

"Who was that pesky boy Jimmy that interrupted my aunt?"

"He is my best friend since childhood."

The sounds from without give signal of the arrival of the most Reverend Doyle.

He enters.

"The lord has spared both of his children here." Greets the reverend.

Ali and the marshal smile in response to his arrival.

"When life fades upon this earth, the angels come to show us the way home to God's reward. I have no doubt that the angels where busy here last night. Let us bow our heads in thanksgiving."

All attending comply.

"You both have a covenant with the Lord. Life so saved together is life to be shared together. We thank the Lord for his kindness bestowed upon these two. We shall have their wedding in your house as soon as they are fully recovered. This we pledge. We ask...we pray...we expect the health of all to rebound by Thy Will. Amen!"

Amen!" Says Ali.

The marshal looks with devotion to the restored Ali.

"Amen!" He declares.

In several days Ali is sitting up.

Her appetite is restored.

Her health is returning.

The marshal is limping about despite much continued discomfort.

He is dressed, armed and ready to take to the high way when he visits Ali.

The woman is not surprised by the marshal's return to duty.

"You're going after the man who shot me?"

"I must...I promised." He replies.

"I heard what Jimmy said. When you return, you will hang up your guns!" She demands.

"Yes! I shall." He pauses before withdrawing. "Just in case Ali...I have never loved anyone as I now love you...or ever will."

"I know Cha! God will see you back to me otherwise he should have never saved my life."

"I'm taking some of our cash and buying some new garments when I get to Fargo."

"Get a new white shirt. It makes you respectable. Keep the hat its fine looking on you." Her eyes glisten with delight.

Despite much soreness the marshal rides straight into Fargo.

Chapter 10

"The Lord's House

Marshal Legs arrives at the federal courthouse.

He speaks with U S Marshal Hull.

"Looking for a gambler what has a lot of cash...small man, baby faced...dresses fancy like." Woody asks. "Goes by the name of J. B. Ledford."

"Dressed like your self but quarter size?" Hull replies.

"Yes! I'm a getting new clothes as soon as I leave your office."

"Saw the man. Left here a day or so ago." Hull confirms.

"He be carrying a lot of luggage?"

"One large box all locked with chains."

"Anyone come into town shot up about the same time?"

"Found a rider out on the road just outside of town. The fellar had been wounded for a while, and died of his injuries. No horse or any belongings found with him." Hull informs.

"That be the last of the Autry Gang. The whole bunch was killed after a robbery down at Eighty Eight's Road House."

"Well that gambler you're after is now ridding with a gun hand called Balzak. They headed out together westwards I believe."

"How does a man get a name like Balzak?" The marshal is unfamiliar with the term.

"He is a gypsy...a kind of folk what dresses different with bright colors, buckles and fancy scarves. They be dark haired and dark complexion mostly. They make real fine music and the men are good fighters."

"Like Mexicanos?"

"No they are from Europe really. Travel together in strange looking wagons, always on the move around the territory. Some of them are camped outside town now." Hull advises. "Be careful they can be dangerous folks. No one knows how they make their living...don't seem like they be the most honest type."

"When I return Marshal Hull I'll be resigning my commission. I'm retiring as a marshal."

Marshall Legs' wounds are healing.

Despite his haste, the marshal is taking time to seek a present to return to Ali.

He seeks a shop with items that a woman should enjoy to see in her house.

"Something small and fine like." He muses.

Near the federal court there is a commercial district. Here the marshal steps.

As he nears a café, a solitary man has just finished his midday meal and is exiting the establishment.

The stranger is tall and lanky as the marshal.

The two men approach each other

In a causal manner each man nods in greeting as they pass.

The stranger notices the elegant boots of the marshal.

"Hold there!" They man yells at the federal lawman. "Those are my boots!"

The marshal turns to face the angry man who threatens with a hand gun

The marshal is stunned.

The stranger studies the attire worn by the marshal.

"Those are my cloths that you are wearing!" He snarls. "You stole them from my school teachers"

The marshal judges the man as capable with a weapon but not dangerous. He does not speak.

"How did you get hold of my garments? Where are my ladies?" The stranger asks.

"Beaudreaux?" The marshal asks.

"How do you know my name?"

"These cloths were given out by Miss Bennet." The marshal declares.

"Ali? How come you to know her name?"

"I'm a going to marry that girl!" The marshal states emphatically as he opens the coat he wears to reveal the federal badge of a marshal.

This information leaves the aggressor without contest. His gun lowers to his side. He is perplexed.

"Why my cloths? Marry?"

"Just a temporary loan." The marshal informs. "Cause I love her!"

"This story calls for a drink." Invites Beaudreaux.

"Be my pleasure." The marshal accepts.

In a near by saloon the men sit and sip whiskey.

"How are the ladies? I thought they would be long gone toward the west by now."

The man fills the marshal's glass. "Call me Alain."

"Well, Mr. Alain" The marshal takes a deep breath.

"Judith married a medial doctor back in West Liberty. Evelyn married a Deputy U S Marshall near a road house about two days ride south east of here. Layla is visiting the village of Many Horns of the Nez Perce. Michele is keeping time with a wealthy chicken rancher and Ali is busy reading our home both reside near the same road house."

Alain is surprised. "Those ladies have done much better without me!"

"You were chasing to catch up with them were you?" The marshal guesses.

"I'm a man of my word marshal. I ran into trouble and sent the girls on ahead. Always meant to rejoin the troupe."

"Girls thought you got married sudden like?"

"You gamble.... play poker marshal?"

The marshal nods yes.

"I won as much as $1500 in one night!" Alain brags. "Lost more than that in an evening as well." He confesses.

The marshal nods in understanding.

"Seems I won more than cash in a game back while I was guiding them ladies." The expression of the gambler shows embarrassment.

"One player put a deed of property on the table as stakes." Alain continues. "It's done all the time."

The marshal nods again.

"I won that there deed...turned out to be for owner ship of his only daughter!"

The marshal is surprised. "That not be legal tender...white slavery be against the law."

"That's what I said and argued for cash payment of the debt." Alain insists.

The marshal waits.

"Well that farmer what owed me came with a shot gun to clear the debt with my marriage to his daughter."

"You sneaked away later did you?" The marshal surmises.

"Nope! Married that girl. It was the best day...the best piece of luck any man could have ever had."

The marshal is astonished.

"Fell in love with that girl at first sight. Can't ever leave her."

"Oh brother!" The marshal is amazed at the change of plans that love can bring.

"The Mrs. is over to the boarding house now."

"Them teachers don't need you any more Alain. Best see to your wife." The marshal advises.

"I'd like to take up preaching marshal by way of thanking the Lord. My wife is very religious and has been teaching me the bible. Them cloths of mine that you are wearing would make fine dress for the clergy." Alain suggests.

"You'll need them right off then Alain!" The marshal obliges.

"Have a church in mind do ya?" The marshal asks.

"We are going to start looking right away!"

"They be building one down at the road house off the Fargo Road near my home. Everyone there be glad to have you and your wife to give out services." The marshal invites.

"We'll get a stage coach in the morning marshal. I want the lady teachers to meet my wife."

Alain adds. "What business brings you to Fargo marshal?"

"Be looking for a gambling acquaintance of yours named Ledford." The marshal answers.

"J.B...saw him a couple of days back. We had one drink for old time sake. He invited me to a game of poker but I done give up gambling. Promised my wife to stay away from all games of chance."

"He be keeping ruff company?"

"He was with a gun hand named Balzak...had a couple of other men with him."

"Say where he be heading?"

"Not sure marshal...he is heading out on the open road looking for a place where there be serious gambling" Alain adds.

"He can be a dangerous fellow for a small man. He's got a mean streak hiding under that boyish grin that's for certain."

The marshal nods in agreement.

"You going to arrest Ledford marshal?"

"Going to hang him if I don't kill him first." The marshal answers

The men shake hands as they part.

"I'll leave your duds over to the dry goods store Alain... reverend."

"Obliged marshal!"

"Is there any thing Ali fancies personal as a gift?" The marshal asks.

The man ponders. "Small pieces of porcelain figurines and such."

"Little people and animal statues?" The marshal wonders.

"Yep, things like that. The smaller the better." Alain recommends.

The marshal returns to his standard attire; brown leather boots, deer hide trousers and a canvas coat. He has purchased a white linen shirt and has bought a new black felt hat.

"Hold them fancy cloths and boots!" He instructs the attendant at the dry goods store before he rides out of town. "A friend of mine will be by soon to collect them."

"Where can I find a place that sells womanly type gifts?" The marshal asks the shop keeper.

A band of gypsies has been camped in a low meadow beside a small creek.

It is dusk and the campfires are bright.

The evening meal is being prepared by the woman folk.

Men gather with drink and smoke.

They make conversation.

The marshal walks into the camp slowly.

The gypsies tense at his presence.

Their eyes follow.

A heavy older woman steps before the marshal.

"Why you come to gypsy camp?" Her tone threatens.

"I'm looking for a man they call Balzak...he's good with a hand gun and is traveling in the company of a small man in fancy clothes...a gambler."

"Why you want this man?" Her tone stays harsh.

"I don't want him. I want to find the little fellow with him. He shot a woman. The lady nearly died and she is not yet recovered. Don't want the gun hand just some information."

"We know nothing! You leave now!" The female orders.

The men seated about the camp rise and place their hands on their weapons.

"What is your name?" The marshal's tone becomes formal.

"Illavina...I am mother to this band of gypsies."

"I am U S Marshal Legs. The small man is called Ledford. He is wanted for robbery and murder. I have no warrant for your fellow gypsy riding with him."

"We know nothing! Go now or there will be trouble." Her threat is final.

"I need to know which direction them boys are be heading then I'll go. If there's trouble then the U S Calvary will hunt your band down. They'll ride in your camp shooting at anything what moves. They'll burn your wagons. Won't make no mind if women, children, dogs, horses or any kind of critter will die. You point your finger for me the way to be followed and I'll be gone. No words need be given." The marshal's offer is final.

The old lady points west.

For several days the marshal is following the main route from Fargo west deeper into the territory. At each town or village he stops for inquiry.

The unusual description of the small gambler and the gypsy make an easy trail to chase.

Five days out from Fargo is a mining town called Silver Spoon.

Here some years back a pair of young men from Dublin arrived.

Both men had little money.

The pair took a job for room and board on a sheep ranch.

While herding sheep out of the nearby hills from the ranch, they wandered into a narrow crevasse among some piles of large rocks.

Shiny yellow specks in the stream nearby drew their attention.

With the little money they had saved, they purchased a few acres of land about their discovery.

They would dig about the secret place on their free days.

After many months of exploration they chanced upon a tiny vein of gold and silver.

The sums collected where not large but enough to permit them to work full time at mining their claim. Ultimately the vein grew to several feet wide and over a foot tall in pure gold and silver.

Much money was extracted from that small piece of ground. Both men returned to Europe, bought castles, married, and lived as wealthy lords for the rest of their lives.

Much gold and silver circulated in the area. When iron came in high demand with its heavy use in the mines then folks made needed cutlery from the precious metals.

The tale remains popular today and many residents search for natural treasure in the area around Silver Spoon. Much gold and silver pass in the town yet today.

Gambling is a major form of diversion in this remote region.

The main saloon in Sliver Spoon is large and well attended.

Piano music, noise, drinks and games of chance fill the tavern.

Looking inward the marshal sees the gambler Ledford busy at a table playing poker.

"This man must be kin to Autry." Whispers the marshal.

Standing to the side is a dark man wearing a tight speckled headscarf, and fancy side arms with silver lined holsters.

"This one is very dangerous with a gun." Decides the marshal.

His thoughts are of Ali and her injury.

He fetches his handguns from their holsters and steps into the room.

Walking directly toward Ledford, he waits to be recognized.

The small gambler turns and spies the marshal's approach.

The gypsy is slow to respond.

As Ledford opens his mouth to call alarm the marshal discharges his two handguns.

Directly they impact into the chest of Ledford.

The small body is blown out of his seat onto the floor at the foot of the gypsy.

In a total daze the gypsy listens and watches as the marshal concludes.

"J. B. Ledford you are under arrest for robbery and murder."

The marshal points his guns to the face of the gypsy.

"I wish no fight!"

The gypsy states as he raises his empty hands.

"Do you want to live to see Illavina?" The marshal asks.

The gypsy does not move. "If you let me leave I will go straight to my people."

"Next time I see you carrying them fancy guns, I'll shoot you on the spot then arrest you." The marshal directs the gypsy to walk toward the front exit of the saloon.

"How many friends be there of yours waiting?"

The gypsy is hesitant. "No one else marshal." He stammers.

This is a lie.

He has two confederates watching.

"You are going to walk out through that door. Any one gives you question I'm a gong to shoot them dead."

The marshal warns as he pulls the firing hammers back on both his side arms.

The gypsy is nervous as he passes through the door to the out side of the saloon.

The marshal strides a few steps at the immediate rear of the gypsy.

The lawman studies the response of the gypsy as he enters the street. Once he is seen the open, two men approach from a distance.

Both strangers stare at the gypsy.

Both men have expressions upon their face that inquire.

Balzak is uncertain.

His hands are lowered.

He steps aside to reveal the presence of the armed marshal at his following.

The two men at the approach freeze. They recognize the threat. Both pull their weapons.

The gypsy turns at the same time to face the marshal.

The marshal steps to keep Balzak's silhouette before him, and behind the view of the two confederates of the gypsy.

The two henchmen discharge their weapons toward the moving marshal.

At the same instant the marshal fires both his hand guns directly at Balzak.

Before Balzk can threaten the marshal, he is struck from behind. Two bullets have been misplaced by Balzak's associates. Balzak is simultaneously hit in his front by the marshal's two shots.

Balzk stands as he shudders in death.

Momentarily his two companions observe their leader as they watch the gypsy begin to slump to ground. This is a mistake.

While the twosome discovers their mislaid attack, the marshal quickly moves to a direct path and unloads his six shooters toward the pair of desperados.

Both attackers fall before the marshal. Neither shall rise.

In a fortnight the former marshal is returned to the road house.

The retired law man yet recovers from his wounds. He is mostly healed.

The man arrives early at first light.

None but the owners stir.

Both of the Freemans are unused to Woody's new appearance.

They measure the man as more ordinary, less dangerous looking.

The retired federal officer hands his guns and holster to the owner.

"Woody, I'll put you hand guns away for you." Bill Freeman offers.

"Put'm in a box. There a present for Ali." Woody asks. "Mr. Legs intends to put away his handguns forever".

"Come in for some coffee marshal." Mary invites.

"Give up my badge Mary. Call me Woody. My marshalling days be over now."

"How is Ali?" He requests.

"Ali is doing right fine marshal...Woody." Mary responds. "She's getting about now pretty near as she did before."

"There's a new preacher what come to the road house, Reverend Beaudreaux. " Mary informs. "He and his wife are staying with Ali."

"Wearing white toed boots is he?" Woody asks.

"Thought the reverend was you at first sight, the way he came in dressed in black." Eighty Eight responds. "Looks like you from a distance he sure do."

"The church will be done in another week, Woody." Mary Freeman advises." Folks will be gathering for your wedding". Mary Freeman is excited.

"Guess you'll be going off to see Ali's after breakfast?" Mary continues.

"Nope! Going to ride down through that long meadow behind the guest house first. I have to make right with my mount what's a coming. We be giving up the open range together now. This spread will be our permanent home."

Mary shed tears for the end of the famous marshal's career and the new beginnings about the road house.

The new church is small but suitable for use as a school house as well.

It is stands just recessed from the road house but visible from the Fargo Road.

Dr. and Judge Bayfield have arrived in a party with J. D. Summer.

Layla and Mara Nar are returned from the nation of the Nez Perce with Little Owl. They arrive in the company of Chief Many Horns.

The newly appointed Sheriff of the community of Eighty Eight, Seth Adams awaits to greet each stage.

The guests have filled the rooms in the road house and the hideaway.

On a fine summer evening, Ali dressed in white enters the church assisted with Bill Freeman's arm.

Waiting at the altar is Michele, Seth, and Woody.

All are attired in finery for the occasion.

A tall preacher wearing fancy pearl inlaid dark boots calls the service to order.

"We gather today to join together Miss Ali Bennet and Mr. Wooden Legs in marriage in the presence of the Lord."

Ali's smile does not fatigue.

Solemn and sober is the bridegroom.

Her eyes and thoughts are of the man to be her husband and the shared life they are to begin.

Woody's is nauseous.

His accustomed life has ended.

He awaits with uncertainty the future.

Many Horns stands at the rear. He sees the call of the Great

Spirit to build a grand village about the home of the famous Sioux warrior, Chicha Mandoa.

"It is good." He thinks.

Evelyn Adams sees her best friend as happy as she has ever known Ali to be. "Michele is next." She is sure.

Bill and Mary Freeman view the marriage as a blessing on the start of a new town. "More settlers will stay now that we have a church." Eighty Eight hopes.

Little Owl wishes that all natives might view the love known by these two settlers. "Will I have the power of such romance?" She asks privately.

Michele views the happiness of her friend Ali, and the suffering of Woody under the burden of the ceremony. "Ali's babies will all be boys." She concludes.

Jeremy Cloug and his two boys are in attendance.

"That bride's maid will make a fine wife for one of you two boys." He whispers.

Mrs. Beaudreaux is delighted at her husband's first performance of a marriage. "Not long till his first baptism." She predicts.

Joe Klinger has arrived with his bride Inot Mai. "There's justice for the marshal in this wedding." He whispers to Inot Mai.

Mrs. Klinger responds. "I was promised to this warrior but for that woman I may have been his bride."

There is a hint of jealousy in her remark.

There is relief for all as the new preacher pronounces, "You are now man and wide. Let us all give thanks to the Lord."

"Amen!" The congregation answers.

For the first time Woody smiles, none have witnessed such joy in the expression of the former marshal.

Several years have passed.

A heavy snow line is moving off the mountains behind the Legs' Ranch.

The preceding bluster of wind blows the occasional large snow flake down the long valley driving steer and horse form the meadow.

"Woody, get the boys to take feed out!" Ali calls from the kitchen. "Snow squalls moving in fast."

"Where's the baby?" Woody barks as he gathers his coat.

"She's watching her mother get breakfast ready."

Pancakes, fried ham, biscuits and gravy are being prepared.

"Get the milking done. Agnes is fusing." The latest of Ali's children is now three months. Agnes is the only girl child.

There are settings for first meal for five other children...all boys.

"Ready!" Ali calls from the kitchen. "Get those boys up pronto."

"I'll take Will and Jessie out to the pastures. Frank and Todd will have to get the milking done before they join us." Woody states.

"Let little George stays in with you until the ruff work is done." He adds.

He's going to raise the devil if he can't ride with his dad." Ali protests.

"He's only four, those herds may get mean like with this harsh change in the weather. I don't want any of them boys in the meadows any longer than need be today. Once the snows be settled them critters will become pacified."

Woody has gathered his rifle as he enters the kitchen.

"You expecting trouble?" Ali is concerned at the need for a weapon.

"Can't take chances with them boys. Could be some varmints move down off them slopes with this storm. I'm going to have the two older boys to take their rifles as well. They be men soon." Woody asserts."

"Keep Todd and Frank near you. Don't let them out of your sight and don't keep them younger ones out in that cold past lunch."

"Be sure to keep the doors locked when we are out. Seth tells me there's been bad trouble further up the Fargo Road."

Ali is concerned.

She looks upon her husband for assurance. "Seth is riding after those what be causing trouble?"

Woody nods yes.

"He asks you to ride with him?"

Woody nods yes.

"When do you leave?"

"Tomorrow first light." He adds apologetically. "If we don't go after them bad men they'll come after some of us...our home, our family maybe."

"You're wearing your side arms with the posse?" Ali asks.

"Nope...I'll keep my promise.... just my carbine."

"They will be asking the boys one day to join a posse?" Ali guesses.

"Man has the duty to protect his family and home. Who else?" Woody replies.

"The boys will need to learn to use hand guns?" The mother worries.

"It be coming time for the older two." Her husband declares.

"You teach them! No one else is good enough. I don't want them running off as lawmen." Her heart aches.

"Will gets that hard distant look in his eyes like you when marshalling after out laws."

"Life's work comes to find a man. It'll find Will if he meant to be a marshal."

The smell of mother's food has roused the boys. The winter's day begins on the ranch.

Seth Adam's posse gathers at the road house.

Some seven men from the immediate community have been deputized.

'Three riders have been robbing, and killing north along

this section of the Fargo Road...We'll pick up any tracks left in the snow and drive on to where they be hold up." Seth directs.

Woody makes no comment.

"More snow be coming. Won't do to track more than a day or so." Advises Jim Travis.

Jim is a local trapper and guide.

"Those desperados will be hurrying to take shelter. They won't be expecting to be chased now." Seth determines.

Woody agrees. "They won't run far off the Fargo Road."

"Snows may have pushed them down our way. They could be held up close." Bill Freeman notes.

"Won't do to take all the men folk away." Bob Dowdy advises.

Bob is new to the area. He and his wife opened a barber shop and beauty parlor in Eighty Eight last year.

"My youngest sons will keep watch and help here." Bill Freeman advises.

Seth, Woody, Jim, Bob, and Bill Freeman with his two oldest sons compose the posse.

The snow of yesterday has covered the land.

Several inches of fresh snow makes tracking easy.

About an hours ride north a narrow trail leads into a well known valley.

"Three horses traveling light." Announces the guide Travis.

"This be our gang." Seth concludes. "Ways out of this valley?"

"One way in, one way out." Notes Travis.

Woody knows this gang will not surrender easily.

"What be our plan?" Bill Freeman asks.

Seth puzzles. He looks to Woody for approval. "Cross fire!"

Woody nods yes.

"Seth has the right instinct for the job." He thinks.

"Freemans to the left, others to the right. You all take positions on each side of their camp. I'll ride straight in alone and draw them out. Make your shots count."

"No other way." Woody agrees.

Up a mile or so is an old cabin.

Hunters and trappers have used this place since the earliest days of the territory.

The narrow trail provides a pathway into and out of the higher elevations where the game is abundant.

The day is cloudy.

Snow still falls.

The outlaws have taken refuge within the old wooden hut. A fire burns inside as the posse closes.

Abandoning all concern to the weather, the bad men keep no watch.

With ease the two columns of the posse have ridden to the sides of the cabin's front. The cross fire is established.

Yet early in the day, the sheriff walks within a hundred paces of the cabin's front. The smell of coffee brewing confirms the three men are within.

Woody sets his carbine. He knows the Freemans will fire their weapons after the first shots are made. The sheriff's life depends on the posse.

"We'll have to place the first shots other wise Seth may fall." He whispers to Travis and Dowdy.

Woody is sure that Travis is a crack shot.

Dowdy is not likely capable with his weapon.

Woody and Travis will have to fire twice with effect to assure the sheriff's safety.

The sheriff watches as his band take firing positions behind good cover.

"Hello in the house." Bellows Seth as he views his posse. All his men have their weapons at the ready.

A muffled conversation is heard within the wood hut.

A tall lean man emerges followed by two others. They wear side arms.

The trio stands spread before the figure of the sheriff in the distance.

"Who's there?" Asks the leader.

The former marshal points to Travis to sight upon the leader.

Woody sights on the second man nearest to their flank.

The third bandit is open to the flank guarded of the Freemans. Woody's side of the posse has no of line of sight upon the third man.

"Seth best pick on the correct one." Woody says under his breath.

The sheriff stands with his hands open and clear.

The bandits are cautious.

"As soon as them boys grip their guns we fire." Woody declares to his companions.

"Who be you?" The tall outlaw blares.

"The Sheriff of Eighty Eight. You men are under arrest for murder and thievery. Raise your hands or prepare to die here." Seth calls in return.

The tall criminal realizes the danger from his sides. He turns to face his left. He reaches for his side arm.

Travis fires.

Woody shoots.

Dowdy hesitates.

Seth pulls his hand gun.

The tall leader is hit by a high powered round from Travis' rifle. He is flung in death.

Woody's gunshot hits the mark of the nearest thug. This bandit turns wounded to the ground.

He shall not rise.

The Freemans collectively fire but they lack target and none of their shots strike the enemy.

Seth has guessed Woody's purpose.

He turns upon the third bandit as two of the outlaws are immediately slain.

Seth and the third robber face each other.

Both fire at the same time.

Seth's shot misses.

The bandit's does not. Seth is struck in his shoulder and falls.

Woody's second shot strikes the last criminal just a Travis' second round follows to hit the same mark.

All three bandits are dead.

Seth is seriously wounded but will live.

His courage and sacrifice have made safe the homes of many.

❧

More years have passed.

Ali is cleaning her home when Mary Freeman's son, Leroy arrives at the house.

"Mrs. Legs come at once!" The boy shouts excitedly. "There's been an accident."

Ali is disorientated by the unexpected commotion. "Accident? Woody?" She fears.

"No mam! The reverend's son Alain, Jr." The boy removes his hat at his entrance."

"Agnes' husband?" Fright overtakes Ali for her son in law. "What happened?"

"There was a bad traffic accident on the Fargo Road" He pauses.

"Traffic? That road has gotten too busy. Where is the man? With Agnes?" She hopes.

"Dead mam! He was kilt." The blunt response stifles Ali's thoughts.

"Seems a horse spooked and ran wild with his buggy. He crashed into one of them over weight wagons. Died instantly."

"Poor Alain.... Poor Agnes. I have to go to her." Ali drops her apron.

"Leroy, will you ride out in the back meadow and inform Woody? Tell him to meet me at Agnes's home right away.

❧

The final years arrive.

"Dad, why don't you take a nap before dinner?" Agnes proposes to Woody.

Woody sits in a rocking chair on the back porch of his home.

He watches the long meadow now full with farms and fenced sections of land worked by his sons and grandchildren.

"I'm not tired. I'm not hungry either Agnes."

"You always ate mother's cooking. You must eat to you kept your strength." His daughter pleads.

"Your mother's gone some number of years now. I've been enjoying your meals ever since.'

"You must eat!" His daughter insists.

"Man my age don't need much."

"Woodrow left for the army yesterday dad. It was his last meal at home. I want you to share the table tonight. That new solicitor, Mr. Jeffers is coming to dinner again. I don't know how to talk to him by myself. All he wants is to hear stories about my famous dad"

"I see him watching you. He might listen to me but his eyes are for my daughter."

Woody laughs at the remembrance of the youngest child of Agnes. He was yet in diapers when they came to live with him. "Seem he was just two or so yesterday."

"Oh dad there was a young boy that came to see you earlier this afternoon but you were asleep."

"A boy? What did he want?" Woody is confused.

"The boy said he knew you. He wanted to talk. It was important he said." His daughter replies.

"He leave his name?" Woody asks.

"Jimmy Doyle!" Agnes recalls. "I told him to come back well before super.

A pause is needed.

"Agnes, bring me a glass of whisky and a small black cigar." Woody requests.

"Dad you haven't had a drink since mother's wake" Agnes is surprised.

"Smoke isn't good for a man of your advanced age." She frets with concern for her elderly father

"When Jimmy comes show him to the back here. I'll have a

talk with him while I sip a little whisky and have a good smoke." Woody looks to his daughter.

He measures the look of his wife in her ways.

Her presence has provided much comfort since the loss of his wife.

"Your mother's death date is coming soon." He states as the cigar, and tumbler of whisky is placed at his side.

"It's today dad...exactly 16 years ago tonight mother died. Seems like yesterday." Agnes frowns

The marshal waits.

His mind relives his first meeting with Ali back in Sweet Creek.

"I'm late Woody." A young boy arrives.

"Ali wouldn't let me come until Agnes' children were old enough." The small boy announces as he skips onto the porch.

"Have a seat Jimmy." The marshal invites.

The child sits but fidgets with a small leather ball between his hands.

"Time is it? Jimmy" Woody's tears flow at the sight of his childhood friend.

"Yep! The boy responds. "Ali says it's time for you to come play with us."

The marshal sips his whisky.

He lights his final cigar.

"Ali needs me does she?" The old man asks.

The small boy nods agreeably. "I've waited longer than she did."

"I've been busy for a long time Jimmy. Lot's of work needed done."

"I was going to come sooner but Ali watched me. She said she would tell me when the time was right."

"She sent you did she?"

Jimmy nods yes.

"Let me enjoy my last cigar Jimmy then we'll be off. Smoke always made me calm, peaceful like. Had my first tobacco from my grand dad's old peace pipe."

"Your grand father has a new pony waiting for you Woody."

The child hesitates in thought. "I'd like a turn riding him Woody?"

The old man on the porch nods yes.

"Never picked up my hand guns Jimmy...kept my word to you, I did."

"Ali says when we return we have to visit your mother and dad first before we can play. We have lots of time to play...she always says that."

The last sip of whisky passes the old man's lips.

The last puff of smoke is released.

"You are a famous marshal Woody. All the kids want to hear your stories when we get back"

"My favorite tales are of being a husband to Ali and father to our children." His mind runs through many precious memories

Jimmy squirms to be released form his seat.

"Ready Woody? Ali doesn't like to be kept waiting. Finally, she is going to get to hug you...that is what she tells everybody."

"What do I have to do Jimmy?" The marshal stands.

"Just follow me!" The child shrugs his shoulders. He turns and walks toward the grave where Ali's rests.

"Dad? Are you going somewhere?" Agnes asks as she reappears on the back porch.

Woody calls for a hug from his youngest.

"I'm going to leave something on your mother's grave...I'll return for you later."

His words chill Agnes. "I don't understand dad. Why do you have to go?" Sadness fills her eyes.

His worn hand caresses her face.

His aged lips kiss her fore head.

"Everyone must answer God's call home. Your mother wants me with her now." He weeps. "I have loved you always, always. My heart, my spirit is with you evermore."

"I love you dad." The woman's tears fall.

Their hug extends.

"Thank you daddy." Her heart is breaking

They part slowly.

Her eyes follow.

Her breath holds.

Woody steps slowly to his wife's grave where his friend Jimmy stands in wait.

As he nears, a young woman walks forth with her arms open to him.

It is Ali.

She appears just as young as when they first met.

A bit more time passes.

Agnes Jeffers arrives at the graves of her parents.

"Quit running about like a wild animal!" She shouts to a two year old boy who scurries near to her.

"You have to tire sometime." She puffs as she begins to plant flowers upon the graves.

"Your father will have to stay up with you tonight. Your mother needs some rest."

The toddler races up close to his mother as she leans over Ali's grave.

As soon he has Agnes' attention, he turns to race away giggling with glee at his mother's consternation.

"On second thought...keep running! Perhaps we'll finally see you fatigued!" She smiles with a mother's love as she watches her precious child.

"He looks a lot like you dad!" Agnes says above her father's grave. "And he has legs of wood!"

Tears of love and gratitude fall from the woman's face to moisten the earth of the marshal's burial mound.

The End

Made in the USA